BESS

TUDOR GENTLEWOMAN

THE ELIZABETHAN SERIES

TONY RICHES

COPYRIGHT

Copyright © Tony Riches 2025
Published by Preseli Press

ISBN: 9798281720434
BISAC: Fiction / Historical
Cover Art by Ashley Risk

ABOUT THE AUTHOR

Tony Riches is a full-time writer and lives with his wife in Pembrokeshire, West Wales, UK. A specialist in the history of the Tudors, Tony is best known for his Tudor Trilogy, which begins the continuous story of the Tudors through to the end of his Elizabethan series. For more information please visit Tony's author website www.tonyriches.com and his blog at www.tonyriches.co.uk. He can also be found at Tony Riches Author on Facebook, Bluesky and Twitter: @tonyriches.

In memory of my mother
Irene Bryant
who taught me to read, and passed away
during the writing of this book

1

RICHMOND PALACE 1590

BESS FLINCHES AS THE QUEEN'S ACCUSING VOICE, RAPIER-SHARP, echoes in the crowded privy chamber of Richmond Palace, silencing the chatterers of court. 'You stare at our ladies, Master Raleigh.'

Walter Raleigh laughs, and Bess notes the glint of mischief in his dark eyes. If the queen wants sport, she will have her wish. He raises an eyebrow and studies each of them in turn, resting on the lined face of the queen's oldest companion.

'Which of your ladies, Your Majesty?'

'Bess, for one.' The queen turns and stares at her with the cold intelligence of a hunting hawk.

Bess prickles with danger, but risks a smile. The queen plays her games with them, yet this time she is right. They have become close since Walter returned a hero from Ireland, but the longer they keep their secret, the better.

Walter bends on one knee, his rich voice confident and sure. 'Ah! My beloved queen and goddess of my life. Who shall me pity, when thou dost me wrong?'

Bess guesses his words belong to one of his unpublished poems, too flattering. She holds her breath and her heart pounds against the confining stays of her tight bodice. The queen is in good spirits and cackles at his quick-witted reply. He knows Her Majesty well, but it's a dangerous game they play. Good men and women have been thrown in the Tower dungeons for less.

The ivy-covered door creaks in protest as Walter pushes it open. He ushers Bess through the arched stone entrance to their secret place, a walled rose garden in the palace grounds. The white roses, reduced to thorny stems, wait for their chance to bloom, and the brick-paved path gleams with the evening frost.

One of the older groundsmen claims the garden was a favourite place of Anna of Cleves, who lived in the palace after her divorce from the queen's father. Bess understands why she found solace there. Once the wooden door closes, the walled garden becomes a tranquil sanctuary, an escape from the world.

To be together unchaperoned is a dangerous risk, but Bess enjoys the innocent thrill of outwitting her overprotective mistress and her gossiping ladies. This secluded corner of the palace gardens is out of bounds to commoners, and the walled garden is unlikely to encourage visitors until the winter chill passes.

Bess is glad of her warm woollen shawl, a gift brought from Ireland by Walter. The River Thames is frozen again, and their breath turns to mist in the still air. She pulls off one of her white gloves and reaches out to caress his cheek – a brief caress, but full of longing.

'Was it luck, or good judgement?'

He takes her hand and kisses it. 'I learned the power of

poetry to turn the queen's head from my friend Edmund Spenser.'

She smiles. 'You took a risk, so luck played a part.'

'As always, but you have to roll the dice to win.'

Bess studies his face, trying to decide if he is a man she can trust, and recalling her late mother's well-intended warning. *The queen is a jealous mistress.*

He grins. 'The Privy Council has yet to pass a law against us meeting – and if they did, I confess I would still be tempted.'

'For the life of me, I fail to understand you.' Bess frowns. 'You are one of the most eligible bachelors at court, yet they call me the plainest of the queen's ladies. You are a gifted poet, but I am not tutored, and struggle with reading and writing. You are wealthy, and I have only thirty-three pounds a year as the queen's gentlewoman—'

He takes her in his arms and kisses her on the lips to silence her. 'You caught my eye from my first day at court, and I know you sensed the connection between us.' He kisses her again, with more passion. Bess holds him close, enjoying this precious moment of intimacy.

Her voice is soft as she speaks. 'I'm surrounded by the queen's ladies, yet I've suffered great loneliness since my mother died. I have four brothers, but even the closest, Arthur, has become a stranger to me, and has his own family.' She smiles at a memory. 'My mother warned me about you.'

'What did she say?' His eyes flash with concern and he holds her closer, as if to prevent her escaping.

'My mother was an astute judge of character, but if I were to believe even half the stories about you, I wouldn't be here now.'

'My reputation as a philanderer is a cruel jest, put about by those who envy my closeness to the queen.' He gives her a mischievous look. 'I've even heard that they say I am the queen's lover.'

She laughs. 'I once thought the rumours could be true. They say my lord of Essex now has that thankless task.'

Walter shakes his head at the thought. 'I've also been lonely for many years past.' He unfastens the silver clasp of his fur cloak, draping it over her shoulders, and whispers, 'My poor mother warns me if I don't marry soon, she might never see her grandchildren.'

'Well, we must be sure not to disappoint your mother.' She kisses him, and whispers in his ear, 'I love you.'

'*Would* you marry me?' Hope echoes in his voice and his eyes hold hers, as if longing for her answer.

Bess chokes back tears. 'My father bequeathed five hundred pounds for my dowry, but my mother was persuaded to lend the money to Henry Hastings. She tried her best to have it back, even petitioning the queen, but told me it is a debt he will never repay.' She shakes her head. 'All I have are my mother's pearls, and goods of no great value—'

He takes her hand and stares into her eyes. 'My income from licences for the import of wines is enough to keep us in comfort. Her Majesty granted me the traitor Babington's confiscated estates, my estates in Ireland show promise, and I own a flotilla of ships.'

'Why do you need a flotilla of ships?'

He looks thoughtful for a moment. 'God willing, my ships can make my fortune with my colonists in the New World.'

Bess knows he can provide for her, but her position as a gentlewoman of the privy chamber means this choice is not hers to make. 'What do you think the queen would say if you ask permission to marry me?' Her voice wavers, and she holds her breath, sensing her future hanging in the balance.

'That question will be the gamble of my life, and put everything I've gained at risk. But what is my life, if not with you?'

Bess gasps as her maidservant Martha pulls the lacings of her pair of bodies tight. The blue silk covering belies the two strips of stiff whalebone which run down either side of the front lacing, flattening her breasts and squeezing into her ribs, making it hard to breathe.

She glances at the simple green gown worn by her maidservant over a linen shift, and envies its lack of constraints. The queen insists on this impractical fashion for her ladies and seems to care little for the consequences.

Martha has served Bess since the age of twelve, and will soon turn eighteen. A bright, inquisitive girl from a prosperous merchant family, Martha sleeps on a truckle bed at her side, so there is little privacy and few secrets between them.

Their bedchamber at Richmond is small, yet preferable to the shared chambers of the other palaces, where Martha is in the servants' quarters. In what is still called the new wing, built after the devastating fire in the time of the queen's grandfather, the room is hot in summer and freezing in winter. More than once they've broken a layer of ice on the water ewer left out overnight, before Bess can wash.

A shuttered, leaded window looks out over the palace gardens, and the only furnishings other than the beds are the heavy camphor chest for storing gowns, and her mother's dressing table with its small polished mirror and velvet upholstered chair. The ewer and bowl are on a washstand behind the door, and everything travels with them when they accompany the queen on a progress.

Like Bess, Martha must complete her limited education herself. Keen to learn the complexities of life at court, she has many questions. 'Can there be any truth in the rumours of the Earl of Essex, my lady?'

'That the earl is a hopeless womaniser and a notorious gambler?'

Martha smiles at her ironic tone. 'They say he has married

Lady Frances Sidney – without permission from Her Majesty.' Her eyes shine as she shares the scandalous news.

Bess frowns. 'You must take care not to repeat such rumours, Martha.' She'd seen Lady Frances as a self-assured, insightful woman, unlikely to fall for a man like Sir Robert Devereux, who seems to be always in debt. The rumours sound unlikely – yet, if true, could make it more difficult for her to ask permission to marry Walter.

Martha looks thoughtful. 'Do you not agree the Earl of Essex is handsome, and has a certain charm?'

Bess hesitates to agree, for that is how rumours start. Martha confessed to falling for one of the young grooms, but Bess has said nothing of her feelings for Walter. 'The earl is careless about who he offends, and has made enemies at court, and there are plenty who envy his privileged place in the queen's affections.' She frowns. 'You can be sure the queen will learn the truth of it soon enough. If this rumour *is* true we will never hear the end of it.'

Martha secures the ends of the lacings, tying them as tight as she can. 'You should know there is talk of little else, my lady.'

Bess gives her a cautionary look. 'The queen thinks of Essex more like the son she never had.'

Martha agrees. 'I've heard how she speaks to him, accusing him of behaving like a spoiled child.'

'They know the rules of the game they play, which is why he'd be a fool to cross Her Majesty.'

The court is in mourning, any talk of the Earl of Essex overshadowed by the death of Lady Blanche Parry – former Chief Gentlewoman of the Privy Chamber and the queen's closest confidante – at the venerable age of eighty-two.

The queen has retired to her bedchamber in her grief, and Countess Catherine Howard, made Chief Gentlewoman since Mistress Parry's blindness, summons the queen's ladies to the privy chamber. She clasps her hands together and leads them in prayer.

'Almighty and eternal God, from whose love in Christ we cannot be parted, even by death, hear our prayers and thanksgiving for Blanche Parry, who we remember this day; through Jesus Christ our Lord. Amen.'

With the other ten ladies, Bess bows her head and replies 'Amen', sensing the ending of an era. Mistress Blanche Parry was the queen's most faithful servant, at her side since her birth. The queen will miss her more than any of them.

Countess Catherine seems satisfied she has done her duty and reads to them from Blanche Parry's will. *'I give to the queen's most excellent Majesty my sovereign lady and mistress my best diamond, and to every of the ladies and gentlewomen of the privy chamber and the grooms of the same, and every of the maids of honour that shall be at the court when God shall call me out of this life, I bequeath silver rings made like hoops with death's head of the value of twenty shillings apiece. I give to the six pages of the queen's majesty's privy chamber every one of them twenty shillings.'*

Bess would rather have the twenty shillings than a death's head ring, yet knows that wearing it binds the queen's ladies even closer. New ladies will come and more will leave, but those who wear the silver ring will have a special place in the queen's affection.

She stares at Countess Catherine as she continues to list the virtues of Lady Blanche, who remained a maid all her life. The prospect of doing the same has no appeal for Bess, but Countess Catherine has shown there is no need to treat the privy chamber like a nunnery.

The queen's ladies are sworn to chastity, silence and absolute loyalty to the queen, but in her five years as the queen's gentlewoman, Bess has seen little observance of the rules, apart from Mistress Martha Radcliffe, keeper of Her Majesty's jewels.

Like Blanche Parry and the queen, Martha takes pride in her chastity, and needs no man to protect or comfort her. Walter calls the queen's ladies her 'witches', capable of doing great harm to reputations with their fickle influence, and of secret communication without the need to speak.

Walter is closer to the truth than he knows. The queen's demure ladies remind her of worker bees. They gather information as bees gather nectar, sweet-talking courtiers and foreign ambassadors into revealing their secrets, which they serve to their queen at the centre of this hive of intrigue.

Bess glances at the younger maids of honour and sees them eye-rolling as they grow bored of the platitudes. She's seen how they flirt with any man with prospects. They gamble at noisy games of cards in the maidens' chambers and gossip like the fishwives of Billingsgate Market, with scant concern for the consequences.

She never joins in, and knows they call her *Boring Bess*, yet now they will see her differently. At twenty-five they no doubt say no man wants her, but can't have missed Walter's affection for her. She senses her neck flush as she remembers his kiss, and the longing in his voice when he asked her to marry him.

An idea occurs to Bess as she listens to the countess. All the queen's ladies are present, so the queen is likely to be alone in her grief. One of the privileges of being a gentlewoman is access to the royal bedchamber, and no one seems to notice as she slips out into the high-ceilinged corridor.

Bess enters the queen's spacious bedchamber with a curt-sey. The tall, mullioned windows are shuttered, and the darkened chamber is lit by a pair of beeswax candles, their honeyed aroma competing with the delicate scent of rosewater and the tang of some exotic perfume.

Few would see their queen in such distress. Red-eyed and without her magnificent red wig, she still wears her nightgown, and lies propped on silk cushions. There is a distant look in her eyes as she stares at a diamond in a gold pendant, which Bess guesses is Mistress Parry's bequest.

She is unsurprised at the queen's state of undress so late in the morning. She often rises late, and even walks in the privy gardens in her nightdress. The queen looks up and studies Bess for a moment, as if making a judgement, and gestures for her to sit at her bedside.

'We have been praying for Mistress Blanche, Your Majesty, and remembering her great kindness and loyalty.'

The queen dangles the diamond pendant on its gold chain, and Bess sees a glint as it catches the light of the candle. 'We will not see her like again, Bessie.'

Bess notes the queen's informal name for her. Until now she has always called her Bess, or Mistress Throckmorton in company. She calls Walter her *pug*, and he once told Bess there are worse things than to be the queen's lapdog, a sign he is in her favour. More often she calls him *Water*, a pun on his name and time at sea.

She calls Robert Cecil, groomed as his powerful father's replacement, her *imp*, and her *pygmy*. At five foot he is only a little shorter than most, but the queen is taller and his hunched back diminishes him. Bess has seen his false smile at the queen's odd humour, and suspects he takes her nickname for him as a cruel jest.

The queen looks up at her. 'Blanche was the last of my ladies who also served my mother. She must have been your age when I was born. She said she would rock me in my cradle and sing me to sleep with her old Welsh songs.' The queen gives Bess a wistful smile. 'She was the closest I had to a mother, as I was not three years old when my poor mother met her cruel fate.'

Bess knows the stories of the downfall of Queen Anne Boleyn, yet in all her years at court has never heard the queen speak of her, and hesitates to reply. 'Mistress Parry showed me great kindness when I first came to your service, despite her blindness, Your Majesty.'

'Mistress Parry could see more than most members of our Privy Council. She will be missed.'

Bess keeps a respectful silence. 'Would you like me to send for something to break your fast, Your Majesty?'

The queen grips the large diamond in her slender fingers, as if to prevent anyone from taking it. 'You are right, Bessie. I must keep my strength up and speak with Lord Burghley. Blanche was his favourite cousin. He will be sure to know her final wishes.'

Bess stands and gives a final curtsey. She longs to ask the queen's permission to marry Walter. This is not the time, but she has seen a rare glimpse of the humanity behind the facade of majesty the queen maintains in every waking moment.

Bess senses a frisson of excitement when she finally meets with Walter in secret. The risk of punishment for them both is even greater if they are discovered. 'Someone has told the queen about the Earl of Essex and, as you would expect, she was furious with him.'

Walter scowls. 'I heard her shouts and thought it best to keep away. What did she say?'

'She counted off his crimes on her fingers, accused him of duplicity, of lying, and of marrying a woman beneath his station who was not well born.' She frowns. 'Their marriage was consummated, and Frances carries his child, so there is little anyone can do about it.'

Walter pulls her close and holds her tight in his arms. 'I

heard he kneeled before the queen and begged forgiveness.' His voice has a note of scorn.

'I was there. He offered to fight for the Protestant cause in France, but Her Majesty forbade him to go, and said if he dared to defy her again, he would suffer the consequences.'

'But she will forgive him?'

'Not yet. She banished him from the court, but everyone knows she'll have him back before long.'

Walter kisses her on the cheek. 'I'm relieved to hear he hasn't been sent to the Tower.'

'Our secret will have to keep a little longer. We cannot ask the queen's permission while the risk of her refusal is so great.'

'Be patient, Bess. I've waited all my life for you. A few more weeks is of little consequence.'

2

GREENWICH PALACE 1591

SUMMER RAIN KEEPS THE QUEEN'S LADIES INSIDE, AND THEY PASS the long afternoon in the comfort of the privy chamber of Greenwich Palace. Some gossip, others read poetry, and the maids of honour play a popular card game, primero. Bess works on her embroidery, which she thinks a more suitable pastime for a gentlewoman.

She tries to focus on sewing a line of neat stitches, the silver thread gleaming in the rich black velvet. She works on a fine doublet, a birthday gift for her elder brother Arthur, yet her mind is on the problems of her own future.

Arthur is well connected, often the first to hear news, and relies on privileged information from Bess to help him sort fact from rumour. He told her Walter secured the queen's permission to return to sea and try his luck against the Spanish, but Walter has said nothing to her of his plans, another worrying sign.

They'd agreed they must be more discreet, and take care not to arouse suspicions. This means some time has passed since they risked being alone together. Bess misses the thrill of their secret meetings, and worries Walter's proposal of marriage seems like a distant dream. If she doesn't take the initiative soon she could be too late, and become another maiden gentlewoman.

She glances up as she hears the queen's shrill laugh. As predicted, the Earl of Essex is back at her side, flattering her with his shallow compliments. It seems she hasn't been told he's having an affair with one of the youngest maids of honour, despite his marriage to Frances, now the Countess of Essex.

Bess frowns as she sews. The Earl of Essex must know they could both end up in the Tower if the queen learns of his adultery – which she will. She stops sewing as she recalls from her own time as a maid of honour that it is impossible to keep such a thing a secret from the other ladies.

Her mind buzzes with conflicting questions. Is it disloyal to the queen to hold her silence? Is her real duty to protect those around her from the queen's vindictive fury? Her conscience prevents her wishing to be the first to tell her, but that's how others win favour. The games they play are for the highest stakes, and most of those who win do so at another's great cost.

She understands Walter built his fortune and reputation taking risks as an adventurer, but not why he keeps his seafaring ambitions from her. The bond between them is tested while they wait for the queen's mood to improve, and she resolves to risk confronting him.

Her chance comes when the queen retires early for the night, and they can meet in one of the many private rooms of Greenwich Palace. She kisses Walter and tries to sound innocent as she asks, 'Is it true you are to command one of the queen's ships?' Her voice is soft, yet her eyes study his as she watches his reaction.

'I'm provisioning Admiral Howard's fleet for an expedition

to the Azores, where he hopes to intercept the Spanish treasure fleet. The queen's warship, the *Revenge*, is without a commander, and Lord Howard offered me the chance to be vice admiral of his fleet.'

He makes it sound like nothing of any consequence, yet Bess recalls the glint of ambition in his eyes when he's told her stories of Spanish galleons laden to the waterline with a fortune in gold and silver, jewels and precious spices.

'What about your promise to me?' She hears an edge of panic in her voice, and senses her promising future slipping away like the ebb tide on the Thames.

He holds her close for the first time in many weeks. 'Her Majesty will not allow me to go – but she takes me for granted.'

Bess feels a stab of disappointment at his lie. Her brother said Walter already had the queen's permission to sail to the Azores. 'But you remain in her favour?'

'Yet the queen refuses me a place on the Privy Council, or to make me a Garter knight.' He mutters a curse. 'She thinks me low-born.' His words echo with bitterness, and his Devon accent is more marked, which Bess takes as a sign of the strength of his feelings.

'That's why you wish to prove yourself worthy?' She feels his body tense, and he is silent for once. She has pushed him too far, but it must be the truth. '*I* never take you for granted, and I would never rest with the worry of your going to sea again.' She frowns. 'Your first voyage to the Azores was almost the death of you.'

He shakes his head as he remembers. 'That was a nightmare I'm in no hurry to repeat, but it pains me to see Sir Richard Grenville sail in my place.'

She smiles. 'You have money to invest in Lord Howard's voyage. Stay safe with me, and you can still have your share of the spoils. Risking your money is better than risking your life, and you know how fickle the queen can be. If you are away too long you risk losing her favour.'

'You are right, Bess. Our spies say the Spanish are improving their warships, and are ready to defend the treasure fleet.' He gives her a wry smile. 'I am honoured by Lord Howard's offer, but I shall invest in the voyage – and Sir Richard Grenville will owe me a favour for recommending him as vice admiral.'

The Earl of Essex rides his fine white charger at Her Majesty's side, restored to his privileged position of Master of the Horse. Walter, placed in charge of the queen's security on the progress, wears a shining silver breastplate over his tunic and follows with a dozen yeomen dressed in royal livery and armed with halberds.

Bess is with the queen's twelve ladies, riding in pairs and followed by the members of the Privy Council, the royal musicians, the queen's doctors, and an army of servants. Behind them is a long train of baggage wagons, laden with everything from beds to gold plate.

The destination for the royal progress is Lord Burghley's mansion house, Theobalds, in Hertfordshire. As grand as a royal palace, with balconies, long galleries and rooftop walks, the mansion was built with such visits in mind.

Bess turns to Countess Catherine Howard, riding beside her. 'I cannot imagine how much this visit will cost old Lord Burghley.' She looks back at the straggling procession. 'There must be over three hundred of us, including all these servants.'

Countess Catherine agrees. 'Hosting a progress as large as this would bankrupt most men. I've heard stories of people having to sell land to meet the costs. Lord Burghley's reward is a knighthood for his son and heir. Robert Cecil is becoming a man to watch out for.'

Each royal progress has its challenges but, for Bess, this one is long awaited. Walter contrived for her to be in an attic apartment at the rear of the top floor, close to his own. There is no room for Martha, who sleeps in the servants' quarters, but Bess is glad of the privacy, as they have a plan.

The evening entertainment includes music on lutes and overlong discourses in verse, during which they hope they can slip away unnoticed. Walter leaves first, on the pretext of checking the guards, and Bess must wait a while before pleading an early night with a headache.

She makes her way up the back stairs to the top floor and taps on Walter's door, saying a silent prayer she isn't seen by any of the queen's household. Walter answers her knock and smiles as he sees her. He takes her hand and pulls her into his room, closing the door and sliding the iron bolt across.

The attic room is lit by a single candle in a silver holder, which casts flickering shadows in a draught from the small window. Bess smiles as she sees two glass goblets and a bottle of wine on a low table at the side of Walter's bed. He has planned well.

They stand in silence for a moment, before Bess gives him a concerned look 'Will they not miss you?'

'My duties include checking the security of the royal party.' He caresses her, his eyes bright with longing. 'It's only right to make sure the queen's gentlewoman is safe in bed.'

Bess feels her pulse race with desire and a sense of danger. 'It's a great risk we take.'

'A risk I am prepared to take – if you are?'

Her answer is to begin unfastening the bright silver buttons of his doublet. 'I am tired of waiting.' She kisses him on the lips, a promise of more to come.

He unties the thin bows of white silk ribbon fastening her

kirtle of embroidered silk brocade, while Bess pulls off her headdress and ruff of fine Belgian lace, stiffened with silver wire. She unties her wide farthingale, which falls to the floor, followed by her petticoat.

Bess unlaces her stays, and sits on the edge of his bed to take off her shoes, her pale silk stockings and chemise. She's dreamed of this moment for weeks, yet is overcome with unexpected shyness as she covers her breasts with her hands, glad of the dim candlelight.

She pulls back the coverlet, climbs into his bed and lies back on his down-filled pillows to watch him undress. Walter pulls off his leather riding boots and lets the rest of his clothes fall to the floor without a care.

He joins her in the bed and she relishes the warmth of his body against hers, holding him close. She kisses him with such passion they forget any risk of discovery, and make up for so many months of longing.

She discovers she can read his mind as they become one, taking him to the edge again and again before surrendering to him in a shuddering wave of ecstasy. She lies on her back, her heart pounding, and understands why people risk everything for love.

He pulls her close. 'You are full of surprises. Why did we wait so long?'

She smiles, and counts the reasons on her fingers. 'Her Majesty would be furious if she even suspected what we are up to. We could both be banished, locked up in the Tower, my reputation would be ruined, and you financially—'

Walter puts his finger to her lips to silence her. 'It would all be worth it, now I know what I've been missing.' He reaches out and pours them both a generous glass of wine, handing one to Bess and raising his as if in a toast. 'To us, and a long and happy future.' He grins. 'This is Lord Burghley's best wine, most generous of him.'

She gives him a shy look as she sips the strong wine, and pulls the warm coverlet over her. 'I hope that won't be our only time?'

'We will have to take care, but there will be more opportunities and, when we can, I *will* marry you, Bess. You have my word.'

'You still have to ask the queen's permission.' She frowns as she remembers the challenges they face. 'Her Majesty watches us like a hawk.'

Walter looks thoughtful. 'I know you worry about the risk of her refusal. It is her way of keeping you close to her, but our time will come, and we must be ready when it does.'

She turns to face him and stares into his eyes. 'I'm afraid there are many who would take pleasure in bringing us down. What do you suggest?'

'We will need allies to support us. I've tried to earn the favour of our host, Lord Burghley, but I confess I find it hard to like Robert Cecil, and as for the Earl of Essex…'

'You must try to put your differences behind you.'

'Essex is impossible.' He frowns at her suggestion. 'His arrogance provokes me, and the way Her Majesty favours him—'

'He could be useful to you, as could Robert Cecil.'

'I'm not sure I want Robert Cecil for a friend … but he would be a dangerous enemy.'

'Lord Burghley grooms his son to take his place. You would do well to have their support.'

She tenses at the sound of footsteps on the wooden stairs. 'You must go, before someone discovers us.' She watches as he dresses, admiring his lithe body, and with one last kiss, he is gone.

~

Bess is awake most of the night, planning when to break her troubling news to Walter, yet in the morning he seeks her out with news of his own. He leads her to the path through the queen's gardens, screened from the palace windows by high laurel hedges. There is a risk they might be seen together, but not overheard.

His face is grim. 'Sir Richard Grenville is dead, and the *Revenge* is lost with all hands.'

'Dear God. How?'

'The crew suffered a fever, and fell behind from the rest of the fleet. They were rammed and captured by a Spanish warship. By all accounts Sir Richard Grenville put up quite a fight with cannon and musket fire, but the *Revenge* was dismasted and lost in a violent storm, which also sank many of the Spanish ships.'

'Where were Lord Admiral Howard's warships?'

Walter frowns. 'I would not be surprised if they fled for safety when outnumbered by the Spanish fleet, leaving the *Revenge* to fight alone.'

'So your venture was a disaster?'

He shakes his head. 'Far from it. They captured eight Spanish ships with at least forty thousand pounds of silver and jewels. I expect a good return on my investment – and, but for you, it could have been me commanding the *Revenge*.'

Bess sees her chance. 'I also have news.' Bess glances back at the palace to make sure no one hears what she must tell him. 'You are going to be a father.'

He stares at her. 'Are you sure?'

'I waited until I was certain before telling you.' She struggles to compose herself. 'We must ask Her Majesty soon, or risk her anger.'

'We will marry, Bess, and leave the consequences to the grace of God.' He caresses her middle. 'You will have proof of consummation soon enough, and it will be too late for even the queen to do anything about it.'

Walter knows a minister he trusts to remain discreet about their secret marriage, and finds a quiet church to the west of the city where there should be less risk of anyone recognising them.

Torrential rain turns the narrow roads to rivers of mud as Bess makes her way with Martha to the old church. Walter paid for a covered carriage for privacy, which also keeps them dry.

Bess recalls the look of concern on Martha's face when she'd told her of their dangerous plan to marry without the queen's permission. 'I have no choice, Martha. I am with child, and cannot become an unmarried mother.'

Martha stared at her with wide eyes. 'You cannot keep such a thing secret for long, my lady.'

'I *must* – until the moment is right.' Bess frowns at the realisation it is unlikely there will ever be a good time. 'I shall have to tell my brother, Arthur. He will know what to do.'

The carriage stops close to the side door of the church and Bess steps out into the cold rain. She wears a hooded riding cape, which Martha takes from her as she enters the church to reveal her best gown, worn with her mother's pearls. Wild roses adorn her hair, an old bridal tradition.

Walter looks handsome in his best doublet, and gives her an appreciative smile as he sees her. He takes her hand and leads her to the altar, where the minister, a dour middle-aged man in the black robes of a cleric, waits with two of Walter's trusted friends who'd agreed to act as witnesses. There is no going back, and her happiness is edged with a frisson of fear. She dreads the consequences of what they are about to do.

The minister's deep voice echoes in the empty church.

'We are gathered together, here in the sight of God, to join this man and this woman in holy matrimony, an honourable state, instituted of God in paradise.' He looks up at them both. 'I require that if either of you know of any reason why you may not be lawfully joined together in matrimony, that you confess it now.'

Bess can think of many reasons, but Walter clears his throat and answers for them in his Devon accent, 'We know of no impediment.'

The minister continues. 'Will you have this woman to be your wedded wife, to live together after God's ordinance in the holy estate of matrimony? Will you love her, comfort her, honour, and keep her, in sickness and in health, and forsaking all others, keep only to her, so long as you both shall live?'

Walter replies in a clear Devon accent. 'I will.'

The minister turns to Bess. 'Will you have this man to be your wedded husband, to live together after God's ordinance in the holy estate of matrimony? Will you obey him and serve him, love, honour, and keep him, in sickness and in health, and forsaking all others, keep only to him so long as you both shall live?'

Bess answers in a calm, clear voice. 'I will.'

She listens while Walter says his vows, and does the same, sensing her life changing forever. The minister pronounces them man and wife. Walter kisses her and whispers. 'I will care for you and our unborn child, whatever the cost or the consequences.'

She is so preoccupied with the wedding that she hasn't thought about their future as husband and wife. 'What are we going to do now?'

He gives her a reassuring smile. 'We must continue as if nothing has changed, for as long as we can.'

She moves her hand to her middle, where there is yet no

sign of their child. 'I can wait until the end of autumn, but by then the truth will be obvious to all.'

Walter looks thoughtful. 'Have you told your brother?'

Bess shakes her head. 'I must, but I've no idea how he will react. He's worked so hard to restore our place at court, and now I risk ruining it all.'

'Arthur is a good man, Bess. Let us hope he will help keep you and our child safe from the gossips of court.'

3

MILE END 1592

Tнe covered carriage rattles and jolts as they ride through narrow cobblestoned streets in wintry rain. Bess moves her hand to support her child. She is on her way with her maidservant Martha to spend her confinement with her brother Arthur and his family in their house at Mile End on the outskirts of London.

Bess worries about involving her brother, and putting all he's done to restore their good name at risk, but she has no choice. The only alternative is to stay with Walter's mother, far away in rural Devon, which would only raise more questions.

Walter said it was best if he stayed at Chatham docks, planning his new adventure at sea. Bess suspects he wants to leave the country – out of sight and out of mind – before the queen discovers they are married. The dockyards are not far from Mile End, yet her only way to contact him is through her brother, as they've agreed letters are too great a risk.

Bess cannot forget the look of astonishment on her brother's face when she found the courage to tell him her news. The weight of responsibility was lifted from her shoulders, but she knows her brother will not think of her in the same way again.

It would have been easier if he had been angry with her. Instead, he'd looked at her as if seeing her for the first time. She remembers how the hurt echoed in her brother's voice. 'It is unforgivable you didn't tell me sooner.'

She'd tried to explain, yet even as she said the words they sounded hollow. 'Walter thought it best, for your own reputation.'

'You continued to serve as the queen's gentlewoman. Did you not think anyone would notice, and report you to the queen?' Her brother's eyes flashed with concern.

'It was easy at first, and I don't think anyone noticed, even later, as I gave them no reason to suspect—'

'No reason?' Her brother was scornful. 'You can be sure someone will have found good reason.' He cursed, for the first time in front of her. 'Let us thank God you seem to have got away with it, for now.'

After his initial outrage, Arthur's tone softened as he began to think how he could make the best of the poor hand they've dealt him. 'There's fever in the city. We shall inform the queen you are unwell, and must stay away from court until you recover.'

'If the queen has the least suspicion, she will send her doctors to discover the truth.'

'Ask leave to tend my wife. Even the queen will understand if your sister-in-law asks for your help.'

Arthur's wife Anne looks weary as she welcomes them, and something in her eyes suggests resentment. 'Arthur has arranged for a midwife, Mistress Collingwood, to attend you during your confinement. He tells me you are not certain when your child is due.'

Bess forces a smile. 'I'm grateful, Anne. It was never my

intention to be a burden to your family. I plan to return to court when my baby is born which, God willing, is within the month.'

'Who will care for your child, when you are at court?'

'I will find a wet nurse, but Walter has a plan for us to escape by sea to Ireland if someone discovers our secret.'

'Well, let us pray it doesn't come to that, and now you must rest, for the sake of the baby.'

Bess's confinement at Mile End is like imprisonment. She is not allowed out in case someone sees her. Arthur forbids her to receive visitors, so her only company is her maidservant Martha, Anne and her servants. It is a relief when the strange pain arrives, meaning her child is on its way.

The midwife, Mistress Collingwood, is reassuring, and encourages her to drink a potion of herbs in warmed mead to help dull the contractions. Bess cries out to God for the pain to stop. Her prayers are answered when her baby, a healthy boy, arrives without complications.

Bess holds her swaddled son and stares into his wide eyes with a sense of wonder. It seems impossible this tiny child has caused so much trouble and changed her life. She expects Walter will wish to name their son after himself, but when her brother rides to the docks to inform Walter, he returns with a surprise.

'The child is to be named Damerei.'

'Damerei?' Bess thinks she misheard her brother.

'Walter said the name is to honour his ancestors, the D'Ameries, who came to England with William the Conqueror.' Arthur smiles. 'He's asked Anne and myself to witness the christening, and urges you to return to court as soon as you're well enough, as questions are being asked.'

'Does the queen suspect us?' Bess studies her brother's face, and her pulse races as she senses he is not telling her everything. 'There is something else, isn't there?'

'Walter told me Robert Cecil tricked him into denying he's married – to you or anyone.'

Bess gasps, but knows Robert Cecil will have left him no choice. 'This could make it worse for us both when we judge the time right to tell the queen.'

Arthur nods. 'I should tell you he also asked me to invite the Earl of Essex to be your child's godfather.'

'Why?' Bess stares at him, her mind racing with the consequences. 'He doesn't trust the Earl of Essex.'

Arthur's hesitation suggests he is as surprised as she is. 'He seems to think the earl will be a useful ally.'

'Walter knows there is a risk he might tell the queen our secret, before we are ready.'

'Let us hope he does not, at least until Walter returns with ships laden with Spanish gold.'

Bess tries to hide her anxiety as she arrives at Essex House, one of the finest mansions in the Strand, with her maidservant, Martha. Her wet nurse, carrying her infant son, takes the servants' entrance. Bess is uncomfortable in her tight-fitting brocade gown, but must wear it when she returns to court.

Now she understands Walter's plan. After making the Earl of Essex part of their subterfuge, his wife Frances, Countess of Essex, and sister, Baroness Penelope Rich, have both offered their help.

Bess greets Frances with an apology. 'I'm sorry to burden you with my troubles, countess.'

Frances smiles. 'I have little to lose. I am already banished from court, as is Penelope.'

Bess returns her warm smile. 'I'm grateful to you. My brother, Arthur, and his wife, Anne, have been kind, but I could not risk staying with them any longer.'

Frances looks thoughtful when the wet nurse arrives carrying little Damerei, who stares at her with innocent blue eyes. 'I've been in your position, Bess, in fear of Her Majesty finding out, but you must know it is only a matter of time before someone tells the queen?'

'Robert Cecil is asking questions, but if I am banished, I won't miss my life at court.'

Frances agrees. 'In truth, I wasn't sorry to be banished, and my husband was *soon* forgiven.'

'Walter is in the queen's favour. She's appointed him Captain of the Guard, and permitted him to return to sea.' Bess smiles. 'He hopes to have another chance to intercept the Spanish treasure fleet.'

Frances puts her hand on Bess's arm. 'Well, let us hope he succeeds.' Something in her tone suggests she doubts he will.

Bess says a silent prayer as she enters the privy chamber for the first time in many months. She's rehearsed this moment, yet cannot help the pounding of her heart as she approaches the queen and curtseys. 'Your Majesty.'

The queen seems to have aged ten years, despite the skill of her ladies. Her red-painted lips part to reveal stained teeth. 'Bess.' She stares, her eyes bright with curiosity. 'We've missed you at court, but your brother tells me his wife is recovered.'

Bess plays her best card. 'Lady Anne will never recover from the loss of her first daughter, Your Majesty, but with God's grace, her second child is strong.' Her conscience prickles at the use of a child's death to explain her absence, but the queen nods and Bess allows herself to breathe again. She steps back, pleased the queen asks no more questions.

Bess senses a coolness from some of the other ladies, and catches them glancing at her with what could be disapproval. She recalls her dilemma about sharing gossip with the queen. She hopes anyone aware of the truth will have the sense to keep her secret to themselves.

By the end of the first week she feels able to relax in the knowledge she has escaped the queen's wrath. She returns to the sanctuary of Essex House, where she finds Damerei safe and well. Frances has shared her secret with her sister-in-law, Baroness Penelope Rich, who in turn has told her lover, Sir Charles Blount.

Penelope has a child by Charles Blount, and seems more interested in news of the queen's failing health than her secret marriage. 'It's typical of her to call it treason if we even speak of the succession.'

Charles Blount raises an eyebrow, and listens to Bess as she tells them about her return to court. 'I caution you to take care, my lady. Your husband has a talent for making dangerous enemies.' He gives her a cautionary look. 'You can use the threat of plague in London to escape the city, while you can.'

Bess is at Walter's property, Durham House – a towering old mansion facing the Strand, at the bend in the river in White-hall – when the Vice Chamberlain of the Household, Sir Thomas Heneage, arrives with two yeomen of the queen's guard. Close to sixty, Sir Thomas suffers from gout, which gives him a stern demeanour.

He frowns at Bess. 'Mistress Throckmorton – or should I refer to you as Lady Raleigh?'

Bess feels her world collapse, yet tries to sound calm. 'I

don't understand, Sir Thomas.' She prays that, like Charles Blount, he only intends to offer her well-meaning but unnecessary advice.

He gestures to the Yeomen of the Guard. 'You are under house arrest, and are not to leave or receive any visitors without permission.'

Bess makes one last effort. 'On what grounds, Sir Thomas? What have I been accused of?'

He studies his shoes, made larger than usual due to his gout-swollen feet, and remains silent. His eyes meet hers. 'Please do not make this difficult for me.'

Encouraged by his more informal tone, she tries again. 'On whose orders am I to be arrested?'

'On the orders of Sir Robert Cecil. I am to detain you until further notice.'

A trickle of cold sweat runs down inside her bodice, which is too tight since Damerei's birth. She curses Robert Cecil having his petty revenge on Walter. Bess has no idea if he is driven by jealousy, duty, or something she has yet to discover.

Her brother Arthur paid for a nurse to care for Damerei, out of sight in Enfield, and a plan forms in her mind. She guesses Walter is also under arrest, so she will ask Countess Frances to help her escape with her son to Walter's mother in Devon, where no one, other than him, will think to look for them.

Bess wakes to a bright August morning, with sunshine streaming through her window. Nothing has happened after a month of house arrest, but she's troubled that she has not heard from Walter, and her guards are unwilling or unable to answer her questions. With luck she faces nothing more than banishment from court.

Sir Thomas Heneage enters her room, grim-faced as he gives her the news she fears. 'The queen has signed the order for your imprisonment in the Tower.' He holds up a hand to silence her, before she can object. 'I have no knowledge of the details, only that your husband, Sir Walter, is recalled from sea and also sent to the Tower.'

Bess gasps. 'For how long, Sir Thomas?'

'I've told you all I know. Please follow me.' He leads her to the river steps, where the two yeomen help her into a boat.

There is no chance to escape, and they travel in silence to the watergate at the Tower of London. Bess has visited several times, and hopes to be shown to one of the better apartments, so her heart sinks when she is led to one of the outer towers.

Her cell's small window looks over the stinking moat, with the gallows of Tyburn Hill visible in the distance. The sight triggers an old memory. Her mother once told Bess that her grandfather, Sir Nicholas Carew, was accused of conspiring with the king's cousin, Henry Courtenay, Marquess of Exeter.

Despite protesting his innocence, he'd been executed at Tyburn on the old king's orders, his lands and property seized. She struggles to remember her own father, a cousin of Queen Catherine Parr, who served as ambassador to France and Scotland. Accused by the queen of involvement in the Duke of Norfolk's conspiracy in favour of Mary, Queen of Scots, he'd been imprisoned at Windsor Castle. He'd died soon after, leaving her mother to raise their family. She'd married again, and Adrian Stokes, widower and former Master of the Horse to Lady Frances Grey, Duchess of Suffolk, became her stepfather. As mother to the ill-fated Lady Jane Grey, Lady Frances was the closest connection Bess had to the throne of England.

The cold stone floor of her cell has a thin scattering of straw, as if to house an animal. The only furniture is an old pallet bed and a wooden chair. A covered iron bucket occupies one corner. She doesn't need to examine the blanket to know it is infested with fleas, and fears bed bugs lurk in wait. She'd imagined her room at her brother's house in Mile End was like a prison, but now she sees the consequences of crossing the queen.

Sir Thomas Heneage is apologetic as he ushers her into the small cell. 'I'm sorry it's come to this, my lady.'

'Will you permit me to send for my maidservant? I must tell her my wishes for my son's care.' A thought occurs to her. 'I will need a change of clothes, and will ask her to bring me a pen and paper. I wish to write a letter of apology to Her Majesty.'

'You are only allowed to be visited by the chaplain, and to exercise in the yard once a day.' His tone softens a little. 'I will send a yeoman to Durham House to fetch you a change of clothes, but I advise against writing to the queen, for now at least.'

The heavy door slams shut as he leaves, and Bess hears a metallic clunk as they lock her in. She'd managed to remain composed on the river journey to the Tower, but now sits on the rickety chair with her head in her hands, and weeps until she has no more tears. Her only hope is that the queen will forgive her, and Walter, before too long.

Bess wakes at the sound of rattling keys, expecting to see her warder with a bowl of cold pottage and a crust of dry bread. She rouses herself, trying to brush the creases from her gown, slept in too often, and sits up ready as the door opens. Her warder brings a plate of freshly baked bread and a chunk of cheese, with a cup of wine.

The delicious taste warms her throat, and she gives him a questioning look. She still hopes for news of a reprieve. 'Who should I thank for this?'

Her warder grunts. 'Sir Arthur Throckmorton. He has permission from the Constable of the Tower to meet with you in the yard this morning.' He frowns with disapproval at this departure from their dull routine.

Bess finds her attempts to question her guards bring scowls and the occasional curse. She learns to recognise the Lord's day from the ringing of the bell in the Chapel of St Peter ad Vincula, and uses the pin of her brooch to scrape a mark in the sandstone lintel of her window.

She doesn't have to count the marks. There are six, so she's been in her bleak prison for more than a month, time enough for even her vindictive queen to relent. She itches the many bites on her arms, and her mind buzzes with questions for her brother while she awaits her chance to see him.

At last, her door is pulled open and she follows her warder into the unseasonably warm September sunshine. Arthur raises a hand as he sees her, but Bess knows him well and, as she approaches him, the sadness in his eyes tells her he brings bad news.

He studies her with an appraising look. 'I hear you've been unwell, Bess.'

She would like to embrace him, but worries about the lice in the folds of her gown, and the fleas which make their home in her plaited hair. 'I feel better now, but for the first few weeks I suffered from lack of sleep, and the food here is not fit for a dog to eat.'

Her brother scowls. 'I paid for them to treat you well, and will have to speak to the constable.'

'It's surprising what you can become used to. I will never again take anything for granted.'

'There is no easy way to tell you, Bess. Plague raged through London and many have died, including your son.' His voice falters.

'Damerei?' Bess stares at him in disbelief. She recalls what a strong little boy he was, so full of life, and tears of grief run down her face. Bess falls to her knees on the hard cobbles, sobbing. Her only reason for living is gone.

Arthur reaches out a comforting hand to help her stand. 'We sent for the plague doctor, but we were too late. Little Damerei and his nurse died in the same night. There was nothing anyone could have done.'

Bess cannot bear to think about how her son must have died, and that he is now buried in some foul plague pit, with no words spoken over his little body. She makes herself a promise he will never be forgotten.

She dries her eyes; she has so many questions, her grieving must wait. 'What has become of my husband?'

'He is not forgiven, but the queen ordered his release.' Arthur gives her a wry look. 'He has the task of ensuring she receives her share of a Portuguese treasure ship, the *Madre de Deus*, which is being unloaded in Dartmouth, so I expect he is being kept busy.'

Bess eyes the leather bag her brother carries. 'Do you have a letter from Walter for me?'

Arthur frowns and shakes his head. 'I regret I have not seen or heard from him, Bess, but I've brought you parchment, pen and ink, so you can write to him, and plead to others for your release.'

'You mean the queen?' Bess frowns. Her brother seems to have forgotten the great difficulty she has with her writing.

'I recommend writing to Lord Burghley first, to make peace with Robert Cecil, and…'

Bess notes his hesitation. 'What is it?'

'I was going to suggest you tell them the fate of your son. If that wins their sympathy and secures your release, his death should not be for nothing. I've paid your guards to bring your letters to me, so I can deliver them in person.'

Bess gives him a nod of gratitude and takes the bag from

him. 'I pray Walter is also trying to secure my release.' She sees her brother's frown.

'Let us hope he is. The queen granted his request for the Sherborne estate in Dorset, so he must be in her favour.'

The guard grunts that their time is up, and Bess raises a hand in thanks to her brother before returning to her dismal cell. The loss of her little son is too much to bear, but her brother's words give her hope, and she resolves to write letters until she has run out of parchment.

She recalls how much Walter wished for the Sherborne estate. There is nothing to keep her in London, and Dorset is far enough away for them to make a fresh start, if she can only persuade the queen to release her.

Bess struggles with her writing, and envies those who can spell the longer words. Her solution is to write them as they sound, and pray their meaning is not lost. It doesn't help that she must appeal to those who have ordered her locked away.

She understands her brother's plan to explain the loss of her son, but as she tries to write his name her tears fall onto the parchment. She takes a fresh sheet and begins her letter to Lord Burghley again. *Most noble lord, I humbly beseech you to…*

Bess thinks Sir William Cecil, Baron Burghley, is her best chance. He is the queen's most trusted advisor and, as Lord High Treasurer, will know the value of the work Walter does to secure the queen's share of the treasure.

His son, Sir Robert Cecil, is quite a different matter. Ambitious and cold, Robert Cecil never liked Walter, and would care little for the hardships she suffers on his orders. Bess spends all day working on her letter to him until the light fails.

Her letters are her best hope of freedom, but Walter's silence troubles her, and she has many questions. If her brother can bribe the guards to see her, why does her husband not do the same? What can he be doing that is more important than securing her pardon?

Bess shivers in the wintry cold, and scratches the bites on her arms. She calculates from her marks she's made on the lintel that it must be the end of December. She dreams of the extravagant celebrations of Christmas and New Year, and prays the queen is in a more receptive mood to her pleas for mercy.

She doubts if any of her letters were even read, and worries she is forgotten. At least her food has improved after her brother's intervention; she is allowed clean clothes and decent food, sent by Countess Frances from Essex House.

She cannot face the prospect of a long, freezing winter in this prison, and has nothing to live for now her son is gone. She hears a shout and footsteps outside her door. There is a rattle of keys and her door bangs open. Her brother Arthur stands staring at her for a moment, as if he has no words.

'I've come to set you free, Bess.'

4

DURHAM HOUSE 1593

Bess wakes at dawn and it takes an effort for her to realise she is back at Durham House. The old bed creaks in complaint when she moves, and the worn ropes supporting the mattress sag in the middle, but after her flea-infested pallet bed in the Tower it seems luxurious.

'Tell me this isn't a dream?'

Walter stirs at her side. 'This is no dream.'

'I can't believe we have Sherborne, after all that's happened. Does it mean the queen has a heart, after all?'

He shakes his head. 'I suspect old William Cecil felt we'd been punished enough.'

'Lord Burghley may be old, but he's never lost his sense of fairness. He still holds the royal purse strings, and you've filled his treasury with gold, so although your profit was stolen from you, he might see this as some recompense.'

Walter places a kiss on her cheek. 'Am I forgiven?'

Bess must think before she can answer. 'I still can't understand why I had to rely on my brother to set me free. Tell me why you could never visit after you were set free, or write to let me know you were well and working for my release?'

'I didn't want to risk raising your hopes until I was certain.'

She hears the lie in his voice, but must let it go – for now. He's changed since their arrest, as they both have. The spark of ambition still glints in his eye, but the hardship he's suffered makes him suspicious of everyone. He will turn forty-one in a week, and his once dark beard is peppered with grey.

'The worst thing was not knowing if my imprisonment would ever end.' Bess closes her eyes at the memory.

'I'm sorry it took so long.' Walter frowns. 'You know we are not even supposed to be here? We are both banished to Sherborne, and must travel there as soon as the weather improves.'

Bess lies back on her pillows. 'Our New Year's gift from our vindictive queen. Freedom, not only from the bleak life of the Tower, but from her dull court – and from the nightmare of the plague, still haunting this city.' A darkness passes over her mood as she remembers little Damerei, but she pushes the thought away.

Walter sits up in bed. 'Banishment to Sherborne seems more like a reward than a punishment.'

She watches him pull on his linen nightshirt. His body is still lithe and muscular. 'One thing I've learned from my time in the Tower is to make the most of every moment, and never to take anything for granted.' She smiles. 'I can't wait to start our new life, and don't wish to stay here in London any longer than we need to.'

'You shall be the lady of the manor of Sherborne, Lady Raleigh, and we will rebuild the castle as our family home.'

'How can we afford to rebuild a castle?' She frowns at the prospect of sinking deeper into debt.

Walter grins. 'You think I didn't profit from the treasure of the *Madre de Deus*?'

'You said everyone had their fair share, except for you, even though you invested more than anyone, and needed to borrow money to pay for supplies.'

'That's what I wished everyone to believe. My assistant, Thomas Harriot, made the records of the treasure inventory.' He gives her a wry look. 'His task was to ensure I had more than my share, in compensation.'

Her eyes widen. 'If they ever find out—'

'There's no way they can, Bess. They know the treasure was being looted before I arrived in Dartmouth, which is why they tasked me to take charge – and *mine* is the official record.'

She brightens. 'I'd thought we would be in debt for many years to come.'

He shakes his head and counts on his fingers. 'I still have the income from wines and my licence on the export of broadcloth. My ships earn their keep as privateers, and I'm owed payment for those taken for the queen's navy. We have the income from my estates in Ireland, and rent from the apartments here at Durham House, which Thomas Harriot leased while I was—'

Bess puts her hand to his lips. 'Let us not speak of it.'

Walter pulls on a robe, and climbs from their creaking bed to fetch a wooded casket, which he presents to her.

Bess sits up, pulling the coverlet around her, and gasps as she turns a small key in the lock and lifts the lid. The casket, lined with velvet, glitters with gold and jewels. She takes a solid gold crucifix, set with gleaming rubies on a fine gold chain, and turns it in the light. 'This alone is enough to keep us for a year.'

'These jewels are my gift to you, Bess. Take care where you wear them, but you are more deserving of them than our vindictive queen.'

She reaches into the box and takes a string of perfect pearls, letting them slip back through her fingers, and smiles. 'I have a gift for you, Walter. One of the few things of value my father left me was his best bed. I shall have it brought to Sherborne.' She gives him a coy smile. 'I fear this one won't tolerate much more exertion.'

Walter had warned her that Sherborne Castle, once the opulent palace of a bishop, was now a ruin. The great gatehouse is still impressive, and the bishop's chapel has retained its decorative carved stonework, but missing roof tiles have allowed damp to affect many of the rooms.

Black mould speckles the cobwebbed corners, and old rushes crackle underfoot on cold stone floors. The air carries the musty scent of decay, and the light is filtered through leaded windows opaque with grime. One entire wing is gone, with only a footprint of neat stonework remaining.

Walter shakes his head. 'The villagers no doubt stole the stone, carting it away to build houses of their own.'

Bess is happy, despite the grief in her heart for her son, the hardship of her imprisonment, and their long, freezing journey in midwinter from London. For the first time since that fateful day of her arrest by Sir Thomas Heneage and his yeomen she feels glad to be alive.

Walter examines the broken windowpanes and shakes his head. 'I learned an expensive lesson restoring Lismore Castle in Ireland. Even Durham House cost me four thousand pounds to make habitable.' He frowns. 'The bills are always many times the estimate.'

Bess is undaunted. 'We can't return to London. I like it here at Sherborne, but we need somewhere to live. We could start with a few of the better rooms.'

Walter leads her out into the frosty courtyard, overgrown with weeds. 'As well as an orchard of apple and medlar trees, we have water meadows and a deer park.' He smiles. 'The deer are long gone, but I want you to see the old hunting lodge.'

They cross a stone bridge over the tranquil River Yeo, and Bess sees a building with good views of the former deer park. Like the castle, the hunting lodge is close to ruin, with tiles missing from the roof. Rooks fly through gaping holes where there were once windows, and a colony of bats haunts the attic rooms.

Walter stares up at the roof. 'This place is too small for our needs, but the poor harvest means we'll have no trouble finding labourers. We could have this hunting lodge pulled down and build a new manor house, fit for the lord and lady of Sherborne.'

She smiles at his enthusiasm. 'What do you have in mind?'

'Something grand, Bess. Four storeys high, with corner turrets, like my study at Durham House, to make the most of these views – and a nursery.'

'A new house, for a fresh start.'

They dine in the old castle refectory, one of the few rooms with glass in the windows. A log fire blazes in the old stone hearth, keeping the wintry chill at bay. Walter brought an oak dining table and chairs, silver candlesticks and salts from Durham House, as well as several bottles of his best wine.

He smiles across the table at Bess and raises his glass in a toast. 'To peace – and happiness.'

Bess raises her glass. 'To a new start in our new home.' She's dressed for dinner in an azure-blue gown with puffed sleeves and a lace ruff with matching cuffs. A jewelled pendant, one of the best pieces from the treasure of the *Madre de Deus*, glints at her neck in the candlelight.

Servants bring platters of freshly baked manchet bread, still warm from the ovens, a dish of wild duck with ginger and pepper, and a gravy of mace and barberries preserved in claret, served with butter and sugar. Bess savours such rich delicacies after being half-starved on cold pottage and stale crusts for so long in the Tower of London.

Walter looks thoughtful as he sips the sweet wine. 'I've not made any apology to the queen for not asking her permission. I thought an appeal to the Cecils would be more worthwhile. Now I fear that was a serious misjudgement.'

Bess helps herself to the steaming breast of duck, and spoons the rich gravy onto her plate. 'You can't rely on either of the Cecils to put our case. Lord Burghley avoids involvement in such matters, and I suspect it was Robert Cecil who revealed our secret, to increase his own favour with the queen.'

'I always suspected it was Essex who betrayed us.'

Bess shakes her head. 'I doubt it. Countess Frances told me Essex nominated you to be a Garter knight.' She sips her wine, savouring the taste. 'Frances said her husband was the only one to do so.'

Walter stops eating and stares at her. 'I didn't know. I must have been in the dockyard, preparing the fleet for the Azores.'

Bess tears a piece of bread and dips it in her gravy. She has learned to waste nothing. 'We have few enough friends now. You must not be quick to judge.'

'There are still those who would bring us down.' Walter frowns. 'The whisperers and gossips of court undermine my reputation – and yours, Bess.'

'That's how the court functions, on gossip and self-interest.'

'Do you think I should write to Her Majesty?'

'I don't see what you will lose, but it's difficult to know what you stand to gain.'

Walter drains his glass. 'There is much to gain. Essex was forgiven within a year. I only hold my estates in Ireland because of the queen's favour, and expect moves are being made even now to steal them from me.'

'Are you saying you wish to return to London?'

'My man Thomas Harriot can look after my interests in London, but I shall write to the queen. As you say, Bess, I have little enough to lose.' Walter smiles. 'There is plenty for me to do here, overseeing the building works and the Stannaries in Cornwall, which is useful income.'

The clink of chisels on stone and voices of workmen echo across the water meadows as Bess crosses the bridge to see the progress. Most of the old lodge needed to be demolished, and the walls of the new house already rise above the height of the mullioned first-floor windows.

She turns as she hears her name called, and sees Walter has returned from his Easter meeting of the Stannaries. He rides up to her and dismounts, watching with her as the labourers carry heavy baskets of stone up the high scaffold. 'What do you think of our new home?'

She smiles. 'The architect suggests the external walls should be covered in a lime render. He says it's a new fashion. As well as keeping the weather out, we save money on ornamental brickwork.'

'It seems I've married a builder.'

She laughs. 'How was your business in Cornwall?'

'I have good news. I've been elected a burgess of the parliamentary borough of Mitchell, which means I can attend the next meeting of Parliament and start rebuilding my career.'

Bess smooths the front of her gown. 'And I have news for you, Walter. I am with child again.'

'Praise be to God.' He wipes away an unexpected tear, and grins at her. 'This time my mother *shall* see her grandson.'

Bess raises an eyebrow. 'How are you so sure the child will be a boy?'

'I'm not – but if it is, he'll be named Walter.'

She stares up at the towering wooden scaffolding of their half-finished house. 'This will never be ready in time for our child to be born here.'

Walter agrees. 'I shall have them prepare our bedchamber in the old castle as a fit place for your lying-in.'

'I shall send for my sister-in-law, Anne, and her midwife, Mistress Collingwood, to keep me company when the time comes for my confinement.'

Walter frowns at her suggestion. 'Anne Throckmorton was one of those who betrayed us—'

Bess holds up a hand to silence him. 'You must not bear her a grudge, Walter. She is family, and we both knew the truth was bound to come out. You couldn't expect Anne to lie to Lord Hunsdon.'

He raises an eyebrow at her tone. 'You are right, of course, Bess. This new house is a fresh start – with everything.'

Bess finds her lying-in less onerous after her months in the Tower, and no longer feels her room is a prison. Once bedchamber to a bishop, faded old tapestries of biblical scenes grace the walls. Walter had the fireplace and chimney restored, and the broken windows shuttered to keep out the autumn breeze.

Her days have been so busy; summer flew faster than the bats escaping the old hunting lodge, and now fallen leaves swirl in a wintry breeze. Her time as the queen's gentlewoman seems like a different life, and Bess has never been more content.

Anne arrives from Mile End in a carriage with her midwife, Mistress Collingwood, and her small daughters, one of whom, little Anne, is only a few months old and cared for by her young nursemaid. Anne looks apologetic as Bess welcomes her.

'Arthur told me how you were treated in the Tower. I am sorry I couldn't deny your marriage to Walter, Bess. I had no idea—'

Bess reaches out to take her hand. 'I understand, and it is

of no matter. Sherborne is a new start for us.' She smiles. 'I am grateful to have you here to keep me company, and that you've brought my maid, Martha, and Mistress Collingwood.'

Anne looks relieved. 'I've tried to bring you everything you will need for the baby, and confess I was intrigued to see where you and Walter are living.'

'Thank you, Anne. I'm afraid we've had to find temporary rooms for you here in the castle, but you must ask Walter to show you progress with our new house.'

Bess cannot tell if it is day or night in her darkened bedchamber, and no longer cares. Her maidservant Martha built a good fire in the hearth to boil a pan of water, but the old chimney makes the air smell of woodsmoke and hot steam.

Mistress Collingwood, a kindly woman with an apron over her plain dress, tucks a stray strand of greying hair back under her white linen coif. The concern in her eyes tells Bess this will not be the same as last time, with little Damerei.

Her unplaited dark hair is plastered to her forehead with sweat as Bess fights the thoughts echoing in her mind. Something has gone wrong. The pains began long ago, yet there seems no end to the delivery of this stubborn child.

Anne sits at her side, holding her hand. 'Have faith, Bess.' Anne tries to calm her as she grips her hand tighter. 'The good Lord watches over us.'

Bess raises her head to have a better view of Mistress Collingwood. 'How much longer?' She grits her teeth and holds her breath as a sharper pain returns.

Mistress Collingwood hesitates before answering. 'All in good time, my lady. You need to push now. Push as hard as you can.'

Bess pushes with all her strength but is weak after so many

hours. She tries again, for the sake of her baby, the effort helping to keep the despair from her mind. She stares at Anne, who has not left her side. 'If it is a girl, I should like to name her after you, and my poor mother. Walter wishes for a boy, to be named after him.'

All Bess wishes for is the pain to end, and she begins repeating a silent prayer between each deep breath. 'Please God, let this soon be over.'

'Good, that's good. Push again, my lady.' Mistress Collingwood sounds encouraging but Bess sees her frown. She closes her eyes and says a silent prayer for God's mercy. She cannot suffer the loss of another child.

Her mind wanders as her strength ebbs. She cries out as she puts every ounce of her remaining energy into one last push. Mistress Collingwood pulls her baby free in a sudden moment of release.

'You have another boy, my lady, a perfect little boy.'

The shrill cry of a baby echoes, and Bess gives thanks to God and smiles. 'A perfect little boy.'

All the hurt and worry ends in an instant. 'He shall be named Wat, after his father.'

Bells ring out in tuneful celebration as they gather in St Martin's Church in the hamlet of Lillington, three miles from Sherborne. By tradition, Bess should not attend the christening, but she will not be parted from her son, and refuses to remain in bed for a month for no good reason.

Walter's mother, Katherine Raleigh, is frail yet her eyes shine with pride as she cradles her grandson. She has travelled from Devon in her ancient carriage, and complains she felt every rut and bump in the road. Also gathered in the church are Walter's elder brothers, Adrian, with his wife Eleanor, and

Carew, with his wife, Dorothy. Bess's brother, Arthur, and his wife Anne again agree to act as godparents.

The minister calls them to the octagonal font, with Tudor roses carved into the Portland stone. Their son's cries echo to the rafters as he is baptised Walter Raleigh. Bess senses her life is changing yet again. From now on, everything she does will be for little Walter, who they agree to call 'Wat'. She looks forward to their new life together as a family, whatever the future might hold.

5

SHERBORNE 1594

WALTER'S FACE IS GRIM AS HE CARRIES HIS MOTHER'S OAK coffin on his shoulder with his brothers. The only sound is of shuffling leather soles on the ancient tiled floor. The bells of the church of St Martha Major are silent; the stunted spire was never replaced after a winter storm sent it crashing to the ground.

Bess stares up at the silver cross on the altar, her mind filled with memories of her own mother, and everything she'd done for her. Her mother was so proud of her when she became the queen's gentlewoman, but could not have known what the consequences would be.

Like Bess, her mother taught herself to read and write, and knew hardship, yet always did her best for her ten sons and three daughters. Bess suspects her mother married her late stepfather, Adrian Stokes – former Master of the Horse and widower of Lady Frances Grey, Duchess of Suffolk – to pay for her court expenses and dowry.

Walter takes his seat beside Bess and she catches a hint of stale tobacco. He'd told her he wished he'd persuaded his mother to remain at Sherborne after Wat's christening, as the return journey to Devon took its toll. He'd planned to visit her, but another harsh winter, and work to finish their new house, delayed him too long.

Walter's sister Margaret, widowed for two years, looks blankly at Bess as if she holds her responsible. Her voice has an edge of bitterness when she speaks to Walter. 'Mother prayed for you, when you were locked up in the Tower of London.' Margaret frowns. 'You should have asked the queen's permission to marry, for our mother's sake.'

Bess would not know how to explain about the queen to Walter's sister, who'd never been to court. She is relieved when the minister asks them to take their places for the service. He describes Katherine Raleigh as a woman of noble wit, and of a good and godly opinion.

Bess remembers her mother's modest pride, and says a prayer for both her own parents as Walter's mother is laid to rest beside his father. Walter takes her hand as he says farewell, fighting the tears. The loss of a mother is the end of an era, but Bess promises herself she will tell little Wat how proud his grandmother, Katherine Raleigh, had been of him.

Bess is kept busy with their growing household. They've taken on more servants, including a housekeeper, Mistress Hull. Their servants include a small army of gardeners, game-keepers and groundsmen who work long hours to tame the overgrown orchards and plant new gardens. There is a rose garden for Bess, and kitchen gardens for herbs and vegetables.

This is not London, where anything she needs is for sale close by; Bess learns to be self-sufficient, and find economies where she can. She enjoys visiting the farmers' market in Sher-borne, but relies on the weekly wagon trip to the county town of Dorchester, eighteen miles away.

While Walter is absent on business, his stepbrother, Adrian Gilbert, arrives with his wife, Eleanor. Eleven years older than Walter, Adrian is heavyset and opinionated, with little of his brother's style or charm. He dresses like a farmer, with riding boots and a leather jerkin, and wears a broad-brimmed hat. Walter is scathing when he talks about his stepbrother.

'He won his fortune through marriage to Eleanor, and risked much of it investing in a silver mine at Combe Martin in Devon. More by luck than judgement he manages to turn a profit, but cares not what he says to any man or woman, speaking his mind regardless of the consequences.'

Bess thinks Eleanor an odd choice of wife for a man like Adrian Gilbert, as she must be close to sixty, but remembers she was a wealthy widow. Softly spoken and modest, her dark brocade gown is old-fashioned, with a high bodice. She wears a starched ruff which reminds Bess of old oil paintings in Richmond Palace.

While Adrian oversees the work to have fresh water pumped to the house from springs in the nearby hills, Eleanor offers to help Bess find suitable furnishings for every room. This is her first guest since the building work was completed; Bess enjoys showing her the new house.

'Our move from the old castle to the new house is quite a turning point in our life at Sherborne.' She smiles as a servant welcomes them to the grand entrance hall. 'We were unlucky to have another severe winter, which delayed the building work. Sherborne was cut off by drifts of snow. The river froze over with thick ice, and flooding after the thaw turned the roads to mud.'

Eleanor studies the tall windows. 'You will need to have shutters made before next winter, to keep the weather out.'

'I must make a note of your suggestions, Eleanor. I've never managed a house before.' She leads Eleanor into the new parlour. 'This place is bigger than we need, but Walter insisted on three and a half storeys, and at least three rooms on each floor. The lower storey includes the new kitchens, a bakehouse, beer cellar, and a fan-vaulted wine cellar, stocked with fine wines from his importers.'

In Walter's new study, high in one of the corner turrets, they stand at the window overlooking the restored deer park. His oak desk, brought by wagon from Durham House, has pride of place, and is spread with parchments bearing nautical charts.

Bess points to one of the charts, showing settlements in the New World. 'Walter plans to explore the Orinoco River on the northern tip of South America. He hopes to discover a lost city of gold and return with a fortune.'

Eleanor examines the chart, which has tiny ships painted on long sweeping lines of the intended route. 'I hope Adrian is not persuaded to sail with him.' She frowns. 'I had to wait a full six months for any news last time, and had no idea if he was alive or dead.'

'I didn't think Adrian was a mariner?'

Eleanor raises an eyebrow, as if she is about to defend her husband. 'He owns a fine ship, the *Elizabeth*.' Something in her tone suggests she doesn't approve of Walter or his risky venture.

Bess leads her across to the opposite tower. 'This is my private space, which I'm calling my closet. It's where I'll work on my sewing and keep the ledgers of accounts. I confess my limited writing makes this slow work, but I must control the household expenses.'

'You are fortunate, Bess. Adrian gives me a modest allowance, but he would never allow me to know how much he is spending.'

Bess raises an eyebrow and changes the subject. 'The view is not so grand as Walter's, but I want new furnishings. I was thinking of a comfortable chair by the window, so I can see anyone arriving and leaving.'

Finally, Bess shows Eleanor their spacious bedchamber and her grand bed. 'This is my only inheritance from my father. The carpenters rebuilt the frame, and I will make a new canopy of silk brocade.'

Eleanor studies the dark wood, carved with the Throckmorton coat of arms and the words *Virtus Sola Nobilitas.*

Bess smiles. 'Our family motto. Virtue is the only nobility.' She traces the carved words with her finger. 'I am a Raleigh, but will always be a Throckmorton.' She points to a side door. 'Little Wat has his own nursery through there. He is sleeping, but is a strong, healthy boy, who shrieks louder than the queen when he wants to have his own way.' She smiles. 'Wat can be quite a handful. He takes after his father, and I am afraid I indulge them both. Do you have children, Eleanor?'

'By my late first husband. Our first son died young, of a fever, but our twins, John and Faith do well, and my youngest, Cecily, has made me a grandmother twice over.'

'I'm sorry. We also lost our first son.'

Eleanor stares at her in surprise. 'I had no idea. Adrian never mentioned it.'

'We kept it a secret, but our son was taken by the plague in London, and didn't even have a proper funeral.' Bess has never seen a plague pit, yet the idea of such a place for her son's eternity haunts her dreams.

Adrian Gilbert speaks to Bess as if she is a child, rather than the lady of the manor. 'We must find ways for your land to make an income.' He studies her, as if deciding how much he must explain. 'Instead of a deer park, you could establish a stud farm. There is always demand for good horses.'

'Walter plans a herd of deer, so we can have venison whenever we wish, but I will be glad of your knowledge of horses.' Bess smiles. 'We have more than enough land, and men in the village will be glad of the work.'

'I could bring my thoroughbred mares from Devonshire, and build new stables, but…'

Bess hears his condescending tone. 'You don't think horse-breeding a suitable occupation for a lady?'

'It will need investment to establish a successful stud farm, Bess. I must speak to Walter.'

She unfastens her gold brooch, set with a blue sapphire surrounded by cut and polished diamonds, part of the treasure of the *Madre de Deus*, and hands it to him. 'You should find this is worth enough for the expenses.'

He raises an eyebrow, studies the brooch, feeling the weight and turning it in the light, and looks up at her. 'I shall have to ride to Dorchester. If I can find a buyer at the right price, I'll make the arrangements.'

Bess finds Adrian Gilbert hard to read, but is sure he looks at her with new respect. She has plenty more jewels from the *Madre de Deus*, and thinks it is time to put them to good use. She likes having control over how she spends her days. Even more, she likes the idea of having an income of her own, and some financial independence for the first time in her life.

Bess is with Walter and Eleanor in the new parlour, finishing their evening supper of roasted pheasant. Their cook has spiced the tender meat with cinnamon, precious cloves and ginger, brought back from Walter's last visit to London as a rare treat. Eleanor nods in approval as she tastes the sweet muscadine wine and raises her glass to them. 'Congratulations on your fine house.'

Bess is about to reply when there is a commotion outside

and the door bursts open. Adrian Gilbert has rain dripping from his riding cape and mud on his boots. 'Forgive my interruption, but I have grave news. There's plague in Sherborne village!'

Bess stares at him. 'Are you certain?'

'There's no mistaking the plague. I regret to tell you that ten or twenty villagers have already died.' He turns to Eleanor. 'We have to return to Devon until the danger is passed.'

Walter agrees. 'We must also leave. I'm not prepared to take the risk of anything happening to Wat.'

Bess feels her happiness drain away. Wat is about the same age as little Damerei when the dreaded plague took him. 'Many of our household servants are from the village.' She turns to Walter as she realises Sherborne is no longer her sanctuary. 'Where will we go?'

'My brother Carew can make you and little Wat welcome at Downton House, near Salisbury. It's some seventy miles from here, which should be far enough to be safe, and Carew's wife, Dorothy, will keep you good company.'

'You're not coming with us?' Bess suspects she knows the reason, yet is surprised at his lack of concern for her.

'I shall send for my man Thomas Harriot, and we'll ride to meet Captain Whiddon in Plymouth. He's due to return from his voyage to the island of Trinidad, and I'm keen to know what he found.' He grins. 'Then we have a fleet of ships to make ready for my next great adventure.'

Bess embraces Walter when they are alone in their bedchamber the night before she is to leave for Salisbury. 'I beg you not to sail on that voyage. Please listen to me, Walter. Winter is coming, and little Wat needs his father.' Her voice carries a sharp edge, and she is close to tears.

The bed creaks as Walter climbs in to join her. 'I must, Bess. I have authority from the queen.' His eyes shine with ambition. 'This could be my best opportunity to make a name for myself, and make our fortune.'

Bess fastens the lacing of her nightgown with unnecessary care. When she speaks, her voice is softer.

'I know little of South America, or this mysterious place up Orinoco River you wish to sail to – but I understand the dangers of such a venture are great, not to speak of the cost. There is still much to do in this house. Will you gamble the money we have left on a sailors' tale of gold which may not even be true?'

'Please try to understand, Bess. Everything we have is a gift of the queen. There are many who wish to see me ruined, and others will profit by persuading her to take her gifts back. There will be nothing I can do about it.' The frustration in his voice is edged with pleading. 'This voyage is my best chance to restore my reputation. It will be my greatest adventure and, if I succeed, the rewards are beyond anything most men can dream of.'

She studies his face as a thought occurs to her. 'You would risk your life, risk everything we have, to win back the queen's affection?' She decides to tell him her great secret. 'I have a confession to make. I wrote to Robert Cecil, begging him to prevent this scheme of yours.'

'You wrote to Robert Cecil?' He stares at her in open-mouthed surprise. 'What did you say to him?'

'I said he was the only one you would listen to, and asked his help in making you see reason.'

'Well, he took little heed of your request. Even the wealthy Sir Robert Cecil can't resist the city of gold they call El Dorado.' He grins. 'Instead of trying to talk me out of it, Robert Cecil has become one of my investors.'

Bess snuffs out the candles, plunging the room into darkness. She lifts the edge of the coverlet and climbs into bed, turning her back on him.

'I believed you'd changed, and that we could be content with our new life here.' She turns to face him. 'What about me? What of our son? Let others take the risks, Walter. If there is a fortune to be made, you can be sure of a good profit.'

'There is little glory in leaving the adventuring to others.' He reaches out to caress her, but she turns away once more. 'I do all this for you, for our son.'

The sadness in her words turns to bitterness as she realises the truth. She'd hoped this would be a fresh start for them both, and that Walter would settle down as the lord of the manor of Sherborne. 'You've not changed, Walter. You risk everything for this madness, and all I can do is pray for your safe return.'

Downton House, near Salisbury, is not as grand as Sherborne Lodge, but Bess is grateful for Walter's brother Carew and his wife Dorothy's hospitality after her long ride. Their home is an old timber-framed house, rendered with flint, the main rooms in a long, single storey, with dormer rooms above.

Bess has one of the dormer attic bedchambers, with low beams and lime-plastered walls. Wat has the other as his nursery.

Dorothy is about ten years older than Bess, with three young sons and a nine-year-old daughter, Catherine. Walter told Bess with a note of scorn that, like Eleanor Gilbert, Dorothy was a wealthy widow, worth a great fortune when his brother Carew married her.

Dorothy has old scars of the smallpox, and gives Bess a despairing look. 'Carew is often away with his duties as vice admiral of Dorset. I'm glad of your company, Bess, and want to hear your news from London and stories of life at court, as I feel quite isolated here.'

Bess understands. 'I've not been back to London for some time, but I've plenty of stories of my years at court. Walter tells me little enough of the news from London, as he is busy preparing for yet another sea voyage.'

Dorothy gives her a look of sympathy. 'What is it with the Raleigh menfolk, Bess? They never seem content with what they have, and talk of making a great fortune.'

'I thought it was typical of Walter, but I see it's all the brothers.' She decides to share her concerns with Dorothy. 'I worry what will become of me if Walter fails to return.'

'You must make sure he provides for you, Bess – *before* he sails.' Her voice has an edge of concern, as if she suspects he has not.

'You mean he should leave a copy of his will?' The thought has never occurred to Bess.

'More than that. You need to find out who his investors are. If his venture fails, you can be sure they will make their claims on his estate.'

'They could force me to sell Sherborne?'

Dorothy puts her hand on Bess's arm and looks her in the eye. 'You must protect yourself – and your son's inheritance.'

That night Bess cannot sleep. She knows Robert Cecil is one of Walter's investors, and would not hesitate to demand compensation. Walter has never spoken to her of a will, not a good sign. Bess worried she might never see her husband again, but *now* she worries there is much to do before he sails, and time is running out.

6

MILE END 1595

BESS SHIVERS AS SHE RIDES THROUGH DRIFTING SNOW IN HER covered carriage. She travels light, with only her maid, Martha, and two grooms as an escort. Her decision to leave Wat in the care of her sister-in-law, Dorothy, at Downton House troubles her conscience, but she has no choice. Her future, and that of her infant son, could be at stake, and she must return to London to consult her brother, Arthur.

She wrote to Walter in Plymouth, begging him not to sail until the winter storms pass, but has yet to receive any reply. Bess suspects she knows the reason. He gambles their future on sailors' stories and the lure of gold. Dorothy advised her to retain the services of a good lawyer, but her instinct is to be guided by her brother, who has himself profited from Walter's earlier voyages.

Although three years have passed since she was last at Mile End, it seems a lifetime ago. So much has happened since, and everything has changed. Grand new houses fill both sides of the avenue as she approaches Mile End, yet she knows the plague still haunts the city.

Arthur looks broader, his beard greying. He listens, frowning, as Bess explains her concerns, and the letter she wrote to Walter. 'His brother, Carew, said storms off Plymouth keep the ships in port. It's unlikely Walter has already sailed, but he will as soon as he sees a break in the weather.'

Her brother thinks for a moment. 'There's still time, but only if we leave for Plymouth right away and find your husband. I will escort you, and hope we find he's made a will, but now is the time to be certain.'

Bess puts her hand on her brother's arm. 'Thank you, Arthur. What can be done to protect me from his investors?'

Arthur shakes his head. 'From my knowledge of such things, there is little you can do. Investors, even Her Majesty, and particularly men like Robert Cecil, like to keep their involvement private.'

'Why is there the need for such secrecy?'

Arthur frowns. 'Walter's search for a lost city of gold could be a convenient cover story. The queen would wish to distance herself from any piracy, but there are plenty who see the Spanish and Portuguese as fair game.'

Bess understands. 'I've seen how passionate Walter is when he talks of his El Dorado. He heard the story from a captured Spanish conquistador, and has a map of the Orinoco which he says shows the city of gold.' She frowns. 'I tried my best to make him see sense. By his own admission, this is his most dangerous adventure, and if he fails to return—' Her voice wavers at the thought of the consequences for herself and little Wat.

The winter gales, which rattle the shutters at the windows, keep them trapped at a small coaching inn halfway across the wilderness of Exmoor. They've been forced to stop while the grooms dig out a snowdrift with only one shovel between them; the weather adds another week to their journey.

Bess has plenty to occupy her mind. Dorothy has opened her eyes to how naive she'd been, trusting Walter not to put their son's inheritance at risk with his ambitious adventures. He'd not said goodbye when they last parted, as if he would soon be back. Now she sees she knows little of what he is up to.

Arthur knocks at her door. He wears his riding cape and boots, and holds his hat as if he is about to leave. 'I must ride ahead and see if I can track down Walter, or we could be too late.'

Bess crosses to the low window. The snow has stopped, but she knows the risk of meeting another drift on the narrow moorland road is too great. 'I can take one of the spare horses and ride with you.'

Arthur frowns at her suggestion. 'I'll cover the ground faster alone, Bess, but you have my word I will return as soon as I have news.'

Two long days pass before he returns with a black-caped rider at his side. Her pulse races; Walter has come to say a proper farewell! But, as they dismount, she recognises Walter's agent and right-hand man, Thomas Harriot.

Well educated and serious, with a neat pointed beard, Thomas Harriot is a skilled navigator and map-maker, and sailed on Walter's Roanoke expedition. Bess knows him as one of the regular residents of Durham House in London. If anyone can tell her the details of Walter's investors, as well as whether he has left a will, it will be Thomas Harriot.

Bess manages a smile of welcome, and asks the question that's troubled her since she left London, although she can guess the answer. 'Has my husband sailed, Master Harriot?'

Thomas Harriot shakes snow from his riding cape. 'Two weeks since, Lady Raleigh. Sir Walter asked me to remain ashore to administer his affairs.' He gives a wry smile. 'I didn't protest, as the conditions were not the best when his fleet departed from Plymouth.'

Bess sends to the kitchens for a hot meal for them both, and must wait until they have recovered from their long cold ride. Thomas Harriot wipes the last drop of gravy from his plate with a crust of bread, and fills his stub of pipe with tobacco from a small leather pouch before lighting it with a spill from the fire, puffing little gasps of smoke until he seems satisfied it is alight.

He studies Bess for a moment, as if trying to decide how much to tell her. 'Your brother shared your concerns with me, Lady Raleigh, but you need not worry. Your husband left everything to your son in his will.'

'That is some comfort, Master Harriot, but I'm concerned my husband's investors will press a claim on his estate, if he fails to return.'

'Anyone who chooses to invest in a venture such as this knows the risks, but the success of the mission does not rest on the discovery of El Dorado.'

'You talk in riddles, Master Harriot. Are you referring to piracy?'

'Your husband would prefer to call it privateering, by way of a little insurance to cover his costs, if the opportunity presents itself.' Thomas Harriot looks thoughtful. 'I can arrange to have a copy made of your husband's will for you, and suggest you return to Sherborne with your son. I shall wait in Plymouth for any ship bringing news, so you can rest assured I will write to you as soon as I hear anything.'

It troubles Bess that Walter does not seem concerned with her own position, but she's not surprised. At least he's made sure to provide for Wat, if the worst happens. It is too late to do anything else this time, but in the future she will.

It feels good to be back at Sherborne, and the first flowers of spring brighten her day as Bess walks in her rose gardens. Little Wat seems happy to be back in his nursery, and she carries a letter which has arrived from Thomas Harriot in Plymouth.

Still sealed, Bess delays learning his news until she reaches her garden seat, a private spot with views over the tranquil fishing lake Adrian Gilbert created by damming the River Yeo. She pulls the fold of parchment from a secret pocket in her dress, and braces herself for bad news as she breaks the dark wax seal.

Thomas Harriot's writing is like the man himself: neat and economical, telling her only what he thinks she needs to know. Walter captured a Flemish merchant ship with a valuable cargo of barrels of Spanish wine. He put her crew ashore unharmed, and Walter kept his prize as a supply ship.

Bess frowns. She doubts it could be legal to seize a Flemish merchantman, despite Thomas Harriot's assertion they were trading with the Spanish, which makes them enemies. It is hard to imagine the Flemish crew were any threat to Walter, so this is piracy. Bess fears there could be consequences once Walter returns.

She reads Thomas Harriot's brief letter a second time, as if some new clue may reveal itself. He says nothing about how far Walter has sailed, and there is no message for her from him. She would like to know her husband is well but, for now, all she can do is pray for his safe return.

Bess picks a bouquet of flowers to brighten the room she calls her closet, and returns to begin the hard work of checking her ledgers. The costs of running such a vast household have grown at an alarming rate in her absence, and something must be done.

She lays down her pen and takes a fresh sheet of parchment. The solution to her problem is clear. She must find a way to make the Earl of Huntingdon, Sir Henry Hastings, repay the loan of five hundred pounds, her legacy and dowry.

Powerful and well connected, Henry Hastings is unlikely to respond to her letters. For a moment, Bess considers an appeal to the queen. Despite all that's happened, she doesn't see what she would lose by asking, but when she starts to write she realises this is going to be one of the most difficult letters of her life.

The thought of writing to the queen brings back unpleasant memories of her time in the Tower. Her grief for little Damerei returns, and she is haunted by the thought that he could have lived if she'd been able to take him to a place of safety. Her tears fall to the page, smudging her writing, and she rips the parchment into small pieces.

Instead, she decides to write again to Robert Cecil, despite her deep distrust of him. Cecil is ambitious – yet, from what she knows of him, has a good sense of right and wrong. Bess also suspects he will disapprove of Henry Hastings keeping her inheritance for so long.

Taking a fresh sheet of parchment, she dips her pen in the black ink and begins to write. Ignoring what Walter told her, she thanks Robert Cecil for his help and support.

Sur Walter's remembranse of me to you at his last deeparting shall add and increese if it wer possibl more love and dew respect to him.

She stops to read back her words, regretting her poor spelling, and undecided whether she should travel to see Robert Cecil, to appeal to him in person. She has spent long enough away from her son and from Sherborne. She will have Alexander Brett deliver her letter.

A Devon man, and distant cousin of Bess, Alexander Brett is bright and capable, taking over the work started by Adrian Gilbert to improve the supply of fresh water to Sherborne. Keen to better himself, he will relish the challenge of meeting such an important man as Sir Robert Cecil.

He is one of the few unmarried men at Sherborne, and Bess is flattered by how Brett flirts with her. The twinkle in his eye when he makes her laugh reminds her of Walter before they married. She suspects Alexander Brett admires her, and tries not to think of what could happen if Walter never returns.

She frowns as she dips her pen back in the ink and continues.

Sur I am in hope ere it be long to hear of Sur Walter, thow not of long time to see him, being for a time thus diseevered from him as I am.

She waits for the ink to dry in the spring sunshine streaming through her window, satisfied this is enough of a preamble. Bess doubts Robert Cecil will be familiar with the debt owed by Henry Huntingdon, but hopes he will realise the seriousness if she threatens to go to law.

I must entreet your favourable word to my Lord Keeper. I desire no favour, only suferance. The bearer of this leter can tell you the matter. I choose this time to follow it in Sur Walter's absents, that myself shall beare the unkindness, and not he, the money being long time past due to me.

. . .

Once the ink is dry, she folds the letter. One way or another, Henry Huntingdon will become aware that she will not forget the money he owes her. With luck, Robert Cecil will find some quiet way to avoid the matter going to law. Bess smiles as she presses her signet ring into the hot red wax. She has rolled the dice, and has little to lose.

Robert Cecil's encouraging reply is unexpected, as is his concern that her brother Arthur seems also to be trying to recover the money from Henry Huntingdon. Since her eldest brother William's breakdown, Arthur is effectively the head of the Throckmorton family, yet five hundred pounds is enough for Bess to suspect his motives.

She's settled into a routine, spending her time with little Wat while she waits. The terse note from Thomas Harriot is delivered by a rider from Plymouth, and Bess includes the news in her reply of thanks to Robert Cecil.

Sur I thanke God Sur Walter is safely landed at Plymworth with as great honor as a man can, but little riches. Kepe this I besech you to your sef yet. In haste this Sunday. Your poure frend E. Raleg.

She calls for her housekeeper to prepare the house and have the kitchens cook a haunch of venison fit for a returning hero. Her maidservant, Martha, helps her squeeze into her gown, and holds the small mirror while Bess studies the result with a critical eye. 'I want to look my best, Martha, but these old gowns belong to the past.'

Martha hesitates to agree. 'We could send to Dorchester for a new gown, my lady.'

'There may not be time. I've no idea if my husband is on his way here now, or whether he will ride straight to London to make his report.'

'Let us make the most of what we have, my lady.' She opens the camphor-wood chest and holds up a dress of blue silk for Bess to see. 'There is plenty of material for this to be more fashionable with a little work, and you could wear your mother's pearls with a lace collar and cuffs, and the white egrets' feather headdress.'

Bess smiles. 'You're right, Martha. You have an eye for such things, but I expect my husband will be too tired to even notice.'

Walter arrives from Plymouth alone, looking well, apart from a bandage on his left hand. His face is tanned by the foreign sun, yet Bess sees the look of defeat in his eyes. She embraces him, breathing in the salt of the sea and a hint of stale tobacco.

She ushers little Wat forwards. 'This is your father, Wat.' Wat stares wide-eyed, and hides behind her skirts. Close to his second birthday, his nursemaid has dressed him to look older.

Walter bends to his knees, and takes his son's hand. 'I feared I may never see you again.' The emotion echoes in his Devon accent.

Bess smiles at the sight of them together. 'I thank God you are back safe, Walter. You must be hungry. Cook has your favourite – venison simmering in a pint of claret wine, with cinnamon and cloves – ready when you wish.'

Walter grins, for the first time since his arrival. 'Then let us eat, Bess, and I can tell you something of my adventures.'

Walter seems not to notice the trouble Bess takes to look her best, and sounds preoccupied with his tales of adventure, as if rehearsing what to tell his investors. Even when the maid serves steaming venison he leaves it untouched on his plate while he swirls his wine in his glass, deep in thought.

'We made the Atlantic crossing in three weeks, and found a good anchorage in a sheltered bay at the southern tip of the island of Trinidad. My plan was to take the Spanish governor, Antonio de Berrio, prisoner, and learn what he knew of El Dorado.'

Bess tastes the venison, rich with cinnamon and cloves, and glances at his bandaged hand. 'I hope you are not going to tell me you provoked them into a fight?'

Walter shakes his head. 'The garrison surrendered before we fired a single shot. Two Indians, half-naked, with feather headdresses and red snakes painted on their skin, rowed out to us in a canoe. They said the Spanish mistreated them, and would hang anyone who trades with us.' He frowns at the thought. 'They led us to the Orinoco River in a shallow-drafted boat. Our ship's carpenters removed everything they could to make her lighter, and fitted four pairs of oars, so they could row her like a galley.'

Walter tears a piece of bread and tastes his venison, nodding in approval. Bess notes he hasn't asked anything about how she coped in his long absence, or even how little Wat is doing. At least the haunted look in his eyes is gone as he recounts his story.

'I'd expected it to be hot, but not to suffer such a deluge of rain, which soaked us all to the skin.' He takes a deep drink of his wine. 'They warned us to watch for monster lizards and giant serpents that can swallow a man whole. I'd hoped they were only stories, but a great lizard seized one of my men and dragged him under the water.'

Bess stares at him, wide-eyed. 'Did you save him?'

Walter shakes his head at the memory. 'The attack happened so fast there was nothing we could do. The next day we spotted natives watching us from the riverbank. We presented them with hatchets and knives, to show them we were friendly, and needed their help. They led us to their village, but as far as we could tell they knew nothing of any city of gold.'

Bess is unsurprised, yet part of her wishes he'd been right about his mysterious El Dorado. 'That was when you turned back?'

'We'd travelled over four hundred miles inland, but could see the river was impassable by boat, and we would have to continue on foot. We had no choice but to risk the river monsters and wade through the water up to our necks. After a day we reached a gravel bank at a bend in the river, where we could set up a camp. We were soaked to the skin, covered in bloodsucking leeches, and exhausted. Worse still, we were running out of food and fresh water. I gathered the men to tell them we'd done enough and had to turn back.'

Bess reaches out a hand to him. 'I, for one, thank God you did.' She manages a smile. 'I prayed for your safe return, Walter, every day.'

He joins her in their dark-wood bed, carved with the Throckmorton coat of arms. *Virtus Sola Nobilitas.* A new canopy of burgundy velvet glitters with gold stars and a crescent moon, embroidered by Bess while she'd waited for him to return.

She reaches out and takes his bandaged hand. 'You've not told me how this happened?'

'I'd become used to easy victories, and was unprepared for the fusillade of Spanish muskets which greeted us when we returned to the mouth of the Orinoco.'

'You were hit?'

'I was lucky. Many of my men fell dead, cheated of life after all the hardships they'd survived in the jungle.' He scowls.

'We rescued the injured, and returned to Trinidad to bury our dead, including my loyal captain, Jacob Whiddon. I promised to ensure Jacob's wife, Anne, and his four children are provided for.'

Bess leans across and kisses him. 'Will the money from your prize ships cover the costs of your voyage?'

He looks surprised at her question. 'No ships were lost, and we've returned with fine prize ships. Once we've sold them I must share the money with the crew – and, of course, my investors – but no one died of sickness, and the Indians proved valuable allies.' He manages a smile. 'The *real* value of this voyage is that I've redeemed my reputation.'

'You think the queen will forgive you?' Bess doubts it, but life would be easier for them both.

He grins at the thought. 'I pray she will. I shall write a full account of my discoveries, and convince investors this is far from the end of the adventure.'

7

SHERBORNE 1596

BESS KEEPS HER FURS AROUND HER SHOULDERS AND WORRIES Wat could catch a chill. The River Yeo turns white with ice in another harsh winter. Flurries of snow cover the deer park, and frost glistens at the windows of Sherborne Lodge, despite the log fire blazing in the hearth.

She also worries about Walter, who suffers with dark moods and spends long hours at prayer in the old chapel. Worse still, he's shown her no affection or tenderness in bed since his return, never taking off his thick winter nightshirt. Bess dare not ask, for fear of provoking his outrage, yet suspects he could have been unfaithful in some foreign port, and paid the sailor's price.

Walter paces the room, his riding boots thumping on the polished oak floor. He utters a curse as he reads a letter from Durham House in London, and waves it in the air as if it might catch fire. 'Thomas Harriot says they accuse me of passing off fool's gold to my investors, and of keeping a great quantity of the real gold for myself, hiding it here in the West Country.'

'Well, they shall have to prove it.'

Walter shakes his head and stares at the letter. 'Unfortunately, they do not. I fear my investors plan to use these allegations as an excuse to seize my assets, and won't be too concerned with the truth.'

'You should not be too quick to think the worst of those who supported you, Walter. Anyone hearing you speak of your expedition to the Orinoco would think it a great success.'

'It was!' His raised voice echoes in the high-ceilinged room, a sign she has touched a nerve.

Little Wat – who had been playing with a toy sailing ship, complete with linen sails and tiny cannons cast from lead, which Walter brought back from his travels – stares up at his father in alarm, and looks as if he might cry. Bess has become used to Walter's aggressive outbursts, which have grown worse since his return.

'I meant no criticism, Walter, only that there is little enough return on your own investment, considering the great risks you took.'

Walter stops pacing and gives her an indignant look. 'What we learned about the country of Guiana is worth more than a shipload of gold, and I've formed an alliance against the Spanish with the local people. Any who doubt the value of our achievements do a disservice to those who gave their lives, like Captain Jacob Whiddon.'

Bess guesses that something about Jacob Whiddon's death troubles his conscience. 'You've been restless since you came back. I thought you were going to write about your adventures?'

'I'm working through Edward Hancock's notes, and have made a good start on a first draft. I've dedicated it to the Lord Admiral, Charles Howard.' He climbs the stairs to his study, and returns with a bundle of papers. 'I'd like you to read it, if you can decipher my writing.'

She studies the frontispiece and reads aloud. 'The discovery

of the large, rich, and beautiful empire of Guiana; with a relation of the great and golden city of Manoa, which the
Spaniards call El Dorado, and the provinces of…' She tries to
form the words and looks up at him. 'I've never heard of these
places.'

'You are not alone, Bess. Guiana is a new empire, which
few even know exists, and even fewer will ever have the chance
to see.' He takes the papers from her and continues to read
aloud in his rich Devon accent, as if to an important audience.
'The provinces of Emeria, Aromaia, Amapaia, and other
countries, with their rivers, adjoining. Performed in the year
fifteen ninety-five by Sir Walter Raleigh, knight, captain of Her
Majesty's guard, Lord Warden of the Stannaries, and Her
Highness's Lieutenant General of the county of Cornwall.'

Bess stares at him as he reminds her of his many titles. 'I
was not aware you are still the captain of the queen's guard.'

'I was never replaced or dismissed, and although it's some
time since I performed that duty, I see this as an opportunity to
set the record straight.' He turns the page and continues reading. 'To the right honourable my singular good lord and
kinsman Charles Howard, Knight of the Garter, baron, and
councillor, and of the admirals of England, the most
renowned.'

Bess gives him a cautionary look. 'Don't forget to mention
your benefactor, Sir Robert Cecil.' She smiles. 'He'll not have
any choice but to support you, once he sees his name included.'

Walter raises an eyebrow at her suggestion. 'I shall do that,
Bess.' He brightens. 'Do you remember me telling you we
brought back the Indian chief's son, Gualtero? Thomas
Harriot is teaching him to speak English, and he says they are
making good progress. When he is ready, he will be useful as
my interpreter, and I shall ask Sir Robert Cecil's assistance in
presenting him to my doubters.'

'Even to Her Majesty?'

'Why not? The queen can see for herself that what I've been saying is true. It's even more important now to reassure investors, but I must take care not to provide information that will allow rivals to discover the city of gold.'

'You promised to return the chief's son to his country, and you cannot forget you also made me a promise you would not return—'

He holds up a hand to silence her. 'I can't afford to, even if I wished. I'm sending my second in command, Lawrence Keymis, and he'll also bring back our cabin boy, who we left with the chief to learn some of his language.' Walter takes her hand and kisses it. 'One of the many things I learned in Guiana was how greatly I missed you, Bess.'

She smiles in surprise. This is the first time he's mentioned missing her. It seems his adventure has changed him, she hopes for the better, yet in her heart she feels it is only a matter of time before he begins to plan another sea voyage and his next adventure.

Bess sees from the scowl on his face that Walter brings bad news from his visit to London. 'What is it, Walter? What's happened?'

He slumps into his favourite chair and pulls off his hat, running his fingers through his greying hair. 'I regret to tell you that Henry Hastings, Earl of Huntingdon, has died of a fever in York.'

Bess looks at him in alarm. 'We must submit our claim against his estate, before it is too late.'

'They are saying he died intestate, and was deep in debt to the Crown, which perhaps is why your brother has had little success in recovering the sum owed to us.' He shakes his head. 'Arthur says we shall have to take our chances with all the others, but he does not hold out much hope for ever seeing our money.'

Bess could point out that the money was *her* inheritance, and nothing to do with her brother, but decides to keep her silence. Walter doesn't seem to notice her frown, as he has more bad news to share with her.

'Few mourn the passing of Henry Hastings, as the talk is all about Sir Francis Drake, who is reported to have died at sea off the coast of Portobello.' He looks up at Bess. 'They say he died a hero, but Thomas Harriot suspects he succumbed to a shipboard fever. He was one of a kind, but if these accounts are true, his passing creates an opportunity.'

Bess lays down her embroidery and stares at him. 'What are you planning, Walter?'

'A Spanish fleet is assembling in Cadiz, with new warships, said to be faster, with better guns, and more than a match for ours. I suspect they could be planning to invade us with a new Armada.' Walter begins pacing, as he does when deep in thought. 'This could be our chance to stop them, once and for all, and not only from the sea. Sir Francis Vere has two thousand battle-hardened soldiers from the wars in Holland and France, and the Admiral of Holland agrees to bring his fleet of twenty-four Dutch warships.'

Bess gives him a look of concern as she sees the spark of ambition return to his eyes. 'You don't need to risk everything with another raid on Cadiz which, by your own admission, would be dangerous.'

'One of the commanders of the mission is the Earl of Essex, and he's put my name forward to Robert Cecil.'

Bess frowns. 'You've never liked the Earl of Essex. Would you work with him?'

'The earl is a hothead, but I must put our differences aside.' He smiles. 'Our fleet is assembling in Deptford, waiting for someone to arrange crews and take care of the provisioning.

They need me, Bess. There are few with my experience of such things.'

She knows he is right. 'You could help with the preparations, then return to us.'

'If I'm in charge, I could have the pick of the queen's new warships, and might even have command of a squadron, which should ensure Her Majesty appreciates my contribution.' He looks at her with new resolve. 'I shall return to royal favour through this venture, so we *must* succeed, even if it means putting up with opinionated men like the Earl of Essex.'

Bess says a prayer of thanks that the rain has stopped and her ride through Exmoor to Plymouth is blessed by bright sunshine. She rides with her sister-in-law – Arthur's wife, Anne – and maidservant Martha, and took the difficult decision to leave little Wat at Sherborne with his nurse.

She last saw Walter when he left for the dockyards at Deptford, although he kept his promise to send word when he sailed for Plymouth. This time she is determined to see him off, yet fears this mission to Cadiz could have even greater dangers than Guiana.

Anne looks older, and has travelled all the way from Mile End, stopping overnight at Sherborne to continue her journey with Bess. She stares out of the window at the relentless moorland. 'Arthur is convinced this foolhardy venture will be the making of him, but I worry this raid on Cadiz is such a poorly kept secret the Spanish will be waiting for them.'

Bess frowns. 'Walter told me the new Spanish warships are faster and better armed than ours.'

Anne turns to her. 'I tried my best to persuade Arthur not to sail this time. Why do they take such risks when they could be safe at home?'

'Walter wishes to redeem his favour with the queen, and resume his post as captain of her guard. He commands a new galleon, the *Warspite*, which he says is faster than any he's sailed before, with thirty of the latest culverins. She has a crew of three hundred, but in his letter he admits many are pressed men, from the taverns and men from the Fleet debtors' prison. Few have experience of sailing or fighting at sea, and many are drunkards who don't know one rope from another.'

She sees her words do nothing to improve Anne's mood and remembers Arthur is also sailing on the *Warspite*. 'Walter brought back a talking parrot from his last travels, as a present for his half-brother, Adrian Gilbert.'

'A parrot?' Anne has a glint of curiosity in her eyes.

Bess manages a smile as she sees she has Anne's interest. 'He meant it as a joke. His crewmen taught the parrot to swear like a sailor, but Adrian Gilbert made a present of the parrot to the queen, with a note that it will sit in a gentlewoman's ruff all day. He said it will eat bread or oatmeal groats, and drink some water or claret wine, and he claims if it is well taught the parrot will speak anything.'

Anne smiles, for the first time since arriving at Sherborne. 'That should raise an eyebrow at court, although I think it will amuse Her Majesty.'

Rain hammers at the windows of the Plymouth hostelry where the four of them share a final meal before the fleet sails. Bess knows Walter well enough to see through his jovial bluster. He'd told her he sailed from Deptford in worsening weather, and there seems little prospect of improvement, yet they *must* depart in the morning.

Walter calls for more wine and refills his glass. 'I have some good news. Lord Admiral Charles Howard persuaded Her

Majesty this mission is too important for Essex to command.' He grins. 'I've also learned Sir Francis Vere, commander of the land forces, is displeased at the prospect of taking orders from me, as rear admiral.'

Bess frowns. 'Does that not worry you?'

Walter shakes his head. 'I don't take it personally. Francis Vere resents anyone who is not a soldier giving him orders, and I shall have my hands full at sea. Our informers say the treasure fleet is now at anchor in the Bay of Cadiz.'

Bess gives him a questioning look, and guesses he knew about the treasure fleet, his *real* incentive to be a commander of the mission. She turns to her brother. 'How did you get that bruise on your face, Arthur?' She sees his glance at Walter before he replies.

'It's nothing of any consequence.' His eyes will not meet hers, and he busies himself with carving another slice of beef.

Walter grins, and takes a deep drink of his wine. 'I heard it was a matter of honour. Whoever it was should be glad the queen has made duelling illegal.'

Bess knows Anne will find out what Arthur has been up to and tell her later, but it seems a bad omen. She's always thought her brother restrained and even-tempered. Unlike Walter, her brother has few who bear a grudge against him, so she guesses someone must have shown disrespect for Walter, or for her.

Plymouth quayside bustles with activity, but the sea conditions are far from ideal. More ships than can be counted are moored several deep, with men shouting to each other as they ready the sails. Bess recalls Walter telling her the fleet includes over a hundred and fifty ships, including the Dutch warships, which is half as many again as sailed against the first Armada, and is the biggest flotilla ever assembled in England.

There is no sign of Walter or her brother but it's easy to find the *Warspite*, with its proud flag of St George flapping in the breeze. Bess spots Walter, dressed in bright-blue silks, trimmed with gold braid, with a silver sword at his belt. Her brother, standing at his side, wears a shining breastplate over his doublet, and his sword looks more like a fighting weapon than an ornament.

It seems they have no intention of coming ashore, so all she can do is stand with Anne, watching as the final supplies are loaded. Bess is glad of her hooded riding cape as it begins to rain. She calls out to Walter, 'Take care, and come home safe!'

He raises a hand in acknowledgement, but his face is grim. This time he rolls the dice for the highest stakes, as victory could be the making of him. Bess says a silent prayer and gives him one last wave with her white-gloved hand, fighting back tears and knowing in her heart he might never return.

Bess is embroidering a new forepart at Sherborne when she hears the dogs barking, followed by footsteps and a knock at her door. Alexander Brett looks serious, as if he wishes he was elsewhere. He's been to London to deliver her letter to Robert Cecil, with news that Lawrence Keymis returned safe from Guiana, and requesting his help with her claim on the estate of Henry Hastings, which she pursues in the absence of Walter or Arthur.

Alexander Brett has none of his usual cheerfulness, but pulls off his cap and wrings it in his hands. 'I visited Thomas Harriot at Durham House, my lady. I'm sorry I must tell you there is talk in London that … Sir Walter is drowned at sea.'

Bess senses her world collapsing yet again. 'Dear God.'

Alexander Brett looks down at his shoes. 'Master Harriot is endeavouring to discover the truth, and asked me to tell you he will send word as soon as he is certain of the facts.'

She sits in silence for a moment, afraid to think about the consequences. If the *Warspite* has foundered, she could have lost her brother also. She waits until Alexander Brett leaves and surrenders to her grief. She cries for Walter, for her brother, and for little Wat, who could now be without a father.

It is growing dark outside by the time she wipes away her tears, and begins to think about her own future. Walter told her he'd left a copy of his will in the desk drawer of his study. He'd been insistent it was only to be opened in the event of his death, but Bess must put her mind at rest and discover what provision he has made for her.

She lights a candle with a taper and makes her way to Walter's study. She has a collection of spare keys and finds one which turns in the locked desk drawer. The will, secured with legal ribbon, is not sealed with wax, but to untie the ribbon means admitting there's no hope of Walter's return. She locks the will back in the desk drawer. Hope is all she has left.

Bess recognises the rider as one of Walter's grooms from Durham House, and her heart misses a beat when he hands her the letter from Thomas Harriot. She sits in Walter's favourite chair holding it in her hand, torn with indecision, afraid to learn the contents. Thomas Harriot would only have written if he is sure of his facts, and the course of the rest of her life could be changed by the contents of his letter.

Bracing herself for the worst news, yet hoping for the best, she breaks the seal and begins to read the neat handwriting. A ship was sent ahead by the Lord Admiral to announce that the

Spanish fleet is destroyed and Cadiz burned. Walter lives and, although wounded, is a hero of the venture to Cadiz.

Arthur distinguished himself in the battle, and is rewarded with a knighthood. Bess allows herself a smile as she imagines how proud Anne will be to become Lady Throckmorton. Her brother's gamble paid off, but she hopes that this can be the last time Arthur and Walter risk their lives to make their names.

Walter uses a stick to walk. His once fine silks are torn and he has a linen bandage on his wounded leg. He seems in a surly mood, and shouts to the men with him to carry his sea chests down to the wine cellar. Bess kisses him on the cheek. 'They told me you'd drowned.'

He scowls. 'I heard there were rumours of my demise, but I've disappointed my enemies. I'll not profit from this mission, but it should be enough to restore my reputation, God willing.'

'Thomas Harriot said the venture was a success, and that you were a hero of the battle. Did you not capture the Spanish treasure fleet?'

Walter curses. 'There were no treasure ships in Cadiz, only the Spanish merchant fleet. We took two galleons, which will please the queen, but the Spanish burned their own ships to prevent us taking them. All we could do was watch.'

She frowns as she studies his bandaged leg. 'How bad is your wound? Do I need to send for a doctor?'

Walter stares at his leg. 'I was lucky. An explosion threw me onto my back. My head struck the deck and splinters of timber were stuck in my leg. No bones were broken. It's only a flesh wound, but it hurts like hell.'

Bess shakes her head. 'I shall send for a doctor to make sure your wound is healing.'

Walter takes to his bed early, but Bess is reassured by the doctor, who seems satisfied with the work of the ship's surgeon. 'The wound will leave a scar, my lady, but men have lost a leg for less.'

She checks on Wat and finds him sleeping, but recalls something which arouses her curiosity. Walter told his men to put his sea chests in the wine cellar. He might have brought back Spanish wine, but usually keeps his heavy sea chests in his study, and would struggle to carry them up the narrow staircase with his wounded leg.

Lighting a candle, she makes her way to the wine cellar and finds the men have placed his sea chests behind the door. She unfastens the thick leather straps and holds the candle closer as she opens the chest. Instead of his clothes, a heap of gold and silver glitters in the candlelight. She picks up a heavy crucifix, and her pulse races as she realises his chests are full of treasure. Bess recalls Walter's words. *I'll not profit from this mission, but it should be enough to restore my reputation.*

8

DURHAM HOUSE 1597

THE SNOWSTORMS PASS, AND BESS AND WAT ACCOMPANY Walter to Durham House in their rattling coach, followed by a covered wagon containing their servants and luggage. For Bess, the long journey seems like travelling back into her past, with all its troubling memories.

Walter still needs to use a stick. His doctor says he will always walk with a limp, but he must re-establish himself at court and reclaim his post as Captain of the Guard. He cannot tell her how long that might take, only that he knows to be out of the queen's sight is to be out of her mind.

Bess is torn between remaining behind in the peace of Sherborne or travelling with Walter. Her sister-in-law Anne's last letter assures her the threat of plague in the city is passed, that it's safe to bring Wat, yet Bess is not so sure. The painful memory of little Damerei is renewed as she sees the familiar skyline.

London seems crowded and dirty after the tranquil Dorset countryside. Brooding houses overhang the narrow streets, foul smells from the River Thames make her feel ill and there are more horses and carriages jostling for room than she remembers.

She finds Walter has spent a good deal of money improving Durham House. Another surprise is that they have separate bedchambers, hers graced with a fine new bed with hangings of burgundy silk. Magnificent tapestries of maritime battles impress visitors in the grand hall. Bess suspects these were looted from some merchant's house in Cadiz, yet another way her husband conceals his true wealth.

They soon settle into a new routine, and Bess is glad to visit new dressmakers and discover the latest fashions. The chance to replace her worn and tired gowns is long overdue. She has mixed feelings about Walter asking the queen's permission for her to return to court, but suspects this could be the reason he's given her such a generous allowance.

He takes a wherry from the river steps to court at Whitehall Palace, and grumbles to Bess when he returns after a long day. 'Far from welcoming me as a returning hero, I'm made to wait like an ordinary petitioner, but I shall not give up.'

'You know that's how the queen shows her power over us. Have patience and, God willing, your time will come.'

Walter slumps into his leather chair and winces at the pain in his leg. He stares at Bess for a moment with unexpected sadness in his eyes. 'I'm sorry to tell you Robert Cecil's wife, Elizabeth, is dead.'

Bess gasps, and puts her hand to her mouth. 'That's terrible. Elizabeth wrote to me to say she was expecting their third child.'

Walter's face is grim. 'She died in childbirth, but the child survived – a daughter, I believe. I must write Robert Cecil a letter of condolence, but I confess I'm intrigued. I've been invited to a meeting with him and the Earl of Essex, at Essex House in the Strand.'

'What are they planning now?'

'I've no idea but, like me, the Earl of Essex has had little enough reward for his success in Cadiz, and is absent from court since he argued with the queen about appointments.'

Although it troubles her, Bess keeps her silence about discovering his chests of treasure. She believes Walter keeps his secret because it must be looted, and property of the Crown. She hopes he will confide in her when he feels the time is right, but what other secrets does he keep to himself?

Walter returns from his visit to Essex House looking pleased with himself. 'I was shown into the earl's study, which once belonged to Sir Robert Dudley. Robert Cecil arrived late, and we were served wine from the Duke of Medina Sidonia's cellar in Cadiz.'

Bess raises an eyebrow. 'Looted wine?'

He smiles. 'Essex is planning to return to Spain and bring home some more, but Robert Cecil suspects the Spanish fleet is preparing to sail to Ireland to establish a base for the invasion of the West Country.'

Bess frowns. 'I hope you've not agreed to sail with Essex to stop them?'

Walter hesitates a moment too long before answering. 'Everything we need is ready. The ships are refitted, the crews are ready for action, and our commanders are rich with experience, if not the spoils of war. The Spanish fleet was sighted at the port of Ferrol, and if they've sailed for Ireland, we should pursue them.'

Bess shakes her head. 'I'd hoped your wound would mean you would settle down – for now, at least.' A thought occurs to her. 'Does Lord Admiral Howard know of your plans?'

'Robert Cecil told us he proposes to recommend the Earl

of Essex as captain general, Lord Thomas Howard, as vice admiral, and myself as rear admiral.'

Bess frowns. 'You will need the queen's permission.'

'Then let that decide whether I go or stay.'

Walter returns from court in cheerful spirits. Bess doesn't need to ask, as she knows she will hear his news soon enough. He calls for wine, and grins as he raises his glass to her.

'To the good health of Her Majesty, long may she reign.'

Bess gives him a questioning look. 'I take it you have her consent?'

'I am restored to my post as Captain of the Guard, and our mission to Ferrol is approved, thanks to my good friend and sponsor, Sir Robert Cecil.'

'How is the queen?'

'Older, but as sharp as ever. She said they told her I've changed, yet she sees little evidence of it, as I never was slow to ask a favour.' He smiles and takes a drink of his wine. 'I said I have unfinished business with the Spanish, and asked permission to command the *Warspite* again, and put an end to the threat from Spain. She asked Robert Cecil for his opinion.'

Bess takes a little credit for keeping Walter in Robert Cecil's favour. 'What did he say?'

Walter grins. 'He told her I'd prove a restraining influence on Essex, and our mission against the Spanish fleet has his support, on condition this adventure is not at the expense of the Crown.'

Bess sees the truth in a flash of insight. Walter's secret hoard of looted treasure is kept back to finance this new venture, which he'd no doubt planned with the Earl of Essex long before the meeting with Robert Cecil. He'd not wished her to know until it was too late for her to try to change his mind.

'You are no sooner back from one dangerous adventure before you sail on the next one.' She looks him in the eyes. 'You have responsibilities, as Captain of the Guard, as Wat's father – *and* as my husband. Will you promise me you will not take unnecessary risks?'

He takes his pipe and fills the little bowl from a leather pouch before lighting it with a taper from the fire. He takes a few puffs of smoke before answering, filling the air with the distinctive scent of tobacco. 'There are risks any time a man puts to sea, but I can promise you I will take care not to put myself or my crew in unnecessary danger.'

Robert Cecil seems pleased with the offer from Bess to help with the upbringing of his young son, William. A little less than two years older than Wat, William will be company for him, and Bess hopes they can share tutors. Robert Cecil agrees to meet Bess at his mansion house in Chelsea to discuss the arrangements.

His stoop is more pronounced and he seems to suffer with pain in his back as he bows to welcome her. 'I appreciate your kindness at this difficult time.'

Although they are close in age, and regular correspondents, Bess finds Robert Cecil unexpectedly intimidating in person. One of the few people the queen will listen to, he has an aura of dangerous power, which has grown as his father's health declines.

She bows her head. 'Please accept my sincere condolences, and I hope your daughter is well?'

'Thank you, Lady Raleigh. My daughter was christened Catherine, and is a healthy child, thank God. My son William misses his mother, so I am hoping he will be cared for in the future by his aunt, Lady Frances Stourton, but your support in the meantime is most welcome.'

She makes a judgement. 'Please, call me Bess.' She manages a smile. 'We have known each other for a good many years.'

Robert Cecil studies her for a moment, his sharp eyes noting the ruby pendant on a gold chain and the flattering cut of the expensive new gown she chose for their meeting. 'Thank you, Bess, and you must call me Robert. Would you join me for a little supper?' He surprises her with a shy smile. 'I confess I find dining alone a somewhat lonely business.'

'I would be honoured.' She finds she cannot bring herself to call him by his first name. Bess can't imagine what Walter will say when he learns she's dining with Robert Cecil, but decides that if *he* can have secrets, so can she.

Robert Cecil's son William has something of his father's dour manner, which Bess hopes is only while he grieves for his mother. He barely speaks, and answers her questions with nods or shakes of his head. William brightens a little when Wat shows him his toy sailing ship, the beginning of a lifelong friendship which could be of benefit to them all.

Bess returns to Sherborne with the boys and her servants. She has no wish to wait until Walter sails, or to see him off, only to know when he is returned safe. The queen is right. Walter has not changed, as his only concern is with provisioning ships. He spends more time with Thomas Harriot and his lists than he does with her or Wat.

He did not once visit her bedchamber in the time she'd been at Durham House. He seemed not to notice her expensive new gowns, and made no mention of asking permission for her to return to court. At one time she would have found this upsetting, but even if Walter hasn't changed, she has.

Her time in the city showed how she misses the freedom of being lady of the manor of Sherborne. She'd longed to breathe the fresh country air and walk again in her rose gardens. The one dark cloud on her horizon is a nagging feeling Walter might never return from Ferrol.

She has no confidence in the Earl of Essex as commander of such a mission, and heard he was arguing with Walter about the proposed course before they set sail. If the Lord Admiral had been in command, he would have mediated between them, but she doubts the capabilities of Lord Thomas Howard as vice admiral.

Bess distracts herself from her worries by checking over the accounts of her horse-breeding venture. After an initial loss, she can see a growing profit, which gives her an idea. She sends for Adrian Gilbert and his wife Eleanor to come and stay. If Walter can spend so much on Durham House without mentioning it to her, Eleanor can help her make improvements to Sherborne as a surprise when he eventually returns.

Adrian Gilbert studies the new foals with a critical eye. 'I must admit you have achieved more than I expected.'

Bess feels a frisson of pride. Although Adrian Gilbert found the grooms and provided the breeding stock, she kept a close eye on the costs. 'I was thinking of investing further, and hope you will return to see the changes made.'

His eyes study hers with interest at the prospect. 'What do you have in mind?'

'Heavy horses, for pulling ploughs on the local farms. The farmers around Sherborne have suffered poor harvests these past years, and I'm told part of the reason is that good working horses are expensive and hard to find.' Bess watches his reaction and is pleased to see his nod of agreement.

Adrian Gilbert thinks for a moment. 'Shires would be best.

They have a docile temperament, which is important, as a stallion can weigh over a ton. They are also hardy in all weathers, and quick to learn to pull a plough.'

'Can you find me some good breeding stock?'

'It won't be easy, and could be costly, but would be a safe investment. You would have to double the size of the stables, and find more grooms to care for them.'

Bess smiles. 'If you accept the challenge and oversee the work, I shall provide the funds.'

The first reports are concerning; word reaches Bess that one of Walter's smallest ships, the *Darling*, returned to Plymouth early and alone. It's said the captain claims Walter is to be court-martialled for disobeying orders. Bess dismisses this as another argument between Walter and Essex. She knows little of such things, but a memory nags at the back of her mind. People can be sentenced to death at courts martial.

Bess takes her pen and writes to Robert Cecil in London.

My Lord, I am most confused and know not what to think. Gentlemen that are come from the fleete bring news that Watter has gone before my Lord General and that his ship is cast away.

She knows there is little, if anything, Robert Cecil can do, but it eases her sense of helplessness to share her own dilemma, and she has nothing to lose by asking. She dips her pen in the black ink and writes.

For God's sake, let me heer from you the truth, for I am much trubled.

. . .

She hesitates to sign her letter 'Bess' and decides it is best to end with her usual formality. *Your poor frend E. Raleigh.* Reading her words she adds a short postscript. *Pardon my haste.*

Bess summons Alexander Brett to deliver her letter. He has taken to wearing a hat of black sarcenet with an iridescent feather tucked into the band. He has a new doublet of black velvet with silver points, and a dagger at his belt, making him look more like a handsome noble than Walter's distant cousin, and her servant.

'I need you to ride to London again, Master Brett.' She hands him the letter and a purse of money for expenses. 'I would like you to try to see Robert Cecil in person.'

'I shall do my best to return with a reply, my lady.' He gives her a knowing look. 'You can rest assured Sir Walter is more than a match for the Earl of Essex.' There is a hint of humour in his voice, and she guesses most of the household speculate about Walter.

Bess has allowed him to become too familiar, but is less concerned than she might have been. She enjoys the independence of her life at Sherborne. If Walter does not return, she will be glad to have a man like Alexander Brett in her life.

The thought fills her with a new resolve, and she climbs the stairs to her husband's study, unlocking the desk drawer and taking out his will. She hesitates for a moment, noting how the legal ribbon is tied around the middle, then unties the knot and begins to read.

She sees that Walter's will was witnessed on the tenth of July, the day the fleet sailed, and one of the witnesses is his half-brother, Adrian Gilbert. He must therefore know he is named in the will to receive the sum of one hundred pounds for as long as he shall live.

Walter seems preoccupied with making provision for Wat,

with only five hundred pounds and her mother's pearls as provision for herself. She scans the legal wording, spotting such things as Alexander Brett's appointment as overseer of the Sherborne estate until Wat comes of age, and that Thomas Harriot is to be granted Walter's collection of books at Durham House, and his best black suits.

Bess frowns as she reads the conditions that she must not plough the deer park, or lease any of the land while their son and his successors live. She is about to return the parchment to the drawer when a line catches her attention. Slipped into a paragraph about the disposal of Walter's share in a ship called the *Roebuck* are the words: *I will that my reputed daughter on the body of Alice Goold, now in Ireland, shall have the sum of five hundred marks.*

Bess can say nothing about her unsettling discovery when Walter returns. He looks thin and pale, and has aged a good few years, his once thick hair now thinning. As predicted by his doctor, his wounded leg means he still has a limp as he thumps up the stairs to his study in his riding boots.

She listens and imagines him checking to see if his will is as he left it, secured with legal ribbon. Bess did her best to retie the knot as it was, but if he asks whether she read it she will not lie. There is nothing he can do, and it is reasonable she should know the contents.

She waits until after they have eaten and he has lit his pipe before asking about his voyage. He takes a few puffs and shakes his head. She can never recall him being so reticent, and prompts him. 'I heard such weather at sea was never seen by man this time of the year.'

'I confess our voyage was a disaster, from which I count myself lucky to return.' He takes another puff of his pipe. 'We saw no sign of the treasure fleet, and gales scattered our ships.

The *Warspite* sprang a leak from the caulking. The men were at the pumps night and day, and I thank God we didn't founder.'

Bess frowns as she hears how close she came to becoming a widow. 'I prayed for your safe return.'

Walter continues as he remembers. 'The storms carried us down past Land's End, but we found shelter in St Ives. We were exhausted and short of food, and returned to talk of a new Spanish Armada heading for Falmouth. After hasty repairs, we sailed back around Land's End, only to find the Spanish were scattered in the same storm we'd suffered from.'

'The captain of the *Darling* said the Earl of Essex accused you of disobeying his orders.'

Walter curses. 'He summoned me to a court martial, but our vice admiral, Lord Thomas Howard, helped him see sense.'

'Is this the end of your seafaring adventures, Walter?'

'I have little enough to show for the hardship we suffered, other than some wine we took in Fayal, and two prize ships laden with cochineal and indigo. My share might not cover the costs of the voyage, and I confess I am glad to be home.'

9

DURHAM HOUSE 1598

It takes Bess a moment to remember she is back in London, and that the snoring figure at her side is Walter, who shares her new bed at her insistence. She's decided to be more assertive with her husband, and take control of her future. He has no qualms about putting so many conditions in his will, so she has no conscience about demanding her own conditions.

At the back of her mind is the knowledge she will be thirty-three in April. She has no idea when her childbearing days will be over, and longs for another child. Bess thanks God Wat is thriving, but she would like a little girl, and hopes to name her Anne, to honour the memory of her mother.

Bess lies awake, thinking of how much has happened in the eleven years since her mother's passing. She has so many questions she wishes she'd asked about her royal connections. She recalls her mother telling her she was related to the queen's mother, Anne Boleyn, as well as Queen Catherine Howard and Queen Jane Seymour, and that her grandmother was a lady-in-waiting to Queen Catherine of Aragon.

She shakes Walter awake. 'Durham House is so cold.' She

shivers, despite the glowing embers of the fire kept burning in the hearth and the extra woollen blanket on the canopied bed. 'When can we return to Sherborne?'

Walter rubs his eyes and stares at Bess as if seeing her for the first time. 'I'm afraid my duties as Captain of the Guard mean we must stay in London, for now at least. But you have my word we'll return to Dorset when we can.'

The bed creaks as she raises herself on one elbow so she can study his face. 'The country air is good for Wat, and he's growing up fast. You can ask if Robert Cecil will allow his son William to come with us.' She caresses the greying hairs on his chest. 'Will you promise to stay at home with us, and not sail off on another risky venture?'

Walter runs his fingers through her long, unplaited hair as she lays her head on his chest. 'I've had my fill of ship's biscuit and salt fish, but I can't make promises. We face the threat of another Armada.' He tenses as he remembers. 'Our plan to strike a blow to the Spanish war fleet was like poking a nest of hornets with a stick. All we've done is to make Spain more determined.'

'Let others go to sea against them. Your place is with your family.' She hears the pleading in her voice. 'You told me you feared for your life in the last storm. Do you not think you've done enough?'

'Would you have me leave it to men like the Earl of Essex to keep our country safe?' He gives her a wry look. 'If so, we might as well surrender to Spain now.'

'I thought you'd made your peace with Essex?'

'I've not forgotten how he charged me with mutiny.' The scorn echoes in his voice. 'I've tried my best to resolve his arguments with Her Majesty about appointments for his friends, yet he refuses to support my bid to be admitted to the Privy Council.'

'I would see even less of you if you served on the Privy Council.' Bess kisses him. 'My brother Arthur told me there is to be a spring progress. You could ask permission to spend that time at Sherborne. I imagine Her Majesty has no shortage of ambitious men to keep her safe.'

'I shall ask her.' Walter returns her kiss. 'You are right. I've dodged Spanish musket balls once too often, and want to be a better husband to you – and a better father to Wat. It will cost me nothing to ask.'

'Is that a promise?'

He kisses her again, more slowly this time, in a way she had almost forgotten. Bess unfastens the silk ribbon and pulls off her thick winter nightgown. She sees his eyes shine as he watches her in the dawn light. He pulls her close, and they make love with an even deeper passion than when she'd been a shy young woman.

Walter seems in good spirits when he returns from Whitehall Palace. 'I found the opportunity to speak to the queen about her progress. She's excused me from my duties as Captain of the Guard. You were right.' He grins. 'Men are queueing up to take my place.'

Bess kisses him on the cheek. 'I've never felt at home at Durham House, and look forward to seeing Sherborne again.'

'I have other news to tell you. Her Majesty discovered Elizabeth Vernon is with child by that rascal Henry Wriothesley, Earl of Southampton.' Walter scowls. 'He's one of Essex's cronies, and they say he seduced Elizabeth Vernon for a bet.'

Bess stares at him. 'Dear God. I remember when Elizabeth Vernon was one of her youngest maids of honour. Has she been banished?'

'Worse. The queen ordered them sent to the Fleet prison,

as well as being banished from court.' He curses. 'The Fleet is no place for her to be with child, and I'll wager the Earl of Southampton is forgiven by the queen soon enough.'

Bess fights off the dark memories of her own time in the Tower. She doubts Elizabeth Vernon is as innocent as the gossips of court suggest, but she does not deserve to be locked in the Fleet. She will not tell Walter, but resolves to sell another of the jewels he gave her to pay for her friend to be well treated.

Walter seems not to notice how deeply his news touches her. 'I've decided to have my portrait painted before we leave London, and invited Master William Segar to visit.'

'As a gift for Her Majesty?' Bess hears the bitterness in her voice at the cruelty of their vindictive queen.

Walter shakes his head. 'For Sherborne. It's been ten years since I last had my portrait painted.' He smiles. 'I shall commission one of you to match.'

'You've changed a little in ten years.'

'I have, and William Segar is the obvious choice. He painted the queen's portrait last year, as well as the Earl of Essex and Sir Francis Drake.'

'Have you decided what you'll wear?'

'I thought my gilded armour. It cost me a fortune and I've hardly worn it.' He pats his broadening middle. 'That's if it still fits me.'

'You'll look too military. You need to look like a statesman if you are to win one of the offices of state. I suggest your silver and pearl doublet, and the silver satin shirt with jewelled buttons.'

'You don't think that looks too grand for a simple man from Devon?'

She raises an eyebrow at his false modesty. 'No grander than your golden armour. You can have your map of Cadiz in the background, and be remembered for your success.'

Sherborne is a breath of fresh air after the noise and dirt of the city. The only sounds are the welcoming song of a skylark, hovering high overhead, and the distant calling of the stags in the sprawling herd of deer browsing the lush green parkland.

Robert Cecil agreed for his son William to return with them. Although he says little, William has become a polite and likeable boy, and is a good influence on Wat. Edward Hancock, a North Devon man who'd served Walter since his voyage to Guiana, also accompanied them as a tutor for the boys.

Walter must travel on to Cornwall, to assess the coastal defences against any threatened attack from the Spanish. He promises to return as soon as he can, but Bess senses he's not telling her everything, as he seems to have a small mountain of luggage.

Bess has a question before he leaves. 'I'd like to convert the nursery into a suitable bedchamber for Wat. He is five years old this year, too old for a nursery. We have enough room for Master William to have his own chamber, and Master Hancock is accommodated in the guest wing.'

Walter gives her a mischievous look. 'We could have need of a nursery.' He smiles. 'Who can say what the future might hold?'

Bess hesitates to spoil his good mood. 'We shall see, but it's been five years since Wat was born.'

His face turns serious. 'I'm sorry, Bess. I've been away for the greatest part of those years, and even when we are together—'

'No one is at fault, Walter, and we should give thanks to God we have a fine, healthy son.'

He takes her hand and kisses it. 'I am always grateful, Bess.'

She looks into his eyes. 'As am I, Walter.' She suspects the trauma of his last adventure has changed him, as this is the first time they've spoken of their failure to conceive another child.

Bess finds Wat practising his archery with William Cecil in the garden. She watches as William's arrow strikes the target with a thud, but Wat's flies wide into the trees. Sometimes the two-year age difference counts, although they look much the same in height. It crosses her mind William could have inherited his father's problems, but will keep her concerns to herself for now.

She calls out to the boys as they retrieve their arrows. 'Would you like to come and see the new stables?'

Adrian Gilbert grins when he spots them. 'I've won a contract to supply post horses.' He looks pleased with himself. 'We are fortunate to be on the route between London and the West Country, and ideally placed to provide fresh horses.' He gestures for them to follow. 'Come and see the new shires.' He grins. 'I'll wager they are the biggest horses you've seen.'

The stables smell of fresh hay and look well run, with two young men busy caring for the great shire horses. The shire stallion is an impressive sight, over seventeen hands tall, with alert ears, bright, intelligent eyes and a flowing black mane. The breeding mare is smaller but still towers over the grooms.

Adrian Gilbert points to the new paddock. 'I've had a field levelled and fenced, and carpenters are building new stalls.'

'You've done well, Adrian. This will all help Sherborne to pay its way.'

He nods. 'The grooms are from the village. It's good to be able to offer them worthwhile employment.'

An idea occurs to Bess as she watches the boys taking a keen interest in the horses. She calls out to William. 'Do you ride?'

'I was taught to ride at my grandfather's stables, when I was Wat's age.'

Bess turns to Adrian Gilbert. 'I'd like you to help find a suitable horse and a good saddle for each of the boys, as a gift from me.'

Adrian grins. 'It will be my pleasure, and I'm happy to help young Wat learn to ride, if you wish?'

'I can think of no one better – but take good care of him.'

The summer heat means they are glad to spend the afternoon by the fishing lake, which Adrian Gilbert created by diverting a tributary of the River Yeo and stocked with carp. He sets up fishing poles for the boys, and shows them how to bait their hooks.

Adrian warns the boys, 'The lake has some fierce pikes, which must have found their way in from the river.' He frowns. 'If you catch one, call for me, as pikes have sharp backwards-pointing teeth, made to grab hold of fish.' He grins. 'Or a little finger.'

Bess watches with Walter from the shade of a line of willow trees, where they have spread out a rug and cushions. 'Wat learns from young William Cecil. Edward Hancock told me they are both diligent students and show great promise with their studies.'

Walter watches them both for a moment and smiles. 'William misses his mother, and his father is so busy I don't think he has much time for him, and his grandfather's health is failing. I'm glad he's come to Sherborne.'

Bess smiles. 'He will remember how we cared for him, and

I hope he will remain good friends with Wat for the rest of their lives.'

'William Cecil is likely to become a man of great influence, and could one day be the power behind the throne, like his father and grandfather.'

Her answer is interrupted by a splash, followed by a shrill squeal. Her first thought is that one of the boys has caught a pike, but she sees a small fish dangling from the end of Wat's fishing pole. Bess smiles. 'I hope Wat hasn't inherited his father's thirst for adventuring.'

Walter watches Wat return the fish to the water. 'Someone will discover El Dorado, the city of gold, and then you'll see why I took such great risks.'

The letter from Robert Cecil signals an early end to an idyllic summer. Walter's face is grave as he reads, before handing the letter to Bess. 'Robert Cecil asks me to bring his son back to London. Lord Burghley is seriously ill and asking to see his grandson.' He frowns. 'I'll return as soon as I can, although we both know that at seventy-seven, William's grandfather is on borrowed time.'

'Wat and I shall come with you. Robert Cecil has been good to us, and William will be glad to have Wat as company on the journey.'

They arrive at Durham House too late. Lord Burghley, the right-hand man of the queen throughout her reign, died the previous night. Walter must break the news to young William, a task made no easier by William's obvious affection for him.

'Your grandfather was the queen's most trusted advisor. Our country owes him a great debt.'

William seems older than his years. 'My grandfather showed me kindness. I shall miss him, Sir Walter.'

Walter's voice softens. 'The funeral is to be held at Westminster Abbey, but your grandfather wished to be buried at St Martin's Church in Stamford.'

William frowns. 'Why is that, Sir Walter?'

'Your family is one of the most important in Lincolnshire, and I expect he has asked to be laid to rest with your great-grandparents.'

Robert Cecil thanks Bess and Walter for returning to London with his son. 'William tells me you gave him a fine grey horse.'

'Please accept our condolences.' Walter glances at William. 'Your son is a capable rider, and a good influence on young Wat. We are happy to have him stay with us any time, particularly during what must be a difficult time for you.'

'Thank you.' Robert checks to be sure no one overhears. 'During my father's final illness, Her Majesty attended him at Cecil House, and sat by his bedside. He told me she fed him each day with her own hand, using a silver spoon.'

Bess shakes her head. 'Her Majesty will miss him greatly. He's been at her side for the whole of her reign.'

'She shut herself away after I informed her of his death, and has been inconsolable since.'

'Forgive me, Sir Robert, but the place on the Privy Council—'

'Is to go to Sir George Talbot, and the position of Lord Treasurer to Lord Buckhurst.'

Robert Cecil's voice is abrupt, and his dark eyes narrow, a sign the conversation is at an end. Bess cannot believe her husband's poor timing, but is not sorry he's lost his chance. If Walter was a member of the Privy Council she would face the impossible choice of moving to London or life at Sherborne without him.

The streets are thronged with the people of London as over five hundred mourners make their way to Westminster Abbey. Bess watches the sombre procession behind the coffin, draped in black and carried by eight men from Lord Burghley's mansion, Cecil House in the Strand.

Robert Cecil marches at the side of his elder brother Thomas, the new Lord Burghley, and heir to their father's great fortune. Walter, dressed in mourning, is at the side of Bess's brother Arthur, their heads bowed in reverence.

The funeral is one of the longest Bess can remember. The procession of the great and the good of England includes many she has not seen for years. She sits several rows behind Robert Cecil, whose shoulders look more stooped than ever, as if he now carries an extra burden of responsibility.

Bess bows her head and clasps her hands in prayer as the dean reads the service, his dour voice echoing to the high-vaulted roof of Westminster Abbey. *'I am the resurrection and the life, saith the Lord, he that believeth in me, yea, though he were dead, yet shall he live. And whosoever liveth, and believeth in me, shall not die forever.'*

Walter tells her Lord Burghley suffered agonies from trouble with bad teeth and the gout in his legs, yet never complained. He had been ill long before his final passing, although he somehow managed to attend the meetings of the queen's council to the end, taking to his bed late in July, wishing for death.

It feels like the end of an era as they pray for the soul of William Cecil, Lord Burghley, the man who'd always overseen the court. Bess stands with the others as the service comes to an end, and watches as his coffin leaves the great abbey of West-minster to make his last slow journey back home to Lincolnshire.

'You cannot go. The risks are too great, and I need you here!' Bess raises her voice in desperation.

Walter shakes his head. 'You spent too long with Her Majesty, Bess. You begin to sound like her.'

'You said only a fool would agree to be Lord Deputy of Ireland. Too many have been poisoned by their Irish servants, including the Earl of Essex's father.'

'There is no proof of that, and I've no intention of staying.' He looks into her eyes. 'I owe it to the hundreds of men and women I sent to Ireland as settlers to do what I can for them.'

She shakes her head. 'You owe them nothing. They knew the risks when they agreed to live in Ireland, and risking your own life will not help any of them.'

'There's been another rebel uprising in Munster, and my friend Edmund Spenser's home at Kilcolman Castle has been taken by the followers of the Earl of Tyrone.'

Bess frowns. 'Unless you plan to take an army with you, there's nothing to be gained by returning.'

'We are sending the biggest army ever to go to Ireland to deal with the rebellion, but I promise you I shall have no part in an expedition commanded by the Earl of Essex.' The scorn echoes in his voice.

'Why would the queen agree for a man like Essex to lead our army? Has he not proved his incompetence to her satis-faction?'

'I heard Essex objected to every name proposed, until he was the only candidate.' Walter scowls. 'It could be that his enemies have seen their chance to be rid of him.'

'They hope he won't return?' Bess never liked the arrogant earl, but counts his long-suffering wife, Countess Frances, as her friend.

'Nothing in Ireland is as simple as it might seem, Bess. I shall try to sell my Munster estates for two thousand pounds. It's time to cut my losses, before it's too late.'

10

SHERBORNE 1599

Bess makes good use of Walter's absence to spend time with Wat's tutor, Master Edward Hancock, who agrees to help her improve her reading and writing for an hour each morning. Her progress is slow, yet she works hard and he is a patient man.

She would once have thought it improper to spend so much time unchaperoned with Master Hancock, but she's changed, and enjoys her lessons. Edward Hancock is charming company, and skilled at building her confidence. Bess has not thought of it before, but her life at Sherborne can be lonely, despite having so many staff and servants.

Her absent husband can't complain if she wishes to improve herself, but she feels she should explain to Wat's tutor. 'My mother did her best to help me and my sisters, but she had to teach herself to read and write.' Bess frowns as she recalls her envy when her brother went to Magdalen College in Oxford. 'My father invested in an expensive education for my brothers, even my eldest brother William who, I'm afraid, will never make anything of himself.'

Edward Hancock raises an eyebrow at her frankness. 'A

familiar story, my lady. Like many of their generation, your parents no doubt expected their daughters would only need enough knowledge to run a household.'

'I was taught how to keep my accounts, and my mother prepared me well for my life at court, for which I am grateful, but I must master the skill of spelling, as I am aware my letters and writing reveal my lack of education.'

Edward Hancock studies her with intelligent blue eyes and gives her an encouraging smile. 'I confess you have some bad habits to unlearn, but nothing which cannot be improved upon, my lady, and you are making impressive progress.'

She blushes at his compliment, even though she knows he's trying to offer her encouragement. She's told no one, but throughout her life she's been held back by her poor handwriting, and every letter she writes is a struggle. Any improvement will give her the confidence she needs.

Bess has mixed feelings about Walter's letter from London, which she reads a second time to help her understand what he's up to. She's prayed each day for his safe return, and worried he could come to harm in Ireland. Now she learns he is back and apparently safe, yet instead of returning home to Sherborne, he writes to her from Durham House.

His friend, the poet Edmund Spenser, is dead. Walter says he can't believe the rumours Edmund was poisoned in Ireland, or took his own life, and believes it likely he was wounded defending his property from the Irish rebels. She understands Walter will remain in London until after the funeral in Westminster Abbey, yet he offers no explanation as to why he travelled to London in such haste.

Walter's letter says nothing about when he plans to return to Sherborne, or whether he was able to sell his lands and property in Ireland. Instead, he writes about how he will miss Edmund Spenser, and the comfort he had from a treasured volume of his poetry when he was imprisoned in the Tower.

In a troubling insight, Bess suspects Walter not only spent less time in the Tower than she did, but was better treated and allowed his books. She never understood why he left it to her brother to secure her freedom, or why he seems reluctant to discuss her return to court.

She has many questions for him when he returns. When the time is right she will ask whether he had time to visit his secret daughter, or her mother, the mysterious Alice Gould, during his visit to Ireland. To say her name will mean admitting she's been in his study and read his will, but she wants an end to these secrets between them.

The visit from her brother Arthur is unexpected but welcome, as she hasn't seen him for over a year. He looks tired after his long ride from Mile End, and arrives with a dozen armed men. He explains he is on his way to Plymouth, where he is to help oversee the defences of the sea port.

Bess notes he wears his fighting sword at his belt, and studies his face. 'I know you well enough to see you bring news I won't wish to hear.'

'You are right, Bess. It could be nothing, but there's talk in London that the new King of Spain, son of our old adversary, is preparing some seventy galleys and one hundred ships capable of carrying thirty thousand soldiers.'

'He's planning another Spanish Armada?' She frowns, guessing the true reason for Walter's prolonged absence.

'Rumours spread that a Spanish war fleet landed on the Isle of Wight and took possession of the island. The news caused such alarm in London people barricaded the streets and chained the city gates. It proved to be a false alarm, but we can't risk ignoring such talk.'

Bess knows why he's made the detour to see her. 'You've come to tell me the queen's ships are being made ready, and Walter plans to sail with them.'

Arthur nods. 'You will not be surprised to learn that Walter has been made vice admiral of the fleet, and is back in command of the *Warspite*.'

Bess cannot hide her disappointment. 'I'd hoped Walter would be home soon, and he didn't mention any of this in his last letter.'

'He's at the docks, making sure his ships are ready.'

'Too busy to spare a thought for his wife – or his son?'

Arthur shakes his head. 'I worry about Walter. It seems he's made an enemy of the Earl of Essex, who accuses him of poisoning the queen's mind against him.'

Bess shares her brother's concerns. 'I'll write to Countess Frances, and see if I can find out what's caused this trouble between Walter and Essex. I worry he still yearns to become a hero, and will never stop wishing for the next adventure. He still talks of one day returning to Guiana and finding his city of gold.'

Arthur has not been gone a week when another unexpected visitor arrives, a handsome man on a fine grey horse who escorts young William Cecil. Bess is pleased to see Robert Cecil has sent his son back to her so soon, and she asks Martha to fetch Wat from his studies.

William Cecil arrives in a carriage with his luggage and two servants, an encouraging sign he is to stay for a while. He smiles when he sees Wat appear in the doorway, and steps down from his carriage. 'My father sends his compliments,

Lady Raleigh.' His young voice sounds more confident since his last visit.

'You must be hungry, William.' She turns to Wat. 'Take William to the kitchens, and you can tell cook we have guests staying for dinner.'

The stranger dismounts with athletic ease, removes his plumed hat, and bows to Bess as if she were the queen. 'Henry Brooke at your service, Lady Raleigh.'

He has the easy confidence of a man used to commanding others, and Bess is sure she recognises him. His name sounds familiar, yet she struggles to recall their last meeting. She notes his silver sword on a low-slung belt, the quality of the embroidery, and the glistening mother-of-pearl buttons on the impractical white doublet under his red velvet riding cloak.

'Have we met at court, sir?'

He smiles. 'You visited my late sister, young William Cecil's mother, Elizabeth.'

'Apologies, my lord. You are Baron Cobham, brother-in-law to Sir Robert Cecil, and Warden of the Cinque Ports. I knew your late mother, Baroness Cobham, a lady of the queen's bedchamber, and you have a reputation as one of the most eligible bachelors at court.'

'My duties as Lord Warden, like my title, were not earned, but inherited from my late father, may God rest him.' His eyes twinkle. 'As for my reputation at court, I have yet to find any lady prepared to take me on.'

Bess raises an eyebrow. Baron Henry Cobham is privileged and entitled, everything Walter resents. She knows Walter would give anything to be a baron, and made Lord Warden of the Cinque Ports. 'I hope you will join me for dinner? I'll be glad to hear the latest news from London.'

'It will be my pleasure, Lady Raleigh, although I'm afraid the news from London is not good. The city is in disarray due to the talk of another Armada.' He follows her into the house and pulls off his cape and hat, running his fingers through his brown hair. He sits in one of the leather chairs and gives Bess an appraising look while Martha serves them both with Walter's best wine.

Bess is glad she is wearing her newer, more flattering gown, instead of the plain dress she wears when not expecting visitors. Henry Brooke could be useful to know. He is good-looking, despite his wispy beard, and there is a kindness in his eyes which makes him seem more like an old friend than a new acquaintance. She sips her wine, relishing the rich warmth, and smiles across at him.

'How is Her Majesty?'

Henry Brooke tastes his wine and nods in approval. 'The queen fears a fleet of Spanish warships will sail up the Thames, which is why she orders men like your good husband to patrol the approaches, day and night.'

Bess raises an eyebrow at his flippant tone. 'Could this talk of an Armada be another false alarm, like when they said the Spanish were on the Isle of Wight?'

'It's all a game, but one with no real winners.' He takes another sip of wine. 'The Spanish test us, but lack the resources for an invasion.' He gives her a mischievous look. 'But there is a secret reason for ordering the fleet to put to sea which must not become another rumour going around court.'

Bess glances around to be sure the servants cannot overhear. 'Your secret is safe with me. I'm banished from court.'

He lowers his voice. 'Someone warned the Privy Council that the Earl of Essex is preparing his fleet in Dublin. They ordered the fleet to stand ready in case he returns against the queen's order with an army.'

Bess stares at him. 'The Privy Council cannot believe the Earl of Essex intends a rebellion?'

Henry Brooke sounds sure of himself, but his story seems unlikely. Walter often tells her the Earl of Essex lacks judgement and is an incompetent leader, but Essex has always been loyal to the queen. If what Henry Brooke says is right, Walter could have the chance he longs for to be a hero, yet will be in no great danger.

Bess lies awake in the darkness, unable to sleep with so many questions swirling in her mind. She is surprised by the unexpected attraction she feels towards her handsome visitor, Henry Brooke, and troubled by the special connection she senses between them.

She has always been loyal to Walter, yet finds herself dreaming about what she would do if anything happened to him. Lord Henry Brooke, Baron Cobham, could not be more different from her husband. Walter seldom mentions news from court, and when she asks, grumbles of the Privy Council, yet Brooke tells her everything.

Henry Brooke was witty and entertaining over their dinner of roast pheasant. He is the same age as her, and as Walter grows older she's become increasingly aware of the thirteen years between them. Walter will be fifty soon, and his wounded leg ages him more than his years. She feels a prickle of conscience as she dreams of the athletic grace of Henry Brooke as he vaulted from his horse.

It seems odd that Henry Brooke remains unmarried, but she knows from his subtle flirting he finds her attractive. Would the queen welcome her back at court if she were a baroness? How long should she have to wait before making her intention to remarry known?

She pushes away her improper thoughts, and says a prayer for her husband, far away at sea, patrolling the coast for an enemy Bess doubts will ever come. New questions keep her awake. Does he know his fleet are like pawns in the Privy

Council's game of chess? Does Walter think of her, and miss her company in the long and lonely nights at sea?

If so, why does he never take the trouble to write or send her any message that he is safe and well? Did she hurt his feelings by not bothering to travel to the port to see him set sail? As she falls into a restless sleep, she recalls the last words he spoke to her. *I am always grateful, Bess...*

Walter returns to Sherborne in a dark mood, using a silver-capped cane to walk, his face serious. 'The Earl of Essex disobeyed Her Majesty's orders to stay in Ireland. His army was much reduced by casualties and deserters, and he came back to London with armed men against the queen's orders. They marched to Whitehall, but learned the queen was at Nonsuch Palace, where Essex accosted Her Majesty in her private bedchamber.' He scowls. 'The queen was alone, and in a state of undress.'

Bess has a recollection of her time as the queen's gentlewoman. 'Her Majesty hated anyone other than her most trusted ladies seeing her without her finery. I remember she banished a maid of honour for entering her bedchamber while she was in a state of undress.'

Walter gives her a disapproving look. 'The man has no honour, and should know he cannot behave in such a way without there being serious consequences. They are saying the queen wore only her nightdress, and was without her wig.'

Bess is one of the few who knows the queen's real hair is greying and cropped short to allow her extravagant red wigs to fit with more comfort. 'Where were your guards, Walter?' Bess frowns. 'The queen could have been in fear of her life.'

'My men failed in their duty, and will pay the price.' Walter utters a curse. 'I should have been there, as Captain of the

Guard, not at sea off the coast of Kent in a leaking ship for more than a month.'

Bess decides Walter is not in the mood to hear that Henry Brooke told her this had always been the Privy Council's plan. 'What did the queen do about Essex?'

'At first, she did nothing, and even allowed him to attend dinner. He was laughing and drinking the queen's wine as if nothing had happened.'

'He got away with it once again?'

Walter shakes his head. 'The Privy Council called him to a meeting which lasted over five hours. Essex is under arrest at York House, and even his wife is not allowed to visit him. He will face trial on numerous counts.' The satisfaction echoes in his voice. 'He is charged with disobeying the queen's orders. There are plenty at court who demand he should face a charge of treason.'

Bess stares at him. 'Treason?' She frowns. 'I wrote to Countess Frances, but had no reply. All this must be a great worry for her.'

'I don't see how the queen can forgive Essex this time, Bess. He overstepped the mark, and has shown contempt for the queen. The Privy Council will show him no pity.'

A thought occurs to Bess. 'If he's brought the army back from Ireland, does that mean the rebels have won?'

'They say Essex agreed a truce with the Earl of Tyrone, but Charles Blount, Lord Mountjoy, is to be sent out to replace Essex. He will not surrender our lands so easily, and my cousin, Sir George Carew, will be made Lord President of Munster, so some good has come from this disaster.'

Bess is relieved Walter makes no mention of going with Charles Blount to Ireland. She hopes his sojourn in the leaking *Warspite* has put him off adventuring, and they will be able to spend some time together at Sherborne – but he has more news for her.

'I haven't come to stay, Bess, but to fetch you and Wat, and William as well. I must prove to Her Majesty and the Privy Council that I'm serious about my duties as Captain of the Guard, and to do that we must return to London.'

Bess's maidservant Martha returns from her daily visit to the market with worrying news. 'They say the Earl of Essex is dying, my lady, and church bells are already ringing for him.'

Bess stops her needlework and frowns. 'The Earl of Essex has a habit of pretending to be ill to have his own way, Martha. I'm sure this is a ploy to win the queen's sympathy.'

'But it's the talk of London, my lady. They say he has dropsy, and Sir Robert Cecil will not allow a doctor to visit him.'

'Then I wish you to take a message to Essex House, for the Countess of Essex. If what you say is true, I might be able to help, but must speak with her first.'

Countess Frances looks tired but elegant as she welcomes Bess to Essex House. 'Forgive me, Bess. I've been meaning to reply to your letter of congratulation on the birth of my daughter, but with all that has happened—'

Bess holds up a white-gloved hand. She has always been a little in awe of the countess, and wears her best gown to give her confidence for this visit. 'I understand, but am glad to see you, as we cannot tell truth from rumour.'

Frances escorts her into her private room, and closes the door so they cannot be overheard. 'I visited my husband at York Place, and found him ill with the flux. He's not eating, and has difficulty speaking.'

'Dear God.' Bess recalls grim tales of men dying from the flux. 'We must do something, and soon, Frances.'

'I wrote to the queen, begging her to show leniency, but her only reply was a refusal.' Frances frowns. 'I asked permission for Robert to see his new daughter, but that small request is also refused.'

Bess knows what she must do. 'With your approval, I can ask Robert Cecil for another favour.'

Frances nods. 'I will be grateful if you can do it soon, Bess. Robert's men are already speaking out in his support in the taverns. There are plenty of disaffected Londoners who need a champion, and I worry what the queen might do if she learns he has the support of her people.'

11

DURHAM HOUSE 1600

BESS BREAKS THE SCARLET SEAL ON THE FOLDED LETTER AND recognises Countess Frances' neat hand. She writes from her late father's home, nearby Walsingham House, and thanks Bess for her kindness and help. She says her husband recovered well enough to be moved back to Essex House, where she is the only person allowed to visit him.

Walter scowls at the news, and seems more concerned with lighting his pipe than the plight of the Earl of Essex. 'I expected he would die of the Irish flux, or be locked up in the Tower.' He points at Bess with the stem of his pipe. 'Who knows what plots against the queen he could dream up with his friends at Essex House?'

Bess dislikes the smell of tobacco smoke, but indulges him. She looks back at the letter with mixed feelings, concerned for Countess Frances and her children. 'He's held there under house arrest, and guarded by Sir Richard Berkeley until he is well enough to stand trial. His friends have been evicted.'

Walter shakes his head. 'There is already talk that the queen says her purpose is to make him know himself, and his duty to her – and that she would again use his service. It's a sign, Bess, that she is minded to grant his freedom, and then he will be able to meet with whoever he chooses.'

'Frances is only allowed to see him at agreed times.' Bess frowns. 'She says these past weeks have taken their toll on his body. His mind seems to have suffered too. He falls into bouts of melancholy and talks of wishing he were dead.'

'Well, that would solve a problem for the queen – and the Privy Council.' Walter puffs at his pipe. 'The Earl of Essex should face his hearing in the Star Chamber like a man, and explain his actions; they say he is recovered well enough.' He scowls. 'There was quite a commotion when the public hearing was cancelled, as a good number turned up, not realising there was nothing to see.'

Bess raises an eyebrow. 'I don't see why the hearing has to be in public, and it's beyond me to understand how he has such a following with the people, having achieved so little.'

'It's all bluster, and some idle-headed ballad-maker had a picture of Essex printed showing him on horseback, with his titles, and two verses underneath that praise his wisdom, honour, and worth.' Walter frowns. 'The Privy Council issued an order against such engravings, but are too late. The ballads are sung by followers of Essex in every tavern.'

Bess keeps her silence about her part in the transfer of the earl to Essex House. Robert Cecil was surprised she wished to help her husband's enemy, but seems to understand it is out of concern for Countess Frances. He asked her to tell the countess to stop writing letters begging the queen's forgiveness, as it does nothing to help their case.

Wat is seven, a new milestone, and now considered old enough to wear a smart new doublet and hose, and is trusted to carry a knife at his belt. He looks like a miniature version of his father, who he worships – for reasons Bess can never understand. She decides it's time to teach her son and William some manners, and explain how they should behave in company.

'We will start with table manners.' She leads the boys into the great hall, where the table is set for dinner. 'First, you must know where to sit. The most honoured place is to the right hand of the head of the house, while the lowliest is at the end of the table to the left.'

William looks puzzled. 'What if there are many lords, Lady Raleigh? How do they all know where to sit?'

Bess smiles. 'It does happen, which can be amusing. In our house it is rare for there to be many lords, but I imagine your father has plenty of important guests. They will know their place, but the host should make sure everyone understands where to be seated. Now, what must we always do before we eat?'

Wat is first to answer. 'We have to wash our hands.'

'That's right. Sometimes there will be a ewery board, where you'll find a ewer of water, a basin and towel. At some meals a servant will bring a ewer and basin to the guests, and at other times, a small bowl and a cloth is provided for each person to wash and dry their hands.'

William looks puzzled. 'What if your hands are already clean, Lady Raleigh?'

'Good manners are all about being *seen* to behave in company, William. If you are observant you will see people make a display of washing their hands, and anyone who forgets risks disapproving looks. You must also keep your knife clean and sharp to cut your bread; do not tear it. Cut your meat into small pieces and wipe your knife on a clean napkin if it is dirty.'

She shows them how, with her own small knife, draping a clean linen napkin over her arm as her mother taught her when she was Wat's age.

'A man wears a hat while dining, but you need to know when to remove it, which you should do with your right hand, changing it to your left hand, and turning the inside of your hat to your leg.' She smiles. 'Whatever you do, you must not hold your hat like you are begging for alms.'

Wat frowns. 'How do I know when I must take off my hat, Mother?'

'When you need to show respect, such as for a lady, or any person of higher status.' She sees his puzzled look. 'Watch what others do, and you will learn soon enough. One day you will be presented to the queen, and must know how to conduct yourself.'

Bess wishes she could be there when that day comes for Wat, but knows it's unlikely she will return to court. 'You must bow, and try not to stare at the queen. A good tip is to look at her slippers, not into her eyes. Do not speak until she addresses you, and take care never to turn your back on Her Majesty.'

Wat frowns. 'I don't think I should want to meet the queen.'

'Most boys never have the chance, so when you do, you must be prepared to make the most of it. Did you know it was the queen who granted Sherborne to your father?'

Wat looks around the room, as if seeing it for the first time. 'Why, Mother?'

Bess smiles as she tries to explain. 'The queen has too many houses, so gives them to her subjects as rewards for their service. This lodge was near to falling into disrepair, until we rebuilt it.'

Bess welcomes Walter back from a long day at court in Richmond Palace with a kiss on his cheek. He doesn't return her kiss, but looks tired, and smells of tobacco. 'How is Her

Majesty today?' She sees the glint in his eye, and worries he is plotting some new scheme she won't approve of.

'I am pleased to tell you our queen is as vigorous as ever.' He grins. 'I calculated she must be sixty-seven this year, yet can you believe Her Majesty danced a galliard in front of the whole court?'

'With you?' Bess glances at his cane, the handle worn smooth and polished with use.

'I regret to say my dancing days are long over.'

'But did you speak with Robert Cecil?'

'I hastened back as soon as I could. I heard there is ill feeling against him in London, no doubt encouraged by supporters of that rascal Essex.'

Bess frowns. 'My maidservant said they sing bawdy songs about Robert Cecil in the taverns, and daubed *Here lies the toad* on the wall of his house.' She gives Walter a cautionary look. 'You mustn't mention any of this within young William's hearing. There is no need to upset him, and he won't understand.'

'I shall write to Robert Cecil and remind him that of all the things he has to worry about, his son is not among them.' He smiles. 'I shall offer to take young William with Wat to see the entertainments in the tiltyard after Whitsuntide.' He grins. 'Her Majesty commanded the baiting of bears, a bull, and an ape. It will be quite a spectacle.'

Bess frowns at the thought. 'I will not be sorry to miss it, although I should like to see the jousting again.' Her banishment includes all events at court. She finds the baiting with savage dogs barbaric, but misses the excitement of the Accession Day jousts.

Walter ignores her hint. 'It's a good idea to offer to take young William in. He's good company for Wat, and keeps us in Robert Cecil's mind.'

'Keep close to Robert Cecil, Walter. Of all those who would call you their friend, his friendship matters most.'

Walter agrees. 'Her Majesty's favour increases towards him. She gifted young William a new coat of crimson velvet, a girdle and dagger, a new hat and feather, and a jewel to wear in it.'

Bess hears the edge of resentment in his voice. 'The queen may gift her rewards to whoever she chooses. Don't forget you are still a favourite of the queen, Walter, and she granted you our houses here and in London, as well as other generous gifts.'

Bess is glad when Walter agrees they can return to Sherborne, and is soon busy with making more improvements to the house and grounds. Walter prefers to spend his time writing letters in his study, and it's not long before he confides in Bess.

'It seems I can sell my estates in Ireland for a good price, after all. I've had to give away those which are already settled, but I could use the proceeds of the rest to fund another search for the city of gold.'

Bess has been waiting for this moment, which she knew would come. 'The risks are too great, not to speak of the costs. Have you forgotten the storms which almost cost your life?' She looks into his eyes. 'Walter needs a father and I need a husband. Would you like to be like Sir Francis Drake, buried at sea with no memorial?'

Walter sits in silence, gripping his cane. Bess is unsure if he's more upset by her outburst, his memories, or the knowledge she is right, and that he will never return to Guiana, or ever find his El Dorado. He looks up at her with an unexpected glint in his eyes. 'I will need to find another source of income to replace that lost in Ireland, and believe I have an interesting solution.'

He searches through the pile of nautical maps littering his desk, and spreads one out for Bess to see. 'The governor of the island of Jersey, Sir Anthony Paulet, is seriously ill, and Henry

Brooke told me there will soon be a vacancy for his replacement.'

'You would go to Jersey?' Bess stares at him in surprise, then studies the parchment map, marked with castles and churches, towns and harbours, trying to guess what Henry Brooke is up to. 'For how long?' Her pulse races at the thought of sailing to the island of Jersey with Walter. She always dreamed of visiting foreign lands, and would like to be at Walter's side if he is appointed governor.

'I don't know, but confess the idea has a certain appeal. Henry Brooke also told me he has become betrothed to the daughter of Lord High Admiral Charles Howard.' Walter smiles. 'Robert Cecil says Baron Cobham has to marry out of necessity.'

Bess hides the pang of jealousy. 'He's to marry Frances Howard?' Bess wouldn't call her a friend, but knew her when they were both gentlewomen to the queen. 'I thought she was married to the Earl of Kildare?'

'She was, but he died from his wounds in Ulster, trying to stop the Earl of Tyrone's uprising.' Walter frowns. 'You have been away from court too long, and much has changed. When I last spoke to Her Majesty, I feared I would be sent to join Lord Mountjoy in Ireland.'

Bess stares at the map, and recognises the work of Thomas Harriot. Walter has already made up his mind about his future, and isn't consulting her but telling her of his intentions. He doesn't ask if she would like to go with him, but studies the map on his desk. 'Jersey is of strategic importance and well defended. As governor, I would be able to make of it what I will.'

Walter's appointment as Governor of Jersey is signed by the Privy Council, although they made no mention of what the queen thought of it. Bess accompanies him to the harbour at Weymouth, with Wat and William Cecil, who've been promised a tour of his ship.

The ship is docked at the quayside, and accessible by a gangplank. Bess stops to watch the men loading sacks of supplies and wooden casks of water and wine. The tang of freshly tarred rigging hangs in the air, and men shout to each other high in the rigging as they make ready the huge canvas sails.

Although the ship is a merchant trader, Bess spots the snub noses of bronze cannons at a row of open gun ports. Several of the men wear swords and others carry muskets, a reminder of the danger from pirates, even on the short sea voyage to Jersey.

While the first officer takes the boys for a tour, Bess follows Walter to his small cabin at the stern. There is barely room for them both, and she frowns as she feels the thin mattress on his narrow bunk. 'It is little wonder you find it hard to sleep at sea.' She takes him in her arms once they are alone, and holds him close. 'You won't forget your promise?'

'I'll return as soon as I've appointed my deputy.' He kisses her. 'Ships often pass Jersey. I'll write when I can.'

The call comes for Bess to find the excited boys and go ashore. She raises her hand in farewell, still troubled that he'd not even asked her to sail with him to Jersey. She resents this last adventure, and will miss him, but wishes him a safe voyage, and tells him to make the best of his new dominion.

Many weeks pass before the first letter from Walter is delivered from a ship returning to Portsmouth. Bess frowns at his formal wording before she realises he could not be sure who else might read his letter. He writes that the winds veered as soon as he lost sight of land, and waves crashed over the bows for two days.

She can picture him lying on the narrow bunk in his cramped cabin, cursing Henry Brooke for suggesting the voyage to Jersey. She reads on, as he complains about how his ship rolled in the swell, and that he wishes he was back in his bed at Sherborne, and is exhausted from lack of sleep.

It seems the weather improved when he arrived at the main Jersey port of St Helier, as he says he was surprised to be greeted by crowds and a fanfare of trumpets in bright afternoon sunshine. The Bailiff of Jersey made a welcome speech and introduced his son, who would serve as a page, as well as his interpreter and personal guide to the island and its customs.

In her reply, Bess tells him of reports of trouble being stirred up in London by supporters of the Earl of Essex. The stables at Durham House were burned to the ground, but it's thought to be the fault of a careless servant, and the rest of their servants put out the fire before it could spread to the main house.

When Wat and William Cecil see her writing to Walter, they ask if they can add their plea for his return. William is older and has the neatest handwriting, so once Bess has finished her letter he adds a short paragraph at the end.

Sir Walter, we must all exclaim and cry out because you will not come home. You being absent we are like soldiers when their captain is absent, they know not what to do. Sir Walter, I will be plain to you. I pray you leave all idle matters and return to us.

William Cecil.

Bess reads his words before she seals her letter with wax. She is surprised at how the boys miss Walter, who is home so rarely and has little to do with either of them, even when he does choose to stay. He is a hero to William Cecil, and Wat is old enough now to need a father figure in his life.

Walter returns from his adventure in Jersey tanned from the sun and wearing a new sword, a gift from the islanders. 'It's good to be back, Bess.' He embraces her. 'The people of Jersey were divided between those who welcomed my governorship, and those who resisted new ideas. I went all that way to escape the petty fighting at court, yet found self-serving men and gossipers undermining my plans, just the same.'

'Well, it's good to have you back.' She kisses him on the cheek. 'We've missed you.'

'I must preside over the meeting of the Stannaries in Cornwall, but am keen to return to court, and wish to be sure there is no damage to my property at Durham House. What news is there from London?'

'I had a letter from Countess Frances. She is in her confinement at Barn Elms.'

'Another child?' Walter stares at her in surprise. 'Does that mean Essex is forgiven?'

'Her Majesty decided he is no longer to be held under arrest, but is banished from court. And you were right: Frances says he has filled Essex House with his rowdy supporters and soldiers from Wales.'

12

DURHAM HOUSE 1601

ARTHUR FAILS TO SMILE AS SHE GREETS HIM, AND BESS suspects this is more than a social visit. Her brother joins them for supper, with a first course of salmon poached in herbs with a sweet sauce of oranges from Seville. Arthur tastes the salmon and nods in approval. 'I heard your stables burned down, and feared you were being targeted by the Essex faction.'

Bess savours the orange sauce and looks up at her brother. 'The culprit was a servant, who was careless when disposing of hot ashes from the hearth. Two of our horses were injured but the fire was put out in time to prevent more damage.'

Walter frowns. 'I dismissed the troublesome old woman, but we could have lost the house, and now I must pay for stabling until we can rebuild. I thank God my family were at Sherborne, and I was away in Jersey, at the time.'

Their young serving girl brings the next course, a steaming side of mutton baked in claret, on a silver serving dish. Arthur cuts a thick slice of mutton with his knife and turns to Walter. 'I've never been to Jersey, but I knew the previous governor, Sir Anthony Paulet, and attended his funeral. What sort of reception did you find there?'

'Some tried to resist everything I did, and I suspect I was sent as governor to be out of the way, but there is a charm about the island.' Walter smiles. 'The weather is much warmer, at least when I was there, and the climate might be good enough to grow tobacco plants, which could be a profitable venture.'

Bess gives her brother a cautionary look. 'Don't let Walter talk you into investing in his schemes, Arthur. You can be sure that men will lose interest in smoking tobacco soon enough.' She watches Walter's reaction but he misses her hint yet again.

Arthur smiles at her warning and gestures for their maid-servant to refill his glass. 'I hear you're planning to double the queen's guard, Walter?' He sips his wine, a fine Bordeaux from Jersey. 'It would seem a sensible precaution.'

Walter helps himself to another portion of the tender lamb. 'If I can recruit enough men I can trust. A surprising number sympathise with the Earl of Essex. The streets are full of his supporters, although God only knows why he's still so popular with the people.'

Arthur looks up at him. 'There is also a rumour Sir Ferdinando Gorges has joined the Essex faction. Isn't he a cousin of yours?'

'A *distant* cousin.' Walter grins. 'As are most men of note in the West Country. Sir Ferdinando commands the fort at Plymouth, which is a concern. He might know what Essex plans to do. If he's in London, I'll ask him to come to see me, and we shall find out what he knows.'

'I've seen a copy of a letter from Baroness Penelope Rich, the Earl of Essex's sister. She wrote to the queen of her brother's love and service to his sacred goddess and admired mistress, and begged her to give him an audience.' Arthur's voice has an edge of sarcasm.

Walter laughs. 'The man is deluded if he thinks he'll ever be welcomed back to court.'

'Lady Rich accuses you, Walter, as well as Lord Cobham, of poisoning the queen's mind against Essex.' Arthur gives Walter a knowing look. 'I would be surprised if the queen takes any notice.'

Bess wipes the claret gravy from her plate with her bread. It is sweet, with rich fruit tones, the precious cloves lending a spicy aftertaste. 'I asked Countess Frances to stop writing to Her Majesty, and to say the same to her sister-in-law, Penelope. I understand her intention, but the only reputation she harms is her own.'

Walter is working at his desk and turns as Bess enters his study. He has a puzzled look and waves a note at her. 'I sent a message to Ferdinando Gorges inviting him to visit, but he says he will only meet if I am alone, and insists on meeting me in a boat in the middle of the river, opposite the steps to Essex House.'

Bess frowns as she reads the brief note, which looks to be written in haste and has the flamboyant signature of Sir Ferdinando. 'Why would he want you to meet him on the river – and why does he wish to see you so early in the morning on Sunday, before church services?'

Walter's chair creaks as he takes back the note and studies it again, as if it has some hidden clue. 'I've known Ferdinando Gorges since we were boys, so I hope he wishes to share whatever new trouble it is that Essex is plotting, without anyone knowing, or risking what he says being overheard.'

'If Sir Ferdinando has concerns about being seen talking with you, to do so in front of Essex House seems a poor choice. He can come here unnoticed, by the river steps at night. I don't understand why you must go to him.'

'It's my duty, as Captain of the Guard, to report any information to the Privy Council. If I must, I can threaten to have Ferdinando Gorges arrested unless he is prepared to tell me what he knows.'

A thought occurs to Bess. 'This could be useful to Robert Cecil. It would be good to show you are keeping an eye on whatever Essex and his friends are up to.'

'I'm sure Robert Cecil has his own spies inside Essex House, reporting all that's said.' Walter looks up at her. 'You are right, it's important to have his support, and young William Cecil treats me like a father.'

'He seems to regard you as some kind of hero, and his father is always too busy for him.' She puts her hand on his arm. 'Can you have your yeomen ready with another boat, in case this meeting is a plan to try to kidnap you?'

Walter frowns at her suggestion. 'All Ferdinando Gorges wishes to do is talk. The worst that can happen is that he decides not to turn up. I can't risk scaring him off with my Yeomen of the Guard.'

'Then be sure to wear your dagger.' She kisses him. 'And keep your wits about you.'

The crowded streets of London buzz with a sense of anticipation as Bess makes her way to Walsingham House in Seething Lane, in the shadow of the Tower. Drunken soldiers spill out of the taverns, shouting and arguing, adding to the atmosphere of danger and lawlessness.

The wintry wind means she wears her fur-lined hooded cape, which also serves to hide her from curious eyes. Bess would rather not be seen visiting the Countess of Essex and start unwanted rumours about her being involved in any plot.

She has brought her maidservant Martha as company, and takes the risk of ignoring Walter's offer of an armed escort.

Yeomen in the queen's livery would only serve to draw unwanted attention to her visit.

Countess Frances welcomes her to Walsingham House with a smile, yet looks pale and her eyes betray her concern. Bess can see she is troubled by her surprise visit, and questions swirl in her mind. Does Frances know her husband is planning something against Walter?

Bess returns her smile and embraces Frances. 'I was out for some air, and thought I would call to see if you are at home. How is your child?'

Frances brightens. 'My daughter is well, thank the Lord. We named her Dorothy, after Robert's sister. She's sleeping now, but you must see her when she wakes.'

Frances turns to Martha. 'You are welcome to warm yourself in the kitchen.' She waits while her servant takes her cape, and then leads Bess into the privacy of her parlour, pulling the door closed behind them.

A welcome log fire blazes in the hearth, and Bess sits in one of the comfortable fireside chairs, glad of the warmth. 'How is your husband? We are hearing all sorts of rumours, but cannot be sure which are true.'

Frances sits opposite, and gives her an anguished look. 'I worry about Robert. He does himself no favours, speaking out against the Privy Council, and spends long hours drinking with his friends, who encourage him.' She frowns. 'He's still bitter about being banished from court, and blames the queen's advisors.'

'Including Walter?'

'It is a great shame, as they were friends.'

Bess studies her friend. 'It's not too late…'

'I fear it is, Bess. I've tried my best, and so has his sister Penelope, but he's like a stranger to us both.'

'You can tell me what he plans to do.' As she says the words, Bess knows she will report whatever Frances tells her to

Walter as soon as she can.

'Robert talks of marching with his men through London to protest at the way he has been treated. I worry he'll be accused of treason and locked up in the Tower.'

'There must be some way to help him see sense?'

Frances shakes her head. 'I've tried, but it's hopeless.'

Bess sees her friend is close to tears. 'There is nothing I can do about your husband but, if the worst happens and you find yourself in difficulty, you will always be welcome to stay as our guest in Dorset.'

Frances stares at her in surprise. 'I would not wish to cause you trouble, Bess, but I'm grateful for your offer.'

Frances never speaks about her husband's infidelity, but Bess knows he's had affairs with several young ladies of court, and his daughter by Elizabeth Southwell caused a scandal. She has questions for Walter about why he makes such a great secret of his illegitimate daughter, but at least that was long before they were married.

The messenger from Walter wears the red-and-gold livery of the queen's yeomen, and demands to see Bess, despite the late hour. 'Sir Walter is safe, Lady Raleigh, but says you must take your son and Sir Robert Cecil's to your brother's house at Mile End as a matter of urgency.'

Bess stares at him. 'Where is my husband?'

'Sir Walter is with Sir Robert Cecil, my lady, and is required to remain at the palace to ensure the safety of the queen. I understand he met with Sir Ferdinando Gorges, and they were fired upon from Essex House.'

'Was he hurt?' Bess holds her breath.

'Neither Sir Walter nor Sir Ferdinando were injured, by the grace of God, but my orders are to be sure you leave Durham

House for your own safety, and I have men waiting in the courtyard to escort you and your son.'

Bess calls for Martha to wake Wat and William, and help her pack. It worries her that Walter no longer considers Durham House safe, but she says a prayer of thanks he is unharmed, and was able to make his report to Robert Cecil. A thought occurs to her. 'Do you know what action Sir Robert Cecil plans to take about this?'

The yeoman nods. 'I understand Sir William Knollys, with Lord Keeper Egerton, Sir Edward Somerset, Earl of Worcester, as well as Lord Justice Popham have gone to Essex House to deliver a summons for the Earl of Essex to appear before the Privy Council.'

The mounted escort of armed yeomen flank their carriage as they rattle through narrow cobbled streets in the darkness. Bess glimpses the worried look on Wat's face and tries to calm him, but her words sound hollow. She breathes a grateful sigh of relief as she recognises the wrought-iron gates of her brother's house.

Arthur must have heard the commotion and comes out to meet them as they arrive. He opens the door to her carriage and calls for servants to help with their luggage. 'I'm relieved to see you, Bess.' He puts a reassuring hand on Wat's shoulder, and nods to William Cecil. 'You are safe here, and welcome to stay for as long as you need.'

Arthur's wife Anne also looks relieved as she welcomes them inside, and calls for her servants to make their guest rooms ready. 'We heard the church bells ringing at an unusual hour and feared the worst.' She glances at the armed yeomen. 'Is Walter safe?'

Bess nods. 'I was told he's at the palace, guarding the queen, which I hope is as safe as anywhere in London in these troubling times.'

Arthur returns from the palace with the news that the Earl of Essex imprisoned the privy councillors in Essex House. They feared for their lives, but Sir Ferdinando Gorges freed them when the Earl of Essex rode ahead of his army of rebels as they marched down Fleet Street.

'I heard people cheered them at first, but there was a fight at the Ludgate. A man was killed, and Sir Christopher Blount was wounded and taken to the Tower. The rest have returned to Essex House, and barricaded themselves in.'

Bess stares at her brother in disbelief. 'Do you know if Walter is involved?'

'He's still guarding the Palace of Westminster. They've made a barricade of coaches to block the road. Men were sent to bring two culverins from the Tower with enough powder and shot to reduce Essex House to a pile of rubble if necessary.'

'I spoke with Countess Frances, and she feared something like this would happen.' She looks her brother in the eyes. 'She tried everything she could to stop this, but her husband wouldn't listen.'

Arthur frowns. 'Countess Frances is one of those barricaded in Essex House, together with her sister-in-law, Baroness Penelope Rich. If they were not both already banished from court, they would be now.'

News drifts across the silent city like a swirling fog of fact, half-truth and rumour. It's said Essex House was surrounded by the queen's soldiers, and the once proud Earl of Essex surrendered on his knees. Bess feels no sympathy for him, as he should know such actions will have consequences. At the same time, she feels sympathy for Frances and her innocent newborn daughter.

Walter arrives late in the evening, exhausted by the drama of recent events. 'It's been a long day, but it's over, Bess.' He removes his hat and rubs his eyes. 'I fear Essex sealed his own fate, and this time no apology can be enough for threatening the life of the queen.'

Bess embraces him. 'And threatening your life, Walter. I was told you were fired upon by muskets from Essex House when you met with Sir Ferdinando Gorges. I suspected it could be a trap.'

Walter kisses her on the cheek. 'Their aim was poor, by the grace of God. They could have killed or wounded Sir Ferdinando, which is why I'm sure he had no idea of their intentions, or he would never have agreed to meet me on the river.'

'Arthur told me Ferdinando Gorges freed the privy councillors from Essex House and took them to safety by the watergate. That should stand in his favour.'

'It depends if Ferdinando Gorges is prepared to give evidence against the ringleaders at the trial.' Walter scowls. 'There will be a high price to pay if he refuses.'

'What is to become of Countess Frances?'

'She will not be using the title of countess for much longer, and is held under arrest at Walsingham House.' He gives Bess a cautionary look. 'She is not allowed any visitors, so I ask you to stay away, for the sake of your own reputation, and mine.'

Bess sits in silence for a moment, remembering her promise to Frances. Walter looks weary from lack of sleep, but she has many questions. 'What has become of the others who supported Essex?'

'Many of those who weren't captured at Essex House escaped to Wales. The nobles are sent to the Tower. Baroness Rich is imprisoned in the household of Sir Henry Seckford, Keeper of the Privy Purse, in St John's.'

'What has Lady Penelope done?'

Walter frowns. 'Lady Penelope Rich stands accused of encouraging her brother, and could face trial for treason.'

Walter has a haunted look in his eyes when he returns from the Tower. He pulls off his hat and cape, soaked from the heavy rain, and slumps into his favourite chair. Bess watches as he fills his pipe from a leather pouch of tobacco and notes how his hand shakes as he lights it with a taper from the fire.

The danger has passed, but Walter has changed in some way Bess can't yet understand. He should be pleased with his part in saving the life of the queen, yet the experience has left scars which will take time to heal. He takes a few puffs of his pipe and seems to calm a little before he speaks.

'Essex had every chance. The Privy Council intended to reprove him for his unlawful assemblies, and have him retire to the country.' He mutters a curse. 'He gave Her Majesty no choice but to sign his death warrant. Her leniency was to grant him a private execution, rather than a traitor's death at Tower Hill.'

'Which you had to witness?'

'I took no pleasure in it, Bess, but was required to be present, as Captain of the Guard. Essex stared out at us, as if searching for someone. I thought he planned to shout a final insult, but I noticed there was no sign of his wife, or any of his family. I could watch no more, and sheltered from the rain in the doorway of the armoury. I heard him shout, *Executioner, strike home!*'

'You should feel no pity for him, Walter.' Bess takes his hand in hers. 'I would like to return to Sherborne with the boys, and you have Stannary business to attend to.'

13

SHERBORNE 1602

Swirling drifts of snow cover Sherborne, turning the gardens to a pristine expanse of sparkling white. Bess watches with Walter from the window of his study. He promised to take better care of her since returning from London, yet still seems troubled.

Bess sees the snow as purifying, cleansing, a fresh start for them both after the dangers of London. Walter worries about the snowdrifts blocking the roads. Dorchester is cut off and, even once the thaw starts, the ice makes the narrow lanes dangerous for horses.

Walter seems older than his years, his once tanned face pale and his hair thinning and grey. He rarely uses his cane but Bess notes the occasional grimace that reveals the truth. He still suffers from his wounded leg, and will never be the energetic man she once knew.

She places her hand on his back. 'You must forget about what happened in London, Walter. I can tell you are still dwelling on the past.'

'I was thinking about the last Parliament, Bess. I've never seen so many good men close to tears.' He stares out at the falling snow, avoiding eye contact. 'No one who heard Her Majesty's speech will forget that day. She was saying goodbye to us.'

She kisses him on the cheek. 'It's her way to retain the support of her Parliament, and it seems to have worked.'

'If you saw her you would understand, Bess. She looks frail, and stumbled with her speech more than once. She will be sixty-nine in September, and is in poor health. I worry about what will become of the country after her days – and what will become of us.'

Bess frowns. Such talk is dangerous, and she is concerned at the thought of him returning to court in such a dark mood. 'You said yourself the roads are not safe enough to travel to London. Even if you could, there is little you or anyone can do about the queen's health.'

Walter surprises her with a smile. 'She doesn't even listen to her doctors, and calls them all charlatans.'

Bess tries to change the subject. 'I've had a letter from my brother. He says the court has moved to Richmond Palace in foul and wet weather, and the cold winds make this the sharpest winter he can remember.'

'Did your brother mention anything about the health of the queen?'

'He did not, but when I served as lady of her bedchamber she insisted we kept her ill health a strict secret. Arthur would know better than to mention such things in a letter.'

'Could you write to one of her ladies at Richmond with an innocent enquiry about the queen?'

She frowns. 'It's been so long I don't know which of them I can trust any more. Why don't you write to Sir Robert Cecil?'

'I have, but Robert Cecil no longer replies to my letters.'

She stares at him in surprise. 'Did you upset him in some way?'

'We had a disagreement in Parliament, about taxation of

the poor to fund defences against the Spanish, and the abolition of monopolies.'

'Which affects your income from the tax on wines?'

'And woollen broadcloth – and Cornish tin.' Walter scowls.
'Since then, he won't confide in me. He agreed to pay a half
share in a privateering expedition, yet he speaks out against
me, although I've never spoken against him. I fear Robert Cecil
has turned our queen against me, for his own purpose.'

'I shall ask Arthur to find out what's going on. He will be
discreet, and is good at uncovering the truth.'

'Be sure to let me know what he says. Our future could
depend on it.'

Arthur visits in person, rather than risk committing what he
has to tell Walter to paper. 'The news is not good, I'm afraid.
There is talk of the succession, and people are already forming
factions.'

'Do they not know how angry the queen will be if she
hears anyone mention the succession? If people are not careful
they could be accused of treason.'

'That doesn't stop the secret meetings. You of all people
well understand how they gossip at court, Bess. In truth, I hear
of little else, even from those who should know better.'

'Well, my conscience is clear.' Bess stares at her brother. 'As
God is my witness, I have never spoken of the succession to
anyone.'

'Then it is time to consider the inevitable, for the sake of
your family, if not your own sake.'

His words make Walter sit up in his chair. 'Is Her Majesty
so ill?'

'She suffers from bouts of melancholy, and takes less care
with her appearance. Sir Robert Cecil seems to be running the

country in the queen's name, and no one dares to question his right to do so.'

Walter glances at Bess before replying. 'I'm not on the best of terms with Robert Cecil, although Bess has a good opinion of him.'

Bess hears the resentment in his voice. It is worrying that Robert Cecil would turn against Walter, and she suspects he would not do so without good reason. 'What are they saying, Arthur?'

'That a possible successor is King James of Scotland.'

Walter curses. 'Her Majesty will never agree to it. He's the son of Mary, Queen of Scots, and favours peace with Spain. To name him as her successor goes against everything she believes in!'

Arthur glances at the door. 'Can you be certain of the loyalty of your household here at Sherborne?'

Bess answers for them both. 'Can anyone be certain of their household?'

'You should presume at least one of them is in the pay of Sir Robert Cecil. Everyone has their price, so you should keep your voices down.'

Bess knows he could be right but the thought troubles her. 'Most of our servants were recruited from the village by Adrian Gilbert, but others travelled down with us from Durham House. I've never had cause to worry about their loyalty.'

'There is a tension in the mood at court, which I predict will soon turn to dog eat dog. We must not offer anyone the opportunity to use something against us – and that includes you, Bess.'

'How am *I* involved in any of this?'

'You correspond with Sir Robert?'

'I have asked him favours in the past, but that is more than made up for by the care we show his son, William.'

Arthur looks concerned. 'All I am saying is we all need to be more careful from now on.'

Bess is looking forward to the spring and seeing her gardens come alive again. The orchards, planted when they first arrived at Sherborne nine years ago, are bursting into bud, and the deer park is greener than she can ever remember.

Wat will soon be nine years old, and is doing well with his studies. Bess is pleased at how he is turning into a confident young man, and she prays each morning that she will be graced with another child – a daughter, to be named after her mother – before it is too late.

The one dark cloud on her horizon is Walter's need to return to Jersey, to review progress on the defensive works. Although he complains that his governorship of Jersey feels more like an exile than a reward for loyal service, she's always known he must return sometime, or resign as governor, but he surprised her with the news one morning.

'I'm thinking of taking you and Wat with me next time. The experience will be good for Wat, and I think you will like the governor's house.' He smiles. 'We can purchase some land, and see if the island is suitable for growing tobacco.'

His plans excite and trouble her in equal measure. Walter is a poor sailor, but his account of the crossing fills her with trepidation. He is right that the experience will be good for Wat, but Sherborne is where she wants to stay.

She has invested all she has in making Sherborne their home but, at the same time, the great adventure of setting sail for Jersey appeals to her. Walter even hinted that once they are settled on the island, they can make the short journey to St Malo and see a little of France.

The barking dogs draw Bess to the window, where she sees Henry Brooke, Baron Cobham, arrive. He looks older, with a hint of grey in his beard, which he has allowed to grow longer. She can't help speculating what Robert Cecil meant when he said Henry Brooke's marriage to Lady Frances Howard was one of necessity.

Henry Brooke smiles and removes his hat as she welcomes him. 'Forgive me, Lady Raleigh, but I need to speak with your husband about an urgent matter.'

As before, Bess senses an unexpected attraction. Henry Brooke is handsome, but not strikingly so – nor particularly erudite or adventurous – yet there is an unmistakable connection between them. She returns his smile. 'You are in luck, sir. Walter is preparing to leave for Jersey, and is expected to be away for some weeks.'

Henry Brooke unhitches his saddlebags and follows Bess into the house. He grins and raises a hand as Walter appears at the top of the stairs. 'It's good to see you, Walter. We need to talk, but first I shall have to beg for something to eat. I've ridden from Cobham Hall in Kent, and confess I'm famished, and would welcome a drink.'

Martha helps Bess dress for dinner in the new gown of blue-and-silver damask she bought in London. Bess studies herself in her small silver mirror. 'Do you not think this bodice is a little too low-cut at the front, Martha?'

'It is the new fashion, my lady, and your blue sapphire pendant would match well.'

'The one looted from Cadiz by my husband? I was thinking of wearing my mother's pearls, but you are right –

although I pray such a fine jewel doesn't draw unwanted attention.'

Martha smiles as she fastens the delicate Belgian lace collar and cuffs. 'There are few enough opportunities to wear your jewels, my lady.' Bess is glad of her company and pleased Martha is engaged to be married to their head groom, a local man of her own age, which means she should be happy to remain at Sherborne.

Walter surprises Bess with a kiss when he sees her in her new gown, and whispers in her ear. 'Of all my discoveries, it's you I treasure the most.'

She blushes at this encouraging sign, and returns his kiss. 'Thank you.' He has been quite distant since returning from London, spending far too much time alone in his study. She still lives in hope of another child, but he either falls asleep too soon or complains of the wound in his leg.

They take their places at the dining table, lit by tall candles in their best silver candlesticks brought from Durham House with Walter's elaborate silver salt. Polished and shining in the candlelight, the salt is crowned with a three-masted sailing ship on a stormy sea, complete with silver wire rigging. Bess suspects it is another treasure looted from the Spanish.

She sees Henry Brooke noting the sapphire at her neck as the first course is served – roasted wild duck in a rich barberry sauce, spiced with mace. Their maidservant pours them each a glass of sweet Rhenish wine, and Henry Brooke proposes a toast.

'To the queen, long may she live.'

Bess hears the note of irony in his voice as she raises her glass, and can contain herself no longer. 'I confess you have aroused my curiosity, baron. Can you tell me what brings you all the way to Dorset?'

Henry Brooke glances at Walter and takes a drink of his glass of claret before replying. 'I'm afraid the factions at court are engaging in much whispering in corridors. You must recall how it is, Lady Raleigh?'

She smiles. 'Please, call me Bess. I presume this is to do with the health of the queen?'

'I shall call you Bess if you will call me Henry.' He smiles as he sits back in his chair. 'It's said the queen believes in her astronomer's horoscope predicting she will die in her bed, and now I hear she refuses to sleep, for fear of dying.'

Bess raises an eyebrow. 'I would not have thought she could keep that up for long?'

'I think it can only last a few days, but I heard Her Majesty has not taken to her bed since.'

'What does she do?' Bess remembers how superstitious the queen could be about people spilling salt, and was once greatly upset by a cracked mirror. She always took too much note of the predictions of astrologers, but nothing so extreme as this.

'I've not seen for myself, of course, but the rumours are that she remains awake until a late hour, and reclines on cushions instead of taking to her bed.' Henry Brooke's voice carries a note of scorn.

Bess glances at the door and keeps her voice low, recalling Arthur's warning about her servants. 'It's the question of the succession which will have the greatest consequences for us all.'

He sips his wine and nods. 'The Lord Keeper, Sir Thomas Egerton, and our friend Secretary Robert Cecil, begged the queen to name her heir. They say as she has no children or any close legitimate relatives to satisfy the role, she named King James of Scotland as her successor.'

Walter scowls. 'Until now that's been no more than speculation. Do you know if the queen *named* the Scottish king as her successor?' His tone suggests he thinks it unlikely. 'Or is that what our friend Robert Cecil would have us all believe? Could it be that he courts the favour of King James?'

Henry Brooke's reply is interrupted by the door opening as

BESS

their maidservant enters with more wine, and bread still warm from the ovens. She refills each of their glasses and, at a sign from Bess, leaves and closes the door behind her.

He keeps his voice low. 'Her Majesty never allowed Parliament to debate the succession and refuses to discuss the matter.' He glances at Walter. 'There is a growing faction who favour an alternative.'

Bess sees their guest in a new light. Henry Brooke's insight into the politics of court seems more astute than Walter's blunt, self-obsessed understanding. Intrigued, she leans forwards in her chair, and asks him in a soft voice. 'Who?'

'The Scottish king's first cousin. Lady Arbella Stuart.'

Bess frowns. 'I recall her as a junior lady-in-waiting, sent away from court after attracting the advances of the Earl of Essex. She seemed a rather dour young lady, lacking in good judgement.'

Henry Brooke smiles. 'Now she is a dour young woman, with a legitimate claim to the thrones of Scotland and England.'

Walter looks thoughtful as he sips his wine. 'Does Lady Arbella Stuart *wish* to be queen? I understand she does not.'

'That's the point of my visit.' Henry gives Walter a meaningful look. 'If anyone were to persuade Lady Arbella to take the throne, she would be sure to remember their loyalty. The rewards could be more than any of us could dream of.'

The servants knock at the door and wait until Walter calls for them to clear the dishes and bring the main course. They bring a shoulder of venison, basted with sweet rosemary butter, as well as a bowl of frumenty – crushed barley cooked in a broth, thickened with egg yolks and flavoured with precious cinnamon.

Walter waits until the servants leave and turns to Henry. 'I'm less concerned about the risk of King James encouraging Catholics than I am his views on reconciliation with

Spain.' He attacks the venison with his knife, carving generous slices.

Bess tries the venison. The gravy has an unexpected sharpness, and she makes a mental note to tell her cook to add less verjuice, made with crab apples from her orchard. 'It is some years since I knew her, but Lady Arbella Stuart seems a poor choice as successor to the queen. There must be other candidates?'

Henry looks across the table at her. 'At least a dozen, but Arbella Stuart is a granddaughter of Margaret Tudor. Other than King James, the only other serious heir is Edward Seymour, Lord Beauchamp. He is descended from Mary Tudor, but his legitimacy is questionable.'

Walter sits up in his chair. 'Have you come here to seek my support in making Lady Arbella Stuart the queen's successor?'

Henry sits in silence for a moment, as if making a judgement. 'It could mean risking everything, making an enemy of Robert Cecil and, of course, King James of Scotland, but the rewards could be immense.' He turns to Bess. 'You could become the new queen's chief gentlewoman, and oversee her choice of ladies-in-waiting.'

Walter grins. 'I could replace Robert Cecil as her secretary, and create a new Privy Council, with men like you, Henry, to advise her.'

Bess thinks they have both drunk too much wine. 'Take care how you speak.' She frowns. 'I know my brother Arthur would say having such thoughts could be called treason.'

Bess lies awake listening to the noises of the house. Much of the work at Sherborne is complete, with the house furnished to her satisfaction. Her stud farm is turning a good profit, and the gardens have never been more productive.

Walter talks of retiring as Captain of the Guard, and relinquishing the thankless task of managing the Cornish Stannaries. Her future seemed settled, but now Henry Brooke's words trouble her.

He may be prepared to risk everything, make an enemy of Robert Cecil and King James of Scotland, but she is not. As she settles into a restless sleep, Bess resolves to tell Walter she accepts his idea of staying out of the way in Jersey for a few years, for the sake of their son.

14

SHERBORNE 1603

ARTHUR'S SHORT LETTER, DELIVERED BY A FAST RIDER, LEAVES Bess numb, with a sense that life will never be the same again. She's always known this day would come, but now it has she cannot believe it is the truth as she reads her brother's words. *The queen is dead.*

Arthur writes that she died at Richmond Palace before dawn on the twenty-fourth of March, after naming King James as her successor. Bess stares at the postscript after his familiar signature: *Long live the king.* Is Arthur positioning himself to be in favour with King James? She knows her brother well enough to be sure it is a precaution, in case his letter falls into the wrong hands.

Bess has never known a time when Elizabeth was not her queen. The news of her death is a turning point, for the country and for her family. The old order will be replaced with new men, with new ideas, and King James of Scotland is the new King of England. She passes the letter to Walter, and remains silent until he's read it.

'He says the queen lost the power of speech in her latter

days. If that is true, I find it had to understand how she can have named King James as her successor?'

Walter stares at her, the letter in his hand, his eyes narrowed with frustration. 'This is a plot by Robert Cecil and his scheming supporters on the Privy Council. I question why our queen would hand the country to the Scots!'

'It makes no matter, Walter. If King James of Scotland has been declared King of England, there is nothing you, or anyone else, can do to change it – but what does it mean for us?'

'It means the end of England as we know it, Bess. The new king will appoint his Scottish favourites.' He curses under his breath. 'Robert Cecil planned this long ago. For much of the past year he's spoken out against me, and I fear he's secured the new king's favour at my expense. We must return to London for the state funeral, and will find out soon enough.'

Bess is glad of her furs as she makes the long journey on wintry roads with Walter to pay their last respects. The queen's heavy lead coffin has been carried at night, on a torchlit barge along the Thames from Richmond Palace, to lie in state at Whitehall until the day of her funeral at Westminster Abbey.

Whitehall Palace, once so familiar, almost like home in her younger days, is full of ghosts, cold and echoing, and the air feels damp as they wait in line for their turn. Bess remembers happier times, when she was the queen's gentlewoman, and the thrill of risking her first illicit liaisons with Walter.

She glances at him and is reminded that her handsome lover is now a hunched, grey-bearded man, limping with the aid of his silver-handled cane. She still loves him, and he needs her more than ever, but she struggles to imagine him as the athletic poet who once turned the head of every maid of honour at court.

The queue trails down the palace corridors. Commoners and nobles, old and young, rich and poor, united in their grief, some with tear-stained faces, others openly weeping. Bess recognises some old familiar faces from her time at court, but most of those queueing are strangers, no doubt curious to see this once-in-a-lifetime spectacle.

When their turn comes, Bess is overwhelmed with sadness at the tragic effigy of the queen, dressed in her Parliament robes, lying on her coffin. Life-sized, but not lifelike, the dark eyes of the painted face stare unseeing at the ceiling, like the wooden doll Bess owned as a child.

With a sceptre in her hand and a golden crown on her head, the effigy is supposed to be the symbol of her monarchy, yet the faded, reddish wig mocks her memory. Money was no object, and the makers would have had plenty of time, yet the face of the queen's effigy looks rushed, a poor memorial.

Walter stands in silence before the velvet-draped coffin, and Bess knows he is struggling to remain composed. She bows her head and says a prayer for the soul of the woman who'd made her life so miserable, and is finally at peace.

Walter stands at the window of his turret study in Durham House, staring out at the misty River Thames. 'I've been summoned by the Privy Council to sign their address of welcome to the new king.' He scowls. 'It seems disloyal to the queen, while she still lies in state.'

Bess takes his hand in hers. 'Can you plead illness, or tell them you have resigned your post?'

'I'm afraid they leave me no choice. This could be the Privy

Council's test of my loyalty to the new king. If I refuse there could be consequences.'

'I don't agree. The matter is a formality, of little consequence.' She looks into his eyes. 'The new king will appoint his own man as Captain of the Guard.'

'You are right, Bess. I will have no place at his court and I'm not sorry. I've heard he smells to high heaven, and never takes a wash.'

Bess frowns. 'Take care with such talk, Walter. Robert Cecil could have informers in our household.' She keeps her voice low and glances at the door. 'You will not help us by making an enemy of the new king.'

'I understand he will wish to replace *me*, but I shall question the king if he tries to replace my trusted guards with Scotsmen.'

'Please, do not *think* of questioning the king. You must think about how easily he could ruin you. If you care so little for your own future, or mine, think of Wat.' Bess hears the pleading in her voice. 'The new king could take Durham House, or even Sherborne from us, if you give him cause to do so.'

'I own the freehold to Sherborne, and my lawyers have put the estate in trust for Wat.'

Bess stares at him in silence as she thinks about the future. This is the first time he's told her their house is in trust, and she feels a stab of concern about what that means for her, if anything were to happen to Walter.

'We could move our family to Jersey until things settle down, which they surely will. You've talked of retiring there to grow tobacco, and I would like to see the island. The warmer weather will be good for Wat, and we would see much more of you.' She smiles. 'You could teach him to sail. He would like that.'

He surprises her with a kiss. 'You're right, Bess. I'm tired of arguments over the Stannaries and the petty intrigues of court and Parliament. My cousin, Sir George Carew, has a buyer for my Irish estates, together with my ship, the *Pilgrim*. I hope for one thousand five hundred pounds.'

'You should ask for double that, Walter. We will have little enough income once you resign your official posts.'

'There is no guarantee I will ever see the money, but I don't have the heart to start over again. My settlers in Ireland are scattered to the four winds, and my fine house in Youghal is signed over to my cousin, George Carew.'

'You should have kept your house in Ireland, Walter. I'd hoped we could spend time there one day.'

'My time in Ireland is over, Bess. After the queen's funeral I planned to ask Robert Cecil to support my continued governorship of Jersey, in return for surrendering my other titles, but I've discovered he's hosting a reception for the new king at Burghley House, and I've not even been invited.'

'King James must have so many to meet.' She embraces him, and knows she must find a way to calm him. 'Everyone must be seeking his favour. You need to be patient, Walter. Your turn will come soon enough.'

'You don't understand, Bess.' He looks at her as if she's a serving maid, who must have everything explained. 'I'm being shunned by Robert Cecil for no good reason.' He curses under his breath. 'I want to see the king myself, to know if the stories I've heard are true.'

Bess shakes her head. 'You can't invite yourself to meet the king. Robert Cecil might not take kindly to it.'

'I have important Stannary papers which require the royal seal. They've waited long enough, and offer me a good reason to see the new king.'

'Will you promise me you won't do anything to provoke Robert Cecil?' She holds him close, as if he might slip away like a thief in the night. In her heart, she knows he cannot wait for an opportunity to challenge Robert Cecil, but that duel can only have one outcome.

He squeezes the breath from her with both arms. 'You have my word, Bess.'

'And will you promise not to question the king?'

He hesitates for a moment too long, but agrees. 'I shall be a model subject. Our future depends on it.'

Walter returns from the reception at Burghley House in a dour mood. Bess can see it hasn't gone well, but keeps her silence until he is ready to tell her. She wishes she'd somehow found a way to stop him going. Whatever happened cannot be undone, but she is sure there must be consequences.

He slumps into his favourite chair and fills his pipe with tobacco, lighting it with a taper from the fire. He takes a puff before looking up at Bess. 'Robert Cecil looked as if he would have me thrown out. I told him I'd brought papers which must have royal assent, but he said to leave them with his clerk.' His voice is scathing.

Bess imagines them, like two old stags in the deer park, ready to clash antlers, neither wishing to be first to show any sign of weakness. 'What did you do?'

'I will not be treated like a servant by Robert Cecil. I decided to find the king and introduce myself.' He takes another puff on his pipe, blowing out a little cloud of grey smoke. 'The stories are true, Bess. The king is an unimpressive, scrawny man, in soiled silks.' He frowns. 'I bowed and told him who I was, and he mocked me, making some foolish joke about my name in front of everyone.'

'The queen often joked about your name. She called you *Water*, and Robert Cecil her *imp*, and her *little pygmy*.' Walter's pride has always been his weakness, and she knows it has caused him trouble more times than she can remember. 'I hope you remembered your promise to me?'

'I left before I said something I would regret, but now I see the game Robert Cecil plays. He feathers his own nest, to the great cost of his friends. If I had any doubts about retiring to Jersey, they vanished at the sight of King James. I fear for what the country will become under his rule, and can have no part in any of it.'

Bess waits with Wat and young William Cecil to see the funeral procession make its way from the palace to Westminster Abbey. She has never seen such crowds keep so silent. They stand on both sides of the roads, at every window and vantage point, a sea of black, bowing their heads as the procession passes them.

In keeping with tradition, over two hundred poor women are paid to lead the way, four in a rank, dressed in black, with linen headscarves. The junior officers of the royal household follow, carrying the royal standards of the red dragon, the greyhound and the lion, the supporters of the arms of England.

The queen's grooms lead two great warhorses, caparisoned with black velvet embroidered with the arms of England and France, followed by the gentlemen of the Chapel Royal. The boys of the queen's choir sing mournful hymns as they follow, their young voices echoing in the still April air.

The city aldermen and justices are followed by the gentlemen pensioners, with their poleaxes pointing down, the Lord Mayor of London and the privy councillors. Sir Robert Cecil walks alone, his back bent and his head bowed, as if overcome by his grief. Bess glances at his son William, watching wide-eyed at her side, and cannot help thinking Walter is right. Robert Cecil is no longer to be trusted.

The queen's coffin, draped with rich purple velvet, is

carried on a hearse drawn by four horses caparisoned in black. Six barons march at each side and six knights support her canopy of state, led by the Master of the Horse with the queen's favourite palfrey.

The chief mourner, Lady Helena, Marchioness of Northampton, leads the countesses and baronesses, their heads covered with black veils. The ladies of the privy chamber, and maids of honour, follow in pairs. Bess is surprised how many she recognises, after so many years.

Walter's place is behind the maids of honour. He carries his cane and limps as he walks alone, his guards following behind, five in a rank, their halberds pointing downwards. Behind him follow Sir Thomas Sackville, Lord Treasurer, and Lord Admiral Sir Charles Howard.

Bess watches the long procession enter the great doors of Westminster Abbey, where the queen's coffin is to be lowered into the vault to join her grandfather, King Henry VII, and his queen, Elizabeth of York. There is talk of building an impressive tomb, but Bess suspects that will not be a priority for the new king.

Now she is gone, people drift away, like lost sheep without a shepherd. Bess clasps her hands together and says a silent prayer for the departed soul of Queen Elizabeth, the Virgin Queen, and last of the Tudor line.

Bonfires blaze by the Thames, lighting up the sky, the tang of woodsmoke drifting through the open windows of Durham House. Walter said there could be riots, but people cheer and call out, 'God save the King!' and, 'Long live King James!' Walter is right. The queen never named James of Scotland as her successor, but men like Robert Cecil would have it no other way.

For the second time in her life, returning to Sherborne is a fresh start for Bess. She is in a happy mood as she helps Martha pack her gowns in her camphor-wood chest. Although there will be little opportunity to wear them in Dorset, she has no wish to return to London.

Martha frowns at the size of the task as she lays a voluminous silk brocade dress on the bed to fold. 'We shall need a wagon to carry all these, my lady.'

Bess agrees. 'I plan to bring as much of Walter's plate and as many valuables as we can, as well as the best furniture, so we'll need more than one wagon.' She decides to confide in Martha. 'I'll not be surprised if the king takes Durham House for one of his Scotsmen.'

Martha stares wide-eyed. 'I thought Sir Walter owned this house.'

Bess shakes her head. 'He's paid a fortune in upkeep, and I don't know how we will afford the new stables. This house was built for the Bishop of Durham, hence the name, but was seized by the late queen's father and granted to her for life, so is owned by the Crown. The new king may do with it as he wishes.'

Martha's answer is interrupted by a commotion below. Alexander Brett, who acts as Walter's secretary, rushes up the stairs and appears in the doorway. 'Please come quickly, my lady.' His face is serious. 'There are men here, and their orders are to arrest Sir Walter.'

'To arrest him?' Bess struggles to understand. 'For what?'

Alexander Brett shrugs. 'They are taking him now.'

Bess turns to Martha. 'It seems we need to pack with more haste. Find Wat, if you can, and have him ready to travel at short notice.' She follows Alexander Brett to the great hall, where yeomen of the Tower surround Walter, as if they expect him to escape.

He sees Bess and reaches out a hand. 'I must go with these men to the Tower, Bess.' He frowns. 'Henry Brooke has been arrested, with his brother, Sir George Brooke, and has implicated me in a plot against the king.' He gives her a cautionary look, but she knows better than to speak of Lady Arbella Stuart.

'What should I do?' She is reluctant to release his hand.

'They told me Wat will be taken into the care of Robert Cecil, as Master of Wards. Be as helpful as you can, for Wat's sake.' He glances at the waiting men, and speaks so only she can hear. 'Take care, Bess. I love you.'

Bess is restless and cannot sleep, knowing Walter is back in the Tower. She writes a letter to her brother, explaining her situation, then another to Robert Cecil, asking for help. She misses Wat, as only a mother can, and can't forget the look of confusion in his eyes as he left with William Cecil. He will be safe, but is old enough to know their future hangs in the balance.

There is no reply from Robert Cecil, but her brother has learned some of the queen's former ladies-in-waiting are chosen by the Privy Council to escort Queen Anna to London. They are riding north to meet her, and include Baroness Penelope Rich, and Henry Brooke's wife, Countess Frances. Bess suspects the countess hopes to plead for mercy on her husband's behalf.

She reads Arthur's letter a second time, and sees his implied suggestion. The idea is audacious, but her best hope. She may be a commoner, not a baroness or countess, but was the queen's gentlewoman, and is prepared to serve as one again, for the sake of her family.

15

BERWICK 1603

BESS MAKES THE LONG TREK NORTH WITH MARTHA. THE journey is the length of the country, and she is glad to be escorted by Alexander Brett, who knows the roads and arranges the many stops and fresh horses. They travel fast and light, hoping to reach the remote town of Berwick in time to meet the new queen.

This is the furthest north she has ridden, and there is only a slender chance the queen will agree to see her, but there is only one way to find out. She'd been surprised to learn that one of those chosen by Robert Cecil to welcome the queen is Lady Penelope Rich, and another is Baron Cobham's wife, Baroness Frances.

Bess plans to find Lady Penelope and try to secure her support. She has not forgotten Walter's hatred of Penelope's brother, the ill-fated Earl of Essex, but Penelope always shows her kindness. As a last resort she will appeal to Baroness Frances, who she doesn't know, but who shares her predicament, as her husband is the cause of Walter's imprisonment.

She recalls the time Henry Brooke spoke at dinner of his support for Lady Arbella Stuart, and the memory troubles her as she rides. She can't believe Henry would put the blame on Walter, and prays he hasn't confessed she was also present when such matters were discussed.

Although she's heard of men being racked in the Tower dungeons until their limbs are so torn they would confess to anything, there would be no need for his questioners to use torture; Henry Brooke never struck her as a man of courage, and the threat of a traitor's death would be enough.

She turns to Alexander Brett as she pushes the image from her mind and tries to focus on the task ahead. 'Our new queen is from Denmark. I hope she speaks English.'

Alexander Brett nods. 'I heard Queen Anna is like the late queen, fluent in French and Italian, as well as Latin, but they say she talks like a Scot.'

'She's spent half her life surrounded by Scots.' Bess steadies her horse as it stumbles on a loose stone in the worsening road. 'I pray she will need women she can trust, to explain our strange English customs.'

'They say the queen is with child, my lady. Do you think we shall have to wait in Berwick until it is born?'

'I would not be surprised. King James appears to be in no hurry to be crowned.'

'Not since three of his servants died of the plague in one day at Hampton Court.'

Bess turns in the saddle and stares at him in alarm. 'The plague is back in the city?' An old fear returns, and she says a silent prayer of thanks that Wat is on his way to Burghley House with William Cecil, over a hundred miles north of London.

The dark towers of Berwick Castle brood over the garrisoned border town like an ancient sentinel, and armed soldiers guard the iron-studded gates. Alexander Brett secured them lodgings in an old boarding house, where rushes crackle under their feet.

Although exhausted from days of hard riding, the creaking beds and slamming doors keep Bess awake until late, as does her worry about Walter. His life could depend on her meeting with the queen, and if she is anything like her husband, it could not go well.

In the morning, she heads out in search of Lady Penelope Rich, the closest she has to a friend in this remote place. Penelope looks as elegant as ever, with a shimmering gown of peach silk, but is surprised to see her.

'I'm sorry to say you've had a wasted journey, Bess. We are forbidden to continue into Scotland, and the queen is unwell, so cannot see any of us.' Penelope sounds dismissive, and no doubt sees the arrival of Bess as more competition for the limited places at court.

'Is her illness serious?' Bess sees her chances of pleading for Walter sink like a stone dropped into a well.

Penelope frowns. 'I am afraid she lost her child.'

'I also lost a child, and know you have. I can never forget that time.' Bess frowns. 'I'm surprised she's well enough to travel, but I expect she has little choice.'

'I have more bad news for you, Bess. The queen's Scottish ladies-in-waiting are accompanying her, and she says she has no need of more ladies at court.'

'You must know I was not chosen by Robert Cecil.'

'Then you are here to petition for your husband?'

'You've heard?'

'I know several people were arrested for plotting against the king, including Sir Walter.'

Bess fights off the wave of despair. 'I don't know what to do. An appeal to the new queen was my best hope.'

Penelope shakes her head. 'Even if you could see her, I

doubt she would change the mind of the king. Your best hope is to appeal to Robert Cecil.'

'He's turned against Walter—'

'But not against *you*, Bess.' Penelope gives her a meaningful look. 'He's always had a fondness for you.'

'I've cared for his son William, but Robert Cecil has never said anything improper.'

Penelope smiles. 'It's not what they say, Bess, and I'll bet you cannot say you've never encouraged him?'

Bess feels her face redden at Penelope's accusation but, if she is right, she must persuade Robert Cecil to help. She faces a long ride home, but what Penelope says makes sense. The king will not be persuaded to show Walter leniency by his wife, but he might listen to his new advisor, Robert Cecil, and time is running out.

Bess stares at the official notice of eviction, and turns to Martha. 'It's not unexpected, but we have two weeks to leave Durham House.'

'Will we return to Sherborne, my lady?'

'I would like to – but, for now, there is work to do here in London. We must send as much of the furniture and valuables to Sherborne as we can, but I need you with me at Mile End, which I pray is safe from the plague.'

The work of packing and sorting keeps her mind off her worry about Walter. The hardest task is to clear Walter's study in his tower overlooking the River Thames. She finds the smell of tobacco evocative, and discovers a collection of old poems in his desk. She hopes they are to her, but sees he dedicates them to *Gloriana*, his lost queen, who cannot save him now.

A metallic glint shining in the dark recess of the desk drawer catches her eye: a silver key. She sees his wooden sca chest, marked with the initials *WR*, is secured with a silver lock. The key turns, and she opens the lid. Under some clothes and nautical maps is a fortune in looted Spanish gold and silver, precious jewels and pearls. Bess forms a plan to secure the support of Robert Cecil, and sends a groom to fetch Adrian Gilbert from Dorset.

Arthur and his family remain far away in Northampton, no doubt because of the plague, but Bess is glad to have Mile End to herself, and is soon writing to Robert Cecil, despite his failure to reply to her previous letters. She remembers Baroness Penelope's words. He is her best hope, if he can be persuaded to help.

She stays up late into the night, but struggles to find the words that can begin to convey her feelings to Robert Cecil. She sobs with frustration as she rips up her draft letter, throwing it in the fire. Taking a fresh quill, she sharpens it with her knife and starts again:

If the grieved tears of an unfortunate woman may receive anny favor, or the unspekable sorrows of my dead hart may receive any comfort, then let my sorrows come before you, which if you truly knew, I asure myself you would pity me but most especialy your poor unfortunate frend which relieth wholy on your honorable and wonted favour.

Bess reads her words aloud, pleased with her improved spelling, but has nagging doubts this letter alone will be enough to change Robert Cecil's mind. She dips her quill in the pot of black, ox-gall ink, and adds another paragraph before she signs her letter.

. . .

For Christ's sake, which rewardeth all mercys, pity his just cause and God for his infinite mercy bless you for ever, and work in the king's mercy. I am not able, I protest before God, to stand on my own trembling legs otherwise I wuld have waited now on you, or be directed wholy by you.

She that will truly honour you in all misfortune,

E. Raleigh

It will take a special gift to change Robert Cecil's mind, and her plan could be her last chance. If it fails, at least she's done all she can. She has no choice but to place her trust in Adrian Gilbert. When he arrives, she takes a canvas bag, filled with gold and jewels from Walter's sea chest, and pulls it open for him to see.

He stares wide-eyed at the fortune collected by Walter over a lifetime of looting Spanish treasure ships. 'A king's ransom?'

'These jewels could save Walter's life, but only if they can be turned into the money I need – and soon, as we have no time to lose.' Bess hands him the bag. 'Will you take these to the goldsmith, Cheyney in Lombard Street, and see how much you can raise for me?'

He stares at the heavy bag in his hand and then back at her. 'I understand, my lady, and will start straight away.'

'You must be discreet, Master Gilbert. No one must know the source, or we could lose everything.'

A yeoman from the Tower, loyal to Walter, delivers a letter from him, and she takes the opportunity to ask how he is coping. The yeoman looks at his shoes. 'I regret to tell you, my lady, Sir Walter is at a low ebb.'

Bess is unsurprised, but suspects the yeoman is holding back. 'Is he being well treated?'

'He is, my lady, but…'

'Speak freely, sir. I need to know, and this is not the time to spare my feelings. Is my husband unwell?'

The yeoman is silent, as if making a judgement, then looks up at her. 'He took a knife he was given to cut his food. Sir Walter tried to stab himself in the heart, and shouted that he wished to end his life.'

Bess puts her hand to her mouth. 'Dear God.'

'The blade struck his rib, my lady, and the knife was taken from him.' The yeoman looks up at her. 'There was much blood, but Sir Walter was fortunate.'

She asks the cook to provide the yeoman with dinner for his trouble, and retires to her bedchamber to read Walter's letter. He condemns Henry Brooke and Robert Cecil for despoiling his reputation. Bess frowns as he calls her an 'unfortunate woman', and Wat an 'unfortunate child'. He seems to have lost all hope, and gives her permission to remarry after his days, to avoid poverty.

Forget me in all things but thine own honour and the love of min. I bless my poor child, and let him know his father is no traitor. And whosoever you choose after me, let him be but your politic husband, but let my son be thy beloved for he is part of me, and I live in him. And the Lord forever keep thee and give thee comfort in both worlds.

Bess wipes away her tears and resolves to find some way to see Walter, even if their meeting must be brief, and watched over by his guards. She wishes to look him in the eye and tell him to fight for his freedom, as he is innocent of treason. She also wants to tell him she will never remarry, because she loves him.

An unexpected consequence of the plague in London is that Walter's trial for treason is held seventy miles away, in the great hall of Winchester Castle. Bess is not allowed to see him, and sends Alexander Brett to learn what he can. She fears there can only be one outcome of the hearing before Robert Cecil and the king's counsel, the Attorney General, Sir Edward Coke.

Alexander Brett returns within the week, and brings the worst news. 'Sir Walter was charged with conspiring with Baron Cobham and others to place Arbella Stuart on the throne of England and dispossess the king.'

Bess stares at him. 'None of that is true.'

Alexander Brett frowns. 'Worse still, Sir Walter is found guilty, with other persons, of conspiring to murder the king and his children, plotting a rebellion and inciting the king's enemies to invade England.'

Bess struggles to speak. 'This so-called trial is an outrage. Walter is innocent, so they cannot have any evidence of these allegations.'

'I heard Sir Walter gave a good account of himself, my lady, and asked them for any proof. I was told he defended himself in Winchester with dignity and courage, but it seems their lordships' minds were made up.'

'And their sentence?' She stares at him, guessing there can only be one answer to her question. 'Have the noble lords sentenced my husband?'

Alexander Brett takes a deep breath, and looks into her eyes, lowering his voice. 'Sir Walter is sentenced to a traitor's death, my lady.'

'He is to be executed in public, like a common criminal?' Bess digs her nails into her palms. She'd once asked her brother to explain what is meant by a traitor's death, and wishes she hadn't.

'There is a chance his sentence will be commuted to a private execution at the Tower.'

Bess can no longer remain composed, and falls to her knees, sobbing. She cares nothing about her worried servants, watching from a distance, and surrenders to her grief and despair.

Alexander Brett takes her arm and helps her to a chair. 'I am truly sorry, my lady.'

Bess weeps as she reads the letter from Walter, sent from his prison cell in Winchester Castle. She expects this is his last, yet his words reveal his anger, pride and self-importance. There is no humility in his letter, yet he seems defeated by his ordeal.

You shall now receive (my dear wife) my last words in these my last lines. My love I send you, that you may keep it when I am dead, and my counsel that you may remember it when I am no more. I would not by my will present you with sorrows (dear Bess). Let them go to the grave with me and be buried in the dust. And seeing that it is not the will of God that I should see you any more in this life, bear it patiently, and with a heart like thy self.

She wipes a tear from her cheek. The depth of Walter's despair is too great for her. He has lost the will to fight this great injustice, and never expects to see her again. She takes a deep breath before continuing.

. . .

First, I send you all the thanks which my heart can conceive, or my words can express for your many travails, and care taken for me, which, though they have not taken effect as you wished, yet my debt to you is not the less: but pay it I never shall in this world.

Secondly, I beseech you for the love you bear me living, do not hide your self many days, but by your travails seek to help your miserable fortunes and the right of your poor child. Thy mourning cannot avail me, I am but dust.

Thirdly, you shall understand, that my land was conveyed bona fide to my child: the writings were drawn at midsummer twelve months. My honest cousin Brett can testify so much, and I trust that my blood will quench their malice that have thus cruelly murthered me: and that they will not seek also to kill thee and thine with extreme poverty. To what friend to direct thee I know not, for all mine have left me in the true time of trial. And I plainly perceive that my death was determined from the first day.

He knew his was no fair trial, but a chance for his enemies to be rid of him. Bess is surprised to learn he refers to Alexander Brett as *his* cousin, and that he was so involved in putting Sherborne in trust. He does not name Robert Cecil, but Bess understands why he ignores her pleas. He was the instigator of the charges from the first day, and chose the judge and jury. She reads on.

Love God, and begin betimes to repose your self upon him, and therein shall you find true and lasting riches, and endless comfort: for the rest when you have travailed and you shall but sit down by sorrow in the end. Teach your son also to love and fear God while he is yet young, that the fear of God may grow with him, and the same God will be a husband to you, and a father to him; a husband and a father which cannot be taken from you.

. . .

Too late, she sees he wishes he'd been a better father to Wat. Bess sobs at the unfairness of his fate. Robert Cecil didn't need to point out how personally the king takes this threat, and wishes to make an example of those who conspire against him. With an effort, she reads on.

Adrian Gilbert oweth me six hundred pounds, and in Jersey I also have much owing me besides. The arrearages of the wines will pay my debts. For my soul's sake, pay all poor men.

Bess has no idea why his cousin, Adrian Gilbert, owes Walter such a great sum, or why Walter waits until now to mention it. She's placed Adrian Gilbert in a position of trust, and prays she made the right judgement in trusting him with Walter's jewels. She's also surprised to find Walter has invested in his plans for Jersey, and doubts she will ever see the island, or any profit.

When I am gone, no doubt you shall be sought for by many, for the world thinks that I was very rich. But take heed of the pretences of men, and their affections, for they last not, but in honest and worthy men, and no greater misery can befall you in this life, than to become a prey, and after-wards to be despised. I speak not this (God knows) to dissuade you from marriage, for it will be best for you, both in respect of the world and of God.

As for me, I am no more yours, nor you mine. Death hath cut us asunder and God hath divided me from the world, and you from me. Remember your poor child for his father's sake, who chose you, and loved you in his happiest times.

Get those letters (if it be possible) which I writ to the Lords, wherein I sued for my life. God is my witness, it was for you and yours that I desired life. But it is true that I disdained my self for begging of it. For know it (my dear wife) that your son is the son of a true man.

I cannot write much. God he knows how hardly I steal this time while others sleep, and it is also time that I should separate my thoughts from the world. Beg my dead body which living was denied thee; and either lay it at Sherburne (and if the land continue) or in Exeter Church, by my father and mother. I can say no more, time and death call me away.

The everlasting God, powerful, infinite, and omnipotent God, who is goodness itself, the true life and true light keep thee and thine. Have mercy on me, and teach me to forgive my persecutors and false accusers, and send us to meet in his glorious kingdom.

My dear wife farewell. Bless my poor boy. Pray for me, and let my good God hold you both in his arms. Written with the dying hand of sometimes thy husband, but now alas overthrown.

Yours that was, but now not my own.

WR

16

THE TOWER 1604

Bᴇss ᴡɪsʜᴇᴅ ᴛᴏ ᴍᴀᴋᴇ ᴛʜɪs ᴠɪsɪᴛ ᴀʟᴏɴᴇ, ʙᴜᴛ ᴛʜᴇɪʀ ᴇsᴄᴏʀᴛ ᴏf yeomen insisted their orders were to bring her son, brought back from Burghley House. She expected life would be different after the passing of the old queen, yet everything has changed beyond her anticipation. Walter was right; nothing is the same since the new king took the throne.

The terrible plague ravages London, with more than five thousand deaths in a week. People no longer talk of how many died, only those who survive. They'd become prisoners at Mile End, scared to leave for fear of the pestilence. Food ran low, and even fetching water was a risk. One of the scullery maids fell ill, and for two days they feared the worst, but it proved a false alarm.

They ride to the Tower of London, through deserted cobbled streets, in a covered carriage, avoiding Whitechapel, where so many have died of plague. Bess understands her son's confusion, as even in her prayers she'd sensed her doubt this day would come.

The coach slows as the familiar high stone walls of the Tower appear through a grey mist from the river. This place holds grim memories for her, which come flooding back. If she had any choice she would never wish to return to this bleak prison, but she is no longer in control of her destiny.

Their escort of liveried yeomen lead them over the stagnant moat and they step from the carriage into a different world. A gruff yeoman with a halberd leads them down a narrow path and unlocks an iron-studded wooden door. The hinge creaks as he pushes the door open and gestures for them to enter.

Walter is a pale ghost of his former self, with tears in his eyes as he stares at them without speaking. Bess had prepared herself for this moment, but now she stares back at her husband, lost for words. He still wears his silk doublet and hose, but the haunted look on his face reveals a beaten man.

He nods to the yeoman, who leaves after locking them in. Bess finds the cell more spacious than she expected, with leaded windows and clean rushes on the stone floor. Thick candles flicker on a trestle table, where an earthenware jug stands next to three pewter cups.

Walter finally speaks. 'I thank God you've come. I've missed you, Bess.' He stares at Wat. 'You've grown, and remind me of myself at your age.' His voice rasps a little, as if he's been ill, but still has the warmth of his Devon accent.

Bess takes his hand. 'I prayed for you, Walter, every day. I prayed they would show you mercy.'

He gestures for them to sit on rickety chairs, and pours them a cup of his weak ale, as if it is his best wine. 'I made my peace with God.' He takes a sip of ale. 'I even forgave Robert Cecil, and this is my reward.'

'Tell me what happened, Walter.' She glances at Wat's pale face. 'We were prepared for the worst. There was little enough news, not even rumours, due to the plague, and when the message about you came—' Her voice falters. 'I could not believe what the messenger told us.'

'Our friend Henry Brooke was to meet his end three days before me. I watched from my window as the carpenters built the gallows in Winchester Castle yard in the heaviest rain I've seen.' He looks across at her, the flickering candlelight reflecting in his dark eyes. 'The messenger with the king's reprieve came at the last minute, a cruel trick to play with a man's life.'

Bess shakes her head. 'They took Henry Brooke to the gallows?'

'At the time I thought he deserved his fate, but he is Robert Cecil's brother-in-law, so I thought he was spared for that reason. I've since come to understand Henry Brooke is as much a victim of circumstance as I am.' He takes another sip of ale. 'I was spared the same indignity, but am not pardoned. I am attainted, and imprisoned here at the king's pleasure.'

Bess wishes she'd been able to leave Wat at Mile End, as she cannot speak freely, but thinks it best she keeps her secret from Walter. His cousin, Adrian Gilbert, helped her raise a fortune from the sale of Walter's gold and jewels, as well as the plate and valuables from Durham House.

She might never know if her generous gift to Robert Cecil saved Walter's life, and possibly Henry Brooke's too. He had good reason not to reply to any of her letters, or offer any clue to his intentions. She had feared she'd not only lost her husband, but squandered his fortune – yet now it doesn't matter.

There is also the cryptic letter from Baroness Penelope Rich, now one of the queen's ladies-in-waiting. She says she begged Queen Anna's forgiveness. Bess sees the letter *W* in the margin, which most would miss, and understands. Her long ride to Berwick might not have been for nothing after all, and Penelope has her gratitude.

She sees Walter is waiting for her reply. 'Does the Act of

Attainder mean we have nothing?' She glances again at her son, who listens to every word.

'I hope Sherborne is protected, by my having put it in trust.' He glances at Wat. 'Our new king can do whatever he chooses, and it will not surprise me if he offers our home to one of his followers from Scotland.'

Bess hears no hint of bitterness in Walter's voice, as if he's given up hope. She kept the best of his jewels, sewn into the hem of one of her gowns for emergencies, and prays they do not have to surrender Sherborne, for Wat's sake as much as her own.

She looks around the bare walls, and at his feet, still in the shoes with silver buckles he wore when he was arrested. 'What do you need, when we next visit?'

'They let me have writing materials, which helps to pass the time. I've written several times to the king but had no reply. I think they've been warned I might try to cause dissent.' He manages a weak smile. 'It would be difficult indeed to further condemn myself.'

Bess sees the single volume on his shelf, which from the gilt cross on the spine looks like a Bible. 'We kept your books from Durham House, as well as all your papers. Would they allow me to bring them to you?'

Walter shrugs. 'They make up the rules on a whim, but I've always followed the principle that it's easier to seek forgiveness than ask permission. I will be glad to see my books, and more tobacco, if you can find any.'

Wat has remained silent, but reaches in his pocket and produces Walter's favourite pipe, handing it to him. 'I rescued this from Durham House, Father.'

Walter holds his pipe and stares at his son. 'That was most thoughtful of you, Wat. I shall think of you whenever I use it.'

Bess sees another side of her son, who'd kept his gift for Walter a secret, even from her. He is growing up fast, and she feels a frisson of pride. She could have expected him to be more troubled by recent events, yet this is another example of how he is thinking about the future.

Walter gestures towards the steps leading to the upper floor. 'Would you like to see my new home?'

Wat follows him up the narrow steps and Bess listens to them talking. Walter sounds brighter as he shows Wat the stone balcony where he takes his exercise, and Wat's replies sound confident. It seems Walter intends to be a better father – and it is not too late, after all.

The idea comes to Bess as she lies awake at Mile End, running through every detail of her visit to Walter. One thing he said repeats in her mind, like the notes of a songbird. 'They make up the rules on a whim.' If so, she could put that to the test in a way no one would expect.

She cannot face regular journeys from Sherborne to the Tower, a four-day ride at best, and over a week in winter. Walter needs nursing back to his old self, and who better to do that than her? She dismisses the idea as impractical, but recalls stories of prisoners being allowed to have their wives and servants stay, and some even being allowed visits from their mistresses.

Bess knows people will think her insane, to surrender her freedom for her husband's sake, but she no longer cares. She will be free to come and go as she pleases, as she will wish to see Wat. There will be business at Sherborne to attend to, but Adrian Gilbert has proved his worth and can take care of her stud farm.

More reasons not to stay in the Tower keep her awake, but Bess dismisses them, one by one. Even the yeomen of the Tower must know the dice were not fairly thrown, with men's lives at stake. She won't miss Durham House, but can't return to Sherborne, overstay her welcome at Mile End, or afford the cost of renting. Countess Frances has a house in Seething Lane, in the shadow of the Tower, but they have not spoken for some time.

By dawn her mind is made up. She will join Walter and do what she can to make his prison seem more of a home, and less of a punishment. She begins by sending one of her grooms to buy tobacco, and spends the morning choosing the books she thinks he will like, and helping Martha pack some of Walter's clothes, brought from Durham House, including linen undershirts, new stockings, and his best shoes.

Martha knows her better than most, and seems to understand. 'Even if they send you back, my lady, you will know you tried your best.'

'You are right, Martha. I will lose nothing, as I have nothing to lose. My only worry is that they'll forbid me to stay as further punishment to Walter – or stop me from visiting.' Bess looks up at Martha. 'When are you going to marry your handsome groom?'

Martha smiles. 'When I return to Sherborne, and we have enough money saved, my lady.'

'You've been loyal to me through everything, and it is time you had your reward.' She takes the string of pearls from around her neck and hands them to Martha. 'I've no idea how much these are worth, but you are to sell them, and put the money to good use.'

'I could not take them, my lady.'

'I have my mother's pearls. We may have to surrender Sherborne, but these can be payment in advance for your new role as the housekeeper.'

'You *have* a housekeeper at Sherborne, my lady: Mistress Hull.'

'Mistress Hull will have a fair pension, and can retire once the running of Sherborne is handed over to you.'

Bess dismisses her nerves as she is granted a meeting with Sir John Peyton, Lieutenant of the Tower. She wears her best gown, a flattering fit in the latest London fashion, and sees his eyes stray to the ruby pendant at her neck.

'Thank you for your kindness towards my poor husband, Sir John.'

He sits back in his chair. 'It's nothing I would not do for anyone of his rank, Lady Raleigh. The Garden Tower was available, and he only has two servants, one for cooking and one for cleaning.'

His face suggests he knows she comes to ask some favour, but she's sure she will surprise him. His job was a strange reward for loyal service to the late queen, and she imagines he can find it difficult at times like these.

'I am concerned about my husband's state of mind, Sir John.'

Sir John Peyton nods. 'Sir Walter is proving to be one of my more demanding charges. I've had a watch kept over him since the incident with the knife – which I witnessed.'

'May I ask, Sir John, if you will allow me to stay with my husband and nurse him back to good health?'

He raises an eyebrow. 'For how long, Lady Raleigh?'

'Until he is back to his former self, and there is no longer the risk he could try to take his own life.'

He sits in silence for a moment. 'Your request would require the consent of the Privy Council, and they may decide to ask the permission of the king.' His tone implies he wishes to avoid either option.

Bess is prepared for his objections, and hands him a gold

pendant studded with diamonds. 'I have no money, Sir John, but this is valuable and should cover any expenses.'

Sir John Peyton examines the pendant and slips it into his pocket. 'I agree on a trial basis, contingent on Sir Walter's good behaviour.'

Bess breathes a sigh of relief. 'Thank you, Sir John. I will not forget your kindness.' She doubts he knows she has nowhere else to live, or that a wagon waits outside the Tower gates, laden with everything she needs to make their home in the Garden Tower.

Walter brightens when Bess explains her meeting with Sir John Peyton. 'You never cease to amaze me, Bess.' He fills his pipe with her new tobacco. 'Are you sure this is what you wish?'

'Yes.' She embraces him, holding him close and whispering in his ear. 'I've missed you, and thought I'd lost you. God has given us a second chance.'

He lights his pipe and takes a contented puff, watching as Bess opens the wooden box of books and begins filling his bookshelf. 'God had little enough to do with it, but I'm grateful to have you here. We only have this tower at the whim of the king. I was moved to the Fleet prison at Christmas, and feared I'd be forgotten.'

Bess places the last of his books on the shelf and takes his hand. 'Then we shall make the most of each day, and not concern ourselves with what might happen in the future.'

Walter kisses her. 'There is one aspect of the future I wish to be concerned about. We don't have much room, but do you think you can persuade Sir John Peyton to allow Wat to stay from time to time? I've seen so little of him, and wish to be a better father to him.'

She smiles. 'I will do my best, and ask if he can have a tutor visit, as we must be mindful of his education.'

He takes the candle from his desk and leads her up the stairs. The only furniture is an old trestle bed and a covered chamber pot. He places the candle on the sill of the small window, where it flickers and sends long shadows.

'This was once the bedchamber of the Constable of the Tower, so I cannot complain.'

Bess unbuckles her shoes and unfastens the bodice of her gown. Walter helps her with the aiglets securing her sleeves for the first time in many years. She sees the glint in his eye, and feels unexpected shyness as she pulls off the rest of her clothes and lies back on his straw-filled mattress.

Walter kicks off his shoes, and pulls off his doublet and hose, hesitating for a moment before pulling off his linen undershirt. The wound on his chest is healed, but will always serve as a reminder of how low he sank. He's lost the lithe muscles of his younger days, but also his arrogance.

He lies at her side and pulls her close. 'I've failed you, Bess. I cannot provide for you or Wat—'

She puts a finger to his lips to silence him. 'This bedchamber is smaller than the rooms used by maids of honour on a progress, but there is nowhere I would rather be.'

Bess settles into a new routine, and finds comfort in her simpler life. Last time she was imprisoned in the Tower she found it hard to be cut off from the world. Now she can come and go as she pleases, but is glad to forget the changes taking place outside their grey stone walls under a new king.

She chooses her moment to visit Sir John Peyton, who agrees to their son staying overnight. Sir John seems sympathetic, and tells her he has six sons and five daughters of his own. He raises an eyebrow when she asks if Wat can also be visited by his tutor, John Talbot, but doesn't refuse, which Bess takes as permission to do as she wishes.

'I should tell you, Lady Raleigh, I am to be replaced by old Sir George Hervey, who might take a different view. I am made Governor of Jersey. Kindly inform Sir Walter I did not ask for the post, but look forward to the improved climate, and continuing the work he started.'

Bess waits for Walter to be in a mellow mood before surprising him with her news. 'I believe there is to be a little brother or sister for Wat.'

He stares in amazement. 'Are you sure?'

She makes a calculation on her fingers, counting the months. 'January, a winter baby.'

Walter stares at her middle, as if expecting to see a difference. 'This prison is no place for a child to be born. You will have to return to Mile End.'

Bess shakes her head. 'It's safer than most. The plague has returned, and continues to spread in the city. My brother has left for the country, as he fears for his family.'

Walter holds her close. 'I should tell you one of the yeomen told me they have a prisoner here who suffers with the plague, and is likely to die.' The note of melancholy returns to his voice. 'I doubt anywhere in London is safe.'

Bess kisses him. 'Have faith, Walter, and trust in God's mercy. We have waited long enough for another child.' She moves her hand to her middle. 'This child is God's blessing upon us.'

17

THE TOWER 1605

BESS SHIVERS IN THE CHAPEL ROYAL OF ST PETER AD Vincula, on the green within the Tower, not only because they've walked from their Garden Tower through a pristine layer of crisp white snow. Built on the site of an older church, she senses the chapel is haunted by the ghosts of the past.

An ancient wooden crucifix stands on the simple altar, covered with a plain linen cloth and lit by a pair of fresh white candles. She wishes Walter hadn't told her that under the tiled floor lie the remains of the late queen's mother, Anne Boleyn, Robert Devereux, the Earl of Essex, and more unmarked graves than could be counted.

Bess thanks God little Carew was born without trouble, early in the new year as she'd predicted. She never told Walter she prayed their child would be a daughter, to name after her mother. She hopes there is still time for more children, and is grateful they are graced with her strong, healthy son.

Wat moved to lodging rooms nearby on Tower Hill, near the old All Hallows Church. His former room in the Garden Tower is Carew's nursery, shared with his wet nurse. A kindly local woman named Eleanor Swift, she has five children of her own, and acts as a maidservant to Bess.

Eleanor smiles as she holds their new son, swaddled in white linen. Walter would have liked his brother to attend as godfather, and Bess wished her brother Arthur could be here, but everyone stays away for fear of the plague. Their only guest is the new Lieutenant of the Tower, seventy-two-year-old Sir George Hervey, who seems surprised to be invited.

Their stern Protestant minister, Doctor Hawthorne, frowns at Bess, but says nothing about her break with the old traditions by attending the christening. Her new son fills the chapel with his cries as he is plunged into the cold water of the font and named Carew Raleigh, after Walter's elder brother, in the name of the Father, the Son, and the Holy Ghost.

Life within the high stone walls of the Tower reminds Bess of a village where everyone knows each other. She soon learned the names of many of the yeomen warders, and a little of their lives. A surprising number are sympathetic to Walter's case, and a few speak openly of the injustice of his life sentence.

There is plenty to keep Bess occupied. She spends more time with little Carew, a strong and healthy baby, already showing signs of his father's adventurous spirit. His nursemaid, Eleanor, is good company for Bess, and copes well with the cramped conditions in the small bedchamber which serves as a nursery.

Wat's tutor, John Talbot, visits twice a week to help Bess improve her reading and spelling, and teaches her a few words of Latin. She could not imagine reading Walter's books in the past, but that was a different world. Now John encourages her to read a few pages each day.

They have a young servant named Dean, who helps with

cleaning and cooking, and brings them their pottage each morning. Walter calls it *servants' gruel*, and complains it tastes too salty. Bess thinks the pottage is often enriched with leftovers from the meals of the yeomen warders, but she never complains. On Fridays they have fish, and on Sundays hope for some meat.

The Tower waterman, Owen Thomas, a cheerful Welshman, brings watery beer and ale each day. He is forbidden to bring wine, yet is always ready with some gossip for Bess about people within the Tower walls. Walter believes Robert Cecil meets the costs of their food and drink, coal and candles by income from the Sherborne estate, although he cannot be certain.

Alexander Brett, now knighted, brings news of developments at Sherborne, and Thomas Harriot keeps them informed about the world outside the Tower. Walter's poor health also means his physician, Doctor Turner, is a regular visitor, as is their dour Protestant minister, Doctor Hawthorne, who leads them in prayer.

Bess can come and go as she pleases, and finds she enjoys her role as messenger, delivering notes between prisoners, and spending time with those who have few visitors. One of these is Henry Brooke, who is kept in one of the furthest towers. Like Walter, he has lost weight, and looks different with his hair cut short and a closely trimmed beard.

'A precaution against fleas.' He strokes his beard stubble and makes light of it when he sees her looking, but Bess recalls how she was tempted by the itching to cut her own hair short during her imprisonment. Henry Brooke manages a modest smile. 'I am humbled you wish to see me, Bess.' His smile fades and his eyes fill with sadness. 'You know I am the reason Walter is here in the Tower? I've ruined you both, as well as myself.'

Bess glimpses the man she once knew. 'It could have been

much worse. Walter told me how they treated you in Winchester Castle.'

He scowls at the memory. 'I confess I was prepared to meet my maker, but it seems King James has other plans for me.'

She sits on one of his chairs and looks around his cell. Sir John Peyton told her his treatment of Walter was the same as he would provide for any other. Although Henry Brooke is a baron, his room looks more like a prison cell, with rusting iron bars at the windows, and bare flagstones on the floor.

'Walter asked me to say you are forgiven.'

'Thank you, Bess. I thought he bore me a grudge. He once had someone throw an apple through my window, wrapped in a note demanding I write a letter to exonerate him from any plot or treason against the king.'

Bess looks him in the eye. 'I also forgive you, Henry, and bear no grudge.'

Henry Brooke seems close to tears. 'They somehow knew the truth, and tricked me into condemning others with their threats. I should have been stronger.'

'Walter was robust in his defence. He challenged them to show him evidence, but little good it did him.' Bess changes the subject. 'Is your wife allowed to visit?'

Henry looks up at her. 'She is, but fails to do so, or to answer my letters.' He frowns. 'My wife was appointed lady-in-waiting to Queen Anna, and made governess to little Princess Elizabeth, but was sent away in disgrace.' He frowns. 'I suspect she has not forgiven me.'

Bess is sorry to see him brought so low, and wants to help. 'I could take a letter to your wife, if she is still here in London, and wait for her reply.'

'I don't know where she is, but suspect she's gone to Cobham Hall, my house in Kent, and there is something you should know, Bess. When I saw Frances for the last time before my trial she urged me to testify against Walter, to save myself.'

Walter stares out at the barren patch of grass and weeds which gives the Garden Tower its name. 'I've been thinking that ground could be put to better use. Do you think Sir George Hervey could be persuaded to let me try growing tobacco plants?'

Bess smiles, pleased to see him recovering from the melancholy that worried her so much. 'We have nothing to lose by asking Sir George, and the fresh air and exercise will be good for you.'

He brightens. 'I've never seen anyone use the old building at the end of the garden, so will you ask if I can make it into a place for growing seedlings?'

'I see no reason why Sir George will object to your request. The land adjoins our tower, and we would not be asking him for extra expenses. As for the old building, I hope he will be pleased to see it put to good use.'

'It would give me a sense of purpose, Bess. I hoped to grow tobacco on Jersey, but if I can show tobacco can survive our climate, it could become as important for our farmers as the potato.'

Sir George Hervey's approval for them to use the garden and the old building marks a flurry of activity in the Garden Tower. One of the Tower yeomen brings them a spade, an old rake and a dozen terracotta pots, and Wat helps with digging the hard earth.

Bess is happy to see them working together for the first time, laughing as they cut down stinging nettles and pull up thistles. They spend all day clearing the old building, and making a bench for Walter's seedlings from old wooden planks.

Their new garden is a quarter of the size of their little herb garden at Sherborne, yet Walter talks as if it were a grand estate.

'I brought plenty of seeds from Guiana – aloe vera and quinine, which are used as medicines – as well as several different kinds of tobacco. It will be interesting to see which do best in this climate.'

Bess encourages him. 'You could grow lavender, to freshen our bedlinen, and could even try growing some strawberries, as a special treat.'

Walter takes one of his books from the shelf to show her. 'It might surprise you to learn that strawberries are herbs. I read that most herbs can cope with poor soil, and need little watering. If we can grow enough, I could try using strawberries to make some of these potions and medicines more palatable. I've never had time to experiment before.'

Wat has mud on his face and dust on his clothes, but is excited as he tells Bess what he found. 'There are Latin prayers and inscriptions on the walls of the old building, Mother.' He glances at Walter. 'We read the name of Thomas Cranmer, and the date 1555 – fifty years ago.'

Walter searches his shelf and takes down an old leather-bound book. '*Foxe's Book of Martyrs* should tell us more.' He finds the page and looks up at them. 'Cranmer was Archbishop of Canterbury, but became a martyr for the Protestant cause, and was burned at the stake in the reign of Queen Mary.'

Bess frowns at the thought. 'May God rest him. I thought that old building was only used as a hen house, not to keep anyone a prisoner.'

'I can only guess they ran out of room in Queen Mary's reign.' Walter looks back at *Foxe's Book of Martyrs*. 'Archbishop Cranmer was moved to Oxford, with the other Protestant martyrs, where he was imprisoned for over a year waiting for his trial. He cannot have been here for long, but he will not be forgotten.'

~

Bess visits her brother's house at Mile End with Wat to retrieve Walter's seeds from Guiana. The threat of plague which kept them within the Tower walls is now reduced, although Bess is wary of contact with strangers, and has a scented pomander at her belt for protection.

Wat stares from the window as they ride in their covered carriage through the narrow streets. 'There are so many people.'

Bess frowns. 'It surprises me how quickly people forget the threat of the plague, and life returns to normal.'

He turns to her. 'Will *our* lives ever return to normal?'

She thinks for a moment before replying. 'You can resume your studies with William Cecil at any time. I hope you will be accepted at Oxford before too long and, if it pleases God, your father and I will spend few enough years in the Tower.'

He rides in silence for a moment. 'I find it interesting in the Tower, Mother. I want to see if Father's tobacco plants will grow, and Sir George Hervey said a baby lion cub could arrive at any time – the first ever to be born in the Tower menagerie.'

She smiles. 'You are good company for your father, Wat, but you must take care with those lions. Sir George Hervey treats them like his pets, but they are dangerous wild animals.'

Arthur's wife Anne welcomes them when they arrive at Mile End. 'I'm afraid Arthur is at court, and is not expected back until late this evening.'

Bess frowns. 'We must return to Walter before sunset. Please tell Arthur he is always welcome to visit us at the Tower whenever he can. We would like to see him, and the new Lieutenant, Sir George Hervey, is quite understanding about visitors.'

They fill a wooden chest with more of Walter's papers and find the seeds, all labelled in the neat hand of Thomas Harriot. Bess sends one of the maids to the market for more herbs, and she returns with rosemary and lavender, as well as several strawberry plants in pots.

Anne looks concerned as they prepare to leave, and hands Bess a basket of baked bread, still warm from the oven, and a cured ham. 'I worry about you, Bess. You are welcome back any time.'

Bess can tell straight away her eldest son is excited. 'What's happened, Wat?'

'The lioness gave birth to *two* lion cubs.' He grins, reminding Bess of his father in his younger days. 'Sir George has written to inform the king, and says it is the rarest and most royal thing that ever happened to any king of this land.'

Walter looks up from his book. 'It is indeed the rarest thing, but we shall have to see how they do. This is no place to raise lion cubs – or young boys, come to that.' He frowns. 'There have been lions at the Tower since the days of King Henry III, but they've never bred successfully. The first cub died before it could be named.'

Wat is undaunted. 'Sir George has improved conditions in the menagerie, as well as the way the lions are fed.'

Bess smiles at his enthusiasm. 'Has he named them?'

'No, but their parents are named Henry and Anne.'

'You could think of suitable names for the cubs and suggest them.' A thought occurs to her. 'You must be the youngest person in the country to see lion cubs, Wat. I never expected such a thing when we moved here.'

Arthur surprises them with a long overdue visit, and his grim face suggests he brings bad news. 'Forgive me, but I stayed away from London because of the plague – and the king has kept me busy since.'

Bess offers her brother their best chair. 'You are always welcome, Arthur, and we hope you can tell us of these rumours we heard about a plot, a Catholic attempt to kill the king. It is true?'

Arthur sits back in his chair. 'It's the talk of Westminster. The plotters secured the lease to the undercroft beneath the House of Lords, where Robert Cecil's men found thirty-six barrels of gunpowder – enough to blow up the king and his whole Parliament.'

Bess gasps. 'Is the king harmed?'

'No, but I expect this business will harden his views on Catholics. Robert Cecil is to be made Earl of Salisbury, and will no doubt become Lord Treasurer as his reward.'

Walter scowls as he lights his pipe with a spill from the hearth. 'I suspect from your tone you know someone who was involved…'

Arthur nods. 'The man accused of being the ringleader was a relation of ours, Robert Catesby.'

Bess sees Walter's confusion. 'His mother, Anne Throckmorton, was our cousin, on my father's side.' Her voice wavers as she sees the danger to them all.

Arthur scowls. 'It's worse, I'm afraid. Robert Catesby's accomplice is another relation, Francis Tresham, the son of another of our close cousins, Anne's sister, Meriel Throckmorton.'

Walter curses and mutters under his breath. 'What is it with you Throckmortons?'

Bess turns to him. 'It is no fault of ours, Walter, that our uncle married his daughters to Catholic families.'

Arthur scowls. 'I pray there will not be consequences, but Robert Cecil is no fool, and sharp enough to know of the connection.'

Walter raises his hand. 'He is also sharp enough to know we are Protestants.'

'Had he lived, the old lieutenant here, Sir George Hervey, would have faced enquiries about the purchase of such a quantity of gunpowder from the Tower by Robert Catesby.'

Bess shakes her head. 'I would never have believed Sir George Hervey's involvement in a plot to kill the king. He seemed in good health for his age, but complained of weakness and indisposition. It was a shock when we heard he'd died.'

Walter agrees. 'One of the yeomen told me he collapsed in the yard, and death came so quickly he didn't have time to make his will.'

Arthur's face is grim. 'Robert Catesby and Thomas Percy were shot by the king's guards and killed. Robert Cecil accuses the Earl of Northumberland, Henry Percy, of funding the conspiracy. He's been arrested, and is a close prisoner here in the Tower, along with Francis Tresham and others.'

Walter puffs on his pipe, blowing out a little cloud of grey smoke. 'They will be charged with treason and, like me, tried by a jury chosen by Robert Cecil.'

Bess stares at her brother. 'There has often been talk of Catholic rebels, waiting in secret for their chance. Could this plot be enough to spur them into action?'

Arthur turns to her. 'Robert Cecil wasted no time. He persuaded the king to send Charles Blount with an army with orders to encourage the good, and terrify the bad. God knows his experience in Ireland has prepared him well for such a task.' He frowns. 'It seems the conspirators planned to kidnap little Princess Elizabeth, who cannot be more than nine years old.'

Bess struggles to understand. 'What would they gain by taking the little princess prisoner?'

'They no doubt planned to put the princess on the throne, with someone like Henry Percy acting as regent until she came of age.'

Walter gives him a wry look. 'There is no longer any prospect of the king showing leniency to Henry Percy, or any of those accused.'

The bells of all the churches in London ring out into the night, and the sky glows orange with bonfires by the Thames. Bess stands at her open window, listening and watching. 'What are they celebrating?'

Walter joins her. 'I expect this means the plotters have suffered a traitor's death.' He frowns at the thought. 'The people are glad of any excuse to light a bonfire, although I question how many truly cheer the salvation of our Scottish king.'

Bess trembles at the memory of her questioning by the new Lieutenant of the Tower – Sir George's replacement, the stern-faced ambassador, Sir William Wade – who shouted at her, 'Confess!'

18

TOWER HILL 1606

EVERYTHING CHANGES AFTER WHAT PEOPLE CALL THE 'Gunpowder Plot'. The Lieutenant of the Tower, Sir William Wade, forbids visitors to stay past nightfall, including prisoners' wives. Bess joins Wat in the lodging rooms nearby on Tower Hill, and makes the short journey to visit Walter each day in all weathers.

She could ask Countess Frances, who is in Ireland, for the use of nearby Walsingham House, but prefers to stay with Wat in the terrace on the hill. Wat and his tutor, John Talbot, move to the ground-floor study and Bess has the chamber under the eaves. The adjacent room is Carew's nursery, which he shares with his nursemaid, Eleanor.

Their modest household also has a taciturn old cook and a shy young maidservant, who looks not much older than Wat. They both seem a little in awe of Bess. She suspects they've heard untruths about her, or perhaps it's because they know she was a gentlewoman of the privy chamber.

The terraced house on Tower Hill is modest compared with Sherborne, but Bess finds managing the expenses difficult. As well as the wages of her household, she must pay for the food they buy in the market and the rent for their lodgings each week.

Bess suspects Sir William Wade is keeping a share of the payments for their upkeep, but she dare not question him, as to do so could put her daily visits at risk. Walter's precious tapestries, his plate and silverware brought from Durham House are stored at Mile End, so she writes to Arthur, asking him to sell whatever he can.

Walter spends long hours in his garden tending his precious herbs and tobacco plants, which thrived the previous year but suffered in the winter frosts. The little grate in the old building is too small for curing the leathery tobacco leaves. He suspends them on twine in front of the Garden Tower hearth, filling the room with their pungent fumes.

Bess frowns at the sight of the brown leaves hanging above the fire like a washerwoman's line. 'How much longer do these need before they cure, Walter?'

'In truth, I don't know.' He feels one of the leaves between his stained fingers. 'I would guess another few weeks. Let's say a month.'

'A month!' His obsessive gardening takes his mind off their worsening situation, but she never imagined his work would take over so much precious space in their cramped tower.

She doesn't mind the aromatic bunches of dried herbs hanging from the beam, and was pleased when he made a present of dried lavender for her as a New Year's gift. The tobacco could become a useful source of income, but not at the cost of their limited comfort.

She knows that to challenge him risks the return of his melancholy mood, and so changes the subject. 'Tell me again what they said about the New World patent?'

'It's simple enough. They've taken advantage of my imprisonment to steal my ideas – and the fortune I could have made in the New World.' Walter curses. 'I sit in this prison while others use my maps and sea charts to claim the lands I discovered – in the name of our Scottish king!' He begins pacing the floor, a bad sign, and Bess makes a mental note not to mention the New World again.

She could remind Walter he never made it to the land he named 'Virginia' in honour of the late queen, yet anyone could be forgiven for thinking he had done so. He'd barely survived his visit to Guiana, when he'd been younger and fitter than the scrawny, tobacco-obsessed man before her now. Even if he was allowed to sail to Virginia, she fears he would never return.

She kisses him on the cheek. 'You've done your part, Walter, and will be remembered as a great explorer long after those who would take your place are forgotten.'

'Being questioned about the Catholic plot unsettled me. I am reminded that, despite my pleading letters, I am still seen as a threat.'

'It was my family who were involved, not you, and Robert Cecil knows it. Give it time, and our new king could issue a royal pardon whenever he wishes, so be careful not to speak ill of him.'

Walter turns back to inspect his string of drooping tobacco leaves, as if he expects to see some change. 'I pray you are right, Bess.'

Bess enters the Garden Tower late in the morning to find Walter still in his bed, his thin body shaking and shivering in a fever. Her first thought is the dreaded sweating sickness. She puts her hand to his forehead. It is as cold as marble to her touch. Bess calls his name and tries to rouse him.

She throws another woollen blanket over him and rushes out into the yard, where she spots Dean, who helps with cleaning and cooking. 'Sir Walter is sick and needs a doctor. Do you know where to find his physician, Doctor Turner?'

'I do, my lady, but—' He glances back towards the kitchens.

Bess presses one of her last silver coins from the purse at her belt into his hand. 'Quick as you can, if you will. My husband's life may depend on it.'

She sits at Walter's bedside and takes his hand in hers. His nails are bitten and his fingers are stained brown, a consequence of handling the tobacco leaves. She leans forwards and kisses his forehead. He still seems to be in a deep sleep, and doesn't acknowledge her. A good fire blazes in the hearth, yet he shivers as if suffering from the cold.

Bess hears the door open and Doctor Turner's cultured voice calls her name. 'Up here, doctor. Sir Walter is in his bed.' She watches while the doctor examines Walter. 'His health was improving, but he has not been himself since—'

She was going to say since he was questioned for several hours by Sir William Wade about the Gunpowder Plot, but that was before New Year. The less she says to anyone about his shameful treatment the better, although she has seen the decline in Walter's health since that day.

Doctor Turner turns to Bess, his sharp eyes seeming to judge her. 'It seems your husband has suffered a palsy.' He studies Walter's pale face. 'How old is he now?'

Bess makes a quick calculation. 'Walter was fifty-four last month.' She senses that the doctor was expecting to hear Walter is older. 'What is the cause of a palsy?'

'It can have many causes, and affects people in different ways, Lady Raleigh. He might not recover.'

Bess stares at him. 'He could die?'

'Let us pray he does not, my lady, but he could suffer from some paralysis, or memory loss.'

'Is there nothing you can do for him, doctor?'

'There is no medicine for the palsy, Lady Raleigh. I could try bleeding him, to remove corrupt humours and restore the proper balance to the body, which sometimes works, although there is no guarantee.'

Bess hesitates. Her instinct is against bloodletting, which seems barbaric, yet desperation leaves her little choice. 'Then do so.'

Doctor Turner takes a small sharp instrument from his leather case, and holds the blade up to the light. Bess forces herself to watch as he pulls up the sleeve of Walter's nightshirt, finds a vein, and makes the small cut in Walter's pale forearm. Walter doesn't flinch or cry out, a worrying sign.

Bess fights her nagging doubt as his bright-red blood spills into a small bowl. It seems wrong to take his precious blood, yet there is nothing else she can do. She thinks it is over, but his doctor pulls up Walter's other sleeve and repeats the operation on his other arm, letting the same amount of blood.

Doctor Turner finally looks satisfied with his work, and binds the tiny wounds with white linen. He puts his hand to Walter's forehead. 'He still feels a little feverish. I will call again tomorrow to see if he shows any sign of improvement, Lady Raleigh.' His tone suggests he does not expect to see much change.

Bess stares at him. She had expected more, and to see Walter open his eyes. 'Is that all we can do?'

He looks surprised at her question as he prepares to leave. 'You might wish to pray for your husband. God willing, he will break the fever in a day or so.' He gives her a curt bow and seems glad to leave.

It is impossible to tell if the doctor's work or her prayers are responsible, but Bess is relieved when Walter opens his eyes. He stares at her for a moment, as if unsure where he is, then reaches out to take her hand.

'How have I been—' His eyes widen and he stares at her as he seems to struggle to find the words. 'How long?'

Bess smiles with relief, yet Doctor Turner's warning echoes in her head: he could suffer from some paralysis, or memory loss. 'Two days. I had to leave you at nightfall, but paid young Dean to keep watch over you.'

'My hand feels—' Walter frowns. 'It's—'

She gives his hand a squeeze. 'Is it numb?'

He tries to form a fist with his right hand, scowling with the effort. He sits and then tries to stand, but falls back onto his bed, as if he no longer has the strength. 'Fetch Doctor Turner.'

Bess is planning to do so, but Walter's bluff tone surprises her. She worries he could fall back into his deep well of melancholy as she helps him lie down on his bed, and pulls the woollen blanket over him. 'I will, Walter, and I'll have young Dean bring you some hot pottage.'

'Servants' gruel?'

Bess smiles, his tired old joke is a relief. 'You must eat, Walter. All you've had for two days is a little weak ale. I shall ask him to bring freshly baked bread – and some stronger ale.'

'Bring my pipe, and some tobacco.'

She thinks the last thing he needs is to fill his cramped chamber with smoke. For a moment she hopes he might forget, but brings his pipe. She has never filled it for him before, and sees him scowl as some of his precious tobacco falls to the floor. She hands his pipe to him, and lights a taper from the embers in the hearth.

He takes a few puffs to light it. 'I shall have to—' He coughs as the smoke reaches his weakened lungs. 'I shall commend smoking a pipe of tobacco to my doctor.' He manages a smile. 'I feel better already.'

Arthur arrives in the late afternoon and looks relieved to hear Walter is sleeping in his bedchamber. He holds up a leather purse and hands it to Bess. 'Five hundred pounds from the sale of Walter's nautical tapestries to the Lord Admiral, Charles Howard.'

Bess takes the heavy purse with mixed feelings. 'I'm afraid Walter will curse us both when he learns who you sold them to, but I thank you.'

Arthur looks puzzled. 'Lord Howard has been a good friend to Walter. He offered him command of the queen's warship, the *Revenge*, and made him vice admiral of his fleet.'

'Walter discovered the king appointed Admiral Howard to lead negotiations for a peace treaty with Spain.'

'Is peace such a bad thing to aspire to?'

Bess looks at him in surprise. 'Walter believes the Spanish have a score to settle with him, for his part in the raid on Cadiz.' She recalls the precious jewels, sewn into the hem of her damask gown, and the chest of treasure she found in Walter's study at Durham House.

Arthur raises an eyebrow. 'I shall leave it to you to explain, but the admiral's five hundred pounds is a generous sum, enough to cover your expenses.'

Bess glances up the stairs, unsure if Walter can hear. 'I've been taking care of our costs since Walter's arrest. It grieves him that he is unable to provide for his family, yet never concerns himself with where the money comes from to meet our immediate needs. Since he was questioned about the plot his only interest is in his herbs and tobacco.'

'I was questioned by Robert Cecil about the Catholic plot.' He made it sound like a confession.

'He cannot suspect you of any involvement, Arthur.'

'I think it was his way to send a message.'

'What message?'

'That he knows about the connection between the plotters and our family.' Arthur keeps his voice low. 'I suspect he knew about the plot well in advance, and allowed events to continue so he could become the hero of the day.'

Bess stares at her brother. 'The risk would be too great. If he'd mistimed his discovery of the gunpowder, the king and all his Parliament could have been killed.'

'Don't make the mistake of underestimating Robert Cecil, Bess, or the extent of his ambition. If I am right, his plan worked well, as he has been well rewarded by the king, and will be made Lord Treasurer soon enough.' He gives her a cautionary look. 'Take care what you say in front of servants, Bess, as Robert Cecil has spies everywhere, possibly even in your household.'

Bess laughs at his warning. 'You are wrong there, Arthur. We can only afford little Carew's wet nurse, who also serves as my maid. There is a cook and a maid at our lodging on Tower Hill, and Wat has a tutor, but apart from that our only servants are young Dean and the waterman Owen here at the Tower.'

'You still have a household at Sherborne.'

'Martha is my housekeeper there. She has served me since the age of twelve, and could not be more loyal. I find it impossible to believe any of my servants would spy on us for Robert Cecil.'

'I was thinking of Alexander Brett.'

Bess sits back in her chair. If her brother is right, Robert Cecil could know everything, as she has trusted Alexander Brett with her secrets for many years.

'Have you not wondered how Alexander Brett secured a knighthood?'

Bess puts her hand to her mouth. 'Dear God. He's a cousin, Arthur, he's family, and would never betray us.'

'Walter *calls* him a cousin, but Alexander Brett is only related by his first marriage and, as you may know, his wife died of a fever some years ago.'

Bess frowns. 'Alexander Brett arrived at Sherborne and made himself useful. He even offered to escort me to Berwick, a long ride, which may have achieved nothing. I confided in him about my plan to petition the queen.'

'I hope you didn't share your views on our king?'

'I told him I was surprised to learn one of those chosen by Robert Cecil to welcome the queen was Baron Cobham's wife, Baroness Frances. I might have mentioned Henry Brooke's view that Arbella Stuart would be better suited to rule England.' A worrying thought occurs to her. 'Could my innocent remark have led to Walter's arrest?'

Arthur shrugs. 'I imagine that is the sort of information Cecil would reward with a knighthood.'

'Walter named Alexander Brett as a trustee in the legal transfer of the Sherborne estate to Wat.'

Arthur looks concerned. 'Did you know Alexander Brett plans to marry Ann Gifford?'

'He used to visit regularly to report on progress at Sherborne, but I haven't heard from him for some months – since the Gunpower Plot, when they began challenging visitors.'

'That's just as well, Bess. Ann Gifford is the daughter of a wealthy merchant, John Gifford, of Weston-Under-Edge in Gloucestershire, and the Giffords are a Catholic family.'

Bess is puzzled by this. 'One thing I know about Catholics is they do not marry outside their faith.'

Arthur nods. 'Which means one of three things.' He counts them on his fingers. 'Either he is prepared to convert to

Catholicism, Ann Gifford must abandon her religion – or Alexander Brett has been Catholic all along.'

'If he is, he would never work with Robert Cecil, who has made a career out of supressing Catholics.'

'You could be right, Bess, but who would be better to secure inside information?'

~

Walter's recovery is slow, and he spends long hours concocting tonics from his exotic herbs to effect a cure. Some come from seeds and roots, brought back from Guiana, and have never been grown in England before. Bess worries they could be poisonous, but there is nothing she can do to stop his experiments.

He struggles to write with his numb fingers, and becomes frustrated, cursing and spilling his ink. Bess knows she must be patient, as must Wat's tutor, John Talbot, who is allowed to visit during the afternoons to write Walter's dictated letters.

Bess pretends to study one of Walter's books, but cannot help listening as he limps and blusters around their tiny room. He scowls as he dictates yet another missive to Sir Robert Cecil, now made Viscount Cranborne and Earl of Salisbury, as reward for his loyal service.

'I lay before your lordship the new cause of my importunity. I am every second or third night in danger either of sudden death or of the loss of my limbs and sense, being sometimes two hours without feeling or motion of my hand or whole arm. I complain not of it, that I shall be made more weary of my life by Lady Raleigh's crying and bewailing.'

Bess sees the long-suffering John Talbot shake his head at Walter's words, and smile as he looks up and catches her eye. Walter does little else other than complain, and Wat's tutor is often the one at the receiving end, as if he is somehow responsible for the effects of the palsy.

Many of Walter's letters are to Robert Cecil and other members of the Privy Council, but others are addressed to King James. He never asks if there is any reply, but Bess knows the reason. The tone of his letters could only make their situation worse. She made a judgement to use them to light the fires in her apartment on Tower Hill, and worries about any of them reaching Robert Cecil's desk – or, even worse, King James.

19

THE TOWER 1607

WALTER'S GAOLER, SIR WILLIAM WADE, LIEUTENANT OF THE Tower, orders a curfew. All visitors must leave by the time a bell rings at five in the afternoon, or face the consequences. He's also put an end to his predecessor's relaxed regime, and orders his yeomen to ensure all prisoners are locked in their cells at night.

Walter seems unconcerned Bess can no longer stay into the evening. He busies himself tending his herb garden, and spends long hours in the old building with his mysterious experiments, which Bess worries have become an obsession.

She is saddened that he has taken no interest in her since the birth of little Carew and, now suffering with his palsy, she suspects he welcomes the curfew bell. Bess struggles to recall when he last kissed her or said anything romantic. She longs for a little daughter, to be named Anne, after her mother, but the chance seems more remote than ever.

She misses her mother, the only person she'd been able to ask about how children were made and why men behave as they do. Bess worries that Walter was made impotent as a consequence of his palsy. She lives in hope, however. The feeling has returned to the fingers of his right hand, and at least he can write again.

She'd worn her most revealing gown, cut fashionably low at the front, to tempt him. She blushed when her maidservant Eleanor said it left too little to the imagination, and she saw the hardened yeomen warders staring like hungry wolves. If Walter noticed he showed no sign, and seemed more interested in his book.

When she looks in the old garden building in search of him, Bess is surprised to find the rows of herb seedlings and tender plants are gone. In their place is a complicated construction made from old copper piping and glass vessels full of strange liquids. Some simmer and steam over the small hearth, filling the air with a strange aromatic scent.

Walter looks up as she enters, an obsessive glint in his eye. 'I'm trying different ways to distil the essence of herbs, to make them more potent.' He pours some of the amber liquid into a small pewter cup with great care not to spill any. 'I believe this could be the way to create a cure for fevers and other ailments where doctors fail us.'

Bess studies the scrawled labels on some of his ingredients in a row of small jars on the shelf. 'Bezoar stone, musk, ground ambergris…' She looks up at him in amazement. 'I thought you were using your herbs and some roots brought back from Guiana. I know these are rare – and expensive. How are you paying for such things? I trust you are not putting us deeper into debt?'

'I have a new patron. Captain Whitelock, Captain of the Guard, was tasked with escorting the Comtesse de Beaumont, wife of the French ambassador, on a tour. The Comtesse was curious about me, and Captain Whitelock commended my cures to her.'

Bess sniffs the amber liquid, which has a delicate scent of violets. 'The Comtesse pays you?'

'No, but I only need to ask for these ingredients, and Captain Whitelock brings them.'

Bracing herself, Bess takes a sip of his tonic, making a face at the sharpness, like a bitter lime, with an unusual metallic aftertaste. She sees he is waiting for her reaction. 'You could sweeten it with sugar, or some honey, or dilute it to make a cordial.'

Walter turns to a page in an old book, and shows her. 'What I need is strong wine, for the distillation, but Sir William Wade forbids it.'

Bess recognises the triangular symbols for fire, water, air and earth. 'This is a book on alchemy.' She frowns. 'You must take care, Walter. If Sir William believes you experiment with alchemy, he could take this building from you, or worse.'

'Alchemy is based on the same ancient knowledge, and my experiments are alchemy of a sort, turning herbs into gold.' Walter laughs. 'This book shows how to distil wine to extract alcohol, and how to concentrate a liquid.' He studies the amber liquid. 'I shall call this the great cure-all, an antidote to poison, the Balsam of Guiana, and make my fortune.'

Bess worries at his mention of poison. 'What if someone dies after taking your great cure-all? Their relatives could sue us.'

He holds up his hand to silence her objections. 'Let them sue. I have nothing else to lose.'

Bess senses an air of anticipation when she enters the Tower gates. An armed yeoman warder is on guard, and she stops as he steps forwards, his halberd in his hand. He calls out, 'Halt, in the name of the king!'

She manages a smile. She knows him well, and is certain he recognises her. 'What is the matter?'

'Her Majesty the queen is coming to see the lion cubs, my lady, and is expected to bring her son, Prince Henry. On the orders of Sir William Wade, only necessary visitors are allowed to enter the Tower grounds today.' He glances over his shoulder, as if to see whether they are being watched. 'You may pass, Lady Raleigh, but you must stay out of Sir William's way – or I shall answer for it.'

Bess is glad she left little Carew with his nursemaid, Eleanor. She keeps close to the ancient stone walls, keeping a look out for Lieutenant Wade. The menagerie is some distance from their Garden Tower, and if the queen wishes to inspect the Crown jewels in the White Tower keep, it will be easy enough to remain out of view.

She warns Walter, but he is determined to continue with his latest experiment. 'I persuaded Owen to bring me a jug of water from the river, which I am distilling to see if I can make it safe to drink.'

'Who would wish to drink water from the River Thames?' Bess recalls the corpses she's seen floating in the river, and frowns at the thought.

'Sailors.' He grins as she raises an eyebrow. 'There is never enough fresh water on board ship. If I can prove my idea works I could make a fortune.'

Her reply is interrupted by shouted commands in the courtyard outside, and they climb the steps to the upper window to see. The queen's visit to the menagerie is blessed with bright spring sunshine, but the Tower Green is deserted apart from a solitary crow, pecking at the grass for worms.

Sir William Wade appears, followed by his yeomen warders armed with halberds, who Bess assumes must be an escort for the queen and her son. The solitary crow flaps to a safe perch high on the Tower wall, its caws echoing around the green in protest.

When Bess sees her new queen for the first time, her reaction is one of disappointment. Queen Anna wears her reddish hair piled high and decorated with large pearls. An upstanding lace ruff frames her face, in an unsettling echo of the late Queen Elizabeth. Her pale green gown is decorated with pink rosettes, and her jewels flash as they catch the sunlight.

Bess looks down at her own gown, a practical russet brocade with her own embroidery on the partlet. She'd thought it one of her best, yet the frayed hem is repaired and the sleeves puff out in the style once favoured by the old queen. Her old lace ruff is yellowing and in need of starch, a luxury she cannot afford.

Queen Anna is at least ten years younger than Bess, and brings much more than new fashions to England. At her side is a striking young man who looks about the same age as Wat, but there the resemblance ends. The young prince is dressed in cloth of silver and gold. A silver sword hangs on his belt in a scabbard glistening with bright diamonds and rubies.

Prince Henry stops and stares up at Bess and Walter with sharp eyes. He points, saying something to Queen Anna, who also glances up at their open window. Bess steps back into the shadows, hoping she can't be seen by Sir William Wade, who has the power to stop her visits.

Walter turns to her. 'It seems they are coming here. I did not think I would meet her, but I wonder if our new queen has any sympathy for my situation?'

Bess takes his arm in unexpected panic. 'I am not dressed to receive a queen, and was warned to stay out of view. If they do come, you should greet them alone.'

Walter smiles. 'I shall meet them in my garden, and show the queen I do not waste my time here.'

Bess moves to the window overlooking Walter's garden and

hopes she can't be seen. She watches Sir William give a disapproving look as he steps aside to allow the queen and young prince to enter the garden. Walter bows to one knee, and the queen smiles as she speaks to him, but Bess cannot hear what is said.

She watches Walter lead the queen and Prince Henry into his makeshift laboratory. Sir William Wade turns to stare up at their Garden Tower, the look on his face failing to conceal his displeasure. Bess prays Walter shows proper respect for his royal visitors, and prays there will not be consequences for his actions.

Walter looks pleased with himself when he returns. 'The queen showed great interest in my work.' His eyes shine with pride. 'She asked me about my voyage to Guiana and told me to send my potion to her at the palace, once it is perfected.'

'Do you think she might ask the king to pardon you?'

Walter shrugs. 'I protested my innocence, and she told me her brother, King Christian, the King of Denmark, is expected to visit London soon, and could be persuaded to ask our king for my services.'

'We could go to Denmark?' She puts her hand on his arm. 'You deserve good fortune, and your writing hand is recovering well. Write the queen a letter of thanks for her kindness, while your situation is on her mind.'

He nods. 'Prince Henry asked my advice on matters to consider when building a new warship. He seems knowledgeable, and wishes me to share my experience with him.'

Bess smiles. 'You must, Walter, and see if we can find a way to introduce Wat. It could be the making of him.'

Walter waves a pamphlet in the air and curses. 'The king has taken against the smoking of tobacco!' He glares at Bess as if challenging her to agree. 'He says smoking is a custom loathsome to the eye, hateful to the nose, harmful to the brain, and dangerous to the lungs.'

Bess understands the king's view. Although she has never smoked, her gowns carry the tang of Walter's tobacco. Yet she feels sympathy for Walter. 'From what I've heard, the king has pastimes far more loathsome than smoking a pipe.'

'Take care how you speak, Bess. The king will charge you with treason.' His sharp tone surprises her.

'And who will tell the king what I say? Our servants? Where are Robert Cecil's spies now?' It annoys her to know he is right, but her shrill voice echoes, like the cry of a hawk. 'If I cannot speak my mind before *you*—'

He holds up a hand to stop her. 'Calm yourself.'

She takes the pamphlet from him and struggles to compose herself. 'How did you come by this?'

'Thomas Harriot thought I should know what the king is saying.' Walter scowls and takes the pamphlet back from her. 'King James goes on to talk of the black stinking fume thereof, and says it nearest resembles the horrible Stygian smoke of the pit that is bottomless!'

'Don't trouble yourself, Walter. The king can say what he wishes, but I've seen how soon you improved from your palsy after smoking tobacco.'

'You are right.' He throws the pamphlet on the fire and she sees the glint in his eye as he watches it burst into flames, but he has a scowl on his face.

She worries his melancholy is returning, and needs to remind him there is new hope of a pardon. 'You said you have letters for me to deliver?' Bess smiles. 'I trust you have one for the queen?'

He crosses to his desk and hands her three letters, written

on his best parchment, folded but not sealed. 'One for the queen, one to Prince Henry, and one for our good friend, Sir Robert Cecil.'

Bess studies Walter's letters in the privacy of her attic bedchamber on Tower Hill. The first, to the queen, reminds her of Walter's overly flattering language to the late queen. She decides to seek the advice of her brother before sending his plea for her to ask the king's mercy, as she has no idea how the queen reacts to such requests.

The second letter, addressed to 'His Highness the most excellent prince', intrigues her. Headed 'Advice to a prince on building a ship', Walter recommends salvaging the timbers of the old queen's flagship *Victory*. Bess reads on.

In a well conditioned ship these things are chiefly required: that she be strong built, swift in sail, and that her ports are so laid out that she may carry her guns in all weathers.

Walter goes on to discuss ideal ship proportions and:

...above all other thinges have care that the great gunnes be foure foote cleare above the water. For if the ports lie lower and be open it is danger-ous, and by that default was a goodly ship and many gallant gentlemen were lost in the days of King Henry the eighth by the Isle of Wight in a ship by the name of Mary Rose.

.   .   .

Bess decides this letter should be delivered, but is disappointed Walter doesn't take the opportunity to introduce Wat to the young prince. She plans to persuade him to add a footnote, but remembers Wat must leave for Oxford University in the autumn, so his meeting with the prince will have to wait.

The third letter, to Robert Cecil, makes Bess gasp. Walter is proposing a second voyage to Guiana, and offering to bear one third of the costs, with Cecil and the queen providing one third each. She cannot believe he has not mentioned this plan to her, and can't imagine how he intends to pay his share. Her mind buzzes with questions as she reads on.

My tymes are not long in this world and I shall not be able to hereafter performe such a jurney. Your lordshipe may have gold good cheap and may joyne other of your honourable friends in the matter if you please for there is enough. Your lordshipe may relieve mee and my distroyed estate and bynde me more than ever to live and dye your servant.

Walter plans to risk his health and his life, and gamble everything on one last reckless roll of the dice. He'd told her the queen asked about his voyage to Guiana, yet it seems unlikely he had time to discuss funding a second voyage. He seems unconcerned about misleading Robert Cecil, and one line from his letter stands out on the page: *Your lordshipe may relieve mee and my distroyed estate.*

Bess is about to throw this last letter on the fire which crackles in the hearth, but stops herself. This letter must never reach Robert Cecil, but she needs it if she's going to confront Walter. She decides to sleep on the problem, but spends most of the night restless and awake. After all they've been through to make Sherborne into their family home, she will not let him throw it away.

He always had an obsessive spirit of adventure, but his imprisonment in the Tower has made it worse. Bess doubts there is anything she can say or do to stop Walter if he believes he has a chance of returning to Guiana. If she burns his letter, he will find another way. Walter is prepared to risk Sherborne for one last desperate chance to prove there is gold in Guiana. Or die in the attempt.

Bess always knew this moment would come, yet now it has, her heart grieves for her eldest son. Wat stands before her in his best clothes, a dagger at his belt, reminding her of Walter in his youth, when she first saw him all those years ago.

Wat will never know she's had to sell one of the last of her jewels, sewn into the hem of her gown, to pay his expenses. As well as his fine new clothes and books, Walter's friend and Oxford graduate, Thomas Harriot, found him lodgings, complete with servants, his first household. They are close to Corpus Christi College, but the rent is more than she can afford.

'Don't be sad, Mother.' Wat's voice is deeper now he is fourteen, and ready to make his way in the world. 'You've always wished for me to go to Oxford.'

'You are right, as ever, Wat.' She fights back the tears. 'I shall miss you, and will worry when you are so far from home.'

'I shall write to you, and look forward to your replies, Mother.' He gives her an uncertain frown, as if there is more he wishes to say.

Bess looks into his dark eyes, and is touched to see he is close to tears. 'What is it?'

'I worry about Father.' His voice wavers. 'I want to make him proud—'

'Your father has been proud of you since the day of your birth.'

'But he's become a stranger to me.'

'Your father is a proud man, and was driven by his ambition. He's lost everything but you, little Carew, and me. He needs us, and deserves our love.' She chokes back tears as she gives her son one last embrace. 'Go to Oxford, Wat, and make your father even prouder.'

20

THE TOWER 1608

WALTER WEARS HIS BEST DOUBLET WHEN BESS ARRIVES, AND whistles a tune as he tidies the room he calls his 'study'. She's pleased to see the improvement in his mood, as she'd worried about how obsessed he'd become with his experiments and mysterious potions.

He looks up at Bess as she enters. 'His Highness is gracing us with a visit.'

'King James?' She smiles at the look of distaste on his face before he sees her joke. Prince Henry is a regular visitor, and regards Walter as a hero, listening to his stories of preparing England against the Spanish Armada, and the capture of Cadiz.

Walter manages a smile. 'Prince Henry wishes to talk to me about my explorations in Guiana, as well as the prospects of setting up a new colony in Virginia.'

Bess kisses him. 'My brother Arthur told me Prince Henry was overheard saying, *No king but my father would keep such a bird in a cage.*' She smiles. 'It can only be you he refers to, Walter. It seems you've acquired another son, and one who can be a useful advocate for you at court.'

Walter nods in agreement. 'Prince Henry is wiser than his years. He is concerned England's navy is being allowed to rot at anchor, when it could be the greatest fighting fleet in the world.' He shakes his head. 'The Lord Admiral gave him a warship, and he's named it the *Disdain* as he says it's out of date.'

Bess worries his tone sounds as if he's on the brink of a new obsession, but advising the prince on restoring the navy would give him a new sense of purpose. Walter's letter to Robert Cecil is in her bag, and she'd planned to discuss the contents when the moment was right. The prince's visit could distract him from risking his life in search of his mythical El Dorado.

A thought occurs to her. 'I could send for Thomas Harriot. You could work together on designing a new warship, to be built for the prince as his flagship.'

Walter stops tidying the books on his shelf and turns to her. 'I've had the same idea. She could be named the *Prince Royal*, and could become one of the finest ships in the navy.'

Bess spots a letter among the papers on Walter's desk. The dark wax seal is unbroken but it looks more like an official document than a personal letter. She picks it up out of curiosity. 'What's this?'

Walter shrugs. 'The Sergeant of the Tower delivered it yesterday. I think it's from my lawyers, from the look of it.' He sounds disinterested and turns back to his books.

Bess breaks the seal and begins to read, then looks up at him, her eyes wide with alarm. 'This is from the Court of Exchequer. They say the Sherborne deed is invalid.'

Walter shakes his head. 'It cannot be, unless—'

'Unless someone is up to no good?' She reads on. 'They claim the wording your lawyer used is incorrect. Your clerk omitted the words *shall and will from henceforth stand and be thereof seised.*' Bess frowns, and stares at Walter. 'What does seised mean?'

'It means Wat is not put in possession of Sherborne, and the entire Sherborne estate, with all the farms and income from rents reverts to the Crown!' Walter curses. 'Robert Cecil's lawyers have outmanoeuvred us this time.'

'But he personally confirmed that Sherborne would not be taken.'

'His promises mean nothing now, Bess.'

'I shall fight this, for Wat and for little Carew. We must not let them take Sherborne. It's our son's inheritance.'

Walter scowls. 'You might as well fight the morning mist from the Thames, for all the good it will do.'

Bess shakes her head. 'My brother Arthur will help me find out who is behind this.'

Walter's good mood is replaced by sullen despair. 'You cannot win a legal argument without lawyers.'

'Then I shall pay for the best lawyers I can afford. I have my mother's pearls, a few tapestries, and will sell what I can of our possessions at Sherborne.'

'You don't understand, Bess.' Walter takes the letter from her and reads aloud. 'The *entire* Sherborne estate reverts to the Crown. That means everything we owned is gone, and they will descend like carrion crows over a dying sheep until there is nothing left.'

'Even my shire horses?'

'They will be the first to go.'

His tone is the last straw for Bess. 'I trusted you, Walter. I cannot believe how naive I've been, trusting you not to put Wat's inheritance at risk. All you had to do was to ensure the legal papers were all in order.'

'I placed my trust in others, Bess. I am no lawyer.'

She pulls the letter to Robert Cecil from her bag and waves it at him. 'When were you going to tell me you were prepared to sacrifice everything for the chance of another voyage to Guiana?'

He looks at his shoes, as if afraid to look her in the eye. 'I made no secret of it. You've read the letter. I believe the queen can be persuaded to help fund this venture, which should be enough to encourage Robert Cecil to invest.' He looks up at her, still wary, as if afraid of her. 'What do I have to lose?'

Bess can't contain her anger any longer. 'Your life, Walter!' Her raised voice echoes. 'You are not fit to undertake such a voyage. To risk everything on a dream of finding a city of gold is madness.'

Arthur reads the letter and scowls. 'We should have expected this, Bess.'

Bess knows her brother well enough to see he's holding some detail back. She puts her hand on his arm. 'Tell me what you've heard at court, please. I need to know.'

He hesitates. 'It's bad news, I'm afraid. I heard the king is looking for good estates in the country to reward his favourites. He surrounds himself with ambitious young men from Scotland, who know how to please him.' Arthur gives Bess a disapproving look, but stops himself saying more.

'You need not spare my blushes, Arthur. The king's liking for handsome young men is the talk of London.'

Arthur shakes his head. 'The problem is that Sherborne is well situated – and now, it seems, available for the king to grant as he pleases.'

'Do you think he's already granted it to someone?' Bess watches her brother's face, looking for the truth.

'It would not surprise me – and if he has, you will find it impossible to persuade the king to change his mind.'

'Who should I go to for help?' Her sense of desperation deepens.

'Could Walter ask Prince Henry for his support?'

'He could, but Walter's lost the will to fight this, and all my hard work in making Sherborne a family home and the shire stud seem to matter little to him.'

'I understand Robert Cecil has done his best to keep Sherborne for you, Bess, but if the king commands it he has no more choice in the matter than you do.'

'I shall petition the king in person. The time for writing letters which are never read has passed.'

Arthur frowns. 'King James might not care to be petitioned by a woman. There is a danger you could make things worse.'

'How can it be worse?' Bess takes him by both arms and stares into his eyes as she tries to understand. 'What can the king do to us that he's not done already?'

'You think there is little left to lose, but you must be mindful that Walter only remains alive at the king's pleasure.'

'Then I must find a way to win the king's favour.' She has no idea how, or if she will even be allowed into the palace, but it is her only hope of saving her home.

Bess can't recall the last time she was at Hampton Court, a regular haunt when she'd been Queen Elizabeth's gentlewoman. The palace looks little changed, yet there is a sense that *everything* has changed. She dresses demurely, in one of her plainer gowns, with no jewels on display, and has her maidservant Eleanor and little Carew with her, in the hope of arousing the king's sympathy.

She knows the elderly yeoman on the gates, and is encouraged as he recognises her and nods her through. He'd once been one of Walter's loyal men, when he'd been the captain of the queen's guard. Spared the indignity of being turned away, she leads Eleanor and Carew to the great hall with the confidence of one who knows the way.

The cavernous hall buzzes like a hive with the subdued chatter of the other petitioners waiting, like her, for their chance to catch the king's eye. Once she could sweep into the privy chamber, her long gowns rustling on the floor. Now she must wait her turn, even it if takes all day, with no guarantee the king will see her.

She'd not expected there would be so many more people hoping to see the king than in Queen Elizabeth's day. The oak benches along one wall are full, and although she attracts some curious glances, no one seems ready to let her have a seat. Little Carew stares wide-eyed at the other petitioners, and Bess is glad his nursemaid Eleanor is skilled at keeping him from crying.

Bess studies the fading tapestries of religious scenes, her mind drifting back to happier times. This great hall would resound with lively music and laughter, dancing and feasting. Even in her older age the queen could amaze them all by dancing the volta, being lifted high into the air by men like Robert Devereux.

The contrast now is stark. Dour Scotsmen stand muttering in groups, hoping for their reward. Others, like herself, look on the brink of desperation, trying to do their best for the future of their families. She sees little Carew beaming at her, trying to get her attention, and thinks of Wat, who is eleven years older and causing quite a stir at Corpus Christi College.

His last letter had seemed scribbled in haste, as if he had better things to do than to write letters to his mother. He says he enjoys his lessons, is doing well and has many new friends. Wat describes his new life as tranquil and studious, but Bess knows better.

Thomas Harriot is well connected in Oxford and tells her

Wat is one of the brightest students, but also has a reputation as one of the rowdiest. He's often been in trouble for his drinking and smoking, and Bess suspects there is more Thomas Harriot has kept from her.

Bess is tired of waiting to meet the king, and little Carew grows restless. She makes her way through the throng around the entrance to the privy chamber, followed by Eleanor carrying Carew, and stares in disbelief.

The stories she has heard about the king are true. King James is an unimpressive figure, with thin legs and grubby silks. His lank hair looks in need of a wash, and his scrawny beard is cut square, in the fashion of the Earl of Essex, a worrying similarity.

He gives an affected laugh at a comment from his companion, a slim, handsome young man with bright-blue eyes and golden hair who he leans on, as if for support. When he speaks to the young man, his effete voice has a soft Scottish accent, and Bess senses the close affection between them.

Ignoring the throng of petitioners, Bess finds herself staring into the watery blue eyes of the king. She curtseys. 'Lady Raleigh, Your Majesty.'

His eyes go to little Carew, still in Eleanor's arms, then back to Bess. 'You want me to bless your child? I am *Rawley* asked to do so.' He sounds mocking, and his companion giggles at the king's weak joke.

Bess takes a deep breath. At least she has the king's attention, after waiting most of the morning. 'I beg Your Highness to take pity on a poor mother and her son, and not take her home from her.'

He stares at her with a look of incomprehension, as if she speaks in a language foreign to him. His thin smile turns to a frown. 'I hae no idea what you speak of, Lady Rawley.'

Bess hesitates, aware the precious moment is about to pass, and recalls her brother's warning: Walter only remains alive at the king's pleasure. 'My home is Sherborne Lodge, Your Majesty, and has been reverted to the Crown. All I ask is that it be transferred to my son. It is his only inheritance, and his future.'

The king stares at her as he finally seems to understand her, and shakes his head, holding up a hand to silence her. 'Na, na, I mun hae the land, I mun hae the land for Carr.' The king waves her away and moves on to the next petitioner.

Bess guesses from the smug look on the face of the king's young companion that he must be 'Carr', who is to be given all she has of value in the world as his reward for loyal service. She recalls Arthur mentioning Robert Carr being the king's latest favourite. A former groom of the king's bedchamber, he'd been knighted and promoted to a gentleman of the bedchamber.

There will be no changing the king's mind, and to try would risk his anger. A new plan forms in her mind as Bess leads Eleanor and little Carew back down the once familiar passageways and out into the cold. She prays that Robert Cecil has a conscience over breaking his promise to save Sherborne for Wat, and is still able to help.

For all his scheming, she once sensed a closeness with Robert Cecil, and counted him as a friend. Her brother also told her that although the king made Robert Cecil the Earl of Salisbury, one of the senior nobles at court, he mocks his deformity and calls him his *little beagle*. Apart from appealing to the self-serving Robert Carr, Robert Cecil is now their only hope.

Walter seems unsurprised when Bess explains what happened at Hampton Court. They decide the best course of action is for Bess to help Walter word a letter to Robert Cecil. They work by the big window in what they both now call Walter's study, with a good log fire in the hearth. Walter writes a draft on the back of a used sheet of parchment and dips his quill in the black ink.

May it please your lordship, I humbly beseech you to give me leave, and pardon too, for the answering of those things you were lately pleased to object against me, and that you will charitably also consider both of my demands and of the reasons which embolden me to make them, that Robert Carr who is so greatly in the king's favour hath many faire fortunes before him.

Bess frowns at the critical edge in Walter's words. Their future and Wat's inheritance could depend on this letter. 'If you name Carr, it could put Robert Cecil in a difficult position.'

'What of our difficult position, Bess? If I am any judge, Robert Cecil despises men like Robert Carr as much as we do.' Walter scowls, but crosses out Carr's name and continues writing.

…that the gentleman who is so greatly in favour hath many faire fortunes before him, and we nothing to look for but misery, and that he is better able to give us the worth of the land.

We humbly beseech your lordship that your compassion and care of honour may be the judge between his prosperous navigation and our ship-wreck, and that your charity but for us may equal the balance between us. I hope so heartily to find all just favour at your hands as I will venture to assure you I will do my uttermost to make my wife and son forget their misery and to be ever mindful of their duty towards your lordship, to whom I hope they will be as I am, a most faithful humble servant.

W.R.

21

THE TOWER 1609

PILES OF OLD BOOKS ARE SPREAD OPEN ON WALTER'S DESK AND he seems in good spirits as he turns to Bess. 'I've found a new purpose – and my patron is Prince Henry. He's brought me a generous supply of paper, and I'm planning to write an entire history of the world.'

'An *entire* history?' Bess frowns at his untouched bowl of pottage, and the stub of candle in a pool of wax. She must make sure he takes care of himself, but is pleased he has a new obsession. He might forget about his reckless plans of returning to Guiana. She smiles. 'You always were ambitious.'

'True enough, but this is not a new idea.' Walter paces the rush-covered floor of his cell, as he did in his study at Sherborne, limping as he recites lines from one of his poems which Bess can't recall hearing before.

'We should begin by such a parting light,
To write the story of all ages past,
And end the same before the approaching night,
Such is again the labour of my mind…'

He grins at the puzzled look on her face. 'It's from my poem, *Ocean to Cynthia*, written for our late queen.' Walter holds up one of his old books. 'This will live on long after we are forgotten, Bess. My history of the world will be dedicated to Prince Henry, and begin with the creation. Ben Jonson has agreed to review the first draft, and the prince could help me have my work printed.'

'Arthur told me Ben Jonson sails too close to the wind, and risks the king's displeasure with his plays and masques for the queen.'

Walter grins. 'His appetite for controversy makes him the perfect choice. Ben Jonson is well connected and influential in the literary world, so to have his name associated with my work can only help.'

A thought occurs to Bess as she glances at his pile of valuable old books. 'We should have your remaining books brought here from Sherborne, before they are all lost.' Sadness echoes in her voice.

There has been no word from Robert Cecil, but they've not been commanded to hand over the estate, so she's not given up hope. Bess is not surprised by Robert Cecil's silence. After all, the Cecil family motto is *Sero, sed serio*. Late, but in earnest.

Bess shows Walter the latest letter from Wat. 'He's heard from William Cecil, who plans to embark on a grand tour of the Continent. Wat says he wishes to do the same when he graduates from Oxford in October.'

Walter raises an eyebrow. 'Do you have any idea how much a tour of the Continent could cost?'

'I have no idea, but from what his tutor, Dr Featley, tells me a tour abroad could be the making of him. He said Wat keeps strange company.'

'Strange company?' Walter raises an eyebrow. 'Does he mean Catholics?'

Bess worries Dr Featley refers to harlots, but doesn't wish to spoil Walter's good mood. 'William Cecil has been made

Viscount Cranborne, and is engaged to marry young Catherine Howard in December.'

'The daughter of Thomas Howard, Earl of Suffolk?'

Bess nods. 'Robert Cecil has planned this for years.'

'It is such a pity the threat to Wat's inheritance means we cannot find him a suitable wife.' The sadness echoes in Walter's voice. 'Any heiress would suspect our motives.'

Bess tries to lift his spirits. 'Sherborne is not lost yet, Walter. If Robert Cecil doesn't answer you soon I shall arrange to see him in person. He cannot refuse to see me, and I shall find some way to persuade him to help.'

Walter brightens a little. 'I believe Robert Cecil is sending William to the Continent to make a man of him before the marriage, which is the least we should do for Wat. Does he wish to travel with young William?' Walter strokes his grey beard. 'Robert Cecil is a wealthy man. He might bear the cost.'

'I thought the same, but William is travelling to Italy in July, with his future brothers-in-law, Thomas and Henry Howard. Wat must wait until his graduation.' She makes a judgement to share the idea that kept her awake for much of the previous night. 'I could sell the stud farm, and all the horses, to raise the money.'

Walter frowns. 'If you don't, there is a risk we could lose the stud farm to Robert Carr.' His rickety chair creaks as he sits back, his brow furrowed. 'It would be good for Will to see something of the world when he graduates. To my shame, I've never taken him even as far as Jersey.'

Bess places her hand on his shoulder. 'The fault is not yours, Walter. It's been hard work to build up, but the stud farm at Sherborne was Wat's inheritance. I can't think of a better use of the proceeds than to give them to him now.'

Walter agrees. 'Ben Jonson would enjoy a tour of the Continent. I shall write to him and ask if he can help Wat complete his education.' He looks wistful. 'I would give anything to be able to travel with them, but know that cannot be, for now at least.'

Bess is saddened by news of the unexpected death of her distant cousin, Alexander Brett, of a fever. She sits alone in the tranquil, echoing silence of All Hallows by the Tower, and weeps for him as she says a prayer for his soul. The wooden pew is hard, and she kneels on a worn and faded cushion embroidered with a golden cross.

Bess wipes away a tear. The questions she had for Alexander Brett can never be answered. Walter never explained why he'd made her cousin an executor of his will. She'd never found out how he earned his knighthood, but suspects it was his reward as the eyes and ears of Robert Cecil, his spy at Sherborne.

'Such things are best left to the past.' With a jolt she realises she's spoken aloud. She looks over her shoulder but sees she is still alone in the ancient church. She remembers Alexander Brett's patience and support when he escorted her to plead for Walter with the new queen, and finds forgiveness for anything he may have done.

Although he'd been older than she was, she remembers how she was flattered by his flirting with her at Sherborne, making her laugh and reminding her of Walter's courtship before they were married. She'd suspected Alexander Brett admired her, and sensed her own feelings for him.

He'd made her feel like an attractive woman, at the price of reminding her how much Walter has changed. In all their years it seems a miracle they'd produced two healthy boys, having lain together so rarely. She cannot recall the last time she shared his bed, and can't help wondering if she ever will again.

Bess pushes improper memories of Alexander Brett from her mind and clasps her hands together in prayer. 'Dear Lord, in the hour of temptation, deliver us from evil. Amen.'

There has been little enough temptation since the birth of Carew. She's become skilled at maintaining the illusion of a successful marriage. At best she can expect a loveless kiss, but never a compliment or affection. She can blame Walter's lack of interest on the effects of his palsy, but worries the years fly past with relentless speed.

Walter is fifty-seven, and looks older. She will be forty-four in April, and before long will be too old to bear the daughter she longs for. It doesn't help that Walter's gaoler, Sir William Wade, is still the Lieutenant of the Tower, and is diligent in enforcing his curfew.

Bess considered hiding in Walter's bedchamber to escape the dreaded clanging curfew bell. It would be easy enough to do, and she could slip the yeoman warder a silver coin to buy his silence. She expects if she was caught there would be consequences.

She'd been banished from the court of the late queen, and could be the first to be banished from the Tower. With a jolt she is reminded how much power Sir William Wade holds over her. If they also lose Sherborne, she could face a lonely life in her lodging rooms on Tower Hill, her only hope that the king might one day pardon Walter.

Her bones creak as she stands after kneeling in the cold for so long. Bess looks up at the figure of Christ on the cross. She cannot help feeling their God has failed them, but is grateful for her boys, and her own health and strength, which she will need if she is to challenge the decision of their king. She clasps her hands together and says one last prayer, this time for herself.

'Have mercy upon me, O Lord, and forgive my offences. Teach me by

thy holy spirit, that I may rightly weigh them, and earnestly repent for the same. Amen.'

Bess reads Walter's plea to Robert Carr.

Sir, after many great losses and many years sorrowes, of both which I have cause to fear that I was mistaken in their endes, it has come to my knowledge that your self (whom I know not by an honourable fame) have been persuaded to give me and myne our last fatall blowe, by obtaining from His Majesty the inheritance of my children.

There was a time when she would have burned this letter on the fire, rather than risk Walter causing upset. Now she cannot see how it could make matters worse. It pains her to even think of all the hard work she put into making Sherborne a family home.

She does not share Walter's faith in the avaricious favourite of the king having a conscience. Robert Carr has won everything and, as in the past, she has to ask Robert Cecil for a favour. She will beg on her knees if she must, but holds out little hope of securing his support.

Her only consolation is that Adrian Gilbert has proved his worth once again, and secured a good price for her stud farm. Bess is saddened to think she might never see Sherborne again, yet at least she has the money to pay for Wat's travels on the Continent, his first great adventure.

The invitation to visit Countess Frances at Essex House is a surprise to Bess. She has not heard from the countess since she left with her new husband for the west of Ireland. She counted Frances as a friend, and now she needs any friends she can find.

Bess is glad of an excuse to wear the fine dress, with her mother's pearls and wired gossamer ruff, she'd bought in happier times. Eleanor ties the ribbons on the sleeves, and stands back to admire the result.

'It fits you well, my lady.'

Bess smiles at her compliment. 'I've had plenty of exercise walking to the Garden Tower since Sir William Wade stopped me bringing my carriage. The style is out of fashion for a meeting with a countess. Do you think I should have bought something new?'

Eleanor shakes her head. 'The new fashions are too revealing for a married lady.' She frowns. 'It's difficult to tell the respectable women from the harlots in the marketplace.'

Bess decides to take little Carew, now an energetic four-year-old, finally out of smocks. Eleanor surprised Bess by proving to be an accomplished seamstress, adjusting one of Wat's old doublets to fit Carew as if it had been made for him. Eleanor is also modest. 'Wat hardly used it before he'd outgrown his doublet, so it was no work at all.'

Bess laughs as little Carew parades in his new clothes, and does a passable impression of his father's limping walk. Countess Frances had to convert to Catholicism to marry her third husband, Richard Burke, Earl of Clanricarde, so Bess hopes Carew's presence will serve as a small distraction and prevent talk of their religious differences.

~

It seems strange to be back in Essex House. The grand portrait of the Earl of Essex is replaced by a new, flattering portrait of the king. Bess can see no sign of repair to the windows or plasterwork. She'd heard there was fierce fighting in the final battle which forced the Earl of Essex to surrender, the windows shattered in a hail of musket fire and many men killed and injured.

A housekeeper dressed in black greets them. 'You are expected, Lady Raleigh. I will inform the countess.'

Eleanor spots a servant she knows, hands little Carew over to Bess, and heads for the warm sanctuary of the kitchens. Bess fights off a frisson of nerves as she waits with Carew. She wishes she knew Countess Frances better, as the favour she must ask of her is no small matter.

Frances glides into the great hall in a silk gown cut low at the front, with a high lace collar in the style made popular by their new queen. She smiles in welcome. 'Thank you for coming to see me, Bess. My husband has business to attend to, and I confess I find it lonely here in this empty house.' Her voice has a trace of an Irish accent, a sign of how long she has been away.

Frances has put on weight since she last saw her, and Bess is unsure if she should bow or curtsey, or even how to address her. 'Thank you for the invitation.' She pushes little Carew forwards, annoyed he's chosen this important moment to be so shy he hides behind her skirts. 'This is Carew, our youngest. His brother Wat is due to graduate from Oxford soon.'

Frances bends to Carew's height. 'And how old are you, young sir?'

'I'm four.' Carew's confident young voice echoes in the empty hall.

Bess prompts him. 'Say, *my lady*, Carew, as I taught you to.'

Carew looks up with his wide blue eyes at the countess but seems in awe of her, so Bess is glad when Frances ushers them into a side room where a log fire crackles in the hearth. She invites them to sit on the burgundy velvet upholstered chairs, and sends a maid for wine and glasses as she sits opposite.

Frances waits until the wine arrives, and signals for her maid to close the door. Bess savours the warm, aromatic taste of the rich wine, a sensation she has almost forgotten. She's also forgotten how many children Frances has, but remembers her eldest is Elizabeth Sidney, daughter of the legendary warrior poet Sir Philip Sidney, and her eldest son is Robert Devereux, named after his ill-fated father.

'How are your children?'

'Well, it's been good to see Elizabeth, but I worry about her.' Frances frowns. 'You know she married Roger Manners, the Earl of Rutland?'

Bess has been closeted with Walter in the Tower for so long she can hardly recall the Earl of Rutland, but remembers Elizabeth as an intelligent and studious girl, with her father's creative spirit. 'I think I met him at court, but he would have been very young, and has probably changed now.'

Frances gives her a knowing look. 'I wish that were true.' She seems keen to change the subject. 'Elizbeth secured us an invitation to the first performance of *The Masque of Queens*, by Ben Jonson, which was quite an experience. The play was performed on a new revolving stage, lit by coloured lights like jewels.' Frances smiles. 'Queen Anna played the lead role. I wouldn't have recognised her if Elizabeth hadn't told me.'

'Ben Jonson is a friend of Walter. He's agreed to take Wat on a tour of the Continent after his graduation.'

Frances frowns. 'I wish we'd asked someone responsible to keep a watchful eye over my son Robin.'

Bess hears her concern. 'What's happened?'

'He left for a tour of the Continent last year, and I've had no word from him since.'

Bess puts her hand to her mouth. If the same happened

with Wat she would never forgive herself. 'There must be something you can do?'

'Sir Francis Bacon has agents on the Continent searching for Robin, and I pray every day to hear he returns to me safe and well.'

'You know Sir Francis Bacon?'

Frances sips her wine before replying in a soft voice. 'He was an advisor to Robin's father.'

Bess can't help thinking Robin's father, the Earl of Essex, was poorly advised, but a plan forms in her mind. 'Sir Francis Bacon is the king's Solicitor General. Do you think he would support my appeal for compensation for the loss of my home at Sherborne?'

Frances nods. 'I am due to meet Sir Francis Bacon soon, and I shall ask him to help you, as a favour.'

Bess smiles at this glimmer of hope in her otherwise bleak future. 'If you can, I will be forever in your debt.'

22

PALACE OF WHITEHALL 1610

Robert Cecil looks pale, and even more hunched in his chair than usual, his hair and beard turning grey. His carved oak desk is covered with books and papers, but Bess sees there is an order to them. He looks up with the slightest smile of welcome as she is shown into his study. 'Forgive me for not standing, Lady Raleigh. My accursed back troubles me again.'

'I'm sorry to hear that, my lord.' It is the truth, as Bess hoped to catch the most powerful man in the country, second only to the king, in a benevolent mood.

'I need not ask you why you've come, my lady, but as I've told you, the king's mind is made up.'

Bess anticipated this. 'There are fine houses more convenient for London than Sherborne, my lord.'

He fixes her with a direct look, as if making a judgement. 'We have known each other for many years, Bess. It might help if I can speak in confidence?'

She sits back in her chair, surprised at his informal use of her name. 'Of course.'

'King James took my family home at Theobalds. The house has great significance for me. It's where I grew up, and the home of my late mother and father. I have many memories there.'

Bess hears the note of sadness in his voice, and recalls the magnificence of Theobalds. 'I—'

He holds up a hand to silence her. 'The king granted me Hatfield Palace, also in Hertfordshire, in compensation. I do my best to make it a worthy home, but I was aggrieved to learn King James made a present of Theobalds to the queen, as if it were some trinket.'

Bess nods in understanding. This is not the outcome she hoped for or expected, but sees his point. 'You suggest I accept the loss of Sherborne, and work for some form of compensation?'

'I make no promises, Bess, other than I will do what I can to support your case.'

'Thank you, my lord. Will you speak to the king on my behalf?'

'I will have to choose my moment, but the king is becoming known for his generosity, so please try to be patient.'

Walter looks like a man with a secret when Bess visits the Garden Tower. At one time he relied on her for all his news. Now the prince is a regular visitor he is privy to more inside information than most men in England, and seems to enjoy surprising her.

Bess kisses him on the cheek. 'Are you going to tell me Prince Henry is to be Prince of Wales?'

Walter grins. 'I wish I could attend the celebrations, but *you* must go, and you can tell me all about it.'

Bess smiles. 'I don't think I'll be invited to the state banquet, but I shall take Carew to see the prince arrive at Chelsea steps. I'm sure it will be quite a spectacle.'

Walter takes his pipe and fills the small bowl with a measure of the dark tobacco he's grown and cured himself. 'My news concerns a certain lady who caused us no end of trouble, through no fault of her own.'

Bess smiles at how he speaks in riddles. 'Are you talking of Arbella Stuart? Countess Frances told me Lady Arbella danced for the queen in a masque. It seems she's been accepted as the king's cousin, and is welcome at his court.'

Walter busies himself with the ritual of lighting his pipe, as if the matter is of little consequence to him. He takes a puff of smoke, and looks up at her. 'Lady Arbella is no longer welcome at court. It seems she married William Seymour, Lord Beauchamp, in secret at Greenwich Palace, against the wishes of the king, and is imprisoned in Lambeth – and Lord Beauchamp is held here in the Tower.'

Bess frowns. 'I have some sympathy for them both, and don't understand why the king has dealt with them so harshly.'

'Lady Arbella has as good a claim to the throne as he does, as a first cousin, twice removed – and he knows it.'

'Dear God, Walter. What will it take for you to learn you cannot say such things?'

He looks around the small cell, as if expecting to see servants lurking. 'Who is there to tell anyone? King James must still see Lady Arbella as a threat, and William Seymour is also in the line of succession.'

Bess scowls. 'Countess Frances says her son Robin was found safe in Italy. He suffered with the smallpox and, although he's recovered, his troubles are far from over. His wife, Frances Howard, is having an affair with that scoundrel Robert Carr, of all people!'

Walter raises an eyebrow. 'I thought Robert Carr was—'

'The king's favourite.' Bess frowns. 'Unfortunately, Robin Devereux never consummated his marriage as his wife was too young, and she hopes for an annulment.'

'Unfortunately?' Walter takes a draw on his pipe and blows a scornful puff of smoke. 'I would say he is well rid of her.'

Bess stares at Thomas Harriot in disbelief. 'Eight thousand pounds?' The huge sum is more than double the compensation she'd dared hope for.

The serious-faced Thomas Harriot gives her a rare smile. 'You've won, my lady, and deserve to be congratulated for your perseverance. In fact, the sum is eight thousand pounds plus interest, with a pension of four hundred pounds a year for Wat after your days.'

Her mind races with the implications. She will no longer worry about how to pay the rent, and can repay the loan from Arthur. Most importantly, she can begin a new search for a suitable wife for Wat. 'Do you know who persuaded the king?' Bess can't believe it can have been her pleading letters, or her brief audience with King James.

Thomas Harriot shakes his head. 'You have friends in high places, my lady. I believe Sir Robert Cecil found the king in a good mood, and was supported by the Solicitor General, Sir Francis Bacon.'

Bess recalls her strange meeting with Robert Cecil. When he told her to be patient she'd thought he meant she would have a longer wait. She has never even met Sir Francis Bacon, and resolves to write a letter of thanks to Countess Frances, who'd been as good as her word. 'How is the money to be paid?'

'I am appointed trustee for the grant, my lady.' He frowns. 'You will not be surprised there are some who lay claim to be Sir Walter's debtors, and would take what they can.'

'Who would do that to us?'

'Adrian Gilbert, for one.'

'I trusted him—' Bess puts her hand to her mouth as she remembers.

'Well, he was the first to lodge a claim.'

'Dear God. How much?'

'Four thousand six hundred and fifty-three pounds.' He must see the look of concern on her face. 'Rest assured, my lady, I consider it my duty to ensure you have every penny to spend as you wish. I have already instructed John Shelbury to act on your behalf in the Court of Chancery. He's a good man, and will also pursue Master Gilbert for costs.'

Bess shields her eyes from the glare of the late spring sunshine reflected off the water as she strains to see the gilded royal barge carrying the prince. She lifts Carew high so he sees above the heads of the crowd jostling for space. Carew is no longer little. A stocky five-year-old, he is heavy in her arms, but the beam on his face is her reward.

Sir William Craven, Lord Mayor of London, and the assembled aldermen of the City Council wait in their fine robes on barges decorated with flags and streamers to welcome the prince. Musicians play a fanfare of trumpets, then drummers and Scottish pipers strike up a rousing tune.

The crowd cheers and men call out, 'God save the prince!' and, 'God save Prince Harry!' as the royal fleet appears. The prince is standing in the bows of his gilded barge and Bess is struck by the contrast between the spindly king and his son and heir.

At sixteen, the handsome prince looks every inch a future king. Tall and broad-chested, he wears a suit of cloth of gold, with the sun glinting from a jewelled sword at his belt. Judging by the reaction of the crowd, Prince Henry is the future of England, and the people have taken him to their heart.

Bess watches as the skilled oarsmen bring the gilded barge to dock at the quayside. Now it is closer she sees the royal coat of arms are supported by a Tudor red dragon and not the chained white unicorn of the Stuarts. Prince Henry has the late Queen Elizabeth's barge, and it seems no one other than her seems to care or even notice.

Prince Henry told Walter he'd wanted to ride into London on his fine white stallion. He'd talked of parading through the city streets at the head of a grand procession of sixteen noble lords, one for each year of his life. The king wished him to arrive at Whitehall from his home at Richmond by river. Bess doubts the king can afford the expense of a state procession for his son and heir.

Instead, a water pageant featuring sea creatures welcomes the prince. A barge is dressed with canvas painted to create the illusion of a great grey whale, and a smaller one resembles a dolphin. Bess laughs at the sight as the 'whale' emits a spurt of water high into the air, but Carew stares entranced, like most of the watching crowd.

A young boy actor of the King's Men players scrambles onto the whale's back. He plays the part of a woman, riding the whale in a golden crown and flowing white robes. His voice resounds across the water as he announces he is Corinea, the spirit of the ancient Queen of Cornwall, and calls out a welcome to Prince Henry on behalf of the city:

'Gracious Prince, and great Duke of Cornwall, I, the good angel Corinea, in honour of this general rejoicing day and to express the endeared affection of London's Lord Mayor and all these worthy citizens, do thus usher them to applaud in this triumph, and let you know their willing readiness by all means possible to love and honour you.'

The crowd applauds and cheers, and the musicians play lively tunes. Street vendors call out, 'Hot pies! Warm mead!' and, 'Fine ale and beer!', adding to the atmosphere of celebration. Bess is surprised at the number of Londoners attending and the warmth of feeling towards the young Scottish prince.

Prince Henry grins as he pulls off his hat and waves it in the air to another rousing cheer and applause from the crowd. Bess hopes to catch his eye, but before she can, it is over. The royal barge heads for Whitehall Palace, followed by the whale and dolphin, and the flotilla of decorated barges, their colourful flags and streamers flapping in the breeze.

Carew is reluctant to leave, and Bess bends so he can hear over the noise of the crowd. 'If you are good, I will bring you next week to see the royal tournament, where men fight each other on horses.'

The third and last day of Prince Henry's celebrations begins at the temporary tiltyard built in front of Whitehall Palace. They are blessed with warm June sunshine, and colourful flags and banners flutter in a gentle breeze.

Bess brings Carew in his new suit of clothes, paid for, like her summer gown, with an advance of the compensation money. They arrive early, and find a good vantage point, opposite the royal canopy of estate, covered with cloth of gold on a raised wooden platform.

She finds space on a low wall for Carew to sit, and promises he can stay up late to see the water battle and fireworks, if he behaves. She looks across at the palace entrance, remembering the many times she'd passed through the high oak doors as the queen's gentlewoman. That life seems to belong to another age.

Bess stays well away from the palaces. She has no wish for another encounter with King James, although he must still be persuaded to grant Walter a royal pardon. She's learned to blend in with the crowd, and has good reason not to draw attention to herself.

Thomas Harriot warned her to be discreet about the amount of compensation. If word gets out she risks being pursued through the courts by men who argue Walter still owes them money for their investment in his adventures.

Carew stares wide-eyed as a knight on a charger canters past with a loud clatter of hooves on cobblestones. The knight wears gilded armour and a flamboyant plume of red feathers in his helmet. His horse is caparisoned in a blue cloth embroidered with silver thread and glittering with pearls.

'When are they going to fight on horses, Mother?'

'Soon, Carew. Be patient.'

A sharp fanfare of trumpets announces the arrival of the king and prince, who take their places. The crowd cheers and applauds, and the purple velvet seats fill with the king's favourites and the prince's young friends.

Bess recognises young William Cecil, as well as Robin Devereux. Colourful pennants she doesn't recognise fly from flagpoles in the light breeze, and she realises they are the garish standards of the Scottish nobles.

The prince looks magnificent in shining cloth of gold, with a gold coronet, studded with jewels, on his head. Bess thinks few would guess King James was King of England, as he looks shabby, with a black felt cap. As if to remind the doubters, the sun flashes from a gold chain around King James's neck.

The Master of the Joust calls out the names of the earls and barons as they ride up to the king and dip their lances in salute. Many of the names are familiar, but Bess is shocked to realise many are the sons of those she once knew. A new generation is taking over, and Prince Henry is their champion.

Carew is spellbound as the first riders charge each other at the gallop and their wooden lances clash on armour. Shards of wood fly into the air and the crowd erupts into another cheer, louder this time, as one of the riders drops his lance and leans in the saddle. The other rider raises his visor to rapturous applause, and bows his head to the king.

Bess recognises one of the riders in the next joust. Robin Devereux wears a scarlet cape over his jousting armour, and it's the first time she's seen him appearing in public as the Earl of Essex. He unseats his opponent, a Scottish noble, to the delight of the crowd. Bess sees Prince Henry stand and applaud Robin's prowess, and calls out to him. His father would be proud.

Carew has never stayed up so late, but the highlight of the prince's celebrations is a spectacular water fight on the Thames at Whitehall. A wooden castle, painted to look as if it is made of stone, floats improbably on the river.

It seems every musician in London plays as the night air fills with music. Bright torches burn to light the scene as ships in full sail bring men dressed as Turkish pirates. Cannons blast wadding at merchants' ships with a deafening roar, but the king's navy comes to the rescue.

Even Carew cheers as the 'Turks' surrender, striking their colours, and retreating to the castle. The crowd gasps as the navy besieges the floating castle, and colourful rockets and fireworks shoot high into the air, exploding overhead with a shower of glowing sparks.

Any doubts Bess had about the king's willingness to meet the costs vanish as she sees the river lit up by dozens of boats and barges carrying flaming torches. The River Thames has become a stage like never before.

Unlike the king, Prince Henry has a way with people, and

even won Walter's loyal support by taking such an interest in his adventures. The king never replied to a single letter from Walter, or from her. Prince Henry is the promised future of England, and the people know it.

23

THE TOWER 1611

THE YEOMAN AT THE TOWER GATES CARRIES A SHARP HALBERD, and bars entry to Bess. 'You are not allowed entry, my lady, on the orders of Sir William Wade, Lieutenant of the Tower.' His gruff voice sounds officious, yet a little unsure of himself.

Bess recognises the yeoman and manages a smile. 'There must be some mistake. I've come to visit my husband and, as you can see, I present no threat to anyone.' She opens the front of her cape, to show she carries nothing, but has forgotten she's chosen to wear a low-cut gown in the new fashion.

The yeoman warder's face reddens as he struggles to look her in the eye. 'I'm sorry, my lady, but I have my orders.'

'Did Sir William give you any reason?'

The man looks uncomfortable, and glances over his shoulder. 'He did not, my lady, but I heard Sir Walter climbed on top of the walls and sought to engage with people passing by.'

'And this is his punishment?'

'I can't say, my lady.' The yeoman makes no move to allow her in.

Bess tries to hide her frustration. 'I must see my husband. He is not well. Would I be allowed to speak to Sir William?'

The yeoman frowns, and calls to another yeoman. 'Will you escort Lady Raleigh to the Lieutenant of the Tower? She wishes to speak with him.'

Bess thanks him and follows the yeoman to Sir William Wade's office. Her instinct is to return home, rather than risk making the situation worse. Sir William Wade can be vindictive, as he's shown with his curfew bell, but she has little enough to lose by trying to reason with him.

Sir William gives her a suspicious glance as she enters his office, and looks troubled. His desk is littered with papers and the empty cup and bowl suggest he's broken his fast. 'Good morning, Lady Raleigh.'

Bess takes a deep breath. 'Good morning, Sir William. I thank you for agreeing to see me, as I know how busy you must be.' She regrets the note of irony in her voice, but he seems not to notice. 'I would like to request your permission to visit my husband.'

He shakes his head. 'Sir Walter is not allowed visitors until further notice.' He gives her an appraising look. 'There is something you might be able to do for me, though.'

Bess feels her neck redden as improper possibilities flash through her mind. She guesses Sir William has somehow heard about the compensation money, and hints at a bribe. With an effort, she manages to keep her voice innocent. 'How can I help you?'

He leans forwards in his chair and looks her in the eye. 'We have a new prisoner who presents me with a difficulty, by refusing her food.'

'A lady?' Bess is surprised and intrigued.

'A *noble* lady.' He scowls. 'I cannot allow her to die on my watch, Lady Raleigh, and hope you might be able to persuade her to see sense.'

'Do I know this lady, Sir William?'

'Her name is Lady Seymour, but you will know her as Lady Arbella Stuart, kinswoman of the king.'

Bess stifles a gasp. She recalls Walter saying King James must see Lady Arbella as a threat, and William Seymour is also in the line of succession. She had not expected to play for such high stakes when she asked to see Sir William. 'I knew her as a junior lady-in-waiting to the late queen, but she was sent away from court after attracting the advances of the Earl of Essex.'

Sir William nods. 'Will you speak with her, Lady Raleigh?'

'If I can persuade her to take her food, will you permit me to see my husband?'

'We shall see, Lady Raleigh. I make no promises, and must be clear: you are not to take any messages to or from Lady Arbella, and she must *not* be allowed to die.'

'I shall do my best, Sir William.'

He sits in silence for a moment, and seems to reach a decision. 'There is one more thing I must tell you. William Seymour has absconded from the Tower.'

'You mean he has escaped?'

'Tell no one, as it could cost me my job, but he was not held under close arrest, and took advantage of that to evade his guards. He is likely to be on the Continent, but I've taken the precaution of keeping a close watch on his wife.'

Bess is not surprised to find Lady Arbella is in the queen's lodgings, part of the former royal palace at the Tower. Someone told her this was where the late queen's mother, Anne Boleyn, spent her last days, a fitting place for a woman who could have been Queen of England.

Bess finds herself thinking how different her life could have been if Arbella had become queen. She could have been her gentlewoman, and Walter the captain of her guard. They could still have Sherborne, and Durham House, and Wat could have hoped for a title, with an heiress for a wife.

A yeoman guards the door, but is expecting her and nods as he selects a key from the bunch at his belt and unlocks the iron-studded oak door. Golden sunlight streams through the large windows on the black-and-white chequerboard floor as she enters. Bess imagines these were Anne Boleyn's privy chambers, and shivers at the thought of them being haunted by her ghost.

Lady Arbella sits hunched in her seat by the window. She turns her pale face to study Bess with dark, distrusting eyes, and looks close to tears. Although ten years younger than Bess at thirty-six, the thick, off-white ruff around her neck and her old-fashioned brocade gown make her look older.

Bess pulls an empty chair closer and sits opposite Lady Arbella. Her well-rehearsed words fail her, now she is confronted by the stark reality of a once-confident woman in complete despair. 'Do you remember me, Arbella? I'm Bess Raleigh.'

'We met at Richmond Palace, in the service of the late queen.' Her voice is soft and well educated but edged with melancholy.

'I remember. You were very young to be at court. I would say no more than fifteen, younger than my son Wat is now.'

'I was fourteen, and quite in awe of the queen. She scared me. I didn't like her, and I think she knew it.'

Bess smiles. 'We were all a little frightened by her. But now she is gone, I find I miss her.'

Arbella lapses into silence, and stares through the iron bars of her window, like one of the caged lionesses. She seems a tragic figure, and Bess feels sympathy for her. She doubts Arbella is aware she once shared her fate, both of them gaoled for marrying for love without permission.

'I was sorry to hear how you have been treated.'

Arbella looks up at her. 'I never challenged King James. I never helped anyone plotting to overthrow him, and considered Queen Anna a friend. Yet here I am.'

'I find the king an unpredictable man, yet he can set you free with a word if he wishes.' A thought occurs to Bess. 'Prince Henry is a regular visitor to my husband, and might appeal to the king on your behalf.'

Arbella shakes her head. 'I've given up hope.'

Bess recalls Sir William Wade's concern, the reason she is here. 'Hope is the one thing that can make time in the Tower bearable. I was taken from my husband and my child, and imprisoned here, in worse conditions, but never gave up hope, and now I am free.'

Arbella gives her an appraising look. 'Why have you come to see me?'

'Sir William Wade, Lieutenant of the Tower, asked me to, but I confess I am concerned to hear you refuse your food. You must be strong, Arbella, or they will have won.'

'They have already won.'

Bess shakes her head. 'I understand something of how you must feel, but you *must not* surrender.'

'I don't understand why you are so concerned about me. Do you not resent me, as the reason your husband lost everything?'

'Walter is the first to say his situation is no fault of yours. His only crime is to have been open-minded to the possibility of your becoming queen.'

'My fault was to have been born a Stuart.' Arbella stares at her, as if seeing her differently. 'My parents both died when I was a child, and I had to live with my grandmother, at Hardwick Hall in Derbyshire.'

'I knew her, when I was at court. I recall she was a formidable lady.'

'My grandmother was ever the matchmaker, and began, when I was only eight years old, to look for a betrothal to some great English noble. She even tried to marry me to Robert Dudley, Earl of Leicester, but her plan was thwarted, of course. My grandmother died of a winter chill three years ago.' There is no trace of regret in Arbella's voice.

'I'm sorry, I didn't know. I've been here in the Tower with my husband for the past six years, and have lost track of what's happened in the world outside.'

Arbella's voice is flat, and tinged with regret as she continues. 'My grandmother lived to over eighty years old, and was one of the wealthiest women in England when she passed away. I rebelled against her wish to control my life and, as a consequence, was written out of her will.'

'That was when you married William Seymour?'

'No.' She turns to look at Bess. 'We married in secret at Greenwich Palace in June last year. I believed King James would understand. But I was wrong.' She frowns. 'Someone told the king less than a month later. He ordered me held under house arrest at Sir Thomas Parry's house in Lambeth. William was imprisoned here in the Tower. He managed to escape, and now I have no idea where he is.' She gives Bess a pleading look. 'Can you take a message to Queen Anna for me?'

Bess thinks fast. 'I can ask permission of the Lieutenant of the Tower, but he forbids messages between prisoners.' She manages a smile as a thought occurs to her. 'He might agree if you will eat the food he provides, as he worries about you.'

Arbella stares at her in surprise. 'I would be grateful.'

Bess knows Sir William Wade well enough to understand that he will wish to be sure Arbella is not on any kind of hunger strike before he will allow her to see Walter. 'I will return in a few days, when you have regained your strength.'

Bess finds herself writing to Walter for the first time in many years. She is guarded in her choice of words, as she knows Sir William Wade could decide he must read her letter. At the same time, she wants Walter to know she is trying her best to be allowed to visit him.

She tells him about her visit to Arbella, but doesn't mention her request for Bess to take a note to the queen on her behalf. She will ask Sir William's permission, but knows she must choose her moment well, and find him in a rare good mood.

Bess hesitates to share her news from Thomas Harriot about Walter's half-brother, Adrian Gilbert. It took a year to resolve in the Court of Chancery, but her lawyer, John Shelbury, had Gilbert's claim for over four thousand pounds dismissed. She tells him Carew has his first tutor, Master Adams, who teaches him to read and write.

Bess sprinkles fine sand over the drying ink and picks up the letter from Walter that one of the yeomen of the Tower gave her. Like all his letters, it is unsealed, and has probably been read by Sir William or one of his men to check the contents. She supresses the pang of regret it's not addressed to her but to another woman.

She cannot resist reading the letter, and justifies her curiosity by telling herself she cannot allow her husband to write anything which might upset Queen Anna. She mutters a curse as she reads the opening lines.

I did lately presume to send unto Your Majestie the copie of a letter written to my Lord Treasurer towching Guiana.

. . .

Walter takes advantage of her absence to rekindle his ambitions to return to El Dorado, and must have somehow sent a letter to Robert Cecil which she had no chance to intercept. As Bess reads on, it seems he must have had no reply, and his old melancholy has returned.

God doth witness that I never sought such imployment, for all the gold in the earth could not invite me to travel after miserie and death, both which I had bine likelier to have overtaken in that voyage.

Bess frowns. Walter is suffering more than she thought.

For my extreme shortness of breath doth grow so fast on me, with the despair of obtaining so much grace to walk with my keeper up the hill within the Tower. I am subject every day to suffer other mens offences rather so desire to dye, once for all, and thereby to give end to the miseries of this life, than to strive against the ordinance of God, who is a new judge of my innocence towards the King, and doth know me.
    Your Majesties most humble and most bound vassal.

W. Raleigh.

Bess makes another visit to Lady Arbella. Walter's worsening condition troubles her, and she must see him as soon as she can, or fears there will be consequences. Sir William Wade told her he made no promises, but she prays he notices an improvement in his troublesome prisoner, and keeps his part of their deal.

    Arbella sits by her window, her long hair piled high in the

fashion of Queen Anna. She wears a gown of embroidered brocade, and has a gold crucifix on a chain around her neck. She doesn't smile when Bess is shown in to her chambers, yet her air of melancholy is replaced by a glint in her eye which suggests a new resolve.

'Good morning, Bess.' Arbella holds up a fold of parchment. 'I have written a letter to the queen.'

Bess takes the seat opposite her. She is pleased to see Arbella's health has returned, an encouraging sign she must be eating again. 'Good day to you, Arbella. I will have to take your letter to Sir William Wade, so I hope the contents are not critical of your treatment here.'

Arbella hands her the note. 'You may read it, if you wish. It's only a plea for Queen Anna to consider the injustice of my situation.'

Bess could tell her Walter made similar pleas to the queen with no success, but remembers Arbella needs hope. 'I must take your letter to Sir William, and if he is in agreement I will try to deliver it to the queen in person.'

'I am grateful to you, Bess.' Arbella shows the briefest smile. 'I will tell you what happened after my marriage was discovered, if you have the time.'

'I confess I am curious, and time is one thing I'm never short of these days.'

Arbella sits in silence for a moment. 'King James sent me off to the Bishop of Durham. I expect he thought that would be far enough to be out of the way.'

'Walter often quotes the old saying, out of sight is out of mind.'

'My husband's servant, Markham, came to tell me William planned to escape from the Tower disguised as a carter, and I was to find a way to meet him at an inn at Blackwall, by the Thames. I faked an illness when we reached Barnet, and escaped dressed as a man.'

Bess smiles at the thought. 'I heard your husband escaped, but they don't know how he did it.'

'I was told he exchanged clothes with a carter, bringing a load of wood in a wagon to the watergate, and marched out through the Byward Gate without a challenge. Markham brought me a wig, a black hat, cloak and even a sword. He had horses ready, and we rode through the night.' Arbella looks wistful. 'We waited for my husband for as long as we dared, then boarded a ship bound for Calais, but I was captured in the English Channel, and brought back here to the Tower.'

'Do you know what became of your husband?'

Arbella shakes her head. 'I can only pray he made it to Paris, and still waits for me there.'

Bess takes a deep breath as Sir William studies the letter from Arbella to the queen. He takes his time, and scowls as he reaches the end. She had decided long ago that the Lieutenant of the Tower was a hard man to please, and an even harder man to read.

His dark eyes stare at her as if she could be up to no good. 'I cannot allow her to appeal to the queen. The risk of angering the king is too great – and *that*, Lady Raleigh, can only have one consequence.'

'I only promised to ask your permission, and hope you will agree that I've done as you asked, Sir William.' She hates herself for having to flatter this cruel man who keeps her from her husband, but Walter's life might depend on it.

Sir William locks Arbella's letter in the drawer of his desk and sits in silence for a moment, as if weighing up his options. 'I am grateful to you, my lady. I would not have wished to order a lady, the king's cousin, to be fed by force.'

Bess manages a smile, although the thought appals her. 'You will allow me to see my husband?'

Sir William nods. 'You will be pleased to know he begs for your return, and claims his life is greatly impoverished by your absence.' He leans forwards in his chair. 'I hope you will ensure your husband learns his lesson. I cannot have him complaining to the public of his situation.'

24

THE TOWER 1612

WALTER IS CHANGED BY HIS TIME ALONE, AND BESS SUSPECTS his eyesight is failing. He leans close to his books to read, and has become absent-minded, forgetting where he's put his pipe and staying in his bed until late. He spends every waking hour working on his history of the world, which fills several thick notebooks.

Bess is pleased he seems to have a new appreciation of her, and even shows some affection. They celebrate his sixtieth birthday at the end of January with a bottle of mulled wine, smuggled in by Bess at some risk. The warmth lifts her spirits, and she raises her cup in a toast.

'Here's to freedom, and the hope of a brighter future.'

Walter lifts his cup. 'To freedom.' His voice lacks conviction.

Bess watches his face as he takes a deep drink of the mulled wine, his first for many years. 'It's time we made a proper plan to secure your pardon.' She tastes another sip of her mulled wine and relishes the rich, sweet scent of honey and herbs, precious cinnamon and cloves – tokens of her new prosperity.

'Our best hope is that you are on such good terms with the

prince. Have you asked Prince Henry to appeal to the king on your behalf?'

'I've been waiting for the right moment. I thought to ask him when my history of the world is published.'

'How long will that take?'

Walter shrugs. 'Another year.'

'That's far too long to wait. When is the prince due to come and see you next?'

'I never know when he is going to visit.'

Bess thinks for a moment. 'My brother believes the king is running short of money. The late queen left him with an empty treasury, and he tried to save money when Prince Henry was made Prince of Wales. It seems it's time to show the prince your maps of Guiana.' She takes a drink of wine, hoping she will not regret her suggestion.

Walter brightens. 'The prince takes a great interest in my expeditions. I can tell him if we wait much longer the Spanish will beat us to any gold that is to be found.'

'You must promise not to sail off to Guiana and leave me and the boys to worry about whether you will ever return.'

Walter drains the last dregs from his cup of mulled wine. 'You have my word, Bess. I was never much hap as a sailor, and at sixty I'm too old for new adventures.'

Wat's visit is the last before leaving for the Continent. Tall and handsome, he's graduated from Corpus Christi College. No longer a boy, he has a new confidence, bordering on arrogance. He reminds Bess of Walter in his youth, with the same jaunty set of his cap and the glint of adventure in his eye.

'Don't worry, Mother.' He grins, an echo of his father. 'Master Jonson promises to never let me from his sight.'

Bess embraces him. He smells of smoke, another of his

father's habits. 'You must write as often as you can, and do as Master Jonson tells you.'

Wat studies her for a moment. 'Keep an eye on Father.' He seems keen to leave.

'I shall pray for your safe return.' Bess watches him go, proud to see her son becoming a man.

Bess is escorted by her brother Arthur, and wears a new mourning dress bought for the occasion, the end of an era. She takes Arthur's arm to steady herself as they climb the uneven path of flint cobbles to the old Norman church of St Etheldreda's at Hatfield.

Bess looks up as the late spring sunshine glints from the high windows of Hatfield House. 'I visited here on a progress with the late queen. She told us she was living at Hatfield House when she was informed of the death of Queen Mary, and she became Queen of England.'

Arthur studies the new windows with an appraising eye. 'Those must have cost a small fortune. Venetian glass, if I'm not mistaken. I'll wager the king will make a present of Hatfield House to one of his young gentlemen.' There is no hint of disapproval in his voice, but Bess glances over her shoulder to be sure her brother is not overheard.

They pass through the silent crowd of villagers, many in mourning, others no doubt curious to see any famous people attending the funeral. Bess is glad of her anonymity, despite her infamous husband, and recalls how Robert Cecil hadn't seemed himself the last time she saw him.

Arthur interrupts her thoughts. 'I think Robert Cecil suffered for many years. I heard the pain in his back was so bad he could hardly ride to Bath to take the waters.'

'Walter says the waters of Bath are of little enough use. He says they are spring water, and are most likely impure, so do more harm than good.'

Arthur nods. 'I spoke with Robert Cecil's servant. He said his master placed great store on the waters, and would sit for hours in the baths.' He falls silent as they enter the gloom of the church and find a space in the rear pews.

Bess raises a black-gloved hand to William Cecil. Now a grown man of twenty-one, he has a new burden of responsibilities as the second Earl of Salisbury. Bess is pleased he's seen and acknowledged her. William is close to the king, as a companion of Prince Henry, and will support the idea of a pardon for Walter.

The bells high in the tower begin a mournful tolling. Robert Cecil's coffin is carried in by six faithful retainers, dressed in black. Bess is surprised by the absence of high-status mourners, or anyone representing the king. Like Walter, to the old families, Robert Cecil would always be a commoner, raised above his proper place in the world.

She also notes the lack of extravagance, for an earl and Lord High Treasurer. The coffin is plain, draped with a black cloth and Robert Cecil's Order of the Garter.

Her mind wanders as the grey-bearded minister begins the formal service. Bess remembers how the queen rewarded Robert Cecil's loyal service by calling him her *imp*, and her *pygmy*. Bess saw Robert Cecil's false smile at the queen's odd humour, a cruel jest. Even at the end, she'd heard King James mocked his hunched back, and called him his *little beagle*.

She always suspected Robert Cecil revealed her secret marriage to Walter to increase his own favour with the queen. It took time to find forgiveness. She'd appealed for his help to prevent Walter sailing in search of his city of gold, El Dorado. Although he must have known the voyage could cost Walter his life, Robert Cecil made no effort to talk him out of it. Instead, he'd made the voyage possible by becoming one of Walter's investors. Bess wasn't sorry to hear he made a poor profit from his betrayal of her wishes.

Robert Cecil was dealt a poor hand at birth, with his crooked back and strange demeanour, yet more than made up for it by becoming a worthy successor to his father. It is possible he planned for King James to rule long before the death of Queen Elizabeth.

The minister's voice echoes in the old church as he reads the prayers. '*Man that is born of a woman hath but a short time to live, and is full of misery. He cometh up and is cut down like a flower; he flieth as it were a shadow, and never continueth in one stay. In the midst of life we be in death.*'

Bess remembers Robert Cecil's gratitude after the death of his wife, Elizabeth, when she agreed to care for William. He'd asked her to join him for supper, and said, 'I confess I find dining alone a somewhat lonely business.' Something changed between them at that moment, and she will miss him.

She clasps her hands together as the minister finishes his prayers. '*Thou knowest, Lord, the secrets of our hearts, shut not up thy merciful eyes to our prayers: but spare us Lord most holy, O God most mighty, O holy and merciful saviour, thou most worthy judge eternal, suffer us not at our last hour for any pains of death to fall from thee, Amen.*'

The lack of news from Wat keeps Bess awake at night, as she cannot help recalling the concerns of Countess Frances. Walter points out that it's no simple matter for a letter to reach her from the Continent, but she still worries.

There is talk of plague on the Continent, and Robin Devereux bears the scars of the smallpox. Part of her longs for the simpler life she'd had at Sherborne, when Wat was content to study Latin in his chambers. Despite herself, she imagines her eldest son robbed and destitute in some foreign town, or suffering a fever with no doctors, or anyone to care for him.

When the letter arrives it is not addressed in Wat's familiar script, and she breaks open the dark wax seal with a sense of dread. The writer is Ben Jonson, and he begins with a long and profuse apology for failing in his duty to their son.

Bess gasps as she reads on. Wat is in Paris, frolicking with ladies of no virtue, and it seems there is little Ben Jonson can do to prevent him. She must take the letter to show Walter straight away, although there is little they can do. She wishes she hadn't listened to Walter. Too late, she wishes she'd sent Thomas Harriot to the Continent with Wat.

Walter scowls when he reads the letter. 'This is *not* what I had in mind when I spoke of Wat completing his education.' His voice is stern, yet Bess hears a trace of pride. 'William Cecil caught the smallpox, but it looks like Wat aims to return with the French pox.'

Bess stares at him in alarm. 'He must come home, before it's too late.'

'It's already too late. If we ask Ben Jonson to bring Wat back, it will take over a week for our letter to reach Paris.' He studies the letter. 'From what it says here, I suspect persuading him to return will be no easy task.'

Bess takes the letter back. 'I shall reply to Master Ben Jonson, and ask him to bring Wat home. We have to think of our son's reputation, or we will never find him a suitable wife.'

The red-and-gold liveried royal messenger arrives at the Garden Tower an hour before the curfew bell. Bess feels her pulse racing. There cannot be many reasons to send a messenger from the palace. Has the king relented and decided to grant Walter a pardon at last?

Walter breaks open the seal on the letter, but sits back in his chair, and utters a curse as he reads. He looks up at Bess. 'The prince is ill, and the queen wishes me to prepare a tonic, as her doctors are at a loss.' He hands the letter to her. 'They've shaved his head, cut open a live cockerel and put it to his feet, and bled him.' He shakes his head. 'The best they can think of now is to send for the Archbishop of Canterbury to pray for him.'

The writing is neat and regular, a well-educated script, but looks hurried, and is more of an informal note than a letter. Written to Walter by the queen, there is no preamble, and it is signed *Anna R.*

The matter is more serious than Walter suggests. The queen says the prince took a swim in the River Thames, for a wager, but a high price was paid. He suffers from a tertian fever from which he struggles to recover, and she pleads with Walter to save the life of her eldest son.

Bess looks up at Walter. 'Would any of your tonics help cure a tertian fever?'

Walter shrugs. 'I can make a restorative cordial of gentian and mace with a little mint and sugar. It is not a cure, but will lift his spirits better than his hapless doctor's venesection, and could be all he needs.' He makes it sound a simple matter. 'We are fortunate the prince is strong, and will recover soon enough.'

Bess is not so certain. 'What if the prince worsens? Is there not a risk they could put the blame on your cordial, to protect themselves?'

Walter looks thoughtful. 'I shall suggest one of them tries the cordial first, to make sure there are only restorative effects.'

The bells of every church in London join the mournful clanging that can only mean one thing. Prince Henry, the shining hope of the country, heir to the throne and future King of England and Scotland, is dead. It falls to Bess to break the sad news to Walter, and he stares at her in disbelief.

'He cannot be.' Walter stares at his pile of notebooks, his history of the world, with its dedication to the prince.

Bess takes Walter's hand. 'There is no mistake. The whole of London is in mourning.'

Walter slumps into his chair and pulls his pipe from the pocket of his doublet. He doesn't speak as he fills the small bowl and lights it with a taper. With a jolt, Bess understands. Walter has not only lost a patron. Prince Henry became like a third son, and one who saw him as a hero. The prince was his best hope of a pardon, and now the prospect is further away than ever.

When Walter speaks his voice is flat. 'Dear God. Such a great waste. Henry should have known the Thames is an open sewer and carries every disease known to man, as well as a few no doubt yet to be discovered.'

Bess sits in silence for a moment. She sees the signs and worries Walter's fits of melancholy will return. 'The king ordered he is to lie in state for a month at St James's Palace, until his funeral at Westminster Abbey on the seventh of December.'

'You must go and pay our respects.'

'My brother offered to escort me.' Bess has a vision of the empty pews at Robert Cecil's funeral. This time the nobility will be vying with each other to attend.

Walter stares again at his pile of notebooks. 'I shall finish my work on a history of the world, but now it is to be a tribute to Prince Henry.'

Arthur guesses there are more than two thousand mourners lining the streets to watch the funeral procession pass through the city of London. They hear the shrill music of fifes and beating of drums long before the procession comes into view.

It seems strange to have a young boy walking, leading the procession, his mourning dress serving to emphasise his slight build. He looks as if he struggles with the weight of the sword he carries at his belt, and his face is fixed in a frown. Arthur must have seen the puzzled look on Bess's face, as he touched her arm to have her attention.

'That's young Prince Charles, chief mourner – and now the new heir to the throne. I believe he is twelve years old, although I confess he looks younger.' Bess studies the boy's anxious face, and guesses he's not leading the slow procession by choice, as he looks as if he would rather be anywhere else.

Bess gasps at the sight of the lifelike, painted plaster face of the prince's effigy, on top of the coffin. Dressed in the robes and gold coronet the prince wore at his investiture as Prince of Wales two years before, the head wobbles from side to side as the hearse rides over the cobblestones.

A black-draped carriage flanked by marching mourners follows, and Bess expects to see the king and queen, but instead sees the pale face of a young woman. This must be the mysterious Princess Elizabeth, the sixteen-year-old sister of Henry and Charles. Her wedding was to be a great celebration, but is postponed by Prince Henry's untimely death.

Unlike Robert Cecil's poorly attended funeral, it seems the entire court rides behind the ornate hearse with its unsettling effigy. Bess turns to Arthur. 'Where are the king and queen?'

'I heard the queen retired to her chambers in mourning, and the king remains at Theobalds.' He frowns. 'The king needs to be seen by the people at a time such as this.'

Bess glances to see if anyone overhears. Like Walter, Arthur seems unconcerned to be outspoken about the king, but she worries there could be consequences. 'I can only imagine how devasting this must be for them both.'

They watch as the coffin is carried through the great doors of Westminster Abbey. The young prince is to be laid to rest in the vault of his grandmother, Mary Queen of Scots, in the south aisle of Henry VII's chapel. The hope of a nation is gone forever, taken before his time. Bess doubts the young Prince Charles, now the Duke of York, can ever be his equal.

25

THE TOWER 1613

CHRISTMAS AND THE NEW YEAR PROVE A STRUGGLE FOR BESS as she tries her best to prevent Walter's mood sinking into melancholy. After some persuasion, he's resumed his work on the history of the world, but puffs continuously on his pipe, filling his 'study' with the acrid smell of tobacco smoke.

The affection he'd shown Bess evaporated like a morning mist on the Thames. Since the death of the prince he's taken to cursing his bad luck, and seems to resent how Bess comes and goes as she pleases. It doesn't help when he discovers she's kept the true amount of compensation from him.

'Thomas Harriot thought I knew, and let slip the details. Do you not trust me with the truth?'

'It's nothing to do with trust, Walter.' Bess tries to keep the irritation from her voice. 'Thomas Harriot told me to keep the amount secret—'

'Secret from me?' His interruption echoes. 'It's *my* money, after all.'

Bess does her best to remain calm. 'He said to keep it secret for fear of claims from those who say you owe them money.'

'And you've been spending it on fine gowns and lace ruffs, while I live in rags?'

'The compensation money pays our rent, and Wat's expenses.' She fights the edge to her voice as she challenges him. 'Where do you think the money comes from for all the tobacco you've been smoking? How do you imagine I pay the fees of Carew's tutors, or feed and clothe your family?'

Walter curses under his breath. 'I can't have any money. I am legally dead.'

Bess frowns, and decides to ignore his outburst, even if what he says is the truth. 'If you ask Thomas Harriot he will confirm the money is safe in his care, and all I've been using is the interest. If Wat cannot have Sherborne as his inheritance, he will at least be able to live in comfort after our days.'

Walter looks up at her. 'Where is Wat now?'

'Still in Antwerp, as far as I know.' The thought worries Bess. 'He wrote, begging for money, but I've only sent enough to enable him to return.'

Walter frowns. 'Have you heard from Ben Jonson?'

Bess shakes her head. 'There was no mention of him in Wat's last letter, so I wonder if they are still together.'

'We must find him a wife, and see him settled. Prince Henry—' Walter's voice chokes, and he seems to struggle to remain composed.

'We must also find him gainful employment. I shall ask my brother for help.'

'Prince Henry was planning a bridge over the Thames at Westminster. He showed me the plans.' Walter brightens. 'I will recommend some good people, like your brother, and Thomas Harriot. Wat can make his name if he leads the scheme, and makes it a success.'

Bess is unsurprised at how little Walter knows his own son. Wat was a renegade before he travelled to the Continent with Ben Jonson. Now it seems he is a drunkard, and Bess would not like to think where he's spent the money she sent him. She nods, but says nothing. It's best for Walter to cling to the hope of better things for Wat.

Carew's eyes sparkle with excitement as the first of the fireworks explode high in the evening sky with a boom and a crackling shower of stars. He joins the cheers and waves his cap in the air as they watch the celebrations for the forthcoming wedding of the young Princess Elizabeth. The grandest wedding in living memory, this is a turning point for the royal family, and for the country.

Although the wedding was delayed for months, the sad procession of Henry's sombre funeral seems too recent to Bess. Carew knows nothing about the untimely death of the prince, and Bess is relieved the sad event is behind them. Looking at the excited crowd, it seems the entire population of London feels the same.

She's heard the fireworks are supposed to represent Edmund Spenser's poem, *The Faerie Queen*, celebrating the reign of Queen Elizabeth. Bess supposes the people of London are intended to see parallels with Princess Elizabeth, but although the princess is named after the late queen, they could hardly be more different.

Young and beautiful, the princess redeems the royal family's absence, and begins to replace Prince Henry in the hearts of the people. She dresses in fine silks and satin. Fashionable ladies copy her taste for plumes of white feathers, wide farthingales and her embroidered bodies, stiffened with whalebone.

A salvo of rockets whoosh into the dark sky from barges moored in a row on the Thames, exploding with a series of deafening bangs to another cheer from the crowd. The royal family watch from the river gallery of Whitehall Palace, which has large windows with views of the water in both directions.

King James, a rare visitor to the city, prefers to hunt with the young groom, Count Frederick of the Palatinate, and his rowdy German companions, in the forests of Theobalds. The word is that the king made Frederick a knight of the Order of the Garter in St George's Chapel, and treats him as more of a son than he does young Charles.

Returned to the Palace of Whitehall for his daughter's wedding, this is the first time the king has been seen in public since the death of Prince Henry. Queen Anna hides herself away in her chambers at Somerset House, and there are rumours she's lost her mind in her grief over the death of her son.

It's said no one dares to mention Prince Henry within Queen Anna's hearing, for fear of sending her into another fit of despair. Bess's brother Arthur heard it was the prince who made the choice of Count Frederick. A Protestant, the young count's ancestors include kings of England, Aragon and Sicily, but the queen is said to be against the match, and says her daughter can do better.

Carew, who will be eight this year, is excited by the prospect of another 'sea battle' on the river. A wooden fort, built on the riverbank close to the palace, will be attacked by a fleet of royal warships. Bess hears there are to be grand masques in the palace as part of the wedding celebrations but, as usual, she is not invited.

A sharp February breeze threatens to spoil the sea battle the following afternoon. Bess and Carew watch from a high vantage point opposite Lambeth Steps, where a cordon of tethered boats keep the river open for the incessant flow of

Thames wherries. There are more crowds than ever, with street vendors doing a roaring trade in hot pies, and cups of ale and mulled wine. Bess buys Carew a colourful flag on a stick, which he waves in the air.

She is surprised to recognise Queen Anna, with her daughter Princess Elizabeth, wrapped in furs at the side of King James. Seated under a red-and-gold canopy of state on the privy stairs at Whitehall, they seem untroubled by the noise of the long silk banners each side flapping in the wind. The royal family must have a good view of the action, while staying away from the crowds.

The show is supposed to be a battle between Christian and Turkish ships, although it's not easy to tell which is which from the riverbank. A brightly painted Venetian caravel, no doubt captured in some real sea battle, defends the wooden castle, bristling with real cannons, with colourful flags flying from high turrets.

Gun crews from the royal armouries dress in fanciful 'Turkish' costumes of red jackets with blue sleeves. They shout curses to the sailors on the ships and call out insults to the crowd. Some brandish great curved scimitars, while others prepare the guns with wadding and gunpowder.

The battle begins with the Christian ships opening fire with a deafening roar and flash of powerful cannons. The crowds cheer, and Carew shrieks with delight as one of the watchtowers is set ablaze. The Turkish surrender in some haste as the brisk breeze fans the flames, which soon spread to the rest of the wooden castle.

Bess will tell Walter he didn't miss much, and many of the watching crowd seem to expect more of a battle. Carew coughs as grey smoke from the burning castle drifts over the crowd, and she decides it's time to go. She later hears several sailors were injured, and plans for a longer battle were abandoned.

The grand marriage of Princess Elizabeth takes place on a frosty morning the following Sunday, in the new chapel of Whitehall Palace. Bess returns with Carew and her maid Eleanor, as well as her sister-in-law, Anne, who brings her daughter Annie, who is good company for Carew. They wear furs over their best gowns, with Carew in a fur-lined cape over a new doublet and hose of blue silk, and a velvet cap with a fashionable white feather.

The wedding procession is planned to circle around the palace of Whitehall so the wedding party can be seen by the watching crowds. A raised wooden scaffold with a walkway crosses the open courtyard, and the crowds cheer as King James appears at the top of the stairs to the court gate. He looks unsteady on his feet as he leads the wedding party along the temporary walkway to the royal chapel.

Bess tries not to laugh as she sees what King James is wearing. He's chosen to dress for his daughter's wedding in the Scottish style, which looks strange to English tastes. The king has long pheasant feathers in his cap, and wears colourful skirts under a gaudy Spanish cape. His long red stockings are possibly a defence against the cold, yet look more suited to ladies of ill repute.

Elderly Baron John Harington of Exton, whose work as her guardian will end once she is married, escorts Princess Elizabeth. Eight young daughters of earls carry her train, all dressed in matching gowns of flowing white satin embroidered with white pearls.

The jewels in the imperial crown shine in rare winter sun on her golden-amber hair, flowing long to her waist as a sign of her purity. Princess Elizabeth looks magnificent in richly embroidered white satin and cloth of silver, with a diamond necklace, her wedding gown glittering with pearls and diamonds.

Behind them follow Queen Anna and her ladies, all dressed in white, with pear-shaped pearls decorating their hair. Bess is ten years older than the queen yet she thinks they look about the same age. The death of the prince has taken its toll on his mother, and casts a shadow over what should be a happy state occasion.

Bess sees the young princess shiver in the cold as she offers a nervous smile to the crowds. She remembers how her cousin, Robert Catesby, and the others plotted to kidnap the nine-year-old Elizabeth. If they'd succeeded they would have deposed King James and raised Elizabeth as a Catholic queen. This marriage, to a German Protestant, would never have taken place.

Princess Elizabeth will leave for her new life in Heidelberg, and it's possible she will never see her parents again. Bess hopes this is a love match, yet in her heart she doubts it. It saddens her to see the beautiful young princess, who could be the future of the country, sacrificed as a brood mare to establish an alliance with the Palatinate.

Walter puffs on his pipe and has the look of a man with a secret. Bess plays along with his game, pretending disinterest, yet before long can contain her curiosity no longer. She worries he's been up to something, and doesn't relish the prospect of being banished from visiting him again.

'What is it, Walter?' She looks him in the eye. 'Have you had a visitor, or another letter?'

'No, but I have news which could change everything. A yeoman warder told me Sir Thomas Overbury is locked up in the Tower dungeons, on the king's orders.'

Bess raises an eyebrow. 'I remember him as Robert Cecil's man, who thought himself something of a poet.'

'Well, now he's the man of another Robert – our friend Robert Carr, master of the Sherborne estates.'

'What did Thomas Overbury do to be locked up here?'

Walter shrugs. 'I can only guess his punishment somehow involves his relationship with Robert Carr. He has aroused the king's anger, and must pay the price.'

Bess studies his face and sees there is more to tell. 'You said your news could change everything?'

'The yeoman warder told me Thomas Overbury vomits every day, and is not expected to live.' He gives her a meaningful look. 'They suspect he's been poisoned.'

Bess sits in silence for a moment. 'There is a chance the king grows tired of Robert Carr since his plan to marry Lady Essex. Do you think someone wishes to prevent Thomas Overbury telling what he knows?' She looks up at Walter. 'I hardly dare to hope this could mean Sherborne is one day returned to us.'

'I thought the same, and there is only one way I can be put into the king's mind.' Walter takes another puff on his pipe. 'The royal treasury must be running short of funds after paying for the wedding of the princess. King James could be amenable to new discussions about a voyage to Guiana – if I mention there is a shipload of gold to be found.'

Bess senses the return of Walter's old obsession with El Dorado, the city of gold. 'I would like to see the letter this time.' She frowns. 'It might be our last chance, so we must be certain to make the most of the opportunity.'

Walter nods in agreement, but is quick to change the subject. 'What news is there of Wat? I had expected to hear from him by now.'

'Not good, I'm afraid. My brother Arthur heard from Sir Henry Wotton that Wat is in the Netherlands, and challenged someone to a duel.' Her throat runs dry at the thought. 'The king issued a proclamation making duelling illegal. If anyone kills someone in a duel it will be murder, yet young men still die defending their honour.'

Walter curses under his breath. 'Does Arthur know who this duel is with – or what led to it?'

'Only that it somehow involves a servant of the Howards and the reputation of Lady Elizabeth Bassett.'

'The heiress he was supposed to marry?' Walter scowls. 'No good can come of that. Wat should put the past behind him, and not make enemies of the Howards.'

'A relative of ours, Sir John Throckmorton, is Lieutenant Governor of the garrison at Flushing. Arthur wrote to him, asking him to prevent any duel, and have Wat returned to us.'

Walter shakes his head. 'Let us pray he can do so in time. When Wat comes home we must find him a role in life.'

26

THE TOWER 1614

WALTER IS UP EARLY AND SITS HUNCHED OVER HIS DESK, HIS face serious as he writes. He turns as Bess enters. 'Thomas Harriot tells me Sir Ralph Winwood is appointed as the new Principal Secretary of State and a privy councillor, taking the place of Robert Cecil.'

Bess sits in her usual seat to warm her hands by the fire in the hearth. Another icy winter has seen the River Thames freeze over, but she's paid for coal to make the fires in the Garden Tower burn hotter and for longer, to keep the cold at bay.

'I'm surprised it's taken them so long. I remember Ralph Winwood when he was a clerk to the Privy Council.' She gives him a wry look. 'He always seemed a bit earnest to me, too eager to please, but it seems to have paid off well for him.'

'I can't say I recall him, but Thomas Harriot says Ralph Winwood is a devout Protestant, and was sent as an ambassador to The Hague, where he made a name for himself through his hatred of the Spanish.'

'You should get on well enough with him then.' Bess smiles as she sees he's understood the note of irony in her voice. 'If you can win his confidence, Ralph Winwood would be a useful ally at court.'

'More than an ally, Bess. I need him to be my advocate. He writes letters for the king, and must have his confidence and trust.' He holds up one of his notebooks for her to see. 'I've made a start on a draft letter to Ralph Winwood.'

'About a new expedition to Guiana?' Bess feels a stab of regret at encouraging him to resurrect his plans.

Walter shakes his head. 'A first step towards the bigger prize: to have me released to oversee the preparations.' His eyes shine in the amber glow from the fire at the prospect. I thought I would begin with explaining how I was working with his predecessor, and hope he replies asking for more information.'

Bess has seen Walter's attempts at subtlety before. 'May I see what you've written so far?'

Walter frowns, no doubt anticipating her criticism as he hands her the draft, and Bess reads.

Honourable Sir, an enterprise which I had heretofore propounded to the late treasurer Cecil, which although at sundry times he seemed willing to imbrace, yet always upon the conclusion he withdrew himself.

'Doesn't that make it seem Robert Cecil was against your plan?'

Walter nods. I thought about that, and decided it's best to be honest. Ralph Winwood is no doubt aware of my proposals for another expedition, and knows Robert Cecil chose not to invest, but you must read on.'

Bess returns to Walter's letter, struggling a little with the alterations and crossed out words.

. . .

It is true my times are so far gone I am unfit, and as I fear unable to undergo so great a travail. I hear of many actions to inrich His Majesty, or at least to supply his present occasions, but some are devised to inrich those who shall be employed in them. This of mine in which I have no other end than to repay His Majestie some part of the debt I owe him.

Walter gives her a questioning look. 'What is your opinion?'

'For once, Walter, I see a plan to have you freed from this prison. I know you hope he will reply with questions, but it can do no harm to send him your previous letter to Robert Cecil – and also your last letter to the king, as proof of your commitment.'

Walter takes back his draft and studies it with a frown. His future could depend on the wording. 'You are right, Bess, and I shall have Thomas Harriot make fresh copies of the maps of Guiana. Ralph Winwood is an astute man, able to reach his own conclusion.'

'There is no one better qualified than you to oversee preparations for a new voyage.' Bess sees the glint of ambition return to his eye. 'But you will not propose to sail on the voyage yourself?'

'I make no promises, Bess.'

'You said you are not fit for such a journey.'

'You know I would rather die in search of adventure than locked away in this dismal gaol.' He gives her a wry smile. 'Let us leave it to the will of God – and Sir Ralph Winwood, Principal Secretary.'

Wat surprises them with an unexpected visit. He will be twenty in November, and his time on the Continent has turned him from a boy to a man. He has a well-trimmed beard and wears a soldiers' doublet of black leather, with a dagger at his belt. The greatest change is his confidence, which reminds Bess of Walter in his youth.

Bess realises she no longer knows her eldest son, and has many questions, not least to know why he hasn't written for months. 'I am relieved to have you back safe, but why did it take so long for you to return?'

Wat glances at his father, and turns to Bess. 'I'm afraid I had to lie low for a while in France.'

Bess frowns, not sure she wants to know the details. 'Ben Jonson has much to answer for.' She shakes her head. 'We trusted him.'

'Master Jonson should not be held to blame. To my regret, I got him drunk, handcuffed him to a wheelbarrow, and rolled him through the streets.' Her son gives her a sheepish look.

Bess is not amused, but sees Walter wink at his son. 'I expected better of you, Wat, and of Master Ben Jonson.'

Wat reaches into his bag and holds up a parcel tied with twine, which he hands to Walter. 'A gift for you from Master Jonson, Father.'

Walter takes his sharp penknife and hesitates for a moment before he cuts the twine, pulling off the paper wrapping. He looks at Bess with unmistakable emotion. 'The first volume of *The History of the World*.'

Bess smiles, although she suspects Ben Jonson paid the costs of publication through guilt over his neglect of Wat. All the same, she can see how much it means to Walter to hold his book in his hands. Rarely lost for words, he flicks through the pages, beaming with pride.

'I wish Prince Henry could have seen this.' He reads from the foreword: '*It was for the service of that inestimable Prince Henry that I undertook this work. It is now left to the world without a master.*' He looks up at her. 'There was a time when I never thought to see this published. I owe Ben Jonson a debt, and shall have to return to work on the other volumes.'

Bess is glad to see his melancholy mood disappearing as he studies his new book. 'You could have a copy sent to young Prince Charles.'

'I've never met him, but think he might be too young.'

'Prince Charles will be fourteen in November, although I confess he looked younger when I last saw him. Your book provides an opportunity to know him. He looks in need of friends.'

Wat agrees. 'One day he will be King of England, Scotland and Ireland, so who better to have as your patron?'

Bess interrupts before Walter can reply. 'I shall ask Arthur to find you gainful employment, Wat. Something suited to your talents.' She adds a note of irony to the last word, but it seems wasted on her son, and on Walter.

'There is no need, Mother. I've made plans. I'm to enrol in the academy of General Maurice of Nassau.'

Bess sits back in her chair. 'You cannot return to the Continent, Wat, after what happened last time.'

'I'm sorry, the arrangements are already made. I'm here to say farewell.' He must see the look of disappointment on Bess's face. 'This is not a decision I've made in haste, Mother. General Maurice founded a new school of military professional practice.'

Bess has misgivings about his plan. 'Would it not be better if my brother finds you a junior position at court?'

Walter must see Wat's hesitation. 'You could become an apprentice to Thomas Harriot. He can teach you his skill of map-making, and will be happy to share his research on navigation at sea by the stars.'

'Thank you, Father, but I've applied to General Maurice to complete my education with him. His ideas on military strategy, with small, well-trained and independent infantry units, will change wars forever.'

'If you wish to be trained as a soldier, we can secure you a commission in the king's army.' Walter looks thoughtful. 'I'm not without contacts who will remember they owe me a favour.'

Wat shakes his head. 'We still arm our soldiers with halberds, while General Maurice has musketeers.'

Bess gives him a worried look. 'You will be fighting in some foreign war before you know it.'

Wat grins at the prospect. 'I have to reach Dover for my sailing, so will say farewell, but I promise to write.'

Bess holds her son close for a moment before he leaves, reluctant to let him go. She wishes her precious boys would never grow into men, but understands they need to make a life for themselves. She slips him her purse, heavy with coins, kisses him on the cheek, and then he is gone, possibly forever.

Sir William Wade asks to see Bess, and she fears Walter has somehow upset the authoritarian Lieutenant of the Tower. Her fear is that Walter will suffer more than last time if her visiting is stopped. Sir William is a man who bears a grudge, and seems to enjoy exercising the power he has within the Tower walls.

Her pulse races as she knocks at his door and hears his gruff voice. Sir William gestures for her to be seated. He gives her his usual appraising stare, and her mind races as she tries to read his intention. He's put on weight during his time at the Tower, and she hopes he's due to be replaced by a younger man.

'I must ask another favour of you, Lady Raleigh.'

Bess lets out the breath she's been holding. Much has happened since he last asked a favour. She tries to disarm him with a smile. 'Of course, Sir William.' It would suit her to be owed a favour by the Lieutenant of the Tower.

'Lady Arbella is…' He seems to struggle to find the right words. 'We believe she is losing her mind, which makes the task of my yeomen difficult.'

Too late, Bess remembers her promise to Arbella to visit when she could. She has no excuse, other than the need to care for Walter, who often complains that out of sight is out of mind. She holds the silence, waiting.

Sir William sits back in his creaking chair. 'I believed I had the solution to my problem. Lady Arbella's aunt, Lady Mary Talbot, Countess of Shrewsbury, also finds herself under my care.'

Bess nods. 'I was surprised when I heard.'

'Lady Mary was found guilty of assisting with the elope-ment of her niece, Lady Arbella. I expect she will be released soon enough but, in the meantime, I asked her to calm her niece, Lady Arbella.'

'Then why do you need me, Sir William?'

He frowns, and leans forwards, his face serious. 'Lady Arbella thinks Lady Mary is an agent of the Catholics, and is plotting to set her free.'

'She could be right.'

'Right or wrong, Lady Arbella is more difficult than ever, and is refusing her food again. I've had one prisoner die on my watch, and don't wish to explain his cousin's death to the king.'

Bess knows he refers to Sir Thomas Overbury. 'I will visit Lady Arbella – I promised her I would – but cannot promise to improve her mood.'

'That is all I can ask of you, Lady Raleigh.'

~

The gloom is made worse by the cold, seeping through the ancient stone walls like a bad omen. Old rushes crackle underfoot and, at first, Bess cannot see Lady Arbella, who could have become her queen, one of the wealthiest, most powerful and influential women in the world.

Arbella's voice sounds weak and rasping, but carries a challenge as she calls from under her woollen coverlet. 'Who is there?'

Bess is concerned to find Arbella still in her bed so late in the morning. She pulls a chair to the side of the bed.

'It's Bess. I'm sorry I've not been to visit for so long, but it's been such a busy time.' She sees Arbella's pale face emerge from the shadows. 'It's so cold in here.' Bess crosses to the hearth and sees there are still glowing embers. Taking some smaller logs from a wicker basket she perseveres until a yellow flame flickers into life. She finds a candle and lights it, then places it at Arbella's bedside, and sits close.

It hasn't occurred to her before, but it is odd that Arbella, first cousin to the king, is still held under what is known as 'close' arrest. This means she cannot exercise outside without permission, and is not allowed to write or receive letters. Worse still, it seems she has no servants to care for her or keep her company.

Arbella makes no effort to rise, but studies her face. 'Did I tell you I was once a water nymph?'

Bess frowns. Sir William Wade said Arbella was losing her mind, but it seems worse than even he knows. 'I think you have been here too long. I shall write to the queen, and ask her to plead for the king's pardon on your behalf.'

Arbella continues with a wistful look in her eyes. 'I danced for the queen, in her masque at Whitehall Palace to celebrate the investiture of Prince Henry as Prince of Wales.' She smiles at the memory. 'I wore a gown of blue and turquoise, as the nymph of the River Trent, with a flowing silken veil which reached to the ground.'

Bess realises Arbella is telling the truth. There was a masque for Prince Henry. There is nothing wrong with her memory, although she could not be blamed for losing her mind after being imprisoned alone for so long, like one of the caged lionesses in the Tower menagerie.

'I watched the prince's procession with my son, Carew, but was not invited to the masque.'

Arbella brightens. 'The stage was made to look like a Welsh harbour, with real boats, and statues of Neptune and Nereus. The dances celebrated the prince as successor to King Henry Tudor, and the tradition of King Arthur.' She sits up a little in her bed. 'Prince Henry was magnificent as the messenger of spring, Queen Anna was Tethys, wife of Oceanus, and Princess Elizabeth was the nymph of the River Thames. Even King James took part as the king of the ocean.'

Bess is not sure if Arbella knows of the death of the prince, or that the queen is still in mourning, and the princess married and gone to Heidelberg. 'One day soon you will dance with the queen again, Arbella.' Bess studies her pale face. 'I will make a deal with you. If you return to eating your food, I will ask a favour of Sir William Wade. You should be allowed out in the sunshine for exercise, and have servants to keep you company.'

Arbella lies back in her bed, in silence, for a moment. 'I would like to see the blue sky again, breathe the fresh air, and listen to the birds singing.'

Bess manages a smile. 'Then we have a deal?'

Arbella nods. 'We do.'

27

THE TOWER 1615

WALTER CURSES. 'THOMAS HARRIOT CAME TO SEE ME. HE SAID King James ordered all copies of my book to be withdrawn.'

Bess knows, but had tried to keep it from him. Once again, his friend Thomas Harriot has failed to appreciate how close Walter is to suffering physical and mental collapse. Any bad news could send him back into fits of melancholy. Bess is not yet fifty, but Walter turned sixty-three in January, and grows less tolerant of his situation with each passing year in the Tower.

He ignores her silence. 'Thomas Harriot told me they are saying the narrow-minded Archbishop of Canterbury, George Abbot, is behind this. It seems he demanded all copies to be seized and publication banned. It's an outrage!'

'Calm yourself, Walter.' Bess takes his hand and looks him in the eye. 'Archbishop George Abbot is out to make a name for himself, and I doubt the king has had time to read your book. When he *does* he will see—'

'When he *does* he will see I've been less than flattering about the cruelty of kings – and, it seems, with good reason.' His voice is raised, with a sharp edge. 'You don't understand, Bess.

I hoped this book would find favour with the king, not turn him against me – and I've still had no reply from Sir Ralph Winwood.'

Bess understands only too well. It is not only Walter, as the queen has not replied to her letter of pleading for Lady Arbella, whose condition continues to worsen. At least Sir William allows Arbella to have a servant, and to exercise on the Tower Green, although only under guard.

'Give Sir Ralph Winwood time, Walter. He must be a busy man, with many petitioners and letters to read, but hold on to hope, and we will write to him again in stronger terms.'

He scowls. 'It is hard to hold on to hope when I work so long for so little reward.'

'I've been giving this a lot of thought, and decided I must do more to support you.'

He stares at her, a look of surprise on his face. 'How do you mean? You have always supported me. What more could you do?' His voice sounds agitated, a worrying sign.

Bess sits him back down in his chair, and hands him his pouch of tobacco and his pipe. She dislikes his smoking, but it does calm him. She watches as he goes through the ritual of filling the bowl and lighting the tobacco with a taper from the fire. He takes a puff, and seems to settle into his chair, his anger at the king forgotten.

She knows he is slowly dying in this prison, and it is only a matter of time before he loses his mind. She's lain awake at night, rehearsing her ideas for a way out, yet now she has to tell him, the thought of the consequences makes her throat dry.

'I've been holding you back, Walter, for my own selfish reasons. I didn't want you to lead the expedition, because I fear you might not return.' She takes a deep breath. 'You must tell Sir Ralph Winwood you are prepared to lead an expedition to find the city of gold.'

'But I have no money. I've no idea what's become of my ships, my captains or my crews.'

'I will help find you investors, and we can use some of the compensation money to prepare your ships and recruit some good men.'

He stands, and takes her in his arms. 'Thank you, Bess. If the king agrees, he will have to release me.' He kisses her, for the first time in a long while.

Bess has a visit from her brother Arthur, who brings important news from the palace. 'Sir Robert Carr and his wife, Lady Frances, have fallen from royal favour and are sent to the Tower.'

'On what charge?' Bess finds her mind racing with the consequences.

'Lady Frances is accused of paying someone to poison Thomas Overbury, who died in the Tower last year, but it seems all Robert Carr is guilty of is being in the way.'

'What do you mean?'

'The king has a new favourite, his cup-bearer, young George Villiers.'

Bess frowns. 'I've never heard of him.'

'Not many had, but they have now. George Villiers is always at the king's side, leads the Protestant faction at court, and promotes war against Spain, which could be useful to Walter.'

'What should we do?'

'Nothing, for now. Let the dust settle and I will find out what I can about George Villiers.'

'I was planning to see Sir Ralph Winwood, now he has taken Robert Cecil's place. He's not replied to Walter's letter, so

I've decided to deliver another letter in person, if he will agree to see me.'

'Would you like me to escort you?'

'I was going to ask Thomas Harriot to accompany me, as he has a good grasp of the details, and is convincing if Sir Ralph has questions.'

Arthur nods. 'Good idea. Thomas Harriot is one of the few we can still rely on, and can also witness anything Sir Ralph Winwood might say to you.'

Bess sits on an ancient wooden bench in the cold, echoing antechamber of the Principal Secretary of State. They've been kept waiting, not a good omen, and she remembers her last meeting there, with Robert Cecil, to plead for Walter's release.

Robert Cecil did everything he could to make sure James Stuart of Scotland would be King of England, yet his years of service to the Crown were soon forgotten. He would be unsurprised at how soon others took credit for his work, but Bess believes he would be saddened by the empty pews at his funeral.

She wishes she knew Sir Ralph Winwood better. Her plan for their future depends on this former clerk made good. Thomas Harriot waits at her side, and holds his new copy of Walter's map of Guiana, a gift for Sir Ralph to show the king. Bess carries Walter's letter, in which he promises to risk his life in the service of the king.

Her pulse quickens as the door opens and her name is called by an usher. With a glance at Thomas Harriot, who gives her a reassuring nod, Bess follows the usher down the gloomy corridor. When she'd left, Walter said he would pray for her. This could be his only chance of salvation.

Sir Ralph Winwood stands as they enter, a good sign. He

lifts his black velvet cap in welcome and gestures for them to be seated opposite him. Unlike his predecessor, his desk is clear apart from his silver inkstand and pen, and a pair of good-quality silver candlesticks, holding flickering beeswax candles.

'Good day to you, Lady Raleigh.' He smiles. 'I understand you have a proposition from Sir Walter?' His voice is cultured, with a trace of a north country accent.

He looks more handsome than she expected, with a dark beard and intelligent eyes. His black doublet is plain, like a Puritan, with only a wide lace collar to stop him looking like an ordinary cleric. Bess allows her hopes to rise, but there is much at stake from this meeting.

She returns his smile. 'I do, Sir Ralph.' She gestures towards Thomas. 'I don't believe you've been introduced to Master Thomas Harriot?'

Sir Ralph nods to Thomas. 'Your reputation precedes you, Master Harriot. It is my pleasure to meet you at last.'

Thomas Harriot removes his hat and bows. 'I'm pleased to make your acquaintance, Sir Ralph.'

Bess lay awake the previous night rehearsing how she would take the initiative at this meeting. 'Forgive me, Sir Ralph, but I know you have much more important business, so I shall come straight to the point. My husband, Sir Walter, asks me to inform you in person of his proposal.'

Sir Ralph strokes his beard. 'I confess I am intrigued. Please continue, my lady.'

'There are gold mines in Guiana, and my husband knows the location.' She turns to Thomas. 'Please show your map to Sir Ralph.'

Thomas Harriot unfolds the map and lays it down on the desk between them. Sir Ralph's eyes narrow as he studies the map. The possible location of the mines is marked with crosses of gold leaf. 'How does Sir Walter know the Spanish have not already taken these mines?'

'He doesn't, but he asked me to tell you that if they have not, it will only be a matter of time, which is why he is prepared to risk his life on an expedition to seize them.'

'At the expense of the Crown?' Sir Ralph's voice carries an unexpected note of challenge.

'We have more investors than we need, Sir Ralph, so there is *no* risk to the Crown, only great profit.' She holds her breath and waits to see if he can tell she is lying.

He strokes his beard again, a habit which could show he's thinking of his options, before he looks her in the eye. 'Tell me, what does your husband ask of me?'

Bess is prepared for the question. 'All my husband asks is to be granted his freedom to serve the king as only he can, Sir Ralph.'

'I might consider a modest investment in this adventure myself.'

Bess feels her pulse race, and takes a deep breath to calm herself. This is the closest they've been to the prospect of Walter's release, but she has one last card to gamble. 'Your investment is most welcome, Sir Ralph, and there is only one condition. I promised my husband I would ask if you would read his letter.'

She passes the fold of parchment to him and holds her breath once again. They spent many hours discussing each word in Walter's latest proposal, but had no idea whether Sir Ralph Winwood would even read it. Bess studies his face as he scans Walter's neatest writing, the final copy after many attempts.

He looks up at her. 'If your husband is right, my lady, the treasury would welcome the profits, but I see a problem.'

Bess tries to remain calm, but senses uncomfortable warmth as her neck flushes at his words. 'What is that, Sir Ralph?'

'You are possibly aware that several members of the Privy

Council bear some grudge against your husband?' Sir Ralph frowns and waves Walter's proposal in the air. 'This can go no further without the support of the Privy Council. I will try my best, but doubt I can change their minds.' He must see her look of disappointment. 'I am sorry, Lady Raleigh, but it would be wrong of me to offer you false hope.'

'I thank you for your frankness, Sir Ralph, and for your support for my husband's venture.' She glances at Thomas Harriot, her sign the meeting is over. 'Please keep this map, Sir Ralph. I hope you might see the opportunity to mention it to the king.' She stands. 'Thank you for your time.'

She bows and leaves, fighting against tears, followed by Thomas Harriot.

Her brother Arthur frowns as Bess explains the outcome of her meeting with Sir Ralph Winwood. 'From how you've described his reply, it seems he's hinting bribes would help, although any attempt to bribe members of the Privy Council could see you locked up in the Tower.'

'What can we do?'

'We need to persuade someone to act on your behalf. They would need to be able to persuade members of the Privy Council, or those close to the king.'

'What about George Villiers? You can't get much closer to the king than him.'

Arthur smiles at her joke. 'Too risky, but I know his elder half-brother, Edward Villiers.' Arthur looks thoughtful. 'Edward is ambitious, and I think jealous of his brother's success. He would like a knighthood, and a role at court.'

'Can you think of anyone else?'

'The Welshman, Sir William St John. He's an influential member of His Majesty's Council for the Virginia Company, and seems to know most members of the Privy Council. They all want a share of Virginia. Most importantly, he's an experienced sea captain and would be a good choice to command this new adventure.'

'Would either of them be offended if I offered payment for their support?'

Arthur shakes his head. 'Edward Villiers is in debt, and Sir William St John has been accused of piracy. Walter could tell him the money is a down payment to secure his commission as commander.'

'I will have to persuade Walter to agree.'

'If he does not, the alternative is to remain in the Tower for the rest of his life.' Arthur looks her in the eye. 'You *must* persuade him, Bess, for his own good.'

The Dean of Westminster, George Montaigne, leads the small congregation in prayer, his voice echoing in the south aisle of King Henry VII's chapel in Westminster Abbey. To see him in his formal robes no one would guess George Montaigne was an adventurer. He'd sailed on Walter's expedition to attack the Spanish fleet in Cadiz, as chaplain to the ill-fated Earl of Essex, and profited from his modest investment.

Bess wears her mourning dress, and bows her head. She should not have been surprised at the news, yet it came as a shock. She'd walked on Tower Green with Arbella, who'd brightened as she breathed fresh air, her eyes shining as she stared up at the cloudless blue sky.

Bess cannot forgive their insecure king. His own cousin, who'd been so full of life, and danced for him as a beautiful water nymph, was too frail to walk far. Arbella asked to rest for a moment, leaning against one of the few trees for support. She said she hoped to hear birdsong, but the only birds were carrion crows, cawing from the high stone walls, birds of ill omen.

Arbella wanted to die, and starved herself until her fragile body wasted away. Her coffin was spirited from the Tower at night by river for this hasty burial in Westminster Abbey. Bess glances around the small congregation, and realises that only these few share the secret. She would not have known if Sir William hadn't sent a message by a yeoman warder.

Bess fights a pang of guilt that she didn't do more for Arbella, and vows to discover what became of her husband, William Seymour. She was only thirty-nine and, but for the cruel luck of the tide, could be safe with him in some foreign land. They might even be expecting their first child, another in the royal line of succession.

Dean Montaigne rushes through the prayers, and a tear runs down her face as Bess joins in with the *Amen*. She watches as grim-faced undertakers carry Arbella's plain coffin into the vault of her ill-fated aunt, Mary Queen of Scots, and her unlucky cousin, Prince Henry, all finally at peace.

28

KING STREET 1616

AFTER TWELVE LONG YEARS IN THE TOWER, LONGER THAN Carew's lifetime, everything changes with one word from the king. Bess is as surprised as Walter when Sir William Wade tells them the news. They can never know if the huge sum of one thousand, five hundred pounds paid to Sir William St John and Edward Villers made a difference.

They say farewell to the yeomen warders, and walk out through the Tower gates. A tear runs down Walter's cheek as he is finally free. At one time, everyone would have recognised him, but no one gives a second glance to the haggard man who walks with a stick for support.

Bess takes his arm and leads him to the waiting carriage. She carries a bag with his precious notebooks and clothes. Two men struggle with a wooden crate packed with Walter's books and some glass bottles of his potions, all he has to show for his long years in prison.

She turns for one last look at the forbidding grey stone walls of the Tower, and says a silent prayer of thanks. Her gratitude is not for the cruel king who took the best years of their lives, or for Sir William Wade. Her thanks are for Sir Ralph

Winwood and others who persuaded King James to give Walter one last chance.

Robert Carr remains imprisoned in the Tower, so Sherborne reverts to the king. Bess judges it too soon to ask if he will return their home. She lives in hope, and plans for when they return to the peace of Dorset. Walter must prove himself worthy of royal favour by returning from Guiana with a shipload of gold. When he does, the king will listen.

Walter stares wide-eyed as they ride through the streets, and mutters to himself, 'So much has changed.'

The once familiar old timber-framed buildings have been replaced by new houses with gleaming glass windows and towering chimneys of red brick. Smart covered carriages jostle for space in narrow cobbled lanes, made for people on foot and single riders on horseback.

The greatest change is in the number of people. London escaped the worst of the plague for the past ten years, leading to an influx of people from the country, looking for opportunity. Bess is used to seeing ladies in the revealing and colourful new fashions, but Walter raises an eyebrow.

'Where are we going?' He gives Bess a surprised look as they head towards the heart of the city. 'I thought I'd be joining you in your apartment on Tower Hill?'

Bess smiles. 'I've rented a larger house on King Street, with room enough for us all, close to Whitehall Palace. It's not to be compared to Durham House, yet has stables, servants' quarters, and a study with shelves for your books.' She doesn't add it is further from the dockyards, but thinks that a small price to pay.

'Anywhere would seem like a palace after the confinement of the Garden Tower.' Walter looks overwhelmed. 'I'm afraid it will take me a while to adjust, but this is what I've longed for. A new start.'

Bess agrees. 'A new start for us all. We must put the past

behind us, Walter, and focus on making a success of your voyage to Guiana. I've told Thomas Harriot to grant you such funds as you need from the compensation money.' Her decision is a calculated risk, but Walter is prepared to risk everything, and so must she.

Bess is soon busy recruiting a new household. Her loyal nursemaid, Eleanor, is promoted to housekeeper, to help make their new house into a family home. Carew is eleven, and pleased to have his own room with an adjoining study. Bess reserves a bedchamber for Wat, who fails to write or find any way to let them know he is safe and well.

She used to lie awake at night worrying about her errant son, but now has new concerns. Bess works in the small-windowed room she calls her closet, keeping a tally of expenditure in one of Walter's notebooks. Half the compensation money, Wat's inheritance, is spent or committed. The expenses continue to increase, and she doubts their remaining money will be enough.

Walter seems pleased with his new study, and spreads maps of the coastline of Guiana on the desk. 'I've waited twelve years for this. I need a fleet of at least a dozen ships, and crews I can rely on. The greatest expense will be five hundred pounds to commission the building of a new flagship.' He gives Bess a wry smile. 'I thought to name her *Destiny.*'

Bess knows there are older ships he can buy at half the cost, but is pleased to see his old enthusiasm return. 'A good name, Walter. She carries the destiny of us all.'

He hands her a note to read. 'I'd like you to look at the draft letter of thanks I intend to send to George Villiers.'

Bess reads the note, which has many words crossed out, and additions scrawled in the margins.

. . .

Sir, you have by your mediation put me again into the world. I can but acknowledge it, for to repay any part of your favour by any service of mine as yet it is not in my power. If the Guiana voyage succeed well a great part of that honour shall be yours, and if I do not also make it profitable unto you I shall shew myself exceeding ungrateful.

She frowns, and looks up at him. 'I'm not aware of George Villiers investing anything in your venture. Is it a good idea to make such promises?'

Walter nods. 'I don't promise a share of the profits, but the credit for the success of the venture. You said I need his good-will, which is an investment in kind. George Villiers has influence with the king – something money cannot buy.'

Bess suspects even George Villiers has his price, but continues reading.

In the meanwhile, and till God discover the success, I beseech you to number me among the number of your faithful servants, though the least able. W Raleigh.

She smiles. 'It can do no harm to keep in with the king's favourite. And it seems you have discovered a new humility.'

Bess wakes at the sound of a commotion in the hall. She wakes Walter, sleeping at her side. A door bangs, and there is a muttered curse as something metal clatters to the tiled floor.

'There is someone downstairs. Are you expecting visitors at such a late hour?'

Walter yawns and rubs his eyes. Before he can answer, Bess smiles as she hears a familiar voice call up the stairs.

'Mother, Father! I'm back!'

His words are a little slurred, and there is the sound of cupboards opening and clunking closed, followed by the clink of a bottle.

Bess feels her pulse race. At last, her prayers have been answered. 'Wat has returned, but it sounds like he's been drinking.'

Walter stares at her, his eyes glinting in the dim orange glow of the embers in the hearth. 'I forgot to tell you. I met with Ben Jonson at the Mermaid Tavern. He told me Wat is back in London.'

She stares at him in amazement. 'You *forgot* to tell me? Do you have any idea how much I've worried about Wat?' Her voice rises with frustration.

'I gave Ben Jonson this address, and asked him to find Wat and tell him to come home. I thought to surprise you, but didn't imagine he would turn up so late.' There is no hint of an apology, but he avoids meeting her eyes.

Bess pulls a shawl over her nightdress and lights a candle with a taper from the embers. 'Thank God he's home.' She sees Walter is going back to sleep. 'You must come down to welcome your son. I was beginning to worry we would never see him again.'

Wat is dressed like a soldier, with a long blue military coat and a musketeer's bandolier with a silver buckle over one shoulder. An ostrich-plumed hat with a wide brim lies next to him on the table. He's found a bottle of red wine and raises his glass to Bess as she enters the candlelit parlour. 'I'm celebrating Father's release.'

Bess embraces him, ignoring the smell of stale beer and tobacco. 'You promised to write. I was so worried about you.'

He grins, and takes another sip of wine. 'I never was a great writer of letters – but I came back as soon as I heard the news from Ben Jonson.'

'I expect you've run out of money?'

Wat drains his glass of wine. 'I put the money you gave me to good use. I've graduated from the academy of General Maurice of Nassau, and am trained in the latest military strategy. All I need now is experience.'

Bess frowns at the thought. 'I pray you will settle down, Wat. There will be time for experience later, but now we need to find you a suitable wife. I've kept a room ready in the hope you would return, and you can help your father plan how to provision his fleet.'

His answer is interrupted by the appearance of Walter, still in his nightshirt. 'Welcome back, Wat.' His voice has an unexpected note of emotion. 'It's good to see you are safe, and looking well.'

'It's good to see you free from the Tower at last, Father, and I hear you are planning a new expedition to South America.'

'My fleet will be the grandest to sail to the Caribbean. I'm having a new flagship built, the *Destiny*, five hundred tons.'

Wat tries to refill his glass but the bottle is empty. 'I'm keen to play a part in your expedition, Father.' He flashes a smile at Bess. 'It will be easier to find a suitable wife when my pockets are full of gold.'

Walter grins. 'I will be glad of your help with recruiting a company of soldiers. You could oversee their training. Most of the men I've seen so far are the scum of the earth, wastrels and misfits. I need soldiers I can rely on. How would you like to be made captain of the *Destiny*?'

Bess stares at Walter in disbelief. 'How can he be a captain?

He's never been further out to sea than a crossing to Calais, he has never been in command of anything, and Guiana is too—'

Wat holds up a hand and interrupts her objections. 'I need to gain experience, Mother. What better way can there be than to learn from Father?'

Walter puffs on his pipe but has a worried frown. 'King James ties my hands behind my back.' He curses at the thought.

Bess is unsurprised at anything the king might do, but her pulse races at the thought of their plan unravelling. 'What is it now?'

'The king gave the Great Seal to my commission, but the terms he's imposed are impossible. I am told any breaking of the peace treaty with Spain will amount to treason, so I must not injure a single Spanish subject.'

'It sounds like a trap, as it will not be easy to avoid the Spanish, particularly if they somehow learn the terms of your commission.'

Walter curses. 'It's impossible to keep our plans secret. Too many people are involved. I can't be sure if some of the crewmen we've recruited are not Spanish agents, spying on our preparations.'

Bess frowns. 'Does this mean the voyage cannot go ahead without great risk?'

'We've long since passed the point of no return, Bess. The money is spent. *Destiny* will be ready to sail next spring, and we've recruited men and placed orders for the supplies.'

She knows he is right, as she keeps the tally of the expenses. 'What can we do?'

'Thomas Harriot is looking into striking a deal with the French. I could put into a French port until I'm sure King James doesn't plan to order my arrest.'

'And if he does?'

'You and the boys will have to join me in France.' He manages a grin. 'You'd best ask Carew's tutor to help you improve your French.'

Bess knows him better than anyone, and sees from the look in his eyes he's holding something back. 'What is it, Walter? Is there more you need to tell me?'

Walter takes another puff of his pipe before answering. 'I am sorry to tell you Thomas Harriot informed me the king has agreed to sell the entire Sherborne estate to Sir John Digby, a courtier and privy councillor, for ten thousand pounds.'

Bess puts her hand to her mouth as she understands the consequences. 'Dear God. That means—' Her voice chokes and she cannot continue.

Walter shakes his head. 'That means Sherborne is lost to us, Bess, even if my venture is a success.' He scowls. 'I know how you longed to return to Sherborne. There is nothing we can do, but it proves the king needs money, and at least he hasn't given Sherborne to his favourite, George Villiers, for nothing.'

The mood at the galley dock at Woolwich is one of celebration, despite the wintry breeze. Bess pulls her fur cape around herself and follows Carew to the wharf. Walter's impressive new flagship, the *Destiny*, made ready in haste, waits to begin her maiden voyage to the other side of the world.

Shouts fill the crisp morning air as men climb high in the ratlines, while others load sacks of supplies and wooden casks. Bess scans the men crowding on the deck, searching for Wat and Walter, when Carew points. 'There's Wat, Mother. He looks like a proper sea captain.'

Bess doesn't agree. Her eldest son is growing a beard,

which makes him look older, and even more like his father. He wears a captains' hat with his blue military coat, and has a silver-handled sword on a low-slung belt, but she knows he is no sea captain. She doubts any of his training with General Maurice prepared him for command of such an unruly crew at sea.

Wat waves his hat and calls something to Bess, but she cannot hear. Walter appears at Wat's side, and raises a hand to wave when he spots Bess and Carew. He grins with pride. He confessed to her that he worries about their fleet being inter-cepted by the Spanish, yet dismisses her concerns about setting out so late in the year.

Walter promised to keep an eye on their son at all times, but Bess still worries. Like his father, Wat is less concerned about making his fortune than with making a name for himself. She always knew Walter was a risk-taker, and has to pass through Spanish territory, but now there is a difference. The lives of her husband and her eldest son are both at risk.

Everything they have is invested in the success of this venture. Everyone she knows – from her brother Arthur to Sir Ralph Winwood, the Secretary of State – also risks their money on Walter's promised gold mines. She raises a hand as the sailors cast off the mooring ropes, and says a prayer for their safe return.

29

BROAD STREET 1617

BESS SITS ALONE IN HER COLD CLOSET, TRYING TO KEEP A TALLY of her household expenses in Walter's notebook. She throws another log on the fire and counts out the contents of her purse. There are forty-five gold double crowns and more of silver. To some this would be considered a fortune, but Bess frowns with concern.

She picks up a gold crown and studies the portrait of the king. Regal, with a fine beard, there is little likeness to the feeble man who has caused them so much trouble. The Latin inscription around the edge reads: HENRICVS · ROSAS · REGNA · IACOBVS. Walter once explained this means: Henry united the rose, James the kingdoms.

She counts sixty-eight silver shillings and two dozen of the little silver sixpences. Some have escallop marks and others are marked with a key, showing they were minted at the Tower. King James ordered even these to be marked with the slogan, *What God has joined together let no man put asunder*. Bess mutters to herself that God had little enough to do with it.

A sharp edge reveals one of her silver shillings is clipped on one side. She turns it in her hand, trying to decide what to do with it. One of the market traders must have passed the clipped shilling with her change. She makes a mental note to be more careful in the future.

Clipping even a shilling is declared an act of treason, an attack on the king. Bess knows men found guilty of clipping or 'coining' are hanged, drawn and quartered at the Tyburn gallows. Women, spared the horror of public mutilation, are burned at the stake as a warning to others.

The gold and silver coins are all that remain of her eight thousand pounds compensation. Apart from her late mother's string of mismatched pearls, this is all she has left in the world. Walter's secret casket of jewels is long gone, a distant memory. She even sold the last of the jewels sewn into the hem of one of her gowns to raise the money Walter needed for his new ship.

With only herself and Carew remaining, the rent of her King Street house seemed an extravagance, but now she thinks the move to the ramshackle terrace in Broad Street was a mistake. Any warmth from the fires goes straight up the chimneys, and the scent of decay from the poultry abattoir hangs in the air like an ill omen.

Her landlord warns her to be wary of cutpurses and worse in the streets. She doesn't ask what is worse than having your purse stolen, but she can imagine. She's told Carew not to venture out after dark, and makes sure the doors and windows are secured and bolted at night.

She scoops the precious gold coins back into her purse. The loss of Sherborne means there is no inheritance for Wat, and he is proved right: his prospect of making a suitable marriage depends on him returning from Guiana with his pockets full of gold.

She sits back in her chair and rereads the short letter from Walter, although she knows the contents by heart. His men threatened to mutiny before they reached the mouth of the

Thames. He doesn't say why, but Walter called them the scum of the earth, so she can only imagine what life is like on board his ships.

Walter writes from Plymouth, where the mayor and corporation of the city organised a grand banquet in his honour. She pictures how he would relish such public recognition after so many years in obscurity, and hopes Wat was invited to attend.

Walter no doubt made a grand speech about discovering a fortune in gold, forgetting he has so far found nothing of any consequence. She also worries he might forget he is supposed to keep his purpose a secret from Spanish spies who haunt the ports.

Bess worries about Wat. Walter passed his sixty-fifth year while at sea, and promised not to take risks, but although Wat will soon be twenty-four, he seems to have no sense of the dangers they face. She takes consolation from knowing they can't take on the Spanish, and prays the Atlantic weather will be kind to them.

Arthur arrives unexpectedly. He is sixty, yet looks older; his grey hair is thinning as he pulls off his hat. 'It's good to see you, Bess. I confess I was concerned. I've not heard from you.'

Bess is conscious of the drab gown she wears around the house. It is practical to save her best gowns, but she hopes her brother doesn't notice the frayed hem. 'I'm sorry I've not been in touch. It's been a busy time, moving house and—'

He puts an affectionate hand on her arm. 'I understand, Bess, but you don't need to live here. You are welcome to stay with us at Mile End until Walter returns.' He smiles. 'Anna will be glad of your company. Another of our girls is to marry, so she'll welcome your help with the arrangements.'

'Thank you, Arthur, but Walter's letters are sent to this

address. There is more than enough room here for Carew and me, and there is a market close by.'

He looks out of the window and scowls at the sight of the stinking conduit running down one side of the narrow street. 'This is not a good area, Bess.'

'I have to make economies, for now.'

She is living a lie. She tells herself her life will change for the better, once Walter and Wat return with a shipload of gold, yet in her heart she knows the truth. Bess sees her brother shares her doubts.

'Do you need a loan?' He studies her face, as if making a judgement. His voice is kind yet firm, like a worried father speaking to a beloved but errant daughter.

Bess shakes her head. 'I am coping, but I might be glad of your help in the future. Walter's voyage cost us everything.'

Arthur raises an eyebrow. 'Have you heard from him?'

Bess takes Walter's last letter from a drawer and hands it to him. 'It's from Kinsale in Ireland. It's dated the end of June, so it's taken weeks to reach London, and I've no idea if he has crossed the Atlantic.'

Arthur gives her a concerned look as he takes the letter and reads it before handing it back. 'Was it his plan to sail to Ireland first?'

'He didn't say, but they waited so long in Plymouth for the weather they must have run low on supplies. Walter knows Sir Richard Boyle, Baron of Youghal, from his time there. At least they were able to take on new provisions before risking the crossing.'

'I don't understand the reference to Admiral Henri de Montmorency being most obliging.' Arthur frowns. 'He's Governor of Languedoc, and known to persecute French Protestants. Is he investing in Walter's venture?'

'Walter must have reached agreement with him to provide

a safe haven in France, if there is trouble with the Spanish before he returns.'

'He could find he is in more trouble if he's allied with Admiral Montmorency. We must find a way to warn Walter. Henri de Montmorency is not to be trusted.'

Bess frowns. 'The king added a condition to Walter's commission. He must not attack any Spaniards.'

Arthur shakes his head. 'You know Walter. He won't be able to resist a Spanish treasure ship if he sees one, but I can't see him enjoying exile in France.'

'Has he spoken to you of his true intentions?' Bess watches her brother, knowing he won't wish to betray a confidence, but also that won't lie to her.

'No, but there is something you should know. The Spanish ambassador, Señor Gondomar, is negotiating with the king for Prince Charles to marry King Philip of Spain's daughter, the Infanta Maria Anne.'

'It's possible Walter could be handed over to the Spanish if he breaks the conditions of his commission?'

Arthur nods. 'I'm afraid the Spanish have a reputation for harsh punishment of prisoners who offend their king.'

The knock at the door sounds official, and Bess fears bad news. She waits in the parlour, and asks Eleanor to find out who it is. Bess holds her breath as she hears a man with an Essex accent ask for her, and announce he is Captain Pennington, of her husband's fleet.

Her pulse races at the name, which she recognises as Walter's vice admiral. Something must have gone wrong for him to return to London so soon. She struggles to remain composed, and stands, smoothing creases from her gown as Eleanor returns, followed by the captain.

A handsome man, with a wide lace collar over his doublet, gives her a questioning look. 'Lady Raleigh?'

'How can I help you, sir?'

He removes his hat and bows. 'Captain John Pennington at your service, my lady.'

Bess studies him for a moment. He looks young to be Walter's vice admiral, and cannot have much experience of command at sea. Not for the first time, she questions her husband's judgement. He should never have made Wat captain of the *Destiny*. 'If I recall correctly, captain, you are also an investor in my husband's voyage, and owner of the *Star*.'

His eyes reveal his surprise. He cannot know Bess kept a tally of every investor in Walter's notebook, and makes it her business to calculate what share of any profit would be due to them. She also knows the name and owner of every ship in the fleet.

'You are right, my lady.' He sounds less sure of himself. 'Your husband ordered me to return to request more funds, as our supplies ran low due to delays in Plymouth.'

Bess frowns at the thought of parting with any more of her money, but asks Eleanor to bring wine and gestures for him to be seated. She's noted he hasn't said Walter is safe and well. 'I would like to hear everything that has happened, captain. The last I heard from my husband, he was in Ireland.'

Captain Pennington sits, and nods in thanks to Eleanor when she brings him a glass of red wine. He takes a sip and looks across at Bess. 'We had to wait until the second week of June before we could sail out of Plymouth.' The captain scowls at the memory. 'Squalls took our fleet to the west. We had to seek shelter at Kinsale, where we were entertained and our ships reprovisioned by Lord Boyle.'

Bess nods. 'I received a letter from my husband when he was in Kinsale, but he said nothing about when he might sail for Guiana.'

'It was late August before the weather improved. We headed due south for the Canary Isles, where we took on water, but after three days of sailing several crewmen died of a fever. I was sent back once we reached the Cape Verde Islands.'

'Was my son one of those who fell ill?' Bess's heart beats faster at the thought.

'He was not, my lady, but your husband's servant, John Talbot, was one of those who died.' He studies her face for a moment, as if deciding whether to say more. 'I regret to say Sir Walter fell sick, and became so ill he was unable to write. He asked me to tell you your son is well, and he will write again once his health improves.'

Bess tastes her wine, glad of the sweet warmth in her throat. Wat and Walter have been in her thoughts since that fateful farewell at the dock in Woolwich. 'Can you tell me how my son is doing on the *Destiny*?'

Captain Pennington smiles for the first time since he arrived. 'Your son is earning the respect of his men, my lady.' He takes another sip of his wine. 'They say there is nothing on board ship he will not try his hand at, even climbing out on the yardarm in the squalls to help reduce sails.'

Bess tries not to imagine the danger he would have been in if he'd fallen, as he never learned to swim. 'It seems my husband was right. This adventure could be the making of him. Was he still in Cape Verde when you left, captain?'

He nods. 'Sir Walter's plan was to make the crossing to Trinidad, a trip of some twelve days, and wait there until I return with money for provisions.'

The letter brought by a London merchant is addressed from Cayenne, a place Bess has never heard of, and headed, *To my dearest wife, Lady Raleigh*.

Dear heart I can yette write unto yew with a weak hand for I have suffered the most violent calenture for fifteen days that ever man did and lived. But God gave me a strong heart in all my adversities. We have had most grievous sickness in our ship, of which forty two have died and there are yette many sick. God I hope will give us comfort in that which is to come.

Bess skips through the details of ports the fleet visited, accounts of the weather, and the names of men who died, searching in desperation for any mention of Wat. At last, she finds it: *Your sonne had never so good health, have no distemper in all the heat under the line.*

The phrase puzzles her before she realises he refers to sailing south of the equator. She speaks aloud. 'Thank God he is safe.' She has to compose herself before she can continue reading. She'd convinced herself Walter was going to say Wat was ill.

Bess reads on: *Remember my service to Master Secretary Winwood. I write not to him for I can write of nought but miseries as yet.* She says a prayer for the soul of Ralph Winwood, one of the few supporters of their cause at court. Arthur told her he'd died of a fever the previous week. She fears this could be the same fever afflicting those on board the *Destiny*.

Walter's letter ends with simple affection.

By the next I trust you shall hear the better of us. Commend me to my poor Carew, my son God bless you. From Calliana in Guiana. 14th of November 1617, Yours Walter Raleigh.

30

KING STREET 1618

BESS WAKES IN THE MIDDLE OF THE NIGHT AND LIES ALERT IN the darkness, listening. Something woke her, but Carew is away at college. The house is silent, and her thoughts drift to Walter and Wat, on the other side of the Atlantic Ocean.

Her brother's prescient words echo in her head. *You know Walter. He won't be able to resist a Spanish treasure ship if he sees one…* Arthur is right. The *Destiny* is well armed, and the crew would consider a share of any booty worth the risk.

Bess has no wish to live in exile in France with the threat of betrayal by Admiral Montmorency. She prays Walter knows better than to attack the Spanish. She has no idea if Wat would also be charged with treason, but would not be surprised at anything their king might do.

Bess tries to put such worries from her mind. She has more immediate concerns which she can try to do something about. The charming Captain John Pennington succeeded in his mission, leaving with most of her remaining funds.

She misses Robert Cecil, and his successor, Ralph Winwood, who would have been able to advise her, but Thomas Harriot continues to sue the Crown for more compensation. If she can't pay the rent she will take up her brother's invitation to return to Mile End. She misses Sherborne, and if Walter returns from Guiana with a fortune in gold, they will buy another estate in the tranquil peace of Dorset.

Bess smiles as she sees the letter from Walter, delivered by the captain of a London merchantman, recently returned from the New World. A dour man, he seems glad to be rid of the responsibility of the sealed letter. He avoids meeting her eye, but she thinks little of it.

She sits alone in her parlour holding Walter's letter, the first for months. Bess prepares herself for bad news, but prays for the best. The letter is sealed with his signet ring and addressed to her in Walter's hand which, although a little shaky, is a sign his health improves.

Holding her breath, she breaks the dark wax seal. Dated the twenty-second day of March, the letter was sent from an island named St Christopher. Bess takes a sharp intake of breath as she begins to read.

I was loath to write because I know not how to comfort you, and God knows I never knew what sorrow meant until now. All I can say to you is that you must obey the will and providence of God.

Her eyes blur with tears. Her mother's instinct tells her the worst news is coming. She sits back in her chair. Wat must be ill or injured, or worse. Her hand trembles as she reads on.

. . .

I refer you to Master Secretary Wynwood's letter, therein you shall know what hath passed, for my braines are broken and tis a torment for me to write of misery. The Lord bless you and comfort you, that you may bear more patientlie the death of your most valiant son.

'No!' Her anguished cry carries a year of dreading this day would come. She drops his letter to the floor and surrenders to her grief, the sobs building until her body aches. 'Dear God, not my Wat!' Her shout echoes and becomes a wail of despair.

Eleanor comes running and stands in the doorway. She stares at her with wide eyes. 'My lady?' She sees the letter on the floor and seems to understand. 'Something's happened to Wat?'

Bess looks up at her, tears streaming down her face. 'My boy is … gone.' She can't continue as the sobbing returns, her body shaking with despair. She remembers when her son was born, and her midwife saying, 'You have a perfect little boy.' Bess recalls her reply. 'He shall be named Wat, after his father.'

'I am sorry, my lady.'

She looks up at Eleanor and remembers Wat was like a son to her too. She finds the strength to compose herself. 'Walter didn't tell me how he died.' An image forms in her mind of the last time she saw him, on the deck of the *Destiny*. Wat had waved his hat and grinned when he saw her, calling out something she couldn't hear. She will never know what he'd said to her.

Walter is coming home, his grand fleet, the biggest to sail across the ocean, reduced to one, his *Destiny*. Arthur is grim-faced as he offers to escort her to meet him. 'I heard some ships were lost at sea, and others returned early, once they knew there was no gold.'

'Did Walter attack any Spanish ships?'

'I tried to find out, but all I know is one of Walter's captains, a man named Pennington, led a mutiny. It seems he reported to the Lord Admiral that Walter ordered an attack on the Spanish fort at San Thomé. It was looted and burned, with many men killed.'

'Captain John Pennington?'

'I believe it was. He has done Walter no favour. The king is displeased.'

'He will return Walter to the Tower?'

'Come to Plymouth with me, Bess. We shall learn the truth from Walter.'

Bess struggles with mixed feelings as she watches the small rowing boat pull away from the *Destiny* and make its way to the quayside. She blames Walter for Wat's death, for costing them everything they had, but in her heart she loves him, and doubts he ever had any choice.

Walter looks like an old man as he is helped up the harbour steps. He still has his silver-handled cane, but walks with a stoop, seeming unsteady on his feet. He looks around, and raises a hand as he sees her. Bess embraces him, and feels how fever and grief have wasted his once athletic body.

'I'm sorry, Bess.' He seems not to care who sees the tears run down his cheek.

She can never forgive him, but there is no point in telling him this. 'Welcome home, Walter.' Her voice chokes and she can say no more.

Arthur's coach pulls up and they are about to join him when a group of yeomen appear. One takes the halter of one of the horses, while their officer confronts Walter. 'Sir Walter Raleigh, I arrest you in the name of the king.'

Walter stands straight. 'Arrested? On what charge?'

'Treason.'

The word makes Bess flinch as if the man had struck her. 'Can you not see he is sick with a fever?'

The officer studies her for a moment. 'He can travel to London in the coach, but my men will escort you.'

Bess waits until they are riding through open countryside before turning to Walter. 'Tell me what happened. I don't know how Wat died, or whether he suffered at the end.' Her voice is cold.

He sits in silence for a moment, and looks from Bess to Arthur. 'It was Saint Valentine's Day. I was too ill to travel up the Orinoco River. I tasked Lawrence Keymis with leading the exploration to find the gold. He had the experience of our last expedition, and knowledge of the river. Wat insisted on going with them.' His voice is flat, and he won't meet her eye as he speaks.

Arthur nods in understanding. 'He was not a child, Bess. Walter had no choice but to let him go after sailing so far.'

Walter gives him a glance of gratitude before continuing. 'I counted each passing day after they departed, praying for our mission to succeed. When Lawrence Keymis returned, I could barely listen to his account, such was my grief. He told me they stumbled on a Spanish fort they call San Thomé. Men began firing at them. I would like to tell you our son was a hero, but the truth is he was killed by a single bullet. You can take a little comfort from knowing he would not have suffered.' Walter falls silent, lost in his memories.

Arthur rouses him from his reverie. 'What became of Keymis? He is an important witness to your innocence.'

Walter looks up at him with bleary eyes. 'Lawrence Keymis

took to his cabin and shot himself with his pistol. He was buried at sea.'

Walter is taken to the Tower, and Bess is not allowed to see him. Held under guard with Carew in the house of a London merchant, she must wait to discover the king's mercy. Carew misses his friends from college, and is confused about their imprisonment.

'What have we done wrong, Mother?'

'I made the mistake of trusting people, and should have known better.' She sees he doesn't understand. 'I tried to arrange for your father to escape to France.'

'But Father is in the Tower—'

'He is *now*, because my plan failed. Worse still, they suspect your father gave me gold from Guiana.'

Carew looks at her in surprise. 'Will they send *us* to the Tower?'

'I pray they will not, and I have another plan. You will write, pleading on your father's behalf, to Queen Anna.'

Carew frowns. 'The queen will not remember me.'

'Never underestimate the influence of a queen, Carew – and we have nothing to lose by trying.'

Bess and Carew are released on the day she is allowed to visit Walter in the Tower. Her heart fills with hope before she realises what it must mean. This is to be her last visit. She wears her best gown and her mother's pearls, and her pulse races as she walks through the gates and is led to the Beaufort Tower.

She would have liked to have brought Walter a pipe and

good tobacco, but she knows what it means to be in the Beaufort Tower. All she carries is her Bible, bound in black leather
and embossed with a small gold cross, the only book he will be
allowed.

Walter surprises her with a kiss. His hair and beard are
trimmed, and he wears a black doublet she's not seen before.
'Dear God, it's good to see you again, Bess.'

She embraces him, with no concern for the yeoman warder
watching through the door grill. 'Is there to be no trial?'

'No court in the land would find me guilty.'

'What did they tell you?'

'That I am to be executed at Westminster, tomorrow.'

'Tomorrow!' She had expected they would have longer.

'I've waited for two months – or some fifteen years since my
trial.'

Bess has the briefest glimpse of the pain in his eyes before
his swagger returns, as if he welcomes death. She hands him
her Bible. 'This is all I was allowed to bring. I would have
brought tobacco, but…'

He takes the Bible. 'I thought to ask for writing materials
and a pipe of good tobacco as my last request.'

Bess had been awake until the small hours rehearsing her
speech, but now words fail her and her eyes fill with tears. 'You
know I have always loved you, and will never love another?'

'I do, and count myself the luckiest man in this cruel kingdom, to have married you for love. You give me strength, Bess.
You always have, and I will love you even after my last breath.'

He gives her a final, lingering kiss, and she knows she must
go. 'I will pray for you, Walter.' The tears run down her face as
she leaves the Tower for the last time.

Walter's words echo in her head as she waits with the sombre crowd in Westminster. The raised gallows look too well made for only one use. There are calls from the crowd as Walter appears with such an escort of yeomen there cannot be many left to guard the Tower. 'God bless you, Sir Walter!' and, 'May God rest you, sir!'

He climbs the wooden steps and stares out at the crowd, like the captain of a ship judging the state of the sea. Bess thinks he's looking for her, but he begins his speech with his old bravado, making light of his situation, and forgiving the king.

The executioner tells him to kneel, and takes out a knife, which he uses to cut the back of Walter's shirt, as if it might be in the way of his grim work. Bess closes her eyes, and prays for Walter's soul.

She hears the thump as the sharp blade bites into wood and the crowd gasps. Bess still holds her breath and feels she might faint. It is over, and nothing can ever be the same again. She has only one thing left to live for: her son, Carew. She will do all in her power to defend the reputation of Walter Raleigh, adventurer, poet, father, and beloved husband.

EPILOGUE

WEST HORSLEY PLACE 1647

B ESS OPENS HER EYES AND SEES W ALTER SITTING AT HER bedside, reading a book. 'Walter?' Her voice is weak, and her eyesight failing. Her mind remains confused by the pain, despite her doctor's bitter potions.

'It's me, Mother, Carew.' He smiles, making him look even more like Walter as she remembers him, in his prime. 'King James used to complain I haunted him, like my father's ghost.'

Bess allows herself to forget her pain and smiles. 'The *late* King James … who got what he deserved.'

'It is little wonder King Charles turned out as he did.'

Bess agrees. 'You know I loaned money to King Charles – four thousand pounds – before the Civil War, as he had none of his own.'

'I've always wondered about that, Mother. You loaned money to the king, paid all my expenses at Oxford and gave me a generous inheritance, yet you had nothing after Father died.'

Bess notes he doesn't say his father was murdered, as he once did. Even such barbarity can mellow with time. 'I want to share a secret. I should have told you long ago, Carew.' She grimaces at the pain, but finds enough strength. 'They were right, when they accused me of hiding your father's gold from Guiana.'

'I always suspected, but wanted to hear it from you.'

'It was looted from the Spanish fort at San Thomé. Your father was ... the only one who knew.' She must rest for a moment, and struggles to find the strength to continue. 'He found it hidden under the bunk of a man who had no further use for it.'

Carew stares at her. 'Lawrence Keymis, who led my brother to his death?'

Bess shakes her head. Her voice is weak but Carew must know the truth. 'Wat died as he would have wished, as an adventurer. Lawrence Keymis is not to blame, and neither is your father.'

Carew sits back in his chair. 'So Father won in the end?'

Bess smiles. 'He returned—' She struggles for breath. 'With pockets full of gold.'

He seems to sense she doesn't have long. 'Is there anything I can do for you, Mother?'

She looks into his kind eyes. His father would have been proud. A soldier, and poet, but he is unmarried. 'You must find a good wife ... and name your son Walter. You can call him Wat.' She sees his smile, as he's heard this many times. 'Will you pass me ... my Bible?'

Carew crosses to the bookshelf and takes the Bible, bound in black leather and embossed with a small gold cross. 'Would you like me to read to you?'

'I gave this to your father, the last time I saw him. Will you read me ... what he wrote inside the cover?'

Carew turns to the inside cover and stares, no doubt recognising his father's shaky handwriting. He glances at Bess and reads:

Even such is time which takes in trust
Our youth, our joys, and all we have,
And pays us but with age and dust,
Who, in the dark and silent grave,
When we have wandered all our days,
And from which earth, and grave and dust
The Lord will raise me up I trust.

AUTHOR'S NOTE

Bess Raleigh died at West Horsley Place aged eighty-two, a wealthy woman and the last of her generation, having outlived two queens. Her story is the sixth and final book in my Elizabethan series. This book also completes the story of the Tudors, from Owen Tudor's first meeting with Queen Catherine of Valois to the end of the dynasty with the last days of Queen Elizabeth.

Bess secured a place for Carew at Wadham College, Oxford, and found him a place at court. He spent the rest of his life defending his father's reputation. When King Charles insisted on his divine right to rule, Parliament and the people needed a hero, and chose Walter. A commoner, from an old family, and a Protestant, he'd defended England from the Spanish.

Bess would have been pleased to know Carew married Philippa Ashley, a wealthy young widow and influential cousin of George Villiers, two years after her death, in 1649, the year King Charles was beheaded. They had three sons and two daughters, and Carew's eldest son, named Walter, was knighted.

Carew sat in Parliament for four years, and fought for the Parliamentarian cause, having his revenge on Sir John Digby when Sherborne was besieged and Digby sent to the Tower. He was eventually appointed Governor of Jersey, and continued the work his father started.

I visited Walter's cell at the Tower of London, as well as Sherborne, for my research. I was shown Walter's study (and his pipe) by Maria Wingfield Digby, who lives in Sherborne Castle to this day.

I would like to thank my wife Liz, and my editor Nikki Brice, for their support during my research and writing about Bess Raleigh and her eventful life. I would also like to acknowledge the invaluable collection of letters (quoted in italics) compiled and annotated by the late Professor Joyce Youings.

I enjoyed telling the stories of the Tudors, and became intrigued by their successors, the Stuarts. In particular, I was fascinated by the life of Queen Anna of Denmark, and am now researching a Stuart trilogy. Details of all my books can be found at my author website, which also has links to my podcasts about the stories of the Tudors. If you enjoyed reading this book, it would mean a lot to me if you would leave a short review.

Tony Riches, Pembrokeshire
www.tonyriches.com

The Tudor Trilogy

THE TUDOR TRILOGY

England 1422: Owen Tudor, a Welsh servant, waits in Windsor Castle to meet his new mistress, the beautiful and lonely Queen Catherine of Valois, They fall in love, risking Owen's life and Queen Catherine's reputation, but how do they found the dynasty which changes British history — the Tudors?

1461: King Edward of York has taken the country by force. Jasper Tudor, Earl of Pembroke, flees to Brittany with his nephew, Henry Tudor. But dare they risk a reckless invasion of England?

Henry Tudor's victory over King Richard III at Bosworth in August 1485 is only the beginning. Can he end the Wars of the Roses through marriage to the beautiful Princess Elizabeth - and unite the warring houses of Lancaster and York?

Available as paperback, audiobook and eBook

The Brandon Trilogy

The story of the Tudor dynasty continues with the daughter of King Henry VII. Mary Tudor watches her elder brother become King of England and wonders what the future holds for her.

Everyone has secrets... but will Charles Brandon's cost him everything? He's fallen in love with King Henry VIII's sister, Mary Tudor, the beautiful widowed Queen of France. Will he dare to marry her without the king's consent?

A favourite of King Henry VIII, Katherine knows all his six wives, his daughters Mary and Elizabeth, and his son Edward. She becomes the ward of Sir Charles Brandon, and when his wife Mary dies, he ask her to marry him and become the Duchess of Suffolk.

Available in paperback, audiobook and eBook

The Elizabethan Series

The enigmatic Queen Elizabeth as seen by three of her favourite men, Drake, Essex and Raleigh, and three of her most interesting ladies, Penelope, eldest daughter of the queen's nemesis, Lady Lettice Knollys, Frances, the only surviving child of the queen's spymaster, Sir Francis Walsingham, and one of her 'Gentlewomen', Bess Raleigh.

Each saw her very differently, as Drake was in awe of her, Essex was like the son she never had, and Raleigh became captain of her guard. Penelope, Frances and Bess were all banished by the queen, yet remained influential and witnessed the key events of the Elizabethan era.

Available in paperback and eBook

Printed in Dunstable, United Kingdom